This Land

~ A NOVEL MEMOIR ~

MARGARET MOORE BLANCHARD

iUniverse, Inc.
New York   Bloomington

This Land

iUniverse books may be ordered through booksellers or by contacting:

iUniverse
1663 Liberty Drive
Bloomington, IN 47403
www.iuniverse.com
1-800-Authors (1-800-288-4677)

ISBN: 978-1-4502-2262-4 (sc)
ISBN: 978-1-4502-2263-1 (ebook)

Printed in the United States of America

iUniverse rev. date: 04/05/2010

"While women hold up half the sky.
they deserve to hold half the land."

--Chinese proverb

"Oh beautiful for spacious skies
For amber waves of grain
And purple mountains majesty
Above thy fruited plains.

America, America, god shed her grace on thee
And crown thy good with sisterhood
From sea to shining sea."

--American song

"Come, my friends, it's not too late to seek a newer world,
....push off...
Though much is taken, much survives. And though
We are not now that strength within old days
Moved earth and heaven; that which we are, we are—
One equal temper of heroic hearts
Made weak by time and fate, but strong in will
To strive, to seek, to find, and not to yield."

--From "Ulysses" by Tennyson

**For my friends from whom and for whom
I have borrowed, stolen or invented
these stories.**

*"Oh my heart's in the highlands,
My heart is not here,
My heart's in the highlands,
A chasin' a deer.*

*"Wherever I wander,
Wherever I roam,
The hills of the highlands,
Forever my home."*

*With gratitude to Kathel,
midwife for this narrative,*

**and to all my *anam cara*, soulmates, heart companions,
friends and colleagues for your inspiration.**

"She is the Wild Girl. Like our natural wilderness she follows her own laws. She is part of all of us, no matter our age or sex. . .. She is freedom and joy, love of the quest and of movement. She is creativity and serenity. She is the seed and the sprout, bursting with life. She is the path through the forest and the forest herself."

—*Patricia Monaghan*

CONTENTS

ROOTS

   1. OVERTURE 3

   2. ON THE EDGE OF CHAOS................................5

   3. BEFORE, US 10

   4. ABBY 19

   5. BETH 32

TRUNK

   6. DULCE 47

   7. CARRIE 64

   8. THIS LAND 85

   9. EVONNE 91

  10. FAITH 109

BRANCHES

  11. THE MOLECULE..125

  12. HELENE 128

  13. GAIL...143

  14. THE OCTAGON 157

  15. US NOW 160

BLOSSOMS

  16. A PLACE FOR US... 165

  17. BEGINNINGS REVISITED 171

  18. THE LETTERS 176

  19. CLOSURE..185

  20. FINALE..191

FRUIT

21. THE KEYS, FIRST AND LAST 195

22. REFLECTIONS AND COMPLAINTS 215

23. OTHERS OF US 235

24. THE STORYTELLER 243

25. THE NUMBERS 249

Roots

1

OVERTURE

Our whole generation was born on, has lived on, the edge of chaos. Only within a larger sphere whose own resonance contained, amplified, and modified our own, could we find the larger order toward which this chaos led us.

Faced with a choice: spend the night on a hard desk or raise the window and leap out, she chose to jump, even though the only exit was through a second story window and the ground below was cement.

We are everywhere. Life begins in us. We contain, carry, and dissolve other molecules. We participate in the chemistry of life, shaping and converting nutrition into energy. We expand when we freeze, bluster out in defense when we're cold. When the heat is on, we disappear into vapor or mist, fog or obscurity. We are ubiquitous, invisible, essential.

We never got around to talking about actually buying land. Despite my fear we might need something like Noah's Ark to rescue us, no one felt like discussing sanctuary. We had no idea how close disaster was or what form it would take.

Each must have followed her own momentum, found her own pivot of balance, though somehow we all swung free together.

Eight are the notes in an octave. Eight are the sides of an octagon, symbol of transformation, of the middle ground in the transition of square to circle, of cube to globe. Eight completes the round, connecting the loop which marks it whole.

We are, modern philosophers tell us, not solid, unchanging substances, but a series of events, "drops of experience." Each one of us alone is her own series of events. Flowing together we form a cascade of experiences, the pattern of which is not predictable. Who we are and what we do, like drops of rain entering a river heading toward a waterfall will change by the end of this story.

Time to remember our scattered pieces and pull ourselves together again. As we bend down again toward our toes, let us gather our fullness within our roundness and fall like a wave, not isolated tears, into that indifferent ocean.

2

ON THE EDGE OF CHAOS

Our whole generation was born on, has lived on, the edge of chaos. We were conceived before or after World War II, grew up in the 50's and 60's, came of age in the 70's. Most of us don't live on the edge of chaos anymore-- but some still do.

The edge of chaos is not the same as being on the edge in other ways: on the brink of, or falling off of, precipitous, extremist, or discriminated against, although we've been there too. No, I don't mean that edge, unless we're talking about the "excluded middle," the hole in the center of everything, the place out of which all things emerge and into which all things vanish.

Edge of chaos, as I understand it, is the place where order and chaos touch, their place of meeting, a place of change. One friend calls this the zone of "biomerge." She knows about molecules, how they share electrons through a figure eight dynamism and how they can mend their hole-y shields by creating together a common umbrella through exchanging electrons.

Some people get a good look at the edge of chaos at an early age and settle way back deep in the heart of order, never again to venture far from the routines, habits, comforts of what has always been, is, and hopefully will always be, traditionally, genetically, culturally. Others, no matter how much they aspire to be regular, ordinary, normal, run of the mill, no matter how much they dream of a common language or search for common ground, or long for a settled life, are drawn like moths to the flames of chaos. They push through boundaries to enter that liminal space, that in-between zone, that place of flux.

Some of these are us.

Of all of us, it seems to me, Dulce lived closest to the edge of chaos in her younger days. I think of her escaping to mountain tops and mesa bluffs to look out at the western horizon in all directions at the vast sphere of possibilities denied her because her little dose of order was so small: the cramped routines of the sickroom, the straitjacket of caretaking when one is still a child. To be rooted in a miniature flower pot on the expansive edge of desert, mountains, sky and stars is a particular relationship to the edge of chaos, one which calls for big eyes and even larger imagination. Particularly if behind you is the experience of death, of the chaos at the heart of life.

Beth and Carrie, on the other hand, zipped around on the edge of chaos as if it were their playground, thanks mostly to their parents' steady hands on the wheels, particularly their mother who managed to build nest after nest in place after place, while cannons and shells and bombs exploded in the background and guns fired incessantly, threatening their father's life and making taut their mother's nerves. There were the war years of four different wars which gave chaos itself a particularly sharp edge. And there were the non-war years when changing horizons beckoned in one direction and orders from the hierarchy of the military sent them into unknown territories. For Beth these moves in themselves threatened chaos; she hated being snatched up and hurried along to somewhere else, away from the known and familiar. For Carrie, the adventure, the lure of the novel and unknown, usually compensated for the loss, but not always. But Beth was agile and knew how to climb the cliffs of chaos while Carrie was terrified of falling over the edge. They both learned that to survive, not be left behind, tossed overboard, be kidnapped, or sent to an orphanage, they needed to step lively, keep their mother's back in sight at all times, and hold onto each other's hands.

For Faith, the chaos was not outside but inside, in the form of entropy, the slow inexorable decline of household openness, liveliness, communication, mood. Since the weather inside was dreary, she found ways of going out to find an easier flow of energy, to her aunts' farms where she could join the miracle of harvesting potatoes from underground, tomatoes from the vines, corn from the stalks or just stare in wonder at the changing face of a giant sunflower. Or better yet, swim in the pond or the river where the intensity of water lifted her spirits, buoyed her body, tingled her nerves, dared her strength, tickled her fancy, let her float like a bubble watching clouds drift in the blue above.

For Abby, it was the order inside from which she escaped to the out of doors. The small spaces of home were thoroughly scoured and tightly packed. Sometimes she felt like just another sardine in the city of life. Everything was squared off, solid, predictable, safe--a multi-chambered container for people who'd escaped the chaos of poverty, pogroms, concentration camps, immigration, unemployment and survived every kind of challenge. They'd had enough chaos. They wanted to settle their village as best they could in the urban fortresses of cinder block and brick rising above the trees in orderly fashion. Always she was grateful, though, to her parents for choosing a building next to a park where she could play with other kids in the loose sand and leafy ground, explore beyond the tree line and discover the many growing, barky things which shed leaves and nuts and sometimes fruits without a care for clutter or neatness, where she could run free, her limbs loose and swinging without fear of knocking over and breaking some precious memory.

For Evonne the chaos was all inside the house: unreasonable demands, inconsistent discipline, irrational explanations, contradictions, fabrications, and a deep, deep well of grief. Retreat was possible only behind the couch or in the basement. So she would ride her bike into the open fields and breathe freely for a change. But the real liberation came with teachers who could parent, from schools where her talents were recognized and applauded (but please, not too loudly), from her odd jobs and from her art where she could make her own lines of order and chaos and meander through the fertile spaces in between. The summer spent in an arts camp with nurturing counselors and talented companions and friendly trees with lots of space in between for games, concerts, word play, drama and expanding images helped her feel fully at home on the edge of chaos where art and nature merge.

For Helene men brought chaos and women, order. There was very little breathing space between. From Mom came tradition, piety, recipes, constriction inside the home. From the nuns, discipline, rigidity, punishment. From Dad came a heavy hand, politics, competition, ambition and no place for a daughter inside all that outside rush of activity. Part of her stayed inside to be cared for and to care for the mother she'd lost and found again. Part of her longed for adventure, travel, challenge, risk. The most fruitful edge of chaos she could find after searching through sex, drugs and money, was radical spirituality. Through intense meditation practice she could soar away from dukka (suffering), and find some transcendence at the edge of chaos, between the hair shirt and the undershirt. Through contact with gurus whose masculinity was softened and made more fluid by their practice, she could discover an androgyny which avoided the extremes of the macho and the martyr.

Gail fled a particular kind of order, the surface order of middle class respectability, covering whatever failures, flaws, and secrets her family had. Her honesty and insight slipped and slid across the cover of financial and psychological well being her parents had constructed over their real lives. Not only did she long to break out, break through the superficial, she wanted to reconstruct those elements into something that could be touched, could move with the wind, could grow, that showed the insides as well as the outsides of life. The random dangers of chaos did not attract her, although she admitted to some fascination with its seamy sides, but the edges of chaos, where forms were as fluid as soft clay or loose as unbleached cotton, ready to be molded into organic forms whose boundaries were limber and mysteries spilled out, messy and authentic, this is where she chose to live.

None of us were rich, powerful or famous, buoyed up by or submerged by the surge at the center of the fountain of life. On other sides, the margins, we had to find our own sources of transformation: renunciation, drugs, sex, resistance, rage, faith. But when we were really at the edge of chaos, it didn't matter how we got there. Some modes allowed us to live longer and enjoy more. Some were healthier than others. But all roads led to the same source, that core of vitality, the merge of pattern with color, movement with shape, light with line.

Some of us still worship at this shrine; some of us have become wary of it. But that's not the point really. However we recognize it these days, ultimately we know we will again shiver with those quivering strings, let that music flow through us once more.

There is, contrary to the opinion of s/he who is living it, choosing it, feeling it, no particular life style more edgy than another. Chaos can be found in the most unlikely places: the untidy head of a bureaucrat; the secret life of a nuclear family; the underside of a preacher. The edge of chaos, therefore, can be about risk, about shadowy selves, about uncertain outcomes, luck, or fate. But for us mostly it was about change, about choices, about fuzzy outcomes, shifting commitments and fluid priorities.

The more we went toward the edge of chaos, the less we stayed in the old order. The more we embraced chaos, the more those orders dissolved. But without continuity, without form, without a certain rhythm, everything dissolves into chaos. We didn't want to dissolve; we wanted to dance.

Only within a larger sphere whose own resonance contained, amplified, and modified our own, could we find the larger order toward which this chaos led us. For me, I was the larger order. For I, we were the larger order. For us, you others were the larger order. For all of us, nature was the larger order. For nature, the larger planetary order is buried in the chaos whose source radiates throughout the cosmic order.

Is our ultimate boundary that margin between earth and sky? Is the human edge of chaos the rim of this world of ours, where we stand and burn, sharing the horizon with other persons, animals and trees?

Maybe our generation was no different than others. Each generation seems to face some kind of major change in its youth, not always disaster.

Maybe ours just seemed especially chaotic. Compared to the one which came after us, but not, perhaps, the one which preceded ours. They were the ones who fought the Great Wars. We were the ones who suffered their comings and goings. And maybe we're the ones in our own generation who've lived particularly on the edge, even after we learned early on how life is rough around the edges.

Chaos is nothing if not edges. Order is smooth, solid, safe. Things come round again. People follow predictable orbits. The universe is systematic. The system is not too shaky. Within chaos, or at its edge, things "melt, thaw, resolve themselves into a dew." They rage. They burn up. Slowly or quickly it doesn't matter. They go back into the dark with a sigh or a cry of joy. We all know this, but those of us who still live at the edge of chaos know it more closely, more deeply, most of the time.

Later we discovered edges of chaos in other places: in the streets, on the road, in ashrams, in communes, in political demonstrations, in gay bars; sometimes, but not often, in our jobs as teachers, counselors, congressional transcriber, artists, saleswomen, social workers, factory workers, real estate agent, massage therapist, college professor, government worker—and usually in some kind of relationship with each other.

3

BEFORE, US

Abby was the scout, the first to leave, the first to arrive in the new land. She'd had it, really had it, with the world of in and out, up and down. She didn't like the idea of people being left out, left behind, excluded, pushed down.

But she felt powerless to change things. She'd organized co-workers, fellow students, tenants, and women of multi kinds--transiting, battered, lesbian, and returning to school--to demand a place for themselves. And they did; some won more rooms of their own, but nothing radically changed. There must be, she thought, another way to get to the roots of all this.

So, congenitally unable to exclude others, in her mind because she was Jewish, but personally wary of inclusion, because she'd been her mother's favorite envied by others, she fled to the woods where alone in her tent she felt at home--free as she had as a child when she skipped away from family tensions to find refuge in the park, beauty and peace in the botanical gardens.

Abby moved quickly and purposefully, whether she was chopping wood or jogging. Short, wiry, she hid her chiseled features and darting green eyes beneath exuberant dark, curly hair. Her voice ran a full range from meek to loud, and it was usually accompanied by hands gesturing rhythmically or emphatically. Her idea of dressing up was a flamboyant set of earrings, a flashy pair of sox, a bright new flannel shirt.

Now that she knew there was a place for her, here on this land, she could welcome others, especially innocent exiles like herself. She could lift her lamp beside the open door.

But in the woods there were no doors. In these woods, no fences, no gates. Only paths and obstacles. Here she was relieved of the responsibility of keeping the lamps burning because there were plenty of lamps already lit: the sun, the moon, the stars, the fireflies.

She knew it was only a matter of time before the others came. How could they resist the beauty of these woods? Secretly she hoped they'd take their time. In her heart of hearts what she loved most was her solitude.

Beth always took her time. Time itself meant nothing to her. From birth on people had torn their hair out over her timing, which was either so quick nobody caught on, or so slow they felt obliged to mutter or scream.

She'd been meditating for months before she arrived on the land so she knew all about timelessness. And she knew how to wait for time to catch up with her.

When she arrived, she knew she would be welcomed and even embraced, but not, not by Abby, smothered. She also knew she had every right to be here. Wasn't this buying land together her idea? Wasn't she the central link, the one everyone else confided in? Hadn't she sent out the others with exact specifications, to find it and buy it?

Beth was slender, athletic with long, soft hair, and vibrant, gracious smile. Whether she was climbing trees, hopping over rocks in a stream, or dancing country, her blue eyes flirting, she was both graceful and sturdy. Her voice was soft, expressive more in receptivity than in articulating her feelings, for which she relied more on body language. She enjoyed dressing up, choosing the appropriate costume: exotic, colorful fabrics, scarves, braided belts, suede boots, robes, shawls, with artful attention to accessories.

Unlike Abby, who was a nomad of sorts, Beth was a settler. Getting in was not as much a problem for Beth as coming out. She knew how to nest. During her mobile childhood, she had plenty of practice. She knew how to make sure that the only shelter on the land, an old shack, was cleared out, insulated and comfortable. A born scavenger, she knew how to salvage just about anything, from ragged psyches to worn-out bathtubs.

Getting Abby to settle in with her was the greatest challenge --Abby whose motto was: "Always look for the nearest exit." But Beth, with the subtlety and skill of a gifted needleworker, had several hooks: being the receptive one, she knew how to listen, something Abby had been starved for since childhood; and, despite her wandering inclinations, she had been true to Abby in her fashion. But Abby wasn't convinced she wanted to count on Beth again, after a series of connections and disconnections.

With winter pressing upon them, however, pragmatism prevailed and having found sanctuary in each other's eyes, and ears, they settled in together. They felt safe in their shelter. Who could possibly want to join them, in their dilapidated shack with no running water, no toilet, and barely enough room to turn around?

Along came Carrie and her traveling animal troupe. Unable to say no to this invasion for reasons of being good girls, Beth and Abby welcomed her with open arms and trembling hearts. Although in many ways a loner, Carrie was, from Beth and Abby's perspective, the quintessential older sister, as well as Beth's actual sister. For others' intents and purposes she'd been groomed for a straight life of wife and mother and although she'd avoided those roles as demands of the patriarchy, she often took her responsibilities, which these days involved causes and animals, very seriously.

Although commanding in Beth's psyche, Carrie was elusive in public, hiding her lively blue eyes beneath hooded lids and long lashes, her fluid feelings within the often moderate tones of her voice. Her sensitivity was concealed in her hands which gestured, created and soothed with silent precision. Her forward leaning thoughts under a slow, wandering walk, her warm smile within quiet features, and her tall, changing body under roomy, shapeless but colorful and comfortable pieces of cloth gave an aura which was both candid and unassuming.

Even though she'd bought into the land, Carrie felt tied down by a thousand tiny strings to her life in the city—to the neighborhood children, to the remnant of friends left in the backwaters of the women's movement, to her political comrades, to dear friends who'd stuck with her through the rise and fall of collective work and struggle.

As a chronic nomad even after growing up on the move, the entire family in tow as her parents traveled from post to post and coast to coast, Carrie had chosen finally to settle down in the working class city where she'd first gone as a member of a commune. After the commune broke up, she stayed as long as there was movement. But finally for the first time in her life, she felt stuck. This, she realized, was the other side of mobility, a sense of stagnation.

As one of two explorers who found the land, Carrie guessed, as soon as she saw the stream and the mountain, this was the place for them. Once they'd discovered the nearby lake and the beaver pond and she'd slept out under the huge pine trees, she knew for sure. She even saw potential in the old gray shack, which the realtor suggested should be torn down

Carrie was an architect of possibilities, virtuoso of the imagination. Once she had a vision, and she had many, she itched to implement it, to ground and grow it. Long before they bought the land, she'd envisioned it, along with the village of friends they could build together. She treasured nature for what it provided of both home and heaven, for herself and for her animals.

Dulce was the other discoverer of the land, While Carrie recognized it as *the place*, Dulce was the one who made it actually happen. She was the one with the know-how, money, and experience in owning land.

Despite her house in the city, her lost farm in the country, her tableland in New Mexico, it took some time for Dulce to feel she really belonged anywhere. When she lived with Beth, she'd felt at home, but that didn't last. In those days she longed to belong to Beth's large, happy family, where she was welcomed but, as an outsider, not fully embraced.

Besides settling in anywhere felt too much like dying, like her mother's confinement, her own caretaking. She had been, from the age of eight, a prisoner of a prisoner of fate. To stay alive, she'd concluded, one must keep moving, like her father, from peak to peak, adventure to adventure.

So even though Dulce bought the land with her friends, she visited there each summer only as a revered guest, full of fascinating tales of her explorations in Spain, Greece, Africa, better even than the kinds of tales she'd heard, or imagined, from Beth and Carrie during their adventurous adolescence, when they traveled around the world with their vivacious mother while Dulce was trapped in one room in one house in one city with her dying mother.

Dulce's beauty featured a handsome delicacy, with straight, long, black, glossy hair, glowing skin and trim frame. Her movements were deliberate and careful, keeping her mind tentatively anchored in a body which guided or tripped her as she gazed off toward distant horizons with searching brown eyes. Her voice was low and thoughtful as it wound its way through complex ideas. Her dress was usually no-nonsense, only occasionally indulging in silk blouses or fancy boots to signal her claim to some distinction in places like classrooms and conferences.

Whether she arrived from a sickroom or from Tahiti, what Dulce unfailing brought as gifts generously shared were ideas. A Johnny Appleseed of the mind, she planted seeds imported from the most vibrant intellectual fields while telling stories and describing books. Always wondering why, she turned over every possible explanation, from depth psychology and quantum physics to ancient literature, for symbol and meaning.

When she saw Carrie inserting herself and her animals into the shack and when her new amore fell in love with the woods, Dulce realized she too needed to make a place for herself there--in the heart of this happy-family-once-removed. This was a second chance. But she knew on the basis of all she had known that nobody was going to make room for her. She would have to do it on her own. And she'd have to challenge the group culture-- poverty as a virtue-- in the process.

Evonne just came along for the ride, to keep Carrie company, or so she told herself for protection. She was wary of commitment, in any sense of the word. Armed with a pencil behind her ear, she was the consummate observer, one who could sketch in a second the telling lines of another person's attitude--as long as she kept her distance.

But she was enchanted with this place, free from the noise and stress of almost all she had known, life in the city. She could sit in a trance for hours by the beaver pond, fascinated, as she had been in the city, with the myriad forms of life. She could for long moments let her guard down.

And she was intrigued with the people, a quirky, cantankerous bunch of women, each as clever, courageous and independent as the next. Even though she was vigilant about their entangled histories and not at all sure she fit in anyway, she recognized her vision of a supportive community of creative people, a potential shelter from her own artistic isolation.

Ev's mobile face was so responsive it took distinctive, as well as lovely, features to secure it: thick, dark eyebrows; deep brown eyes flecked with gold; generous lips; thick, auburn hair. Her sturdy legs and sculpted shoulders suggested a stability which was reinforced by her forceful stride, longer than one might expect from someone her size. In the tapered beauty of her hands and fingers one discovered her agile, artist soul. The intensity of her voice matched the mobility of her face as she listened and leapt from connection to connection. Her discriminating, albeit idiosyncratic, taste in clothes, tuned to trend without embracing it, was usually satisfied by some unique item purchased at a yard sale.

As an outsider Ev would have no way of anticipating that she was destined to be the catalyst for these people becoming not just a collection of old friends but a renewed group. Gifted with both fire and water, warmth, wit and compassion, she became one element which alchemically allowed a transformation from aged, frayed connections to new unity. This sparked reaffirmations of early beliefs in friendship and inspired others to join the circle thus created. The more they discovered who they could be together, the more integral Ev became to the group functioning. When she wasn't there, the best they could do was celebrate what had been.

But as the catalytic substance can vanish into the new formation, Ev sometimes found herself disappearing. No longer the observer on the rim of the group, she'd dissolved into it. She was so busy helping them untie their various knots and manage their breakthroughs that she could find little time to paint or sort out her own issues. Tuned by years of sitting on the edges watching adults act crazy, she could often tell people's secrets before they even knew them. Unencumbered by past connections with these people, she could see them more clearly than they saw each other and thus could help them negotiate around their projections and resentments. But how would she find more time for herself?

Faith protected herself by buzzing in and out of this group of friends she'd known ever since she met Carrie, both of them fresh out of college. Predictably she'd arrive without warning just when the group had stopped believing in itself or just when all its collective energy was needed for some project, she'd take charge with characteristic humor, skill and bossiness, and then after a few good meals and a round of hugs, she'd disappear.

She served as their messenger from the regular world where she was firmly planted as a single mother, teacher, realtor, the surviving female head (now that her mother was dead) of a large, extended family.

Faith was direct, with no artifice, no frills. She was the picture of health with her friendly face, cropped golden hair, trim, athletic body. Many people spontaneously trusted her open smile and honest gaze. Nothing about the way she moved or talked was pretentious. Her voice was often enthusiastic, engaged in whatever was happening that very moment. Her clothes were simple and practical, putting no barrier between herself and the rest of the world. When you got to know her, you noticed her hands: strong, quick, digging into earth to plant seeds, deftly slicing onions, swimming with bold strokes into choppy waters.

Although holding it all together was a precarious balancing act for Faith as she leapt from job to job and lover to lover, she devoted her life to providing an enduring home base for her sons. But unlike many busy mothers she also remained loyal to her old friends and finally when they started marching, she marched with them and when they started falling in love with each other, she fell in love with them too. So when they bought land, she bought in too, even though she had to borrow to do so.

But having grown up in the middle of the country, landlocked, she loved the ocean most of all and, once grown, had never lived far from the beach where she swam, fished or hiked almost daily. The woods, which reminded her of her girl scout days, were for camping, not for living.

It was the group which counted, a place of refuge and consultation, comfort and advice, a place where she could share both the harsh secrets and the colorful nourishments she brought them from the regular world, where some part of her belonged and some part of her never would.

Gail was more enamored of the trees than the people. When Dulce first brought her to the woods, she fell in love with the graceful birch clusters, many armed cabbage pines, arched hemlock. As a sculptor she felt restored to the source of those organic forms which poured out of her imagination.

Gail was the only one of them who would probably have been just as happy wearing no clothes. She was proud of her slender, attractive body and moved gracefully as someone who understood from the inside about balance, dimension, leverage and shifting form. If the nude descending a staircase were herself an artist, she might share insights from the body out which were expressed in Gail's sculpture. Gail's own classic features were framed by a simple style of light brown hair straight to her shoulders. She spoke easily, honestly and with assurance. Carefully steering between the bourgeois and the gauche, with an eye for color, quality and texture, Gail mostly kept her clothes pragmatic: pants you could wipe your hands on, shirts you could get in and out of quickly.

She loved the land, but she didn't quite know what to do with the land people. She was an introvert, hiding under a thick, lustrous shell. The last thing she had time for was group dynamics and the clutter of past connections. Besides, she figured they were all lesbians while she was, essentially, straight. Dulce was the only woman she'd been with and the only serious relationship at all since her marriage.

When her marriage ended, she'd made it clear to her parents that she had no intention of living a conventional, bourgeois life. She planned to devote her life to art and she had: from her loft in Soho to gallery openings to bronze pours to a hand-to-mouth existence as an art teacher. She'd made her priorities clear to Dulce and she'd make them clear to the group as well. Art was the only way out for her.

But here was Dulce wanting to build a house on the land with no one to help her. There was no way she could do it by herself. Gail would have to help her. But if she did, she was going to make sure it was a work of art.

Helene was the last to join the group. . .as Beth's new meditation friend. Beth insisted on drawing her in, forcing her to negotiate past everyone's curiosity.

Helene was, by nature, friendly. Her attractive face was framed by short, curly hair, distinctive for its fine porcelain complexion and good-humored countenance. Soft and full, she moved at a leisurely pace but approached chores with zest and methodical efficiency. Surprisingly strong, she lifted rocks or carried the sick from bed to bathroom--despite a back which kept giving out from too much giving. Plagued with health problems, Helene wrestled with the secret traumas her body was hiding, while with sensitive, skilled fingers, through giving massages, she healed such traumas in other bodies. Her voice danced over a verbal keyboard as she told fascinating or hilarious stories. A connoisseur of t-shirts, each week she wore another colorful and original design ordered by mail.

She lavished the land group with presents, stories, massages and meals, but she kept her distance. She felt like a stranger here, just as alienated as when she was sent away to boarding school and couldn't leave on weekends when the other girls went home, had to stay with the severe nuns, a bunch of "sisters" like this group.

Besides, she had other commitments, the care of her blind and aging mother, her own spiritual development, her schooling. To feel pressure to spend her precious little time with Beth in the context of the group was too much to ask, even of her generous soul. It was wicked bad.

So what kept pulling her back in, aside from the stubborn Beth? Was it the secret springs which reminded her of sacred springs on family land in Quebec, now devoted to the worship of St. Anne, the grandmother goddess? Did this gifted group of women remind her of her maiden aunts, country French psychic healers? Or was it the land itself, the circle of ancient maternal pines which offered refuge from a cruel world?

These sketches are the seeds of the plot of this story: what happens, in a nutshell, if one has imagination, and the desire to crack it open. Fuller portraits emerge from what happens when these persons interact.

This is, of course, only one of eight or thirteen possible versions of this story. What is spoken only hints at what is unspoken. And this telling is only one of many trails of experience which give shape to our changing selves and to our changing worlds.

We are, modern philosophers tell us, not solid unchanging substances, but a series of events, "drops of experience." Each one of us alone is her own series of events. Flowing together we form a cascade of experiences, the pattern of which is not predictable. Who we are and what we do, like drops of rain entering a river heading toward a waterfall, will change by the end of this story.

But even drops have their own unique shapes, sizes, colors, histories and contexts. Out of respect for the contemporary way of telling a story this long, we also serve as characters in this novel, individuals with characteristic ways of moving and speaking. I've tried to describe us without giving away our identities, which, despite all our efforts at ego transcendence, are still precious and, in many ways, private. Here I can only give you snapshots, not fully painted portraits.

This is our story, or part of it. We are eight of a movement of women who risked exile to escape oppression. We were part of the first generation of women to make this choice--or so we thought when we made it. Unaware at the time, we were following a tradition of independent women whose history had been erased. With partial consciousness, we were following our own American roots as daughters of immigrants, servants, pariahs, scapegoats and wanderers. We were also daughters of soldiers, skilled laborers, shopkeepers, politicians and, of course, mothers.

We were born into wartime and faced dire predictions: nuclear holocaust, population explosion, and destruction of the planet. Yet we counted ourselves among the lucky ones. As we grew into our lives, the stigmas attached to the choices we made ebbed and flowed in the world around us, but in our own minds gradually diminished.

Ours is a story of exclusion and belonging and the treacherous paths between them--in other words, a story of ins and outs. Most importantly, it is a story of friendship and the choices which make and break it.

Where we are the girl who was banished by her father because she would not acknowledge that all power flowed through him. She was sent into the wilderness with other outcasts and eccentrics. And there she made a world of her own, a world of harmony and equality, a realm which came eventually to rival her father's kingdom (adapted from *Wild Girls* by Patricia Monaghan).

4

ABBY

One never knows, she thought, looking up at the clearing sky as she pulled herself out of her soggy tent and stretched her long arms toward the rising sun. She was eager to climb the mountain, but not if it was going to rain some more.

Everything sparkled as the sun sang through the dripping leaves and spider webs after three days of rain. The birds were chirping their little hearts out and a few chickadees greeted her from the nearest branches. The air smelled so fresh she was sure this was the day for the climb. She'd never lived anywhere else with such changeable weather. Or maybe she was more tuned to weather since she was out in it all the time. She imagined herself running up the mountain and down again before the dark clouds of the last three afternoons could gather to gossip and scold, warning her to lay low. But then she saw herself sliding down the muddy slopes and decided to wait until noon for the ground to dry out.

She gathered wood for a small fire--not for breakfast which she never ate, something she wished her mother would realize before waking her every morning she was home for a visit to ask what she wanted for breakfast--but for her one true addiction, coffee. After quickly building the fire, she went down to the stream to wash her face, brush her teeth and fill her canteen for the hike. She loved the simplicity of this life in the woods: water from the stream, potential fire from sticks on the ground, a tent for shelter, and the trees for conversation.

In preparation for her hike, she threw an extra pair of sturdy socks, the bright ones her friend Elena had given her for her birthday, and a long-sleeved sweatshirt, the one with the wolf on it, into a small knapsack, along with a couple of apples and some t.p.. She was wearing her shorts, t-shirt and hiking boots. Then she brewed her coffee, poured in a generous dollop of milk from a container cooling in the stream, and, her mind a rare and pleasant blank, sat there sipping as she watched the rising light reach more and more of the pine needles around her.

By midmorning the sky was such a pure shade of Adirondack blue that she couldn't wait another minute. She was ready to take the risk. She fluffed out her untamed hair, leapt up, slipped the knapsack over her shoulder, hopped across the rocks in the stream and strode up the old logging trail to the foot of the mountain. Ahead of her she heard scurrying and looked up to see a raccoon scamper up a tall tree, surprised by her sudden appearance. Equally curious, they peered at each other for a few minutes, then Abby kept going. Three days cooped up inside the tent had put cramps in her legs and she was eager to stretch them before the climb got steeper. She glanced up a few times to search for the owls who'd hooted all night across the stream from her tent, but didn't really expect to see them.

When the logging trail ran out, she followed what looked like a deer path. Sure enough, as she rounded a curve next to a huge outcrop of rocks, two deer leapt across her path, amazing her by their grace and the rich reddish brown of their coats. She passed tiny waterfalls, their sides lined with plush green moss, small caves full of eyes, and trees so entwined you couldn't tell where one began and the other ended, though one was a birch and the other a maple. She sighed, remembering Beth and their first idyllic days together.

As the deer trail angled up the mountain, she felt the presence of a sheer rock cliff looming above her and decided to veer off the path and up onto the ledge above the cliff. This proved easy enough if she watched her feet carefully for loose rocks and exposed roots. She loved the pounding of her heart and the sprinkling of sweat as she climbed, that exhilaration of feeling cleansed as her lungs pulled in fresher and fresher air.

As she wound through the trees rooted on the ledge, she looked out over the valley she had just left behind. She found that if she climbed out on a large grey rock, she could see sunlight shining from the beaver pond below, could hear a car winding along the dirt road near the spot where she was camped. The breeze moved its soft fingers through her hair and she felt a glimmering of peace.

All this in front of her was their land. She still couldn't believe it. This is ours, she said to herself and to the generations before her, her people dispossessed, confined to the villages/shetels between pogroms. But as soon as she said it, *this is ours,* she whispered "Kunahara," to placate the evil eye who scorned such claims as "mine" and "ours," who would snatch something away before one had scarcely received it: *Enough already. You should be so lucky?*

So instead of glorying in ownership, albeit collective, she started to worry:

about who would take care of her aging mother now that her father was gone, about her sisters' money problems, job problems, husband problems, about her nephews' school problems, job problems, about her friends who were sick, lonely, heartbroken or broke. Abby had a talent for worrying: not only could she imagine just about anything happening, she could picture each event in realistic detail. And for her family, at least, the only way they seemed to value her was when she was caretaking for them.

She focused on a scrubby pine whose roots had to reach around the huge rock it was growing on. It was only a matter of time before a powerful wind or torrential rains wrenched it from its tenuous grip. So much for the view, she finally thought, leaping up.

Continuing up the mountain, she found another animal trail which circled around the southern curve of the slope. She started to follow it. But a voice inside told her instead to follow the light and as she looked up, she saw sun rising above the hemlock grove above her, so she headed straight up without much effort. Her legs were strong already from hiking and climbing and exploring this land they'd bought together last fall. None of the others had come yet to stay, but as soon as the deed was granted and black fly season over, she arrived to camp for the summer.

Beyond the hemlocks she came to a clearing, a tangle of downed trees and underbrush and wondered what could have caused so much destruction. A monster storm? Trees that were left standing had huge gashes on their sides, as if bears had been clawing them. Then she saw muddy tracks of huge trucks and realized that loggers must have bulldozed their way all the way up here to take down the straight trees and leave those which were crooked or dying, too large or too small. It looked like they'd come this spring, in fact, after the land had been sold--log poachers.

How can we protect this land from such invasions? she wondered. With ownership came responsibility. But would protecting it, and us, mean keeping people out? Building fences? Drawing lines? Making this beautiful, unbounded place into private property? Wasn't private property the root of capitalist exploitation?

Quickly she scrambled across the fallen logs and through thick berry bushes which had grown up in the cleared space and headed for the woods again. Beyond the trees she could see the summit and perhaps a view of the other side of the mountain. She loved this feeling of stretching out into new territory, both the physical release of freedom of movement and the discoveries that followed.

The higher she climbed, the more her sense of responsibility dropped away. What wasn't at hand to be fixed or comforted fell from her mind's eye. The more she focused on following the sunlight which darted through the trees, at times peeking over the highest leaves, the easier it was to forget the troubles which lay below her: *the teaming masses longing to breathe free.*

At the summit was a grassy meadow full of wildflowers. A surprise. No view to speak of because it was surrounded by towering trees. But such a peaceful spot.

She stretched out in the grass, soaked up the sun and watched the sky. Only the wispiest of clouds drifted by. No sign of rain. She was startled to notice her eyes were damp with relief. Rather than dwelling on her feelings, though, she entertained herself by watching the rainbows which played through the sunlight on her wet eyelashes.

This was bliss. All one needed to do was rise above it all, get the bigger picture, let the worries drift out of one's hands and into the eye of G-d or the all-that-is.

She sat up and propped herself against a rock. Never one to loll around she was surprised at how easy it was at that moment. Just then she heard something coming down the trail. She sat very still and watched. It was a dog. What was a dog doing way up here all by itself? She hoped there wasn't a person with it.

The dog was a mix of brown and black, medium sized, lean. But as it came closer, trotting along quite calmly without apparently noticing her, perhaps because she was up wind, she noticed that it had long fangs which dangled down outside its mouth. Not like any dog she'd ever seen, not that she was much of a dog person. No, this couldn't be a dog, this must be a coyote or perhaps a wild dog. (Later she heard out from a neighbor that this must be a coydog, a mix of dog and coyote, packs of whom were believed to live on top of the surrounding mountains.)

She froze in sudden fear, but this wild creature just glanced at her and trotted on. Chances are he'd never seen a human being before. He didn't know enough to be afraid. He didn't know how dangerous she could be. Or perhaps he hadn't seen her at all, she'd been so still. Relieved as she watched him with her penetrating green eyes disappear over the crest of the hill, she realized that one reason she felt such contentment up here was that she was free from the Eye of Others: the judging, the comparing, the envy. As long as one focuses on the eye of others, she reminded herself, one is trapped in their expectations.

Whether you make yourself invisible or hide behind a mask, you are captured by that gaze, like a deer paralyzed by headlights. Trapped, sometimes in the false self which tries to please, placate, take care of others, whether it wants to or not. Internally that false self can be so alluring, so popular, you don't know what she really wants, what she really feels, aside from "Get me out of here!" when none of her clever problem-solving or people-pleasing works.

What a gift that coyote had given her, just a glance free of expectation or judgement, free of fear or aggression, or even recognition.

The light by this time was directly above her. There was no place on earth she could follow it further. High noon. She took out an apple and ate it down to the seeds, then wandered across the meadow and through more woods to a rock ledge overlooking the other side of the mountain. It looked, as the song implied, much like the first side. Down below the light bounced off the surface of a pond or lake. No houses were visible, nor a road, but off in the distance she could see more mountains and a road winding between them. Awed by the magnitude of the vista, she felt her lungs expand, filling up with the thinner air.

To explore new territory without getting lost she decided to curve around the mountain where she'd been following the animal trail, perhaps along the same path the coyote had followed. Even though the sun at noon provided no compass, she knew from the direction she'd already come that this was south and that if she curved around 180 degrees she would be heading back down toward the stream and her campsite which was now west of her.

Above her she heard a squawk. Looking up she saw two hawks circling quite high. She admired how they followed the lead of the wind, not fighting it but curving with it while maintaining their own vigil. At one with that element, like the coyote on the earth. At peace with themselves.

As she descended she recognized the layers of the mountain she had climbed: the grassy meadow, the devastation zone, the hemlock grove, the rocky ledge, the high cliffs, the zones of birch. But she made discoveries as well: a huge flat sunny rock big enough for several people to sunbathe on, free from prying eyes; fallen rocks full of dark red crystals; a cluster of eight birches in one connected circle.

But when she came to the valley, the stream was flowing in the wrong direction. And when she crossed the stream, there was no road running parallel to it. There was a path where none had been before, but no matter how far down or up it she wandered, nothing seemed familiar. She was lost. But only, she told herself, in the eyes of others. True, she had no map and couldn't locate herself on one if she had. But she knew where she was. All she had to do was follow the sun as it led her west to the road and to home.

But first she decided to follow the path which led along the stream. Perhaps if she just followed the stream down, it would eventually come to a road, maybe not the right road, but any road would eventually lead her back to camp. The path wasn't going west but it was going south and that might be good enough. To the south lay human habitation while to the north was, she knew, vast reaches of wilderness. True, she reminded herself, the native peoples have no word for wilderness, but whatever you call it, this land was probably uninhabited by anyone who could show her how to get back to where she started.

But eventually the path ran out. And the stream turned into a series of waterfalls, each steeper than the last. What should she do now? As the stream descended, another mountain rose up to the west of her. If she were to follow the sun, she would have to climb that mountain first, without a trail to follow, and who knows where that might lead her? She decided to stick to the stream. But this wasn't so easy.

With every waterfall came a cliff to climb down. Being small, light and athletic, she wasn't afraid of climbing, but her hiking boots were clumsy for this kind of delicate maneuvering and sometimes the drop was so steep she felt she was stepping into a void. One time she slipped and slid down a rocky incline toward the crashing waters, stopping herself just in time by grabbing onto a berry bush. Although the berries weren't ripe yet, she remembered a story Beth had told her about a monk who was trapped on a cliff by a raging tiger and who risked his life to reach out and pick a ripe berry which was hanging from a bush in front of him. A story about "being in the moment."

Although she didn't loosen her grip on the bush, she certainly felt like she was fully in that moment. It wasn't likely that even if she slipped, she'd plunge to her death, but all she needed was to twist her ankle, with noone to know where she was or even that she was missing. But she really couldn't take time to worry. She concentrated instead on each foot as she inched her way down the slope to a clump of rocks which provided a more solid though still somewhat treacherous footing. If you stepped on the rocks, you risked hitting against their sharp edges and if you stepped between the rocks, you risked plunging down to your ankles or even knees, spraining or breaking them.

Between waterfalls there were intervals of level ground, traces of trails which meandered along the stream and then back into the woods, the comfort of solid earth beneath her feet. But slowly the sun was sinking beyond the nearest mountain and she didn't feel any closer to civilization, which now had a certain appeal, the eyes of others notwithstanding.

Finally, as she was stepping off the side of another waterfall into pure darkness, she realized she had reached a zero point. She was going to have to stop moving. She was going to have to spend the night on the mountain.

At least she had water and another apple to sustain her, so if she didn't die of exposure or get ripped apart by wild animals, which was unlikely, she should be ok. But why hadn't she brought along her sweat pants? Her shorts had been fine for the upward climb, but not so good in the fading light.

As soon as the sun sank, she could feel the air shift to coolness. She took off her boots to put the new orange socks over her old green ones. Over her thin t-shirt with its portrait of Rosa Luxemburg, she pulled on the sweatshirt she had stuffed into her knapsack and folded her bare knees inside it. Suddenly she felt vulnerably small.

The benign face of the wolf on her breast as she looked at it upside down was comforting. Perhaps it would guard her tonight, perhaps it would be her ally. She was a kind of lone wolf herself, a pathfinder, loyal to her pack but glad to be ahead of it too. But what kind of path had she found for herself now?

"The obstacle is the path," she recalled from her reading. If so, then she had found the perfect path, full of every kind of obstacle imaginable. Looking around before the light went out completely, she spotted a soft hollow in the earth surrounded by sheltering trees. It looked like a bed for a deer. It was well padded with dead leaves and pine needles. Yes, further over, off the path, she saw deer droppings. She hoped they wouldn't mind her sleeping there, and that she wouldn't wake up like Goldilocks staring at the three deer, or worse yet, bear. The local mechanic had told her that there were bear and moose in these mountains, but she hadn't been sure whether he was teasing her or not.

Shivering she automatically reached into her pocket and pulled out the matches which she had used to light the morning fire. What luck. Tormented briefly by the thought of coffee, she busied herself building a fire pit with rocks, then collecting twigs and branches and birch bark. Using these she built a small teepee on top of the rocks. Then cupping two matches she lit them together and touched them to the birch bark which ignited immediately.

And so as the dark closed around her, she had a light of her own, and warmth as well. Never before had she appreciated so much the properties of fire. The little fire also provided some protection. Even though it might attract the eyes of others, it also would keep most wild eyes at bay. The only one she had to fear was the proverbial Man, and while it was unlikely he would be lurking in these parts without a revealing light, she figured it would be easy enough for her to slip away into the darkness if threatened. She felt much safer in the woods at night than if she were trapped alone in a house. But she did wish she had brought along her flashlight. Never again would she set off so unprepared.

The only threat so far were the bugs, mostly mosquitoes with their irritating whine. She tried to listen with buddhist detachment to what was after all just another sound, but it was such a demanding qvetch full of such intense expectations that she couldn't rise above it. And when they started to bite, she lost respect for their life form and started swatting, albeit half-heartedly. She kept remembering what Beth had told her about them: only the females bit, in order to collect blood to feed their young. A noble pursuit, cut short whenever she squashed one. Death not just to this one invader but to the whole family. Life when viewed from the perspective of the very small or the very large is pretty much the same, she thought: complicated.

She was by now very hungry. She rarely ate much before dark but then she was usually ravenous. All she had left was the one apple and perhaps she should save it in case she couldn't eat for another week. She reviewed what food nature could provide: bark if she was desperate (Adirondack apparently meant "bark eaters"), berries if they weren't poisonous, fiddlehead ferns which were edible only in the spring and didn't grow up this far--not much of anything which was close at hand. So with great restraint she ate only half of the remaining apple, saving the rest for the unknown tomorrow. She drank freely from her canteen though. Water up here was plentiful and pure and as long as she wasn't dehydrated, she knew she could live for several more weeks.

As it grew dark, she could hear scurrying sounds suggesting various weights. Judging from the sounds alone, she'd just parked herself at the center of some incredibly busy crossroads, like Grand Central Station during rush hour. But as long as they didn't run right over her, she ought to be ok. She knew from listening to herself how loud her own footsteps were on the forest floor and as long as none of these sounds were louder than that, she felt safe enough.

Curled in the deer's nest with the fire burning low, she fell asleep, her head resting on her backpack. She woke to a huge light shining in her eyes. Damn, she must've camped right next to a highway without realizing it. The headlights of some huge semi-demi-monster truck were gunning her down. Then she realized it was only one light, one bright white light--the moon. Another sigh of relief.

As the moon lit the trees and the rocks with streaks of radiance, she was surprised at how clear everything became. She could see where she was in relation to the stream and the next waterfall, how far she was from the nearest rock cliff and the thicker woods, and how uninhabited this place looked to be. Whoever was making all that noise earlier must be invisible.

Then from behind her, further up the mountain, she heard howling. Not the howling of dogs, up from the valley, but the howling of wolves from the top of some moonlit bluff. One voice followed another in a musical sequence as if they were not just communicating but singing to and with each other. At times they all seemed to join in, at times they followed one after another. It was both eerie and comforting.

Perhaps, she thought with a chuckle, she should join in. What would they think? Aside from the quality of her singing voice, they might be threatened, they might be angry, but chances are, like the coyote whose glance at her was so benevolent, they wouldn't care and they wouldn't judge the quality of her singing.

She leaned her head back and howled. It felt great. Her tonsils throbbed, her sinuses resonated, her lungs cleared. But she mustn't do it again. Their howling had stopped. What if the pack came looking for her? She started humming instead.

Her older sister had been the musical one. Sometimes Abby longed to run her fingers over the piano which sat there untouched, a symbol of her sister's resistance to their parents' unrelenting desire for her to practice. Had Abby expressed the slightest interest in it, she would be labeled a traitor by her sister, the one whose good wishes she aspired to more than anybody in the whole world. So the piano, bought on the installment plan at great sacrifice to her parents, remained untouched except by her mother's dust rag.

Then out of the humming as if from some source outside herself emerged a song:

I am the doer, I am the giver,
I am the earth, I can receive.
I am the sunshine on the mountains,
I am the shadow under the tree.
I am the bird who's in that sunshine,
I am the snake who's in that shade,
I am the bird who sings so softly,
I am the snake who moves so still.
I am the sound that turns to silence,
I am the silence that can be heard.
I am the roots that go deep under,
I am the bough that sways so high,
I am the old one who seems so foolish,
I am the child who seems so wise
Sometimes I know my life's a circle,
Always flowing, returning home.
But sometimes I feel I have no center,
I am a spot, lost and alone.
Then I go to my own mother,
Touch her earth and breathe her air,
Drink her water, breathe her fire,
And I know my home is here,
And I know my heart is here.

Like a child the song came out whole and entire, fully formed. She was amazed. She sang it over and over so she wouldn't forget it.

It came from someplace other than her tough conscious self, someplace pure and innocent, not jaded with an awareness of all the injustice and persecution in the world: holocaust, apartheid, gay bashing, pollution, you name it.

Sure, she had sung the songs of movement hope, we shall overcome, song of the soul and so on, but deeper than those notes of affirmation was the underlying bed of resentment in which she'd been bred, the trauma of her father's flight from Russia at the age of 13 in 1917 at the outbreak of Civil War because he knew from history that any political unrest results in hostility, even violence toward Jews, his long wait in Rumania, his life in America working doggedly selling fruits and vegetables at small stands in the Bronx to save enough money to bring over his parents and siblings before it was too late for them. Later his grandson, exploring family roots, discovered that his grandfather's shtel had no Jews left. They had been systematically murdered in the village or deported to concentration camps by the White Russians, the Germans, the Ukranian police. She recalled the heated discussions of politics at home, her sister and she always more to the left than the parents, who knew better that America, though no dream, was less oppressive, compared to the rest of the world they'd come from. Hadn't the camps proven that? But what could they say to these girls who were themselves so thoroughly American, the experts on everything modern.

She fell asleep chanting the "I am" song and dreamt that she was standing on a high ridge giving a speech, not to the trees but to a multitude of upturned faces, enraptured by her words. She tried to hear what she was saying, but she couldn't.

She woke up laughing. She who spoke with her hand over her mouth to hide her broken tooth. She who whispered in front of a group. She with her odd jobs and their inadequate pay, no benefits and zero visibility. The Malka of Anonymity. What grandiosity to think she would ever be speaking to the multitudes. Neither Moses nor Aaron, she hadn't been chosen to lead anybody into the promised land.

She glanced up and saw a star flickering through pine needles. And it spoke to her, not in a voice she could hear although she would swear later that it had a yiddish accent.

"You are a great teacher. Not to hide behind that mask of good girl and you will have much of great wisdom and beauty to share with many people. Don't be afraid to open your mouth and speak from your heart and your mind. Lead people back into wildness."

She was too stunned to laugh again. Where was the voice coming from?

Her father never spoke like that. Her sister always called her a goody good, but this message wasn't from her sister. She felt like crying, it was so far from the truth, but tears did not come easily to her, so instead she fell asleep again.

In her dream she was dressed in a plain robe, like an Arab, making a speech, a man it seemed; and then she was in quilted pajamas, apparently pregnant, leading more Asian people in the same drab pajamas across a mountain pass; and finally she was in sandals and a torn cloak being pushed by guards armed with machetes into a windowless hut from which she tunneled to freedom.

She woke again when the sun rose over the eastern mountain. She felt wonderful, as if this was the first day of life and she was the first person to greet it. She took a swig of water from her half full canteen and leapt up to face more adventure. She was ready for anything. As she wound down the path, she remembered that past life reading she'd gotten from a psychic friend of Beth's, about how she'd been a revolutionary many times, always speaking up for justice and often being persecuted as a result. Was the reading just a bunch of hooey? Now she wondered about the dreams: was she that impressionable?

She zipped down and around the next waterfall and then the ground began to level out. Eventually she found a path which led to a log cabin which turned out to be locked and empty. She thought of breaking in to find a phone, but doubted there would be one and besides who would she call? Everyone she knew lived at least four hours drive away.

The path led her south, down along the stream where she needed to go. Sure enough, she finally came to other cabins and a dirt road which she hiked down until a pickup truck drove by. She hailed the driver and asked him what road this was. When he told her, she'd never heard of it, but together they identified a common landmark and from there she could figure out where she had camped and how to get back there. He offered to give her a ride to the main road and she accepted. Turned out he was a welder, had a shop down in the village and a camp up near the lake. He'd just dropped his wife and kids up there for the day.

Drawing him out, she realized how relaxing it could be just to chat with regular people instead of worrying about what they think of you, whether they are anti-Semitic or homophobic. Chances are they were, but when you're face to face just talking, it doesn't matter so much. He was curious about where she was from, but she was vague and he didn't pry. She'd already found out how prejudiced the locals were against anyone from the city. He let her out on the main road and pointed her the way to her road with a friendly smile. She hiked back from there, about six miles, arriving at the land as the sun began to slant for its descent into the hills again.

This was the first of many homecomings. She crawled back into her tent with satisfied exhaustion. The only missing ingredient was somebody to tell about her adventure. But she wasn't used to anybody ever listening, except Beth, and Beth was gone, off with somebody else, somebody more beautiful, it seemed, more spiritual, more alluring in every way.

Over the summer and into the fall Abby climbed many more mountains, many with spectacular views and exciting trails, she heard wisps of her own songs and saw fragments of her own dreams which were just as intriguing, but none of her experiences was as full of vision and promise as the time on her own mountain she called her "lost and found."

But as the leaves turned and fell and the days grew shorter, she found herself growing sad. Soon she'd have to return to the city and some dull job. Soon she'd be living again with the eyes of others watching her every move. Soon her consciousness would be imprinted again with images of poverty, racism and the abuse of women and children.

Sometimes as she stared through the woods at the setting sun, she saw shadows moving from behind trees. Sometimes what she thought was a tree stump would stand and turn as if it were an elf or sprite. Sometimes arms would beckon to her, silent gestures of welcome. Sometimes she was afraid she'd be lost in the shadows if she stayed much longer.

She dashed into the city to celebrate Roshashana with her mother, but scurried back to the woods to celebrate the birthday of the world by herself--with the round and the sweet of the earth, an apple from the old tree and honey from a local hive. The crisp air, blue skies and sunny days of early fall were the perfect time for the new year. What would this year bring? Was this the beginning of something really new or just an interlude before she returned to her old life? Playing the Kohl Nidra on her flute by the fire, she kept the fast, honored the memory of her father, blessed the light, and wondered about the future.

When the hunting season came, threats to her safety became audible--loud bangs echoing from hill to hill. She bought dozens of square red warning signs and posted the land from border to border, but she knew it was hard to break habits and these men had been prowling through this land for decades. The old abandoned shack was full of their refuse: girlie magazines, cigarette butts, crushed beer cans. She wore red, stayed closer to home and prayed for the hunters to get stuck in the mud.

But the mud was turning into ice. The nights were getting colder and she shivered even in her down sleeping bag. Still she didn't want to leave. If only she could stick it out until Thanksgiving.

On the day before Thanksgiving she was sitting on the rise above the beaver pond when she saw a neighbor's dog walking on the water which was partially frozen. She worried for the beavers when the dog started sniffing around the beaver lodge, more accessible to predators now that the pond had turned to ice. Beavers really didn't have much protection aside from their powerful teeth. They were the most peace-loving of animals, preying on no others. But the dog seemed merely curious and scampered off after drinking in the various smells of beaver and muskrat and whoever else hung out near the lodge.

Suddenly the dog, who must've been young, skidded to a halt as the ice began to crack underneath her, but she couldn't stop in time and with a desperate scratching of nails on ice, she plunged into the freezing water. Abby stood up, not sure what to do. She prayed that the dog would be able to climb out on her own because there was no way anyone could walk out there to rescue her.

Then as she stared into the distance, worried, she saw a shadow detach itself from the roots of a huge sugar maple and crawl across the beaver dam toward the struggling dog. With total calm, silence and agility the slight figure edged over the intricate tangle of peeled sticks, moving as close as possible to the dog without having to step onto the thin membrane of ice. But even when this person was directly opposite the dog, there was at least ten feet of ice between that position and the dog.

Abby held her breath, then started to run, calling out a warning as the figure stretched out across the ice and inched like a lizard or snake toward the exhausted animal. Abby ran down to the edge of the pond, ready to help but powerless, watching with wonder while the person eased across the ice, spreading out body weight so that no one section of ice bore too much of the burden. Abby thought of running back to her tent for some rope but was hesitant to leave so she stood amazed as the figure worked its way over to the jagged edge of ice beyond which the dog had sank.

Then this mysterious stranger reached out with one arm and grabbed the dog by the collar and slowly, steadily pulled the dog out of the water and onto the ice. Once on a solid surface the dog scrambled over to the beaver dam, her ears flailing, where she shook off the water and turned to look back at her rescuer who was slowly pivoting on her stomach, rotating back toward the dam, then sliding slowly back toward safety. As Abby groaned, suddenly recognizing who it was, the figure stood on the ice and ran while a huge crack in the ice chased her to shore.

Then Beth turned with a smile and waved to Abby. *"You burst on the scene already a legend. The original vagabond, you strayed into my heart."*

How Beth loved to play with danger. Abby grinned, waving back. When she opened her arms, what leapt into them first was not Beth but a wet bundle of fur.

Where we are the girls playing thunder, sisters who wouldn't keep still when they were told to, who clapped their stones together until they were sent outside in the dead of winter. Jumping up and down to keep warm, they bounced up to the sky. There they settled in, shouted thunder down to their village, sparked their stones into lightening, and never grew old.

5

BETH

"You know what?" Beth had been keeping Abby waiting for a couple of hours. Here was another distraction. "I think that dog reminds you of yourself when you were younger and wanted to tag around behind your sister."

Abby narrowed her eyes. Not only was this a distraction, it was a sore point. But Beth, in her discarded role as counselor, often touched sore points, gently of course, but nonetheless incisively.

Ever since she had been rescued from the frozen pond, the dog had attached herself not to Beth who had saved her but to Abby who hadn't. Despite how many times Abby had jogged her back to her home down the road, she'd returned, to sit in front of Abby gazing with her soft brown deer's eyes or to sleep all night outside her tent, no matter how cold it got. Now that they had moved into the shack, she sat on the doorstep, day and night, without hope of either entrance or food. They joked that instead of "Lassie, come home," the refrain was "Doggie, go home." But the dog was in love and no matter how cool the welcome, she was convinced that Abby was her leader of choice, her Alpha and her Omega, with jaunts home for food in between. And Beth was convinced that Abby's antipathy toward the dog echoed the internalized attitudes of dismissal her older sister had expressed toward Abby when she didn't want her following her around.

She was a pretty dog, with her mix of colors, soft face, and agile body, but she seemed, to Abby at least, desperate for attention, fawning and obsequious, in the presence of people anyway. When out in the woods she was everything one might want a dog to be, adventurous, athletic, at home swimming, climbing mountains or jogging along the road. But Abby didn't want anything in a dog; she wasn't used to animals unless they were in zoos or in the wild. She didn't like the idea of condemning one to domesticity. Beth was the dog person, a fact which seemed to have gotten lost in this conversation. And what about Beth's older sister? Had she ever hurt Beth's feelings by telling her to get lost?

All this was beside the point. The fact was they were supposed to go hiking to the caves at least two hours ago. But time for Beth was a tangle of distractions, each one of which offered opportunity to reflect upon those proceeding. Each moment recapitulated every moment which came before it, providing an endless expanding possibility for philosophical discussion about the coulds and woulds and shoulds, the might-have-beens and if- onlys of life. One could imagine Beth at the end of her long life as a large round Buddha ball of yarn.

Take this moment, for instance

Abby had been waiting to go to the caves ever since they'd shared their dreams in the morning. She'd taken out the compost, emptied the pee pot, chopped wood and made a fire, jogged down the road with the dog, gone to the outhouse, installed a storm door, and put plastic over the windows. For Abby, there was little slip between cup and lip; as soon as an idea occurred to her, she was ready to carry it out.

For Beth, all was one slow, luxurious moment. It was hard to tell if this was her natural pace or if it was a response to having been jerked around as a child by her traveling parents. Every time she tried to root into some place, she was pulled away, almost always without warning, without time to anticipate the change, time to adjust, time to grieve. If this slow thoroughness was her natural pace, then the violation was that much more intense. She had learned to curl inside herself, winding through the corridors of the one dwelling they couldn't remove her from, her own mind, or gazing at the larger, less tenuous realities of sky and horizon. She had a poetic or scientific talent for observing with loving attention mundane realities, which unfortunately with so much motion blurred with the constantly shifting landscape.

Had she not traveled, however, she, like a tree, might never have moved further than the first place she rooted. Who's to say? If that had happened, perhaps she would not have had such an interesting mind. She speculated, for instance, that linear time was an illusion, that somewhere at the source of things, we lived simultaneous lives, where oneself as an Egyptian slave could effect the welfare of oneself as a 20's flapper and reverberate into the voyages of oneself as a medieval Chinese merchant. So why not slow down so you could tune into these deep connections?

"Listen to this," Beth said. Abby looked up from the book she was trying to read.

"We are embodiments of the Universal Dreamer... The Council of Nine... said that we create God to the same extent that God creates us."

"Who are the Council of Nine?" Abby asked with predictable disgust, which made Beth laugh.

"God only knows. 'If God created us, in the Universal inspiration, as equivalent fractal elements, then in return we will create God. God is not some other person existing apart from us. God is the collective consciousness of us all.'"

One would need a micro-micro meter to measure the amount of time Abby spent thinking about G-d, or Goddess, compared to Beth, for whom the concept or reality or whatever God was to her was a favorite point of rumination. Abby attributed that to Beth's Catholic upbringing although she knew other Catholics not so inclined.

Beth read on, as Abby knew she would: "As we return to source, we pool ourselves, our wisdom and collective experiences, insights and understandings to become, in the moment of Oneness, a new being, totally fresh and completely unique, a new God; a new collective wisdom emerges, wiser and richer than the God before because of all we have contributed from our many individual lives."

"Is that what it felt like when you were meditating--a return to source?" Abby was still trying to find out what it had been like for Beth to meditate for a year and, and was also puzzling over why Beth had left the ashram. But prying such revelations out of Beth was a little like trying to persuade a snail to move out of its shell.

"Occasionally--but other times sitting was torture. The point is in the allowing, to observe whatever is, without trying to change it."

Abby tried to try changing her expectations, set up by Beth when she suggested that very morning that they hike up to the caves which they hadn't explored yet. The weather was supposed to be warm and sunny. If they didn't get going soon, it would be too late; the sun would be going down again. But the more she tried patience, the less it worked. "Beth!" she muttered.

"No, listen, you'll like this part: 'The merging into Oneness is not an annihilation of self. It is the communion of self. It is the arrival home for billions of selves, after a great adventure. It is the pause of rest, recuperation, and sharing tales after voyages of discovery. We are the front line of experience. We represent God breaking new ground and sailing into unchartered waters. We are God the Adventurer. Our experiences nourish God as we are nourished with love. If we refuse to change, grow and evolve, if we hang onto stagnant physical situations and refuse to return to source, then we are starving God as surely as we starve ourselves."

At the suggestion of starvation Abby put her book down and started packing her knapsack: two bananas, two apples, some sunflower seeds, flashlight, t.p., a canteen full of water, and two extra shirts. "Ok, oh divine one, it's time for our adventure. If we don't move it, the Goddess will lose it."

It took another half hour for Beth to get dressed. Even when she was wearing her old clothes, considerations of texture, warmth, color and overall elan had to be weighed and choices made. When heading out into the public eye, Beth was quite a dresser, but even when they were going into a cave, selections must be pondered with particular attention to dampness, cold, and darkness. One thing which Beth had learned from the mobility of her childhood was that if you can't carry it with you, you don't have it. You can't count on a drugstore in a foreign country, you can't depend on them having your favorite food or a comfortable pair of shoes or even cow's milk if you crave it. So wherever Beth went, she went as a bag lady. Even when hiking, when she could count on Abby, with considerable guidance from Beth, to load up the knapsack, Beth's pockets were packed full.

Finally they got out of the shack and locked the door. Abby waited for Beth to rummage around in her car, in which many of her possessions were still stored just in case orders came down, as they had in her childhood, for her to be in some place like Sumatra the following week--not that she could drive to Sumatra. After much rustling, she emerged with her Tibetan bells which she wanted to play in the caves. As they finally started down the path, Beth, as usual, ran back inside, after getting the key from Abby, to fetch one more item, a soft blue cap.

Then like two Chinese monks, anonymous in their tattered layers, both innocent and wise in their simplicity, small among the towering trees, they set off for their adventure at the caves, the dog loping ahead of them.

They had heard about the caves from the caretaker at the boy scout camp who'd seen Abby trying to install stovepipe at the shack and stopped to help--a g-dsend. While they worked, Beth, in her quiet, receptive way, pumped him for information about the area. The caves were old iron or graphite mines, now played out, which set up in the hills beyond the scout camps. He told them how to get there and they planned an exploration for the next sunny day which, as it turned out, didn't come along for another week.

They hadn't gotten far before Beth called Abby's attention to a spider web in the sunlight. Abby glanced at it, eager to move on, but Beth insisted she look more closely. There in the middle of the web was the spider. They stared at her golden body, thinking of Spiderwoman, the creator of the world according to Navajo mythology. Abby then started to leave. "No wait. She's weaving." They watched, fascinated, as the eight legs moved around the inner circle of the web, each foot with its own separate mission in the weave, one pulling out the thread from her belly, one setting it onto one of the radiating lines, another fixing it there, another stretching it across to the next one, others maintaining balance while others moved the huge body around the circle. It was precise and rhythmical. "It's like a dance!" cried Beth, herself talented in that genre.

"Amazing," murmured Abby, ready to move. Although she usually preferred forward movement when at all possible, she found it much easier to sit still with these interruptions when they were outdoors than when inside. She watched Beth with amused tolerance. Beth had fallen into a trance as she stared at the spider in the web. Something philosophical was, no doubt, forthcoming. Something, perhaps, about composition, coordination and pattern.

Beth glanced at her and smiled. She said nothing. But she did reach out and gently released a struggling fly from the edge of the web. Abby hadn't even noticed it. The fly, surprised to find itself severed from the entangling thread, washed its face with one arm, then the other, gave a buzz and flew off.

As they walked on, Beth reminded Abby of her dream, which Abby had told her then promptly forgot. It was another of Abby's schlep dreams, not anything she wished to dwell upon. But Beth was after her to integrate the schlep, to allow herself to be less than super competent in everything she did.

"That's easy enough for you to say. You don't have a schlep bone in your entire body."

True, Beth had never been anything but graceful physically. But how many times had she felt like an alien, awkward with the customs of the country whether they were as severely challenging as foreign languages or as momentously trivial as teenage sock customs. She'd been laughed at for saying "Merde" when she meant "Merci" and for wearing her socks rolled down when the local fads dictated they be straight up. You didn't have to be a schlep to feel like one.

Beth shrugged. She knew the futility of arguing with Abby and decided to save her energy for more significant issues, like why they should stay the winter there in the shack, together, something Abby was resisting for any number of reasons.

"What about *your* dream? The one about the earth falling. What was happening?"

"I was walking along on top of a cliff and suddenly the earth started collapsing beneath me," Beth said calmly.

"Sounds scary."

"Naw." Beth had learned at a young age that fear was not one of the tolerated emotions in her family. The only thing, she'd been convinced, they had to fear was fear itself. It might be ok, even normal to feel some trepidation, but anyone who expressed fear was a sissy. --except her mother whose job was to worry about everybody else. Most girls were called sissies; that's why she was a tomboy. "It was exciting. I just sort of rode it down."

"Where did you land?"

"I don't know. I woke up."

"What do you think it means."

"Landslide--whatever that symbolizes."

"Maybe it has something to do with your leaving the ashram."

Beth nodded, then shook her head.

"Something to do with having the ground jerked out from under you."

Beth smiled. "That fits my whole life. Besides, I chose to leave."

"Why?"

"Too many people. Too much structure. I just didn't feel at home there."

"But weren't you one of the inner circle?"

"Nope." Actually, now that Beth was talking about it, she realized she *had* felt at home there in some ways; that was the problem. Not that there had been anything wrong with her home, she loved her family and all, but she didn't need another mother, she had one who was more than good enough. And the deepest appeal of Guru Ma for so many of Beth's comrades at the ashram was that she served as the Great Mother. Beth needed to be free of familial needs, vulnerabilities, desires, opinions, expectations and judgements, not trying to second-guess and please even an inspired version of the Holy Family.

The dog ran back to make sure they were following, wagging her tail as she gazed anxiously into Abby's face. Abby gave her a perfunctory pat.

"What about Rebecca?" Rebecca was Beth's sangha companion; they'd discovered Guru Ma together.

"Rebecca's one of Guru Ma's favorites. She'll probably be there for life."

Distracted, Abby remarked on the tenacity of the luminous beech leaves, still clinging to their twigs when all the other leaves had fallen and turned to a mottled brown on the path.

Beth was just as glad; this distraction gave her pause to reflect on why she'd actually left the ashram. It was, perhaps, just too noisy. She liked the all night chanting and she liked the depth of search, but she didn't like that much emotionality, hysteria and gossip, people freaking out and focusing so much of their attention on what Ma did or said. She preferred the quiet of meditation, sitting still or walking mindfully. By disposition she was more Buddhist than Hindu. And, after years of Catholic schools, she didn't like feeling guilty if she wanted to "escape," to walk on the beach or call a friend. She didn't like all the rules and regulations, being assigned chores, although most of the chores were pleasant enough, an opportunity to focus upon something besides the guru's mood or one's own uncertain path. Group life was useful for providing a sort of discipline, but she preferred one-to-one relationships with both divine and human.

The incline was getting steeper. Beth started singing, "Tea for two and two for tea, me for you and you for me." This was their hiking song; it provided a perfect rhythm for walking up a mountain.

"Two for tea and tea for two," Abby sang, joining in.

Beth heard a whir behind them and stopped to listen. Bird wings in flight--one of life's sweetest sounds. A ground feeder. Grouse or quail? If so, there would probably be others. She signaled to Abby, to listen, Abby who was resolutely marching on to the tune of "Two for Tea." But all they heard was the wind stirring the leaves.

They hiked on in silence. A loud hammering stopped Beth again. She and Abby both looked around for the perpetrator: a huge pileated woodpecker, its red crest striking in more ways than one above its distinctive black and white head. As if aware of their attention, it left the decayed birch it had been drumming upon and flew away, its wide wing span causing a cry of admiration from Beth and Abby.

The land next to them began to drop away as they climbed. The dog sat waiting for them at a fork in the path. She looked excited, as if she'd discovered something. Down the left fork was the first cave. Abby expressed disappointment at the shallow cavity, but Beth went up closer to look. Under the roof of the indentation was a small green pool, full of moss. As Beth sat there in silence, she could hear water dripping into the pool from the moist rocks above. The sound echoed like chimes. A line from a poem, "Peace comes dropping slow," fell into her mind.

Abby, eager to discover a bigger cave, pulled her away. Around the next bend they found it, like the open mouth of a huge whale. As they crawled around its rocky teeth onto a narrow shelf, they found a deep pool in the front of the cave, impassable except by swimming, and the water was much too cold even for wading. A thin layer of ice covered the innermost surface of the pond. But deeper into the cave they saw light coming in from the right side.

Exiting through the teeth rocks, Beth climbed around the ridge to the right and through some huge boulders, looking for another entry. Once she found it, she snuck quietly inside the opening so she could surprise Abby. As she anticipated, Abby looked startled to see her there on the other side of the pool, then quickly disappeared from the mouth of the cave so she could follow Beth into its ear. Waiting for her Beth gazed out across the water through the mouth of the cave. From the dark perspective of the cave, the outside landscape seemed very bright, almost too bright. A white line of birch, green splash of pine, gold flecks of beech were reflected in the pool.

Inside the cave they could see, once Abby joined Beth and their eyes adjusted to the dark, where someone had built a fire. In the damp and chill of the cave Beth shivered and pulled her blue cap down over her ears for a moment. A fire was appealing. The dog poked her head inside the cave, sniffed around, then ran off outside again. Apparently not originally a cave dweller.

Seeing that Abby was ready to exit with the dog, Beth pulled out her Tibetan bells and signaled for Abby to listen. As she struck the bells, she closed her eyes and relaxed into the darkness. The sound reverberated so intensely she could feel herself expanding with it. Like a drop of water striking the surface of a pond and circling out from it, her spirit unfurled in every direction, circling out toward eternity. She listened until the sound disappeared into silence. She felt energized and inspired.

Only when I'm perfectly still, she remembered, can I feel this fullness. "The still point of the turning world." Only when I stop pushing, dragging, driving myself here and there, up and down, back and forth, can I know who I really am at the deepest core of my being: nobody and everything.

She struck the bells again and sailed out with the sound. This was the only movement which mattered, the transcendent motion of being. What you did, what people say you've done fade to insignificance in this context.

As she sat savoring the silence, she could hear Abby's restlessness. But Beth wasn't ready to leave. She wanted to stay there with the darkness and the silence, listening, as she did so well. But even if she made it official and called it "meditation," she doubted if she could persuade Abby to stay with her. She could feel Abby's intense desire to be outside in the sun. She'd have to appeal to the adventurer in her.

"Let's see how far it goes back," she said, gesturing with enthusiasm toward the heart of the cave.

Abby cocked her head and squinted. "It's too dark. You can't see a thing."

"Our eyes will adjust. All we have to do is trust our feet. Maybe we could unwind string to lead us back out of the labyrinth."

Abby shook her head with a slight grin. "What string? Something else to trip over?"

"A schlep is not a klutz, amigo."

Abby reached into the knapsack and pulled out a flashlight. Beth took this as a sign of compromise and turned around to head into the pitch black of the cave. Her feet led her along a path next to water. She could hear a soft trickle and burble to her left.

"Promise you'll stop if you run into water," Abby said to her back. "I for one have no gift for walking on water." This referred to a discussion they'd had the night before about mind over matter; Beth believed that one could do just about anything if her faith was strong enough. That's how she was able to spread her weight on thin ice to save the dog. Abby had no such illusions.

Even though Abby was a worry wart, Beth noted once again, Abby also had little use for whiners. Beth could count on the fact that Abby didn't care to think of herself as shrinking from exploration. Nor acting like a sissy.

Inside the cave time seemed to stand still. It was impossible to tell how long it took them to creep along before they stumbled into a pile of rocks. To their left they could hear a louder dripping of water. To their right they could palpably sense the density of damp rock wall. Now in front of them was a clutter of jagged rocks. Beth reached into her jacket pocket and pulled out a tiny flashlight. With it as guide, she spotted a ledge beyond the rock pile where they could crawl.

"I don't think it's going anywhere, Beth," Abby opined plaintively

"Then we'll run into a dead end. But wouldn't it be exciting to find a way out?"

"Or buried treasure?"

"Or a vein of crystals."

"Chances are we'll discover this is a fox den or a place where bears hibernate," Abby stated realistically.

Beth had already scrambled over the pile of rocks, calling back to Abby to assure her that if she just trusted her feet, it would be a breeze.

"What about your dream? What about the earth falling?"

"No problem. I was on top of that earth, not underneath it."

"But I wasn't," muttered Abby.

As Beth crawled onto the ledge, she saw a glimmer of light further back, down a long tunnel. Two eyes? No, not that focused. As she curled up to wait for Abby, she was suddenly overwhelmed with a desire to weep, the same feeling that threatened to overcome her at the most inappropriate times during last year's meditation. Where was this sadness coming from? What did it mean? She wasn't premenstrual and she had nothing to feel sorry about. But here it was again, this deep sadness, like the sadness of all the people she'd ever counseled, the grief of the world weighing upon her. Here in this darkness she couldn't restrain the sobbing and a shudder of grief passed through her like a sudden earthquake. Then she was still, calmer than she'd felt in ages.

She didn't say anything to Abby about what she'd seen, waiting for her to make her own discoveries. She didn't tell her about the grief.

"Light!" Abby exclaimed.

"See! I bet that's the end of the cave. I bet we can get out that way."

With renewed enthusiasm they crawled down toward the glow as the cave narrowed in around them. But when they reached the hole in the rock, they saw that it was set up in the roof of the cave, through a shaft whose opening was several feet above where they could reach. They tried piling rocks up but the rocks were too uneven and the pile kept falling back to rubble.

"How did Jonah get out of the whale?" Abby asked.

"I think he started a fire and the whale sneezed," Beth said.

Imagining being sneezed out of the cave they started to giggle, somewhat hysterically.

"If we get too giddy, we won't have the strength to climb out of here," Beth finally gasped.

"There's no way we're going to climb out here; we'll have to go back the way we came," Abby exclaimed.

"Wanna bet?" They bet.

Then Beth persuaded Abby, against her own wager, to cup her hands so she could hoist Beth up into the shaft. After several tries, it worked. Beth wedged herself into the cavity, bracing herself with her feet, then inched her body upward.

A slight feeling of suffocation, a definite feeling of constriction, a hope that the earth would hold together while you crawled out of her reminded Beth of what it must have felt like to be born. The difference was that this time she was rising rather than falling, she was heading for freedom rather than sanctuary. This was the way out.

A country song echoed through her mind:

"So it's time to set you free,
let you sail away from me,
though I'll miss you when you do,
I'm with you, I'm with you.
Turn your face into the wind,
let your greatest dream begin,
take the high road, win or lose,
I'm with you, I'm with you.
I was there in the morning light
with a love that could last
and I'll be there on your darkest night
when the sun's long gone
and your heart is sinking fast.
When you struggle, when you fall,
when your back's against the wall,
after all the rest are through,
I'm with you, I'm with you.
I've done all that I can do."

She paused for a moment to catch her breath and felt comfort in the solidity of the rock enclosing her. Nothing much to cling to but assurance that with the right leverage it would hold her. As she reached the top of the shaft, she stretched up and grabbed the edge of the rock, hoisting herself high enough to prop herself up with her elbows until her right knee could pull itself up and out, dislodging the rest of her body as she grabbed a tree trunk for security. Once up she lay there gasping, gazing at the blue sky. There was nothing more to do.

"Beth." Abby's voice echoed out of the cave.

Beth rolled over and peeked down the opening. "Yes, oh oracle, what is the answer?"

"What is the question?"

"Who are we and where are we going?"

"I am Abby and how am I going to get out of here?"

"I could hang by my feet and pull you out--"

"No."

"Or I could come back the other way and lead you out."

"I'll meet you back at the mouth of the cave."

Beth took her time wandering over the knoll she'd landed on, wondering if she was walking on top of the cave. On the way she whistled for the dog, but apparently, unwilling to follow them into the depths of the cave, she'd gone home. With an unfailing sense of direction and a now lighted path Beth arrived back at the mouth of the cave before Abby showed up. She sat there on a rock in the sunshine, soaking up the silence with her eyes shut.

When she heard a slight rustle on the path, she figured it was Abby and kept her eyes shut, not wanting to move yet. Hadn't she just been reborn? She felt fingers lifting the flap of her shirt pocket and smiled. Somebody was looking for the chocolate kisses she'd stowed in there. Someone with very small fingers. She opened her eyes and tried not to flinch as she stared into the soft, intelligent eyes of a young raccoon. Then she held still as he pulled out a kiss, unwrapped it delicately and ate it, obviously pleased. She wasn't sure how good chocolate was for animals, so she reached very slowly and carefully into her other pocket and took out some almonds. As she handed him an almond, she was fascinated with the softness of his little hand which she touched as the almond passed between them.

He apparently had no fear at all. He must not have ever met any humans. He probably wasn't more than a year old. But how then did he know so much about pockets and candy wrappers? Would that she herself, who tended to dive for cover whenever a stranger knocked on the door, had such trust.

In the distance she could hear Abby approaching. Abby was shocked at the sight of the raccoon and hesitant when Beth motioned for her to come closer. The raccoon, munching on almonds, glanced at Abby with only mild curiosity.

"Aren't you afraid she'll bite you?" Abby whispered.

"Look at her hands. She's just like us."

"She's a wild animal."

"Come on, she's as good as a person."

Abby kept her distance. Beth could see Abby's mind whizzing around issues like disease, filth and rabies, deciding she was just as glad for her detachment. When Abby didn't experience life the way she did, though, it was disappointing. She would have liked to share the experience more fully.

Above, an airplane droned. The little raccoon, satisfied that all Beth's pockets were empty of food, though otherwise full of odds and ends, and unable to pry open the fist which clutched the remaining two chocolate kisses, wiped his mouth with his dainty hands and wandered off.

Beth started oming with the drone of the plane and Abby joined her. While not as purely transcendent as the sound of the bells in the cave, the chanting provided a more grounded experience of oneness.

"Guess what the buddhist said to the hot dog vendor?" asked Abby once the chant was done.

Puzzled, Beth shook her head.

"Make me one with everything."

Beth laughed. "See--doesn't that make it kosher?"

"And have I got something to show you," said Abby, leading Beth back through the cave's entrance.

The afternoon sun was at just the right angle to pour into the cave. Striking the water sunlight shimmered and sent ripples of light onto the cave's walls and roof. The birch, pine and maple outside danced in the pool while mist rose from the surface of the water, giving a mysterious glow to the scene.

They were spellbound. Entranced at first with the effect of the whole, they then began to notice details: how the surface light and reflected light merged into each other, creating layers of pattern in the water, how the rocks seemed to become liquid with light, softening and melting as the mist rose around them, how the sun reached all the way across the water to touch each of them with its warmth.

What a light show. What a blessing. What a sign from the goddess that all was well and all manner of things would be well, including their life together.

They stayed until the sun had sunk beyond the hill and the cave was darker than when they'd first discovered it. Then they ate the two chocolate kisses and hurried back down the trail, trusting their feet over the fading ground in the rapidly falling dusk until finally their flashlight led them back to their sweet shack, embers still warming the stove. The dog was waiting for them.

And there they spent the next nine months in their own cozy cave. While Beth concentrated her energies on just being, Abby was fond of doing things. She maintained contact with the outside world, providing a buffer zone for Beth while shopping, chatting with neighbors, keeping in touch with old friends, following the world's political crises. Beth, the preserver, puttered and cleaned, saved and salvaged, producing from one of her many bags the most surprising objects like electric blankets or coffee makers whenever they needed them. As they eked out the last of their savings, they ate very simply and lived the most frugal of lives, relying on radio and tapes and long conversations for entertainment. Daily they ventured out to slide across the frozen pond or to wade through the steadily mounting snow. Together they managed to keep the wood chopped and the fire going while watching snow flakes gather and swirl, icicles stretch and melt, sun rise and sun set. In their shared nest they grew closer than they'd ever been.

Their idyll was shattered in spring by the advent of mud season, by dwindling resources which precipitated job searches, and by a phone call from Carrie, Beth's sister, telling them about her friend Ev and announcing that they were planning to spend the summer on the land. This, on top of a note from Dulce, Beth's former partner, saying she also planned to visit with her new honey, Gail.

The intrusion of grimy reality in the form of mud-locked tires and job interviews was adjustment enough, but the impending invasion of family, friends and strangers was positively threatening in ways they could only imagine as they felt themselves momentarily shrink into the old familiar molds from which they thought they had escaped. They looked at each other in alarm.

Trunk

Where we are, at the same time, the orphan girl challenging the Queen of Death who stole away her friend. She walked all the way to the magic blue mountain and through the gate of death to ask for her precious cow back. Even when she was transformed into a lake, her power won out over Ms. Death's, for as a lake she could see everything and she herself would never die.

DULCE

Dulce was here for the people, not for the woods particularly. If she were to build a house, it wouldn't be in a place already crowded with trees. It would be high on a mountain overlooking a mesa or an ocean. Besides, she had no stomach for building. She'd rather be reading or writing. But she figured that if she were going to join her friends, she needed shelter. And since there was none yet, it would have to be built. The shack was a stinking tomb of mouse shit and germs. She'd spent too many nights in a soggy tent or cramped in the back seat of a car.

The trouble was that her idea of shelter was not just a few branches tied together over a damp ground or a leaky mosquito net hung over a frame. She felt the need for a decisive distinction between in and out. At the high of noon or the dark of midnight she wanted to be inside, safe, protected from predators of any sort, humans, mosquitoes, or scorpions. She wanted a roof to keep the rain out, walls to keep intruders out, a level floor you could depend upon.

She had no illusions about finding room enough in the proposed cabin to meet her needs. Too many times lately space she'd shared with another had been taken away from her: the seaside apartment she'd shared with Beth relinquished so Abby could move in; the Vermont farm she'd shared with Eleanor taken away completely, gone with their relationship. No, no, she needed her own space.

So, reluctant always to disturb the peace, she tried to pretend she didn't understand what all the fuss was about. She'd given them every warning: the story she'd written about cutting down trees on the farm; the sword she'd brandished with Tai Chi grace; her request at the meeting that they help her with her shelter, like they'd helped each other. Beth perpetually encouraged her to ask for help instead of toughing it out on her own, but when she did, they waffled as usual: "Well, maybe." Except Carrie who uncharacteristically said "No."

And now in true womanly victim fashion they were screaming bloody murder because she'd hired the bulldozer. She wasn't going to cut down the trees herself, for chrissake. Beautiful as the trees might be, they were crowding too close to what would soon be her house. One good storm and any number of them could easily come crashing down through the roof, crushing her.

Besides they obstructed the view. Why she'd agreed to buy these dense woods when what she really longed for was the vista, the green rolling hills of Vermont or the long lavender stretches of mountain in her native New Mexico sometimes puzzled her. It wasn't the land but the people she finally bought into, the old lover and friends, the group, the family of choice: singing old songs all night around the campfire; long, leisurely discussions of the meaning of life, growing old together with a place to share.

But now it was beginning to feel as if the group was crowding in like the trees, and she would have to split off from them, one by one, just to free herself from the ever encroaching people trap she'd grown up in. She needed more space, it was bad enough she lived in the middle of one of the world's largest cities, she needed open space. "Give me land, lots of land, under starry skies above, don't fence me in." Wasn't that why they bought the land in the first place?

Now this mouse had bitten her. At least she assumed it was a mouse. And instead of making progress on the building, she had to rush to the hospital emergency room for a tetanus shot. The porch where she slept when the mouse bit her was overrun by mice; the shack was overrun by mice. It was Beth's fault for not getting rid of them in the first place, for substituting abstract piety for care of her friends.

"I'll get rid of any pests in *my* house," Dulce muttered. She refused to eat anything the mice had munched on. As a child she'd been terrified of a mouse biting her. Even though the doctor assured her there hadn't been a case of rabies among rodents for 20 years, she felt little comfort: what about plague? What about other diseases scientists hadn't discovered yet?

She was angry at Beth for imposing her life choices on everyone else and assuming that, since of course they were right, whatever followed was "just life." Back when they'd been together, she'd bought into Beth's saintly acts as if they were justified by reality itself. A mouse-infested house was not "just life." St. Francis wasn't the only ideal.

Ironic that the red-headed man she'd hired to clear the road and the site was named Mr. Twist. As he maneuvered the clumsy bulldozer around a big rock, she watched with some detachment as he shoved a huge maple with his machine and it fell with an enormous thud. Oddly she felt a sort of satisfaction in the pit of her stomach as the tree toppled. She wondered why. One can't help but be impressed, she thought, with the power of destruction, even though something in her heart protested and something in her head needed to justify this cutting down of trees to make room for people.

Making oneself at home in a place where one is not naturally comfortable is never easy. This time she was determined not to settle for what somebody else wanted, as she had with the house in the city and with the farm, but for what she really needed: safety, space, and comfort. She used to depend on Beth for these, assuming that Happy Familydom carried with it comfort insurance until she discovered that Beth could barely fry an egg by herself and could just as easily live forever on crackers and cheese or rice and beans. For all her advice to others to just go with the flow, Beth seemed to resist any change she hadn't herself initiated, even when it represented improvement.

But if she had to destroy in order to create, Dulce was willing. Secretly she recognized that she was more able than the others to integrate her own shadow. She'd lived long enough with creative guilt. She also knew that sometimes to cure you have to cut into flesh. This stage of building was, perhaps, a kind of operation. The metaphor satisfied, although the action still troubled. How had the rest of them gotten away without knocking down trees? Or had they done it all in secret before she got there? Why were they so addicted to innocence?

After the mouse bite, Beth, without of course taking any responsibility, did help Dulce clear away some of the shattered limbs on the site and this morning Abby cut some trees with her chainsaw until Twist's ribbing about her dull blade irritated her and she stomped off. Turned out, Dulce found out by listening to him more closely, that his father had been seriously injured by a dull blade. And of course Gail was there, steady and efficient, supervising the whole production. Touched by their willingness to help, Dulce offered the others the cut logs for their planned octagon house and they gladly accepted.

Satisfied with this generosity Dulce turned back to the portable typewriter she'd set up in the woods, in the midst of all the hullabaloo, and continued writing her essay on Flannery O'Conner. Every once in a while she stared off into space, wondering how, restricted as she'd been, O'Conner saw so deeply into the human psyche. Dulce had a gift for getting lost in such thoughts.

The next morning Sam, the dowser who was also a psychic healer, arrived to redowse, since Twist had knocked down the original marker for the well site. When Sam told her he'd been working with a psychic surgeon, Dulce said she'd almost called on him that spring because she'd been told she might have cancer and her breast might have to be removed. This had been a secret, nagging worry even after the shadow on the film was biopsied as benign.

Although she depended mostly on western medicine, Dulce was sometimes open to the alternative healing favored by most of the group.

Immediately Sam stood still to concentrate, then told her it was an inflamed lymph gland and that she should massage it toward the heart to keep the fluid moving and leave the toxins behind. Then he concentrated some more and said that there was still some inflammation left. She wondered how he knew. With his right hand he touched her breast, as if to draw the illness out through her nipple--explaining later that the healer must move the energy blocks or disease out through the nearest opening. She felt calm in his presence and pushed back her skepticism so she could receive whatever healing he had to give.

That same afternoon, the well man came with his huge ten ton rig. Twice he got stuck driving up the hill, but each time he calmly and efficiently worked his way out of the ruts. The next morning he started drilling. They all made bets about when he would strike water. For three days Dulce sat at the site listening to the beat of the drill. She hoped for a geyser and didn't want to miss the moment.

In fact, the water never surfaced without a pump. At sunset, on the third day, just as Sam had predicted, the well-man hit water at 75 feet. Everybody came up the hill to listen to the water.

Watching him fill the hole with pipe, Dulce asked: "Will the water be muddy?"

"Nope. Water runs in veins through rock. That rock's what we've been drilling."

The idea thrilled her. "Imagine," she said, "the earth having a circulatory system so powerful it courses water through rock. What could account for such intense energy?"

Carrie quoted from the *I Ching*: "One draws from the well without hindrance. It is dependable. Supreme good fortune."

"Well?" said Abby.

"Well--that's a deep subject," said Beth and they laughed. Making merry, they took turns ohming into the pipe which reverberated up from the earth. This spontaneous celebration touched Dulce's heart.

With her friends as witnesses, Dulce said her thanks to the universe. They hadn't made room for her down along the stream, but now she was where she really wanted to be, at the foot of the mountain. She had water of her own, a precious source of life for a desert native such as she. And maybe she was "well" too. If Sam was right about the location of the water, maybe he was also right about her breast. There were times in the past she'd just as soon slice it off in amazonian fashion; right now she was feeling rather attached to it.

But the promise of health symbolized by the well was fragile. The next day the whole group gathered to finish moving and stripping the maples which Dulce had asked Twist to haul down into the meadow with his back hoe. Under Beth's supervision, they lined up along the largest log so they could roll it over onto the log in front of it--simultaneously moving it closer to the building site and exposing the side from which they had not yet removed the bark.

But after they'd pushed it, it swung back at one end and pinned Beth's hand between the two logs. She yelled with such ferocity that Dulce, Gail and Carrie ran around to the other side so they could lift it to free Beth.

When her hand was freed, Beth, too quickly dismissing her own fear and pain, yelled for everybody to push it on over, despite the fact that at that point both Dulce and Carrie were standing right in front of it, still locked in the concentration of holding it up. Beth had automatically succumbed to the bravado she'd developed within her family's stiff upper lip code of conduct. As a result, she acted impulsively, without considering the consequences or the circumstances.

Everyone heaved while Carrie hopped out of the way, but Dulce, who had braced herself to lift the log off Beth by placing her foot on the log they were rolling the tree over, was right in the line of the tree's trajectory. It bounced off the top of her right foot. Clutching her leg, Dulce rolled over backward onto the ground in intense pain.

"Why did you do that? I was trying to help you," she yelled. Her voice sounded young. "You hurt me and I was trying to save you."

How could Beth be so careless? Dulce believed firmly there were no accidents in life, that people were as responsible for their unintended acts as for the ones they did consciously.

Looking up she saw tears of sympathy in Ev's eyes and compassion in Gail's face as they bent toward her. Beth, still in pain herself, recoiled from the blame. Carrie rushed to the shack for ice while Abby ran down to the stream for cold water.

When Gail tried to help Dulce stand, Beth moved to her other side so they could lift together. The pain in Dulce's foot was excruciating. Nothing any of them did could take away that fact.

She dangled her foot in a bucket of cold water from the stream before Ev and Beth made a chair of their arms and, with help from Gail and Abby, carried her to the shack. Being lifted made Dulce nervous, but eventually she felt comfortable they could bear her weight. Despite the throbbing in her foot, she tried to relax and even managed to chuckle at the game of trust it represented. At the same time her bruised foot was beginning to swell.

Once she was settled inside the house, she was administered aspirin, crystal healing, ice, and chicken soup, along with tender concern. During this fuss, old friends arrived as scheduled, and Abby, Ev, Carrie and Beth greeted them, serving them lunch outside, not on the porch where Dulce sat with her foot in the bucket. Attended by Gail, she listened to the party and contemplated trying to carry her share of the building of their house with a crippled right foot.

Finally Gail drove her into town to the emergency room. No bones were broken. The doctor said she was damned lucky. Her tendons were badly bruised and that it would take at least a month for her foot to heal. He gave her a pair of crutches.

That night she dreamt about her mother, the weight of that paralyzed body as heavy on a young girl as the heaviest of logs. Her mother's illness pinned her down, crushing her feet, immobilizing her. Because she was expected to care about her as well as take care of her, Dulce couldn't lift her mother off, push her away, free herself. In the dream her mother's face was tearful and swollen with need, and Dulce felt torn between pity and rage. When she woke, she wondered if she'd ever be free of that weight.

At dinner in the shack the next evening one of the cats who wasn't much of a hunter caught a field mouse which had gotten trapped in the shack. When Carrie yelled at the cat, he looked up with surprise, opened his mouth to talk back, and the mouse escaped. Dulce wondered why Carrie tried to suppress the cat's natural instincts--and related it to a previous discussion of parents suppressing children. Meanwhile the mouse kept jumping around as if injured or terrified. Finally Beth tried to rescue it.

As far as Dulce was concerned, it was better off dead. And she said so. She didn't care at that point how fond Beth was of the mice or how much she identified with them. In fact she was beginning to think Beth cared more about an anonymous mouse than she did about her.

Beth told Dulce to "shush up" and then, when Dulce refused to, said she didn't like Dulce's "lack of compassion." Dulce wondered why Beth, who could hurt people's feelings without a qualm of guilt, was so identified with the mouse. Annoyed they weren't catching the mouse they were all so concerned about, Dulce got a paperbag and tried, one-footed, to scoop up the agitated critter--a feeble and pointless attempt. Everyone chased the mouse until finally it hopped out the front door to safety.

Then Dulce shouted at Beth that she was furious that she should accuse *her* of lacking compassion when it was Beth who was responsible for the log falling on Dulce's foot, and it was Beth who was responsible for Dulce getting bit by the mouse.

"If it weren't for your sentimental attitude toward vermin, they wouldn't have overrun our house." She repeated her threat to kill any pests in her new house. Beth replied by objecting to the term "body count" Dulce had used to refer to the dead mice. Campaigning against such callousness, Beth and Dulce had both been arrested protesting the Vietnam war.

Gail tried to bridge the gap by telling whoever was listening about a pet mouse she'd had as child which she was forced to get rid of when it produced too many offspring.

Soon Carrie, Gail and Abby went off to sleep, leaving Beth and Ev to continue the discussion with Dulce. Having vented her rage, Dulce was content to listen, with slight amusement, to Beth's loyal defense of the mice, whom she argued were, like indigenous people, living there long before invaders arrived on the scene. Not these particular mice, Dulce argued, ironically aware that of all of them she was probably the only one with a possible drop of native blood, and depended on it not one whit for a claim to being at home in this crazy country. None of us are really native, she thought. She wondered why Americans needed to hold onto that illusion.

The next morning Gail was fixing Dulce's crutches for her when the others came in for breakfast and decided to try them out. "Crutches never fit me," Dulce explained. To her surprise none of them had ever worn crutches, whereas this was her sixth time, always for her right foot, broken once, sprained five times. She expressed her appreciation that they were all, empathetically, taking on her injury. She wondered why she'd had more than her share of injuries while they had none.

"Why do you suppose you're so susceptible?" Beth asked, reading her mind.

"Maybe from when I had polio."

Ev expressed surprise. "When?"

"The year after my brother died. I was four and a half. I was paralyzed from the waist down and nobody knew what it was at the time. The doctor thought it was tonsillitis. By the time they'd taken my tonsils out, and I was back home, I could walk again. Thirty years later, a Rolfer who couldn't get a quiver of movement out of my right hip said I must have had polio as a kid."

"No wonder your foot feels vulnerable," Ev said.

That time of paralysis was why Dulce was so taken with flight, why the swallow's graceful glide was so numinous for her, why Pegasus was her muse.

Carrie gave Dulce a walking stick she'd carved for her so she'd have some support when the crutches had to be returned. Beth applied hot compresses to her swollen foot.

Pleased with their care, Dulce arrived at a compromise regarding the mice by sacrificing some of her treasured red peppers. She crushed them into powder and asked everyone to scatter it outside around the house, like people did in Vermont, to keep the mice out. It was fun, like casting a circle witch fashion (fun, she thought, as long as you didn't get caught and burned at the stake). The trouble was that the mice were already well nested inside the house.

Later she was rewarded for this attempt at problem-solving. Gail, Ev and Beth transported her in the garden cart up the hill to her site. They pushed and pulled the cart over boulders and through mud so she could watch the next stage of the building, preparation for the big concrete pour. Even though every bump on that rocky trail jarred her foot painfully, she appreciated their support. She wished for more time to heal her foot, but she couldn't abandon Gail at this crucial juncture.

Sam came again to lend his truck for the pour and, while they waited for the cement mixer, he did a healing on Dulce's foot and then told her to throw away the crutches. While Sam's healing didn't ease the hurt in her foot or alter her dependence on her walking stick, it did bring a flash of insight. When she'd discussed her polio with the group, someone asked what the six injuries to her foot had in common. She wasn't sure. Perhaps everytime she'd tried to be heroic? But now, at the prospect of gleefully tossing away her crutches, she remembered: the injuries occured anytime she did something full out, with gusto. That intensity was the kind of energy a kid would have at the age she was when she got polio. Were the accidents the result of a child's ignorance of limitations?

That night, energized by these revelations, Dulce cooked as only Dulce could cook, the joy she took in providing both tasty nourishment and aesthetic pleasure as appealing as the food itself. She decided it would be a cookout, once a necessity but now a special treat. As she hobbled over to the fire with various ingredients, she sang, despite the ache in her foot. "All I want is a room somewhere, far away from the cold night air." She enjoyed using the cockney accent.

Later while they ate the bluefish, roast potatoes, salad, corn, and chocolate chip cookies, Dulce told everybody about Sam's kindness in trying to heal her foot and about her insight into the source of her injuries. From there, they progressed into a discussion of archetypes of illness and healing. As a Jungian scholar, Dulce was often called upon by the group to explain Jungian terminology. This night Carrie asked her what James Hillman meant by "polytheism," and Dulce explained in her calm, clear manner how Hillman was reacting to the monomyth of the dominant culture, how what he described as "polytheism" honored the richness of diverse perspectives, values and beliefs possible through recognizing "many gods."

"And goddesses," added Ev.

Dulce then provided an example by talking about a class discussion she'd recently led on *Oedipus,* which brought out the multi-cultural interpretations offered by her diverse community college students.

Then at Ev's urging, to discover their own multiple archetypes, they drew tarot cards. Dulce's was the Chariot. They joked about the garden cart but she, of course, imagined something a bit more symbolically significant.

Later in the dark, after they'd improvised with various instruments and sung her old favorites, Dulce told a story about a Native American boy being chased by a hungry bear.

"Bears are vegetarians," protested Carrie, ever the defender of animals, albeit sentimentally.

"Not grizzlies," replied Dulce, an expert on the perils of nature. "Anyway, what happened was that his feet stopped working because he hadn't taken good care of them."

"And he got eaten?"

"Yup."

"Sounds more Germanic than Indian," commented Ev.

Abby told a similar story where the boy turned into a bear, then Carrie made a joke about "bare feet," and they laughed and started singing again, rounds and spirituals at this point.

"Hey ho, nobody home, no eat, nor drink, nor money have I none, but still I will be merry."

"All I want is a room somewhere, far away from the cold night air, lots of chocolates for me to eat, lots of coal making lots of heat."

"Swing low, sweet chariot, coming for to carry me home. Swing low, sweet chariot, coming for to carry me home."

"Hey ho, nobody home." She had never been homeless, but she might as well have been--far away in the cold night air. She hoped this new chariot the cards had given her would take her someplace wonderful, not toward the death which the "home" in the spiritual represented.

Dulce went to sleep that night soothed by her own generosity in cooking, everybody's obvious pleasure in the meal, the music and storytelling. These deep connections were why she risked so much of her protective solitude to join this group. It was rare that she could relax and enjoy that fleeting sense of belonging.

That night she dreamt that Ev was going off to Wisconsin for six weeks and Beth was running off somewhere and she woke up feeling abandoned. When she saw Ev and Carrie, she asked them for hugs which they gave warmly, but when she spoke to them of Ev's maternal, nurturing presence and her fear in the dream of being abandoned, she could feel Carrie's nervous possessiveness coming between her and Ev. Nonetheless, both Ev and Carrie shared with her some difficult issues they themselves were dealing with so that Dulce wouldn't feel alone with scary feelings.

When they went outside the shack, she and Carrie found a bloody bird in the old rusty birdcage, usually empty. They didn't know who put it there. Except for a wound in its beak, the phoebe seemed healthy and eager to escape, so Dulce coaxed it out of the cage while Carrie held the cats. When it flew away, Dulce felt, instead of relief, an odd sadness. She wondered why.

But the sadness dissipated with the excitement of the Big Pour for her foundation and the satisfaction of having her friends help: mixing, shoveling, gathering rocks and tossing them into the hardening soup, tamping, measuring, leveling. Everyone was there, working hard together, with seemingly endless energy and wonderful teamwork. The foundation was coming together: the "footing" was going to be solid. Dulce finally breathed a sigh of satisfaction.

She caught her breath when a butterfly landed on the wet surface, afraid it would be trapped there, but seconds later, the butterfly fluttered off, leaving as blessing a faint trace of wings. What a good omen for my house, she thought.

But then Gail got upset because the wall wasn't coming out perfectly level. Dulce suddenly felt exhausted, Carrie became irritated when the rocks they were tossing splattered cement on her, Beth finally told them to change their angle when she too got splashed, and Abby left to go prepare a class. Gail had totally taken charge, inspecting the trench to criticize or, occasionally, approve, while the others hopped to fulfill her orders. When they finally stopped for the day, Dulce gave Ev a big kiss to thank her for all her help and the others clapped in recognition of Ev's sturdy contribution.

The next few days, however, were tense and exhausting. Gail was obsessed with getting the foundation level, but nothing seemed to achieve it. Dulce felt she had to help, but she could hardly walk and besides, she didn't know what to do. The others were supportive but bored or off doing their own things. And then somebody asked for one of their godawful processing meetings where everybody says how they really feel, which is never good. Dulce longed to be on a mountain top reading a good book.

Carrie started by talking about a downward spiral of negative feelings she'd been struggling with all summer, releases from childhood which she hoped people wouldn't take personally. Abby talked about how busy she was. Beth talked about how the group didn't seem to be working and how they needed to get together more often to cultivate more depthful relations. Gail challenged this perception, observing how often Beth seemed to be fleeing the group and avoiding people. From her perspective of living alone, Gail was impressed with how much group activity there actually was. Ev shared a dream in which they'd removed a small boulder from a hole but ignored a huge boulder in another hole.

Dulce described how positive her own experience had been: the fulfillment of her life's dream to build a house; working closely with Gail; the group support, particularly Ev and Abby's help with the building. But she went on to interpret Ev's dream of big and little boulders as the Big House, the group's octagon, and the Little House, the one she and Gail were building. Dulce expressed her distress that instead of working together on the Little House first, her house in the country, they were dividing their energies by working on the Big House at the same time.

She reminded them that the injury to her foot came during the first and only time they'd all worked together on the Big House. When she started to blame Beth again for the injury, Ev commented on the issue of "footing," referring to their discussions of her various foot accidents. Sometimes, Dulce thought, wincing away, Ev seems to think her intuitions are infallible.

Dulce, feeling the group focus on her in a way which reminded her of the grillings she'd received in school from the nuns, then dismissed Ev's comments as "psychologizing," and accused them all of being of one mind, the "mystical unity" of which she wanted no part. She knew all too well how the Collective could scapegoat deviants for its own purposes. And she knew she was violating group values by building her own house first instead of sacrificing herself for the common good--and by doing it right instead of accepting whatever rundown shack life doled out to her.

Ev, hurt and angry, protested by fleeing from the fire around which they had gathered, muttering, "You're so rejecting."

Dulce replied, "Don't be so overdramatic."

"I feel like screaming," Ev murmured.

"That doesn't sound like a scream to me," Dulce taunted.

"Cut the bullshit," Ev screamed, "and talk about what's really bothering you."

Dulce felt trapped. No one agreed with her and because they didn't, they wanted her to say something else. Besides, the last person she wanted to fight with was Ev, who had been the most generous to her during this difficult summer. She sent Ev a sympathetic glance, but didn't say anything lest it be pounced upon.

Ev rejoined the group around the fire but retreated into silence

"Why does there have to be judgment about the log?" asked Abby cautiously.

"Why does there have to be blame?" echoed Carrie.

Dulce insisted that Beth was responsible for what she had done. All she wanted was for Beth to own up to the consequences of her actions and to apologize for the damage she'd done.

"Yes," said Carrie, "Beth made a mistake. She's not perfect and she was under duress. We've all acknowledged it was a mistake, she knows that-- but so what? Is it some unresolved anger from the past?"

Dulce bridled at Carrie's attempt to paint her reaction to a present wrong as unfinished business. And at Carrie's asking "So what?" Why did Carrie feel such a need to protect Beth? How could she talk to people who didn't have a clue what it meant to have Beth so unrelated to her, so bent upon her own purposes that she pushed the tree on top of Dulce's foot, thus crippling her for the summer's work of building her house? At the very moment when she had put herself in danger in order to save Beth from the same tree?

None of them seemed to want to acknowledge the pain or the extremity of effort it had taken for her to carry on sharing building and group duties. Couldn't they understand, at least, how much her foot hurt? At the heart of the problem was that none of them except her seemed to believe there's no such thing as a accident. Instead the shadow of the group--conscientious to a fault--was shucking off responsibility in order to feel entitled to pursuing their own lives.

Beth turned the subject. She assured Dulce that they had no expectations about her helping build the Big House that summer. Upon being released from doing the impossible, Dulce felt enormous relief. It had taken all her courage to bear the pain in helping Gail. It had been particularly hard to lift the cement blocks and carry them to her. Getting clarification from Beth that she was not expected also to help in building the Big House almost made her cry.

Then Gail opened up about how difficult the adjustment to group life was for two solitaires like Dulce and herself. At the same time she assured the group of Dulce's affection for and interest in each one of them. Dulce felt gratitude to Gail for negotiating a closure and couldn't wait to escape to their tent.

That night Dulce couldn't sleep. She kept replaying the scene around the fire. She could see Ev being so characteristically Ev: relational, funny, helpful, one step ahead of others in perception. But there was also a shrillness in her voice as if her personality was fraying at its edges. Dulce was moved as she realized how Ev was trying desperately to stave off loss with her insights. Simultaneously she felt a deep appreciation of who Ev was and she realized the limitation and mortality of that unique energy.

She then turned her attention to each of the rest of the group, and felt a similar grasp of the limits of each being, in strength and in time, and a gratitude for each: Beth in both her caring and her resistance to change; Gail in her passion and her ambition; Carrie in her courage and her envy; Abby in her intelligence and her evasions.

Each with her distinctive features was special, as different as lion, elephant, gazelle, giraffe, and eagle. Each was precious, a particular and beloved elephant or gazelle. Each was bound within her particular form. And each was mortal, limited in time-- and therefore all the more cherished.

She couldn't expect any one of them to be different or better than who they were--anymore than she could expect herself to raise buildings in a single breath, especially with this bum foot. She breathed a sigh of relief and finally fell asleep.

The next day, trying to reconcile the conflict between them without necessarily coming to agreement, Dulce and Beth went into the woods to talk. They walked slowly, adjusting themselves to Dulce's limp. It was a relief for Dulce to have Beth's undivided attention. Having for years been the sole recipient of Beth's sympathetic ear and careful, caring responses, Dulce found it jarring to be among so many others clamoring to be heard. Beth did not apologize for her carelessness over the log, nor did Dulce expect her to, but her concern now for Dulce's pain, and her kindness in helping her move forward, helped compensate for that blind spot. Dulce sometimes secretly admired Beth's apparent freedom from guilt. They fell easily into their old custom of reflecting together on the beauty of nature and the meaning of life.

Nature colluded with them, and magically they spotted three raccoons-- an adult and two kids--sashaying through the trees. Beth followed them, and Dulce gimped along behind as best she could. They were rewarded by seeing the three disappear behind a massive rock. Beth and Dulce conjectured there must be a den back there. As Beth told Dulce the story of the young raccoon at the cave picking her pocket, two adults and four baby raccoon emerged from the den and climbed quickly up the cliff. Nothing delighted Dulce more than seeing animals in the wild.

Over dinner that night Dulce told the story of her battles with nuns at the school where she and Beth first met. She'd been expelled for insubordination— she had refused to take off her jeans jacket when one nun ordered her to-- and then had to apologize publicly: "I'm sorry for whatever I've done wrong," she'd said. They never got her to admit that she'd actually done anything wrong. She claimed to have been so in love with Beth that she accepted the humiliation of apologizing rather than transferring to another school as her father suggested.

This story inspired Helene, who was visiting Beth, to tell about the time she'd been sent to boarding school and did everything she could to be sent home, including breaking her ankle by smashing it against a wall--which only, she said, made some of the nuns treat her even more sadistically. Touched that she wasn't the only one with foot problems, Dulce entertained them by telling about the nun who ordered her in for smiling lessons.

The next day, admiring their new foundation, both Dulce and Gail became enthralled with the contours of the land framed by the cinderblock wall. It looked like a woman's body. She needed more in the way of breasts and she lacked a head, but there was nonetheless something comforting about this symbolic connection between womb and room. "Mother Earth provides for us," as the song said.

Even more thrilling was a caterpillar going through transformation on the dry cement wall. At first they thought it was a cocoon turning into a butterfly, then realized it was becoming the cocoon. Not the end but the beginning of transformation. Dulce marveled over the fact that a caterpillar completely dissolves inside the chrysalis.

During those years when her mother's dependency and dying weighed so upon her, Dulce's hero was her father who had refused to be yoked to death. Even though she was linked inevitably to women, branded by her own hand a lesbian, she shared his cultural distaste for the despair and martyrdom associated with the female.

Dulce was driving back from the store when she pulled up near the shack and heard Carrie calling Ev's name. "No, it's Dulce," she replied. She got out and they looked over the beaver pond together, hoping to see the heron but spotting only a few frogs. She told Carrie about the red-dot spiders and toads up at her place. She and Gail were thinking of calling it Red Spider or Toad Hill. She described how the toads leapt out of the way in fright everywhere she walked by, scaring her, and how the spiders busily kept getting in the way.

She also told Carrie about how one of her ex-lovers, a woman she still adored, befriended chipmunks. So fully that her cabin was overrun with them, just like the shack with Beth's mice. Dulce described those little creatures ferociously running around eating everything up. She was still trying to understand why these two friends tolerated these invasions, why they were so addicted to squalor, so unable to claim a safe place for themselves in the world or so unable to imagine themselves saying "no" to any such invaders.

That night an emergency message arrived that a friend of Abby's had been part of a peacekeeping group kidnapped by contras in Nicaragua and the contra leader had threatened to kill them. So after supper they did a healing circle to bring Abby's friend back safely. Ev sent white light, Beth sent courage, and Dulce sent ferocity for survival. The peacekeeping group was released the next day.

The following week Dulce and Gail spent installing wire mesh under their joists and sewing the pieces together to keep animals out. Days of lying in the cramped crawlspace stapling and hammering left them both exhausted and grumpy.

Around the campfire one night Abby's nephew and Faith's boys started imitating nature and animals sounds in the dark. Everyone joined in to whoosh like the wind, squawk like a crow, patter like the rain, hoot like owls, howl like wolves. Dulce could feel a tension within her between keeping the animals out and letting them in. She was, had always been, the wind, the swallow, the wolf.

Suddenly a storm broke, scattering them to their different shelters. Great flashes of lightning struck down at them, roaring and pouring. She and Gail were soaked by the time they crawled into their tent. So much for their audacity in trying to imitate nature.

My life has closed many times before its close and still I am afraid, Dulce thought as she nodded off against the warmth of Gail's body. And yet, at the same time, I am beyond fear.

When they raised the first wall frame, it was too high because they hadn't measured it quite right. Dulce and Gail argued about whether to leave it up or lower it. Dulce argued that they could add those couple of inches to the next walls, but Gail was adamant. It had to come down.

Irritated by Gail's exactitude, Dulce started tossing heavy cinder blocks off the deck until one smashed into another. Gail walked off, refusing to continue. Dulce blew off steam verbally while the others listened. Then they helped her lower the wall again and left.

Finally Dulce helped Gail dismantle the wall. For every up, she thought, there's a down. For every exuberant moment, a fall. The next day they made the corrections and raised it again. Everyone helped and all went smoothly. The wall towered over the clump of birches which for Dulce represented the most sacred spot on the land, the inner circle. An inside which did not close in upon her but instead opened up to the sky as it grew. At last a place where she belonged?

Abby provided coffee and Beth, mints for the celebration. They danced on the new floor and took photos through the new studs.

Dulce noticed that a few leaves had started to turn. The summer was almost over. Time to go back to the city, to the job, to the more serious responsibilities of her life. She began to worry about the courses she'd be teaching, the novel she was revising, the committee she was chairing, the tenants who were moving.

One night Dulce became a silent witness as the others discussed her novel, which they'd been reading all month. Some hadn't fully understood it, some described it as cryptic, too subtle. But they agreed it was brilliant, had great potential, and they made some helpful suggestions.

Even though she was pleased they'd taken the time to read it, that people were listening carefully to her story, Dulce felt discouraged. She'd thought it was finished. But by the time she woke the next morning, she'd already started revising it in her head. She felt buoyed by the possibilities. The book was a way of saying goodbye to her mother, who had died more than twenty years earlier.

Seizing one final opportunity for play before they all went their separate ways, the group decided to have a costume party. Beth brought out material she'd saved for the past twenty years. Dulce was touched when Beth produced an old velveteen cloak which Dulce had worn when they were in school together, so long ago.

Beth modeled some of her offerings: first she was a clown, then a pregnant woman, shaping up her pillow/baby even in the womb, then a dashing "je ne sai quois" with a red beret. Carrie put on fake fur and fuzzy boots. Gail was a pirate with a hook for a hand, using garden claws. Ev wore a red and black striped skirt on her head like a turban, a huge spiral on her ear, like a gypsy. Abby was Harvest, in a long black robe and straw hat topped by a sunflower, with Indian corn pinned at her breasts. Dulce was an Indian, wearing the old blue cloak and a green band around her head with a feather in it. She'd let down her long black hair for the occasion.

After they cavorted around the fire for awhile, Dulce and Gail shared the gifts they'd gotten for everybody: a footpump for Beth's rubber boat, needlenosed pliers for Ev; an angle measure for Abby; and a fancy ruler for Carrie. The recipients were delighted.

Then they played music and sang and sounded more wonderful than ever, as if they were instruments for the harmonies of spirits. In the background they heard coy dogs howling and owls hooting as the full moon rose, others joining from afar their celebration.

As she was playing an African drum, Dulce noticed it was made from an animal skin, with brown and white stripes: antelope or zebra?

Suddenly as the rhythm intensified, she felt the spirit of the animal speaking to her. She thought she heard it asking to be released so it could go on to another life. It told her that if it were eaten or buried, it could be freed, but preserved like this, it was trapped. It needed to be liberated through the music *by the drummer.*

Dulce silently agreed, but, still holding it captive, asked it first to describe its life. It told her of an idyllic existence in a fertile valley, an oasis surrounded by desert, with its mother and siblings.   Buoyed by the energy of the drums as she, Beth and Carrie shared the steady rhythm, Dulce released the animal.

Before it disappeared, it turned to look back at her. In its antelope face she saw her mother's eyes, saying goodbye. Her heart leapt as the graceful creature dashed into the dark.

Next day she and Gail finished the framing of the house. The others joined them afterward to give a cheer and to partake of one of Dulce's special posole suppers.

Everything was prepared with love: the blue corn posole cooking all day, the red and green chili, chopped onions, watercress and cheese, and authentic Anasazi beans. "This is *real* Mexican food," Dulce ritually announced as they gathered around the table.

The beans were extraordinarily sweet, either because of the New Mexico soil in which they grew or because they were happy to have been found in some ancient canyon ruin and finally planted. The fact that the beans had not died, but had only been dormant for several centuries, tickled Dulce's imagination.

Then Dulce and Gail presented gifts--a shell and a geode--to the cluster of birches next to their new house. Gail invoked a blessing: "May we be rooted together and grow separately toward the sky as this birch does."

The group, including now the two of them, concluded with a song Dulce had written in Hawaii before her first visit to the land: "Uri, Uri, bless our journey." Uri was a Hawaiian god of plenty.

Although this wasn't the first summer they'd sung her song, it was the first summer Dulce hadn't felt slightly left out. Which is not to say that in some key ways she didn't still choose to be at the edge of the group.

As Dulce, standing at her site, watched her friends walk back down the hill, the dogs trotting along with their human pack, she recalled the backward glance of the antelope as she said goodbye.

Maybe one of these days, she thought, I'll get me a dog.

And maybe, she thought, Hillman is both right and wrong about the validity of archetypes. Archetypes may not be universal, but they are still useful—their creation and recognition can provide a positive processing of grief.

Where we are the girl floating in a void between space and the river, suddenly filled with longing for movement and change, which inspires her to plunge into the river, thus creating a new world in which a duck lays three eggs in her lap, eggs which hatch the magic of moon, sun, stars, and transform the girl into one who can sculpt mountains, islands, continents out of the mud of this new land.

CARRIE

Carrie woke to light as the rising sun touched the mesh peak of Ev's spacious tent, borrowed from an affluent friend. Her mind grasped at a wisp of dream which had left her feeling sad, but the images eluded her. Time to get up, cross the stream and head back to the shack to take the cats on their daily walk. Her dog, Moxie, who slept at her feet, was already eager to go. As quietly as she could, she pulled herself out of the zipped-together sleeping bags she shared with Ev and got dressed in the chilly morning air. Even though it was summer, the northern mornings were cooler than the steamy city ones she'd left behind.

She slowly unzipped the tent door, hoping not to wake Ev, a light sleeper. Her dog bounded out, eager to explore a new day. Ever since he'd gotten stuck in the little beaver pond one stormy night, she'd kept him securely closed in after dark whenever possible.

She'd woken that time after midnight in the midst of a driving rain to hear, far away, his bark of desperation, and she knew immediately he was in serious trouble. This was not the usual howling at the moon, disciplining of a cat, or discovery of a squirrel—this was a high pitched cry for help. She'd leapt up, thrown a raincoat over her pajamas, jumped into her boots, and hurled out into the pitch dark with her flashlight, pursuing his insistent barks along the stream and down into the muddy flats next to the little beaver pond not far from her shelter site.

Soon, as she maneuvered across a series of small beaver dams, between flowing water and still pools, the footing became treacherous. One step and her foot would plunge into mud that threatened to suck her down into it, like that horror movie she'd seen as a child where some famous actor disappeared slowly into muck, his rubber face a silent scream. But despite her own fear she knew Moxie was in serious trouble so she slowly advanced in the dark toward his cry. Finally she came upon him, his black coat barely visible in the starless shadows, his voice a whimper now. While comforting him with her voice, she reached down into the gap between two beaver dams where he was lodged and, making sure her feet were firmly supported by the weave of beaver poles, dragged him out by the collar. Later she couldn't understand how she'd managed to haul him back over the crosshatching of beaver poles and mud, since she was neither particularly agile nor strong, but she had--refusing to let him down until they both could set all six feet solidly on ground.

She wished he could tell her how he'd gotten trapped that way, but there was no mistaking his gratitude for her rescuing him as he eagerly followed her back to the tent where Ev awaited them with a dry towel.

Carrie greeted Moxie affectionately now as he leapt around her, ready to lead her into another adventure. But she was planning nothing more than their usual morning routine. Her cats were ensconced in the shack for the summer, as usual. Despite her romantic notion that she was liberating them by bringing them to the woods, they ventured out only as tourists. Traumatized by the long car ride north, they knew instinctively, better than Carrie, the dangers which awaited them in the woods, from owls to fisher cats.

But they loved this morning walk to the stream, protected by their dog and their person. The animals followed Carrie as she and her siblings had followed their mother during their childhood travels. The cats ran along fallen logs and up sturdy trees, chasing and teasing each other. Her city dog was delighted he didn't have to walk on a leash or be contained behind a wire fence. At the stream the animals could drink or stroll from rock to rock, their fur glistening in the slant of morning sun.

Carrie was surprised how at home she felt in the woods, how content. She'd never been an enthusiastic camper. Most of her adult life she'd lived in various kinds of community, patterned after her close family but larger, more expansive. Even when she'd lived alone, she rarely took much time for herself. But now she was relieved to be away from lots of people, to be living, instead, with lots of trees, who did not comment on her activities, judge her moods, distract and worry her, expect her to take care of them. These tree cousins were older, like guides and friends, more rooted than she. The wild animals were fascinating neighbors whose appearances brightened her days and nights, some of whom she encountered, many others she simply heard, their soft, scratchy movements audible in the evening air. Her mostly tame animals were family, whose playful antics made her laugh, with their warm, graceful bodies, their fur she loved to touch, and their tolerances of human moods.

As she watched the cats negotiate the stream, Carrie imagined how she might construct the roof of her new shelter. Over the last five summers she and Ev'd been on the land, she'd put up multiple shelters. Even though they'd cleared out the shack debris and had fixed up the two-rooms, one on top of the other, and built a new porch on the side, where the cats hung out, Carrie wanted to live deeper in the woods, not so close to the road.

Carrie was one of two explorers who, with the assistance of a yoga teacher/ realtor, found the land. Once they'd investigated the lake and the beaver pond and slept out under the huge pine trees, she knew this was the place for them. She even saw great potential in the old gray shack, and later helped Abby clear out the debris of rusted appliances, beer bottles, playboy magazines and mouse droppings. But the land wasn't, at that point, the place for her.

Like Gulliver in Lilliput, she was tied down by a thousand tiny strings to her life in the city—to the neighborhood children, to dear friends who'd stuck with her through the rise and fall of collective work and struggle, to Ev, who herself was tied down to her job, her friends, and life in the only place she'd ever lived.

A sense of stagnation had sent Carrie deep into depression.

The only way she could get out of there was to imagine herself as a guide in a situation which called for evacuation. She'd rehearsed plenty of evacuations in her day, from the time the ship in which her family sailed to Greece almost sank, to the disaster at Three Mile Island's nuclear reactor which sent shivers of flight plans throughout the city. Formal evacuation plans were actually drawn up during her first two years of college on a military base in Europe when a series of diplomatic crises and civil wars threatened to send all Americans packing asap.

It was no doubt a stretch to imagine a need for exile just because the city was growing more and more oppressive, and threats of gay bashing were more easily heard now that the shouting of the women's movement had died down. The cramped space of her two room apartment, the despair of her low paying dead end job, the fact that she had recently been assaulted were not in her mind sufficient excuses for abandoning ship. After all, she did have a place to live, she did have a job, and her attacker had not been a drive-by shooter, just a drugged out stranger. But the revelation of homophobia brought home by a friend's recent death still lingered.

To see herself metaphorically as a guide was not so far fetched. The role of tour guide, leading folks across borders, the role of midwife, assisting people in their passages, fit her teaching, her activism, her part in helping animals, and a few people, be born and die. It was gratifying also to imagine herself as someone who might guide people back to their natural home, this garden of Eden she'd so recently discovered in the woods. She knew how much Ev longed for greener pastures, for travel and adventure, and she wanted to be the person who helped her get them. And it certainly helped Carrie's radical paranoia to think she might, like Harriet Tubman, be able to lead her people to safety and refuge, a kind of 'bean heaven even though she wasn't always sure she was herself a 'bean. Like Emma Lazarus, she longed to lift her lamp beside the stone wall, if not the golden door.

The pilgrimage to the land itself was somewhat less romantic. Her dog, of course, was delighted to accompany her just about anywhere, but the three cats she brought along on their first summer jaunt to the land were less than thrilled with the car ride and settled into the safety of the shack as soon as they arrived. They brought along their considerable paraphernalia of food, toys and kitty litter, which soon began to stink up the shack, offending the sensitive noses of the human inhabitants. Even though Carrie's own nose was mercifully numbed by what she called "odor fatigue," caused by her having suffered the scents of too many smelly places, she worried about how welcome the cats were in this only communal shelter.

With Carrie on these summer adventures was Ev, who shuddered at the thought of any kind of explicit commitment but was nonetheless there whenever Carrie needed her, even for the hot ride up from the city with three yowling cats and one restless dog--an ordeal for all involved, particularly Ev who was "not an animal person."

While Carrie had been busy extracting herself slowly from the ties that bound her to city life and collective living, the shack had been taken over by squatters, disguised as caretakers--Abby and Beth. Even though the shack and the land was owned by four of them, squatters rights were honored by Carrie because she didn't really believe in private property--not just because she was a socialist of sorts but also because she remembered how often she and these same friends had been chased away from camping spots or beautiful vistas or intriguing trails because they were on private property. Now would they be the ones putting up "No Trespassing" signs? It just didn't feel right.

One look at the cozy crowded shack which Abby and Beth already inhabited so fully and Carrie realized she and her entourage would have to seek shelter somewhere else on the land. Suddenly she, who knew all about trespass, having spent much of her childhood asking the Powers That Be to forgive her her trespasses, was again a trespasser. If she weren't careful, she who first set foot on this land might be the last to inhabit it.

As an older sibling, she had a primary grasp of what it means to have your territory invaded by strangers. Now the script had been twisted around so that she, Ev, and the cats were the invaders. Again she was plagued by her recurring dream of a banquet which ran out of food before she, at the end of the line, arrived at the table. She wasn't convinced that if she hung around, like the dogs who hung around her, she might eventually get some scraps.

Filled with a nameless anxiety, she became obsessed with finding a place for her own furry family within the place she'd found for everybody else.

This was always the tension for Carrie, getting her own needs met while helping everybody else meet theirs. Often it seemed she pushed her own needs out of the way to accommodate the needs of other, sometimes going far beyond the call of duty to create something communal for all. On the one hand, as a loner, she'd rather camp out on her own, with just Ev and the animals. On the other, she felt more responsible for the well-being of the whole group than any of the others seemed to feel. This puzzled and irritated her.

But despite the difficult human dynamics Carrie wasn't about to let her oldest friends have this fabulous adventure without her. She'd longed for land at least as long as Beth and Dulce had, ever since together they'd been chased off their first encounter with Private Property. She who had so much wildness hidden within her wasn't about to miss out on this exploration of wildness. And she certainly couldn't miss this opportunity to carry out her secret mission to rescue other wild ones and guide them to safety.

With characteristic resilience and enthusiasm for the what-might-be, not to mention an impulsive single-mindedness, she set about creating a series of shelters. What she discovered in the process was more valuable than what she created. She discovered how flexible space could become when you worked with branches and vines to make a shelter. She loved realizing how different spaces feel and what they mean, inside and out. She relished the physicality of building, the rewards of hard labor. She enjoyed having the freedom and resources to experiment, to construct, and to imagine what might come next, asking "What else?"

She started with a tent, which enabled her to sit outside in the woods in the rain and listen to the birds sing. Living in a tent, as distinguished from camping in one, made her feel closed in, claustrophobic. But she didn't want to disturb the woods with her presence. She believed, as the nomadic person she was, we should leave natural spots as we'd found them, hopefully unscarred by human habitation. So first she kept it simple, tying fallen branches to standing trunks of trees to make her first shelter. Given the configuration of those live trees, her first, triangle-shaped shelter provided limited protection, exposing her legs, feet and toes to multitudinous elements: wind, rain, lightning; buzzing, biting insects; curious, indigenous animals. After the first porcupine waddled by, she decided she needed something which would keep her and her sleeping companions up off the ground. High enough so the other animals could still meander by—even under-- without losing their ancestral paths.

The second summer, guided by the *Tao* to the perfect spot between the muddy and the clear streams, she actually sunk posts (roots at last), and made a platform over which, inspired by the beavers, she wove wild grape vines across radiating branches into a spiral to create a roof. She covered this frame with clear plastic from the hardware store. She knew plastic was tacky and environmentally suspect, but she couldn't figure any other way to keep rain out while letting so much light in. When the spaces between branches formed deep pockets of water, even that protective function seemed too flimsy. But for all her design enthusiasm, she couldn't, at that point, imagine building a permanent roof. It seemed such an intrusion between earth and sky. And she shuddered at the image of walls rising up around her. (Later, during winter, she treasured those walls.)

Carrie was intrigued as she watched Abby, Ev and Beth build their own shelters. Abby's was a sturdy, attractive pentacle made of two by fours bolted into metal braces with five slots each, to form five pentacle-shaped walls covered with cedar shingles. Ev's was a beautiful wigwam woven of curved saplings covered with ferns, like a basket, with a fire circle in its center. And Beth's was a glass cabin whose walls, roof and door were recycled windows, like a pauper's greenhouse. Abby's was the most practical, but none were suited for winter living. Still they gave individual meaning, privacy and protection in the summer, and each structure embodied the spirit of the person creating it. Meanwhile the shack could be used for visitors in the summer, served as a kitty hangout, and facilitated dry meals and warm bodies on wet, windy evenings.

As the sun rose higher in the Adirondack blue sky, Carrie heard the sound of Dulce's bulldozer grinding up the hill. The squeal of its giant tires was the sound she and Ev first heard when they arrived that summer from the city. Beth had greeted them with the news that Dulce had hired a man to clear the road and knock down trees for her site up at the foot of the mountain. Clearly Dulce's idea of a shelter was different than anybody else's. They all looked at each other in amazement.

As she heard the thud of one more tree hitting the ground, Carrie winced. That pounding retrieved the dream image which had escaped her that morning: *two little faces sad and confused, two little hands waving goodbye.* The image flashed back of Robbie and Lisa at the airport as she put them on the plane to return to their father. As their nanny, she'd cared for them for over a year, first as a live-in companion, then as a daily babysitter. Robbie was five and Lisa was three. He was golden haired, anxious and smart; she was serious, dark eyed, and artistic.

Carrie thought taking care of them might help resolve her ambivalence about not having children of her own, now that she'd given up the mother archetype recommended by all her elders in order to embrace the sister archetype, which seemed key to her personal quest for authenticity and mutuality. But being a nanny had proven to be no solution at all.

Fond as she was of these particular children, the job itself was problematic. She lived in the basement of a brick row house in a dull semi-suburb, away from the women's community and friends who served as family-- with only one tiny window. The chronic darkness was gloomy and she didn't relish feeling like a servant.

When it became clear the children's aunt couldn't manage their care, Carrie moved out and picked the kids up from school each day. When the aunt decided, predictably, to send the children back to their dad, Carrie debated whether she should try to keep Lisa, who'd been adopted from Korea in an apparent attempt to glue the parents' marriage together. She and Lisa were pretty compatible, almost as close, it seemed then, as mother and daughter. And unlike Robbie who was already molded into his family role, Lisa was still open to change. But Carrie couldn't bear to think of Robbie continuing to fall through the cracks all by himself. She didn't know what she'd have done throughout the frequent moves of her childhood without her siblings. So that spring, before coming to the land, she'd driven the children to the airport and on the way home, blinded with tears, rammed into the rear of another car. This was a loss nobody would even notice, a grief unrecognizable, except by the person suffering it—unless, of course you counted the person whose car she'd just rear-ended.

She tried to keep in touch with the children, but as a nanny, she'd been invisible; none of her stamped, self-addressed envelopes ever found their way back to her. Along with the children she'd never had, she'd just lost two very real children. But here on the land this summer her grief was as veiled as her role had been. The group never spoke about the children they hadn't had, only the few they did have.

Carrie rose from the log she'd been sitting on next to the stream, called to the animals and headed back up to the shack to feed her crew. She hoped she could get in and out before the other people arrived for breakfast—rarely a warm, communal moment. But when she got to the shack, she found Abby oiling her chainsaw. When Carrie asked her if she and Beth might be free that afternoon to measure the dimensions for the Octagon they'd planned over the winter to build, Abby looked conflicted and Carrie guessed she'd already volunteered to help Dulce clear the limbs off the downed trees at her site. Abby, Carrie noted, was especially eager to help Dulce build her house, her enthusiasm, Carrie guessed, fueled somewhat by the fact that Abby had taken Dulce's place as Beth's significant other, as well as motivated by her own natural kindness.

Carrie sighed. Just as she feared, Dulce's house building was going to take precedence over the building of the group house. When it became apparent at the end of the previous summer that Dulce, along with Gail, who loved the woods, might want to spend more of their summers with the group on the land, it seemed a good idea to build something together, a communal home. Nothing fancy, just a place for all seasons, with a bathroom and running water, conveniences for older visitors like parents, along with more room so they wouldn't be bumping into each other, trying not to step on each other's toes as they moved about in the shack at meal times. Given their limited resources and desires not to mar the environment with too many human made structures, almost everyone agreed this was a good idea.

They picked out a site in the meadow, with its solar potential, flat terrain, access to the road. Carrie suggested the shape of an octagon, symbol of transformation between the practical square and the spiritual circle, eight sides for potentially as many as eight, or even sixteen, people. This place in Carrie's mind symbolized where and how their lives joined. She built a model out of popsicle sticks. She knew how to articulate her vision of common ground only that far. The others would have to help carry this shape through to completion. She had no idea at the time how challenging it would be to create.

Abby suggested a second roof to let light into the interior. They drew up plans which Abby checked with an engineer friend. They calculated measurements, and figured out on paper where they needed to sink posts for the framing to rest upon.

Carrie was more excited than she could ever have imagined about the prospect of building a real house. She'd never owned a house. She never had an enduring home, a physical place that lasted more than a couple of years, having grown up, with Beth, on the move. As the oldest girl, Carrie helped her younger sisters pack and unpack their stuff—pjs, stuffed animals, dolls, books, toys, clothes and various tidbits. She comforted them about stuffed animals and broken toys which had been dumped at the last station, and helped guide them into new adventures. Her mother remembered her as the one most eager to explore, to discover what lay around the next bend, but she didn't realize how much Carrie had disguised her longing for a place to come home to, a house which wouldn't disappear in the rear view mirror.

This longing showed up in Carrie's migration dreams, of suddenly having to move, gather up all her belongings, stuff them into a couple of bags which could disappear at any moment, while worrying about the animals; fearing disconnection from key people; actually losing and sometimes finding people, animals, children; misplacing keys, cars, pocketbooks, even shoes. Some of this anxiety originated in abrupt family moves, especially during times of war and separation.

Their vision of building such a home with their own hands was even more exciting, Carrie thought. They could shape the space they would live in, symbolically escaping the established square forms of gender, marriage, and career by moving out of those boxes toward a true circle. This structure could express, become an extension of, an affirmation of the life choices they'd made

Then the following spring Dulce called them together and asked them to put off building the communal house so they could help her build her own shelter. Carrie felt resistant. Inwardly she railed. It was ok that Dulce had chosen to travel every summer instead of being on the land with them, but since she and Gail had arrived, the shack could not accommodate them all. Why not build the octagon now while they were all together? She had no confidence that Dulce, given her track record, would ever be more than a visitor. Why not combine their limited resources?

Still, as she watched Abby head up the hill with her chainsaw, Carrie felt some guilt that she wasn't helping. But the sight of those fallen trees, still in their prime, made her sad. And the postponement of her dream of a common house made her mad. So she decided instead to take Moxie for a hike up the mountain, above and beyond Dulce's building site. She looked for Ev to see if she wanted to come along, but Ev, meditating by the beaver pond, wouldn't have wanted to be disturbed.

Breathing deeply after a vigorous climb almost straight up, Carrie perched on the wind chime ledge, with a view of nothing but sky and tree tops as the breeze ran through her hair. She could hear working sounds from Dulce's site. Dulce had chosen a more elevated location back toward the mountain on what they all agreed seemed like sacred land, marked by blessings of birch clusters and powerful boulders. It was there they'd often gone for solitary meditation. It was there Carrie had been startled by a silent voice which said, "I am Mohawk," reminding her, psychically, they were neither the first people on this land, nor would they be the last.

Carrie felt pleased to be above it all, despite a nagging disappointment with the group and with herself. With Moxie, panting, snuggled next to her, she realized that their age of innocence on the land was over. They could no longer pretend their presence had no impact on the environment. She thought of Blake's three stages—innocence, experience, higher innocence-- and wondered what "experience" would bring, what "higher innocence" might feel like in their relations to the land.

What was foggy down below, she mused, became clearer up here as her irritation dissipated with the energy generated by her climb. Divisions of territory now seemed ridiculous; they each had so much to give and to gain from each other; one person's abundance did not cause another's deprivation.

She was glad Dulce was finally joining them on the land, not just breezing through on her way to or from some more exotic location. She'd missed her.

Fondly she recalled their first campfire by the lake after they'd found the land. She sometimes hummed the song Dulce composed, to which they'd all added verses--the one they called *the land song*: "Oh, fire, warms the aches inside of me...Oh, lake, cooling waters healing me."

What she herself needed to do, Carrie realized, was dig down to the roots of her own emptiness. It was time, finally, to weed them out. First step was not to give up on her dream of a shared house. Whether or not Dulce joined them, the rest of them could not afford to build separate houses. They would have to share. Even if they started tomorrow, it could take years to build a house. And they weren't getting any younger. How much longer would they have the energy and desire to dig holes, saw wood, and hammer walls together? Carrie had pointed this out to Beth several times, hoping she'd prevail on Abby to commit at least to measuring the site so they could break ground this summer.

Finally one day when she and Ev were weeding the garden, Beth and Abby came to get them for the measuring. The four of them, plus the two dogs, Moxie and the neighbor puppy who had adopted Abby, tromped over to the meadow site they'd selected for the communal house. As soon as Carrie and Beth started hassling over the size of the house, Carrie felt relieved. Maybe they might really do it. When they actually started laying out the measurements with sticks and string, Carrie's excitement mounted. Beth and Ev, keener on exactitude than either Carrie or Abby, found measuring frustrating, but Abby enjoyed the challenge and Carrie was impressed with Abby's natural mathematical ability. The two of them solved problems of feet and inches while Beth and Ev chatted about group dynamics. After lunch, they cleared the circle and marked possible rooms. Carrie was exultant. The dogs chased each other through the wild flowers, delighted to have so much of their pack outside together.

The next day Carrie bought a special loaf of bread for a groundbreaking ritual: it was round with six sections, one for each of them. When they all finally gathered for the ceremony, before she passed it around, she broke off her own section first, rather than her habitual last. *No more Ms Martyr.*

Beth suggested they sing: "From thee I receive, to thee I give." Carrie smiled when Abby cried out, "May our home rise like bread."

That night she dreamt about a fourteen year old who was acting out. At 14 Carrie'd been a sophomore in an all-girls Catholic high school in New Mexico. That's when Beth and Dulce were so tight the Mother Superior called in Beth and Carrie's mother, apparently to warn her about their "special friendship."

What their mother told Carrie was that Dulce apparently lacked adequate parental supervision. Fortunately their mother wasn't all that trusting of nuns, so she consulted Carrie who assured her that Dulce was ok--not one of those "bad girls" who played hokey and cruised around smoking cigarettes or picking up boys. Carrie admired how Dulce stood up to the nuns even though it involved her in endless rounds of trouble. And Carrie had no idea, in those days, what grown-ups meant by "special friendships." But she responded by telling her mother what she knew about Dulce's home life, her mother's illness, her father's frequent absences. Both ended up feeling for Dulce. Her mother expressed indignation that this nun was so lacking in empathy.

At that age Carrie's own conflicts were not with the nuns but with her mother, during a time when her mother was stretched to the breaking point with worry about her husband in harm's way in the middle of the Korean War. During one move, Carrie and her sister had boarded at their school for about a month while their parents dealt with temporary orders which kept shifting—one minute they were supposed to go east; the next, west; one minute their father was to go alone; the next, his family could go with him. The dormitory where the girls stayed was one big room with rows and rows of beds, each one surrounded only by a green curtain. Under the curtain, you could see the black shoes of the supervising nun or the bare feet of a peer on her way to the communal bathroom. You could hear everyone coughing, snoring, muttering in their sleep. It felt like an orphanage. Carrie'd read books about orphanages. Now she knew how real they could be. She wasn't about to end up in one. This brief stay was a lesson Carrie learned quickly. Rather than being kicked out of the family vehicle for bad behavior, she stopped acting out and started acting right. She didn't exactly become a good girl, but she was no longer overtly rebellious. All the more reason to admire Dulce's courage.

A few nights later Carrie dreamt some guys had left a huge snake in the refrigerator. When Carrie opened the door, the snake opened one eye. After slithering out, it turned into a huge, menacing black dog which grew long hair and wagged his tail, looking more and more like Moxie. Dulce, Carrie suspected, would probably name this snake her *shadow*. If so, perhaps Carrie's shadow was not as formidable as she feared. She recalled the snake she'd seen yesterday by the pond, swimming on top of the water. Floating, lovely in motion, its fluid body reflecting light.

Later, wondering why the snake had been in the icebox, she remembered a tale Dulce told about how some guy had walked up to her in Washington Square and handed her a flight bag, asking her to hold it for him before disappearing into the crowd. After waiting in vain for him to return, Dulce opened the bag and discovered, curled inside, a huge python. After she'd taken it home, she was advised by animal rescue people to put it in the freezer so it would remain dormant but still alive until they arrived to carry it off to the animal shelter. This Dulce did gladly.

Meanwhile, Abby's and Beth's nightmare projections about Big Sisters were apparently being triggered by Carrie's insistence on building the big "cabin," as they called it then. One evening, after a day at the lake, Abby and Beth returned, still blatantly discussing what they called their "sister thing." Feeling vulnerable, Carrie didn't dare ask what that "sister thing" was. When Gail inquired, they explained they'd decided they had to incorporate the qualities of "the older sister" so "she" wouldn't have so much power over them.

While this seemed like a sound strategy, Carrie suspected it was also psychologizing to cover up their anger at her--but she tried to keep an open mind. Her suspicion was confirmed by Beth's furtive reluctance to look Carrie in the eye while Abby, glancing boldly at Carrie to gauge the impact, scornfully described her own older sister's flaws. Even though Carrie was very different from Abby's sister, she felt attacked by this barrage.

Fighting back tears, Carrie leapt up and said goodnight, compelled to exile herself.

Ev whispered to her, "Don't go. You are loved. Stay." Touched, Carrie held on for a little longer, but she felt so fragile, she finally left, standing outside to listen to the ratatattat of "she," "she," "she," surprised that the "she" of her could inspire such fervor.

The next day Carrie woke up feeling like she'd been ambushed. Beth was sullen and withdrawn, her grumpiest self, which reinforced Carrie's interpretation of hidden anger. Beth was usually so even-temperered.

Carrie felt like a fool. She'd played into their need for an ogre, she'd set herself up, once again, to be the scapegoat. She clung to the tolerant, affectionate Moxie who forgave all her moods with a wag of his tail. But the land no longer felt safe. She didn't feel at home anymore. She should've known better than to trust these friends who'd hurt her plenty in the past.

She dreamt about having to move again, saying goodbye to her stuff because it wouldn't be protected or saved, worried about how to gather up and transport the animals. This was how the kids, Lisa and Robby, must've felt as they disappeared into the wing of that airplane.

Feeling like a pariah reminded Carrie of her untouchable status as a teenager in her family. After one of her eruptions she'd feel encased in an invisible shell of exclusion. As the most emotionally expressive person in her large family, it seemed she risked being ostracized whenever she released an emotion threatening to the others, usually those labeled negative: anger, fear, disappointment, blame, or envy--feelings stirred up by the stress of their mobile life, yet suppressed by other family members.

That morning Carrie burnt her fingers on the toaster oven. She immediately sought solace from Ev. After soaking up Ev's sympathy, Carrie decided to share some of her recent reflections. Why, she wondered, did she feel more responsible for the well-being of the whole group than others seemed to feel? Ev wasn't sure that was true. She described how Carrie sometimes disguised her own desires by couching them inside the rubric of group need. She wondered if that wasn't a result of Carrie's family dynamic. She pointed out how this seemed to lead Carrie into many a pretzeled situation: trying to convince everybody else to do something because it met her needs.

Ev wondered why they couldn't just hang out in the woods like they'd done the summers before or why they couldn't do both--help Dulce *and* break ground for the big house. Why did everything have to be either/ or?

Carrie confessed how she felt a bit stuck in the sister dynamic. Sometimes she'd resented having to be the big sister and take care of the younger ones. Her own babyhood, after all, had been pretty much shattered by war, evacuations, and worry about their father getting killed. But who was she to feel deprived?

"You were the backup mom, the invisible servant behind the supermom."

Carrie was touched that Ev understood this. "I've always been afraid no one would care for me if I didn't do what I was supposed to do. Share, share, share."

"Care, care, care," Ev said with a smile and they both laughed.

As a member of a happy enough family, Carrie realized she'd probably seemed to others a privileged insider. But Carrie also knew what it felt like to be alienated, to stand outside the inner circle looking in. Understanding that split between insider and outsider was, perhaps, how she'd learned to negotiate borders, to serve as a guide across them.

The trouble was, in the face of others' hard times, Carrie felt guilt. In her travels she'd seen so much poverty and suffering that guilt was almost an obligation in exchange for her privileges. But guilt numbed her to her own pain and produced self-judgment instead. She couldn't allow herself, compared to others less fortunate, to be self-pitying or a whiner. Sometimes, as a result, she felt resentment, even envy for the abundances others enjoyed. Lack of empathy for her own deprivations sometimes blocked compassion for the struggles of others.

Ev already understood all this on some level but she was relieved to hear it acknowledged by Carrie. She admitted she had trouble with Carrie's sometimes blaming or victimy tones because she couldn't feel the love behind them. Then she made one of her characteristic leaps. "Why do you ask for so little from life?"

"But it feels like I ask too much. That's why I'm often disappointed."

They shared a look of puzzlement. Both knew both were true: Carrie did ask too little and expected too much. Later Carrie thought of this as the deprivation within privilege syndrome, or "the American itch."

Assisted by Ev's clarity, Carrie realized how often she held back stating her own desires because, despite her having labeled herself "the bad one," she was still trying to be "good," like Beth, or nurturing and self-sacrificing like her mother. But her mother, who had sacrificed much, had not sacrificed marriage, children, or home, all of which Carrie had apparently given up. And Beth's goodness, Carrie observed, not always with the greatest objectivity, seemed to serve as a magnet for love. Beth seemed to be surrounded by people vying to take care of her

"Maybe you were waiting for someone to take care of you like you took care of the other children. Maybe you were trapped inside that responsible little self of yours, afraid you'd never receive the affection being showered on the younger children."

"Or deserve it," added Carrie pensively. "But my parents did take great care of us! Compared to everybody else I know, I've *no* right to complain!"

Carrie's passion for fairness and equality had fed her concern for the poor and hopeless. It had also demanded she give up whatever privileges she'd been born to. This commitment to justice had fueled her political work, especially her caring for children and animals. Now, suddenly, it was lit with a different light. Not quite so golden.

"All I want now is for you to hug me." Safe in the warm circle of Ev's arms, Carrie could let the tears well up. She felt enormous gratitude for Ev's wisdom, honesty and protection.

That night at the campfire when she strummed a sad, sweet tune on her autoharp, she was touched when people started humming along in layered harmonies. Later after Abby told some of her camping stories about encounters with bears, she called upon Carrie, who was identified with bears, to dance. Reluctantly, afraid she'd look foolish, Carrie, wrapped in her Mexican serape, stood up and danced in her fuzzy boots with a clumsy but steady rhythm as she felt a bear might move. The others seemed to enjoy her dance. In the rhythm of her stomping she felt an energy surge up within her, a wildness spontaneous and free, a joy which could be shared. This was an energy which connected her with others rather than those dangerous rages which split her off.

Later as they watched the moon rise, Carrie, standing at the entrance to her shelter, touched Ev with her left hand, her three burnt fingers resting in the soft curve of Ev's sturdy shoulder. Suddenly she felt a rush of energy as if the top of her head had lifted off. There was no separation between her and the trees, wind, stream, stars. Her body felt emptied, no longer full of that depressed "nothing" state of previous days. Through only three fingers she felt an intense emotional and sensuous connection to Ev as if Ev's body rooted Carrie to that time and place while she luxuriated in a silent and timeless expansion.

The next day she woke up with the realization that Dulce was probably right to be building her own house. Dulce knew what Carrie, trapped in her family role, had been denying: the only person who is really going to take care of you is you. So, in a fervor of self-interest, she began to work on a new roof for her shelter, something more reliable than the fragile branches and leaking, sagging plastic which now stood between her and the weather.

Later at her secret spot by the little beaver pond not far from her shelter, she saw three herons flying over the rippling water. Their interactions in flight were like a dance—graceful, rhythmic, in tune with wind, water, earth and sky as they dove and swooped around and between each other. This experience reminded her of a time the summer before when she'd spent the night on a full moon at this same place and woke to see a huge bird flying directly over her. She felt its shadow pass over her resting body as the bird crossed in front of the moon. This was one place on the land where she felt fully at home and fully herself. And it wasn't even a shelter.

Several nights later she and Ev went into town for dinner in order to avoid the communal meal. One of the men helping Dulce and Gail with their house building had offered to cook them venison. Carrie could barely suppress her predictable outrage. To kill one of those beautiful, defenseless creatures who shared the land with them seemed like a violation. My friends, she told herself, are planning to eat one of our closest neighbors

Dulce waxed enthusiastic about how much she loved venison. Gail described how Jake was "such a good hunter," citing how he'd crept up on an unsuspecting deer in his truck when they'd gone out for lumber. Carrie recognized how a certain macho detachment served those who had to hunt for survival, but she wasn't convinced her friends' desire for venison emerged from such a need.

Even though Ev felt Carrie was being rigid, she indulged her need to get away from the barbecue. Both Beth and Abby, in sisterly opposition to Carrie's obvious disapproval, declared they wanted to taste the venison. There was no place left to go but out.

The day after the meal, Dulce complained of nausea but described her discomfort as flu, dismissing its possible connection to the venison she'd eaten.

That day Carrie was in the shack revising house plans with Abby when Abby pulled something out of the refrigerator and started munching on it. When Carrie asked what it was, Abby muttered, "the steak," then added sullenly, "the venison." Carrie knew from Abby's defensiveness that it was futile to make a reasonable protest. She was prepared to argue that you shouldn't eat another animal unless you were willing to kill it yourself, but as a consumer of chicken and fish, she knew such a position would backfire. She couldn't imagine wringing a chicken's neck or, worse, chopping off its head.

That night Carrie dreamt someone with two kittens handed her one which had been wounded and told her to cook it. But it was still very much alive. She was horrified. She couldn't do it. She also dreamt of searching for the entrance to some underground railroad where she met a woman shaman who was evasive about why she was there. Carrie asked her if they were from the same soul and when the woman didn't answer, Carrie said in the dream, "Well, we're all from the same spirit."

Early the next morning, emboldened somehow by this dream encounter, Carrie snuck into the shack, took out the foil wrapped package of "steak" from the refrigerator and, in a rush not to be detected, ran across the road and hurled it into the beaver pond. To her dismay it did not sink but instead floated, rather glaringly, to the surface of the pond. She should've, she realized, released the meat from the tinfoil. She'd just committed an environmental atrocity. She felt, nonetheless, greatly relieved, even exhilarated. Maybe later she could fish out the foil.

That night, after Abby raved about how good the venison was, there was much talk about their "need for protein" and considerable flurry when nobody could find the rest of the deer. Although she had confessed her crime to no one, Carrie could feel Ev studiously not giving her away by looking at her--but it was Dulce who actually covered for her, asking her in a joking way where it was so that Carrie could just smile and say nothing. When Gail the following day continued to wonder what happened to the venison, Dulce shifted attention to some other leftovers while Ev protected Carrie by calling her out of the shack. Clearly Dulce had not shared her hunch with Gail and for this Carrie was grateful. No one had really been hurt by what she'd done, they'd had three days to eat it, and if she herself had eaten some, it would probably be gone by now anyway.

Later Carrie realized her guerilla action had echoed the kind of "acting out" she'd repressed at the age of 14. At that age she'd been prone to absorbing emotions negative emotions unacknowledged by other members of her family. After being punished for expressing them directly, she was driven to articulate them through some symbolic action, its meaning rarely understood or recognized by others. After one of those eruptions, unable or unwilling to completely ignore her, her siblings talked politely with her or around her, but still she knew she was being shunned.

She wondered why she'd regressed to this kind of behavior now. It wasn't just Beth's familial presence which had been a constant in previous summers. Was it the conflict with Dulce whom Carrie had known so long she seemed like a sister?

Whatever, this time, even though she remained a furtive agitator, she felt she'd reclaimed some buried adolescent energy. No doubt she still could be accused of being "overly dramatic" in her response, but she wasn't ashamed of what she'd done, and she was grateful to those who'd covered for her.

Later Carrie, secretly feeling saved, was glad to go up to Dulce's house to admire the progress they'd made. She realized that Dulce was not only a worthy opponent but in many ways an ally, even a guide. Feeling this renewed surge of friendship, she was tempted to reveal her sabotage to the whole group but decided instead to respond as a deer might--in silence.

In her spare time, when she wasn't working on her own new shelter roof, Carrie continued to dig the holes for the foundation of the Big House. One day Beth joined her while she was working on the trench for the fireplace stonewall. They each choose an end and dug toward the middle, helping each other lift out the heavier boulders. As they dug down toward the required four feet of the frost line, they talked about family: illusions, hurts, insights, messages about achievement and service--the hard things about their common ground as they sank these symbolic roots together.

"Remember the story about Jack having a fit when somebody said something about 'her daddy,' meaning our dad?" Jack was their older brother.

"Yeah, he said, 'That's not *her* daddy, that's *my* daddy.' They laughed together at this family story.

Fortunately, unlike girls in some countries, they hadn't been set out on the hillside to die, but had only been taught to serve--each in her own way, which was, in its own way, a curtsey to uniqueness.

That night in a dream Carrie worried about getting back home to the hotel where she was staying. Suddenly it seemed she was in some foreign country. Ev came along in a bus to help her. Ev kept telling Carrie the name of the street where they should get off but she couldn't remember because it was in another language. Finally Ev shouted, "It's where the Africans bring the placenta after the birth." Carrie still didn't know where that was. So she hopped off the bus to run into a store to buy paper so she could write down the name of the street. She was afraid the bus would leave without her and sure enough, before she could jump back on, the door of the bus closed and it started to move. Concentrating on the name of the street, reminding herself of her memory for places, she got off the next bus at the right place, a wide plaza with a hotel which turned out to be the same place the group had just met. Its name was Pilgrim's Rest--or was it *Nest*?

Beneath the name, a sign said, "Leaders dream the dreams of dead men." Peering at the blaring focus on just "men," Carrie looked beyond the sign and saw inside the window a stiff, hollow figure of indeterminate gender lying on its back. But superimposed on that form was the figure of a woman curled on her side, very relaxed, her body transparent, like a medical doll, with all parts visible. The woman's liver was vibrant, a dark red brown as apparently it should be. Was this the live leader who was dreaming the dream of the dead man?

She didn't know what the dream meant, but as the dreamer she found it reassuring, both about her own basic health and about the land as sanctuary. The live woman in the dream was one of them, not some stiff, hollow stereotype of feminists or lesbians.

The next day Carrie invited Beth, Ev and Abby to her shelter for a fire so she could share her dream. Dulce and Gail had planned to meet some friends of Gail's who were visiting from the city so there was no danger of them feeling left out. Carrie was looking forward to showing her more hospitable side. She recalled the early days on the land when the four of them had wandered up and down the stream, up and down the mountain together, sat around the campfire sharing their dreams, their fears, their hopes. Perhaps, despite the tensions of this summer, she could renew that deep sense of connection.

She built a fire pit next to her shelter and made sure there were enough comfortable seats for all of them. But when she went up to the shack to get some treats, she discovered her plans had been changed by Abby who'd separately agreed with Dulce on an alternative plan--Dulce's offer to cook a campfire supper for everybody, including the guests. This was innocent enough, but Carrie, who'd been counting on a different agenda, hadn't been consulted. Unconsciously it reverberated with a recent dream of hers in which God, who was a woman, "said no" to some plan cooked up by Abby and Beth without consulting the rest of the land group.

Although she knew she was being rigid, Carrie felt disappointed, then hurt by Abby's unilateral decision-making. When Abby apologized, Carrie muttered angrily, so Abby said, "I just can't exclude anyone." The question of exclusion seemed odd, given the fact that Dulce and Gail had originally announced they were taking Gail's friends out to dinner. Carrie felt she was being unfairly labeled as one who excludes others.

"You're excluding me!" Carrie murmured, then stomped back to her shelter. She should've realized at this point that she was being set up. After a recent visit from Abby's sister everyone was on tip toes around Abby. Although Abby was always extraordinarily accommodating to her sister, these visits inevitably left Abby with smoldering rage, which inevitably spit out at one of them. What better target than another older sister?

A little while later Beth, Ev and Abby came down to Carrie's shelter to find her. Locked into her disappointment, Carrie tried to walk away, then gave up and charged back instead, shouting at Abby, waving her arms around wildly. Abby held her ground, arguing that she had done nothing wrong.

"Words, words, words, they drive me crazy," Carrie replied, grabbing Abby's arms before Abby wrenched away. Both Beth and Ev burst into tears.

Abby backed off looking shocked. Frustrated, and aware that she was playing the villain, Carrie threatened to use every dirty trick in the book: biting, kicking, scratching, pulling hair. This alarmed Abby, as Carrie knew it would. She knew Abby was afraid explicitly to "fight dirty," even on this level of silly threats. Carrie sliced her arm in the air, as if to cut through Abby's false, goody-good self. If Carrie had fallen into the trap of acting out Abby's older sister, Abby was also serving as a stand-in for Beth.

Abby kept shouting, "I'm not afraid of you, I'm not afraid of you. I'm NOT AFRAID of you."

Suddenly Carrie saw herself as she was at that moment, totally exposed in her grrrr state, a trapped animal--her hunger/anger fully visible, her teeth bared like fangs, her claws curling into the earth, her fur standing out. The more Abby cried that she wasn't afraid of her, the more Carrie knew she was. *Was she really that scary?*

Carrie collapsed on all fours and then wept, first because Abby was afraid of her, then about fear itself, the fears they all shared but expressed in different ways--defensiveness, false innocence, secrecy, furtiveness, self-centeredness. How alone each of them felt much of the time. How vulnerable in a world which crushed women and despised gays.

First Ev, then Beth, then Abby put their arms around her, rocking her, murmuring words of comfort and safety. Dropping into a deep cradle of feeling Carrie realized this fear was linked to her experience of being a stranger in so many strange places. The xenophobia she'd encountered every time she had to brave the unknown was the border she crossed every time she encountered another strange part of herself.

Afterwards the four of them talked about various issues they'd avoided processing in the chaos of the summer: how Carrie sometimes pushed people to their edges; how Beth's protectiveness of Dulce sometimes increased their resistance to Dulce's assertiveness; how the rest of them resented Abby's dumping her sister tension on them; how Beth and Abby's compulsion to include everybody in everything muffled their own ambivalence; how Ev was wary of depending on the group, especially when connections seemed so tense. Most of these issues had previously been named, but Ev's wariness was a new revelation to which they felt compelled to respond by making her lean back on the rest of them, as in encounter groups they'd all experienced, so she could feel "trust." This engendered much joking and teasing to cover Ev's discomfort.

Then Carrie brought out treats and they ate in the sun by the stream, played in the water, meditated, chanted, admired the wild asters. Finally they exchanged a group hug, and rushed to the campfire to greet the visitors and enjoy Dulce's delicious stuffed zucchini. Carrie got what she wanted and nobody was excluded. Another lesson about the both/ands of life.

When Carrie finished building her new roof, she invited everyone over to see if the rafters would hold up without the temporary support she'd used to build them. The eight rafters came together on a central plate. She was counting on the tension at that meeting point to hold the roof up, without the center pole which at the moment connected the roof with the floor. If this engineering solution didn't work, she could put the pole back in the center, but if it did, if the force where the rafters met could serve the purpose of holding the roof, the space would really open up.

Before testing it, she brought out some crystals she'd dug up in the Ozarks rock-hounding with Ev and offered them as gifts. She delighted in how her friends observed, admired and carefully chose crystals, particularly how Gail, who'd kept her distance all summer, joined in the process with keen appreciation.

Then with a dramatic flourish, while the others stood back, Carrie pulled out the center pole. Everyone cheered as the roof, indeed, held up. She was touched when Dulce said this event had given her "a thrill."

From there they climbed the hill to give a cheer to the finished framing on Dulce and Gail's house.

The next day Carrie was taking a nap in her shelter when Ev came in carrying a tiny wet animal. "The dogs were fighting over it," she said holding it out to Carrie.

Why me? Carrie moaned. *Aren't I supposed to be getting rid of my Responsible Self?*

"Everyone said you'd know what to do," Ev murmured tentatively, understanding Carrie's reluctance to take care of yet another little creature. "We think it's a possum." Carrie examined the silent, wide-eyed creature with its matted golden fur and ears sticking out from both sides of its head. "The puppy caught it and brought it to Abby." Carrie examined the tiny critter for bites but there were none. It was so small it probably still needed to nurse. *What's that formula?* she wondered.

When it mewed, she laughed her rippling laugh. "It's a kitten," she said, stroking its soft soggy coat before taking it in her hands and nestling it into the warm spot between her breasts. She realized, for all her complaints, this foundling was a gift for her. This time God (S/he) was saying *Yes.* This baby would be allowed to stay.

8

THIS LAND

"is your land,
this land is my land,
from the Red Wood Forests to the New York Islands,
this land was made for you and me."
--Woody Guthrie

"I've been to the mountaintop; I've seen the Promised Land."
--Martin Luther King

"As long as the sun shines and the waters flow, this land will be here to give life
to men and animals. We cannot sell the lives of men and animals; therefore we
cannot sell this land. It was put here for us by the Great Spirit, and we cannot
sell it because it does not belong to us. It belongs to its creator."
--Northern Blackfoot Chief

The higher we climbed, the more things became whole. Boundaries dropped away. Cutting across country sharing similar shades and hues, fences between this man's farm and that man's homestead faded to thin scratches. Roads were empty spaces. Trails disappeared.

Higher still, borders were evident only between elements like water and earth-- pond and beaver dam, stream and meadow, mountain and sky. Margins were marked by natural shifts of light and shade, clusters of varied tree textures. The lines were round as they connected the entirety. They didn't divide along the straight and narrow. Like lines on our palms, they identified this place. Like lines on our faces they gave character to this land.

To share land with others seems natural, as contrasted perhaps, to shelter which is, ideally, more private. Something about land, something about the country, something about the earth is inherently co-operative. Communal like water, air, sunlight. Yet to own land is fundamental to the American Dream.

85

Private property is the right of free men. "Forty acres and a mule" was the promise made, although not kept, to freed slaves. Another American dream, of course, is to live together without dominating, suffocating, neglecting or shunning each other. To share "a place for us," a U.S. who's not the us in "us and them." A place like America was, perhaps, before the American dream.

To share a place was our dream for the land a group of us purchased collectively a quarter of a century ago. The story I'm telling here is another variation on the American Dream plot, but this time, for a change, it's just about women, a group of women, an unusual but not unique alliance. Throughout this nation in those days when the women's movement was still vital, but beginning to ebb back into the contexts from which it had emerged, groups of women were buying and sharing land in the country. This is our history, or a slice of it. On one level, it's just another American tale of hunger, greed, curiosity, fear, love, grief, exile, belonging, adventure and security. On another level, it's something more. "Something different," as my mother might say.

We thought of ourselves as dreamers, exiles, adventurers, explorers, fugitives. We were people who enjoyed playing the edges, even camping on the edges (but maybe not always abiding on the edges). We appreciated the company of other talented and accomplished edge-walkers. As friends we did not come, as family groups do, from a single source. We were each of different soils, different roots, each trying to keep our own balance in worlds through which we, almost simultaneously--at that time anyway-- traveled. We'd been carried along by movements which had changed both our shared and our different worlds. We were used to flowing together, frequently, for exchange, familiarity, interaction. Displaced from our homelands, we depended on each other.

In times of mobility, we moved, as animals do. In times of stability, we sought roots, like plants. But where did we assorted mavericks belong? What happens when people who have been on the move for more than a decade decide to settle down?

The only home we recognized collectively was the earth. So we chose the natural world, a "wilderness" as challenging and engaging as the urban world where our movements originated. Although our understanding of this place was not intimate at first, we discovered, within her welcome, a deeper, fuller, more grounded reality.

Whether we call this natural world Mother Earth, *ground* of our being, *soil* of our harvest, *the land, this country, nature, the environment, the biosphere,* all these names depend on and recognize *common ground.* For a few owners property is "sacrosanct." For others the earth may be "sacramental." For some the land is simply sacred. For most creatures, sharing land involves issues of turf, claims over meeting places, questions of territory. Yet all of us who live together on this earth understand the lure of emergence, coming out, blossoming, moving freely outside as well as in.

Those of us in this story are all Americans, native born but from different roots. Our experience tells us that diversity tends, in the best of times, to enrich the soil, nourishing all who share it, but in the worst of times to cause conflict over scarce resources. Some of our ancestors barely escaped the gangplank, some were daughters of the American Revolution, some arrived scared and poor, a few barely breathing, some were displaced by new arrivals while others strode in rich and beneficent, and some ones with ancient genes waited for the rest to adapt.

We all, root-wise and in our own lifetimes, have been driven out or fled places we thought we owned, or that owned us or owed us, then forgot us. We also personally had been kicked out of places we thought were either home or, at least, open to the public, accessible to people like us as well as people like them. We had been kept out of or ejected from forests, beaches, mountaintops, riverbanks, as well as houses, schools, workplaces--public *and* private locations.

We were sick and tired of being considered "trespassers". We wanted to own our own property, claim our own privacy. We wanted to belong somewhere. So we found our refuge in the woods. Finally, at last, in this haven we had a shared territory we could enter freely, with a promise of security and a prayer of relaxation. A place of our own where, if anybody ever trespassed, *we* could vent our indignation at *their* gall.

At the same time, perhaps paradoxically, we vowed to reclaim this land for the glory of the Earth herself. We hadn't yet realized the impact of our presence on this environment. We hadn't yet experienced the sweep and flow of earth in winter, fallen in love with a particular tree, communed with our fellow moving creatures. We had no idea how much we would be changed by settling down in this place.

It didn't sound like much in the realtor's description, but the realtor himself, a yoga teacher on the side, moved through the land, across the stream, up toward the foot of the mountain, like a native. We followed, entranced. We fell in love with the circles of birch, the meandering creek. More than two thirds of the land was up the mountain, good only for logging, commercially speaking. Since we weren't interested in cutting down trees or increasing real estate values, it wasn't a wise investment. We were looking for sanctuary, not profit. A drive down a winding road to the undeveloped side of the lake and we were ready to sign the deed, once we'd consulted with the rest of the group.

Apparently, originally, this land, our property and adjoining tracts, was a single place, a farm with sheep mostly, dotted with circles of huge cabbage pines. The growth of these ancient trees, we guessed, had been assisted by sheep cropping the woods clear of rival growth. We weren't sure where the original homestead had been, but psychic glimpses of the past suggested that this land was, even more originally, inhabited by an extended Mohawk family or tribe. And, of course, it had been continuously inhabited by all the creatures who still dwelled there, or passed through there, from mice to deer, from raccoon to the occasional moose.

Most of the places on the land, when we bought it, and later as we explored it, were communal: the Shack near the Beaver Pond, the Campfire, the Indian haunting grounds, the Grassy Knoll, Wind Chime Ledge, Buddha Rock, and Top of the Mountain, all were common ground. We had a dream of reuniting its separated parts, fragments of the original whole which a century before had been cut into plots and sold off in lots. We almost fulfilled that dream before things started falling apart again.

At first we built "shelters," flimsy contraptions which rocked and swayed during storms, catching and dripping rain drops upon us, more like protective clothing than housing. Then we fixed up the dilapidated hunter's shack—full of dirt and debris. A couple of us stayed in this raggedy but cozy structure all winter long. This adventure more or less inspired the rest, still apprehensive about living out in the woods for a whole year, or more.

Ownership promised safety. At last someplace we could roam free outside, through woods, up mountains, across and down streams, along fertile bogs, without feeling frightened. This isn't to say we didn't feel lots of fears, but just not that constant, numbing anxiety many of us often felt as women in a man's world. Sometimes, it seemed to some of us, the nature of womanhood included this addiction to fear, even those hardy souls who were "counter-phobic." But out in the woods, once we got over our worries, once we realized that if we moved slowly and like shadows through the trees, nobody, not even a man with a gun or knife, would know where we were, or even *that* we were there. The woods, full of other presences, protected us.

In addition to communal settings each of us had our own spot, a personal place we chose which evolved its own structures, or lack thereof. Even though each of our places was unique and individual, we called them by generic, communal names: the Shack, the Hut, the Pentacle, the Wam (wigwam), the Octo (gon). Collectively these were *our* places, as real for us as the natural places like the Grassy Knoll, the Transformation Tree, the Kali tree, the Place where the Two Streams Meet.

Throughout this extended process of exploring and building, we discussed issues of private and public, ownership and sharing, as we tried to reconcile what we were experiencing on this land with what we knew from collective, populist movements and spiritual, native perspectives about common ground. Our conversations still sound in my head:

"This talk about *our land* is fine and dandy, but what happened to our commitment to the common good?"

"What about the actual fact that the earth owns herself and should not be chopped up into bits of mosaic claimed by individual ones of us?"

"Yes, we've got to keep all these pieces together to get the whole picture."

"I still need my own half acre where I live the rest of the time. Even though the bank owns most of it, it's mine. Having a 'mine' is, somehow, crucial to my survival."

"What does Woody Guthrie mean when he says, 'This land was made for you *and me?*' The whole land, the country itself?."

"'You and me' consists of, or should take into account, not just you and me but everybody, including peoples here before 'we' arrived on the scene."

"'We the People' should mean all of us, *especially* those who were here in the first place. *The People.*"

"What about the animals? Other species? They were here before we were."

"Yeah, but, ultimately even the natives who were here before the western explorers arrived came here from someplace else--especially if you consider where we were before we were born."

"Migration, disruption, displacement are changes Americans may not be able to control as we arrive and depart. Often people--and animals-- had no choice but to flow."

"Change, control, choice are not just American themes. Look at migration, disruption, displacement in the rest of the world."

"Control depends on who "you and me" are, of course. No more than 3% of the land across the entire globe is currently owned by women."

"Same for a lot of other folks who don't own much. I wonder what percent of land is owned by what percent of the population."

"These days, more and more of it is owned by private corporations."

"And in some places women are still owned."

"Around the world children are bought and sold—animals, too."

"What is it to 'own' land?"

"I don't know about you, but my dream used to be 'to have some land of my own.' But frankly I couldn't afford that, so I bought in with the rest of you."

"Possession is ninth-tenths of the law, they say."

"And yet to possess for oneself alone seems a limited goal."

"—unless one is trying not to be possessed or repossessed."

'It's good when we can own our houses, I guess. Better than renting."

"Saves us from evictions."

"But when do my property rights violate yours? When does my need for space intrude on your sense of privacy?"

"When do my movements disrespect your boundaries?"

Apart from these personal concerns of mine and thine, we all recognized, fairly quickly once living on the land, that beyond our claimed spots of habitation, most places we occupied in common with others—animals, birds, rocks, trees— where artificial lines of possession disappeared, where we entered into a world we couldn't fully or individually claim, a world marked more by spider webs and shifting lights than recorded deeds.

So, what about private property when it comes to the land, much less the Earth? There's nothing really "private" about land, and we certainly don't own it, in the sense of possession. Sure, we can put up fences and signs, sure we have a right to privacy, but we also have, rightly so, little control over who's sharing it.

Property is an illusion and ownership is a dream, but place is potent. Belonging, even more so. Some of us were in love with the land; some of us just wanted to belong. What we belonged to, of course, was bigger than any one piece of land. Yet owning the land together helped us discover our own "us," and that, for all its fragile stability, moved us, inside as well as outside.

For some women of our generation, the back to the land impulse merged with the women's movement, spirituality quests, politics of identity, searches for equality and authenticity-- and out popped the eight of us. We were only some of many others of us, numbers which connect beyond the unique land and people I'm revisiting here.

We may no longer live on the land, but the land lives in us. "The earth moves under our feet," we used to sing together. That motion is why it's hard to get back to where we belong, like I'm trying to do now, get back to "This Land."

This impulse is no longer about ownership. It's about home.

"Farther along, we'll know all about it, farther along we'll understand why.

So come all my sisters and sing in the sunshine,

We'll understand it all by and by."

Where we are the seventh daughter, rejected even though dragons danced at her birth. Rescued from a box in the ocean by golden turtles and raised by a poor, old woman, she grew up with special powers. Told by a soothsayer that only their seventh daughter could cure them from a fatal illness, her birth parents sought her out. She forgave them for abandoning her and journeyed past many obstacles to the magic well for water that would heal them.

9

EVONNE

Ev questioned her right to be here. She wasn't one of the owners of the land, she was connected to it only through Carrie, and her connection to Carrie, though deep, was bound to change, as all things did. As long as Dulce stayed away, Ev could serve as a substitute for her, but now Dulce was back, apparently to stay, and Ev felt unsure how things would unfold. If she made herself useful, maybe she could stay.

Opportunities for making herself useful were abundant: helping Dulce and Gail with their building, cooking, making special presents for everybody, cuddling with Carrie. She could also aid in articulating feelings.

One night she and Carrie were teasing each other about "negative" emotions. The others were curious. This willingness to face their own shadow sides inspired everybody to list five emotions they considered most negative, a discussion of which eventually but inevitably led to a confrontation between Dulce and Gail about Dulce's "paramour," the person sending her mail almost daily. Evonne could feel Gail's frustration and fear; she could also see how Gail was trying, with re-enforcement from Dulce, to dismiss and rationalize away those feelings. At the same time Ev could feel Dulce's guilt and, beneath her defensiveness, Dulce's own fear of loss.

Sensing other people's feelings could be burdensome. If she named those feelings for them, Ev could get into trouble. If she acted them out, like Carrie sometimes did, thing could really get confusing. Sometimes she wondered why Carrie was so willing, like the scapegoat, to carry the cast off feelings of others without recognition or reward. Didn't she get tired of folks resenting or dismissing her?

People tended to deny their "bad" feelings. Sometimes they even cast them back on Ev, resented her for exposing them. As Dulce and Gail argued,

Ev listened as she usually did, but this time she could feel Beth carefully listening with her, so she felt support for encouraging Gail to express her disappointment about this situation and others she'd been in, including her marriage.

Later Ev provided Dulce a way out of her stiff self-protection by expressing some of her own vulnerabilities, allowing Dulce to get off the hook and offer some helpful feedback to Ev. Finally Gail fell asleep while Dulce spoke of irrevocable loss, how the sweetness of trust and innocence, once lost, can never be recovered. Somehow the way Dulce described this loss of innocence, it sounded like beautiful sad music.

Ev wondered, as she listened, when she'd lost her own innocence. Had she ever really trusted any of the adults who'd supposedly raised her? Although some had been more well-meaning than others, they'd all been *totally* incompetent--except perhaps her grandmother, who, nonetheless, hadn't had the wherewithal to hold onto her. The few photos Ev had seen of herself as a child made her cringe: large, luminous dark eyes staring at the camera in innocent confusion, hesitant shy smile. Only the earliest days with her grandmother had been sweet and innocent, she recalled, although now, trying to explain to others, she couldn't always pinpoint why the rest of her childhood had been so difficult. Other people she knew had much worse childhoods--abuse, death, extreme poverty. True, she'd been taken away from her grandmother, who loved her, and given back to her birth mother, who didn't, but she'd had enough food, clothing, shelter, education to survive, if not thrive. She'd had friends and teachers, and teachers who were friends. That helped a lot.

One night Ev and Carrie cooked at the campfire for a Fourth of July celebration, which was to include a post-ground breaking ceremony at Dulce's house. After dinner, someone offered around some smoke for the house blessing. Ev passed as usual; a contact high was more than enough for her; she didn't trust drugs. They discussed current events while watching the headlines from several newspapers curl into flame.

Then Ev distributed a multi-colored sparkler to each person and while they were still peering into a world of ashes, she ignited her sparkler and danced off away from the fire twirling it in the dark, writing illuminated hieroglyphics in the air--surprising and delighting the others. In that moment a flash of how she felt when she was deeply engaged with her art work returned to her. For several years lately, jobs, the women's movement, relationships, the land group processing had jostled for attention with her art, pulling her creativity in multiple directions.

Drawing forms in the air, she wished she could communicate this way more often. It was a way of translating feelings without the stigma of stating them explicitly. Ev considered herself at core a translator, one who negotiates among images and words, between different temperaments, across various differences. Ev loved languages which read "backwards" or up and down, hieroglyphics, evocative letters from different traditions, universal languages like Esperanto.

Carrie suggested that they carry the fire from the main campfire to Dulce and Gail's home via sparklers, relay fashion. Despite initial stoned enthusiasm this proved unworkable. So, finally, with Abby bearing glowing coals on a sturdy plate, they set off toward the bridge to cross the stream and climb the hill to Dulce's building site.

In the dark, with dim flashlights and slightly altered states of consciousness, they got lost. Amid much giggling, Abby exclaimed, "No one knows the way!" What was a familiar path seemed at that moment completely new, even to Ev who was not stoned. Anxious to get where they were supposed to be going and feeling the responsibility of making sure it would happen, Carrie led them even further astray. Finally Beth recognized a landmark and guided them back to the bridge. After they'd crossed the bridge, they split into two groups, wandering in different directions until Ev found the dirt road by feeling its fresh, newly dug softness under her feet. She called out to the others, brought them back together, and eventually they all arrived at the building site, gathering in a semi-circle to gaze at the curved ditches and mounds surrounded by the concrete foundations of the house.

In the center, like the body of a woman, was an island of earth, sculpted by the backhoe. On top of it Gail had constructed a pyramid of sticks for a fire. When they lit some birch bark from the still burning coals Abby had carried up from the large campfire, the flames rose up, illuminating the earth's body with an intense, magical light.

In the light they could see severed roots which still occupied the ditches, reaching out toward them like arms. The roots seemed like children torn away too soon, too abruptly, from their homes. As the fire grew, one root which stuck out from the earth started to smolder.

That's what happens if you hold on too long, Ev thought, thinking not of her mother from whom she was wrenched almost as soon as she was born, but of her grandmother who had so abruptly let her go, dropping her from the comfort of a warm lap and loving eyes she'd taken for granted into the alienation of a cold, punishing, even irrational mother, a dispirited and touchy father and siblings who were suspicious strangers, as she was also.

While Beth and Dulce wandered through the ditches whispering and giggling as if they were teenagers together again, Ev could feel Gail's sadness. Then Gail asked Carrie, Abby and Ev how they felt about the felling of trees and gouging of earth at the site. Tenderly, they tried to express their reservations without hurting her or provoking guilt. But as Ev already knew, Gail herself felt awful about the devastation and started crying as soon as Ev asked her how she felt. Ev went over and stroked her sobbing back which was curved like an overturned empty bowl.

She comforted her as best she could. As another person attached to one of the owners, Gail had as little right to be there as she did. Although cutting down trees, much less building a house, was beyond Ev's own expectations, she couldn't help empathize with Gail's distress. When you're not sure if you really belong, you're damned if you do and damned if you don't do--anything. She marveled at Gail's trust and confidence that it was ok to make major changes, as well as her tender feelings about the consequence. She admired Gail's extraordinary vision and capacity to turn these raw materials of earth and wood into a work of art.

When Dulce and Beth came back, they did an Om for blessing and then the Malte chant--Ev thought of it as the empathy chant-- which translated means, "The universe and I are one." As they chanted it over and over, they added trees, fire, roots and water, each other, other people, animals, birds, insects.

Dulce commented, when they were done, that she felt surrounded by "a lot of angry trees." She complained of being overwhelmed, there were so many of them.

"Like neighbors in the city?" Ev teased, then murmured that she didn't sense trees were much into anger, though she did wonder if they didn't feel pain.

"I've never seen an angry tree, I never hope to see one," joined Beth.

"They probably absorb our anger along with our other waste products," mused Carrie. "Their symbiosis is generous that way."

Ev figured that *symbiosis*, given Dulce's forged connection with her mother, might not be a selling point. Her own symbiotic bond with her grandmother, was ripped away before it could become oppressive. Nonetheless Ev could understand Dulce's wariness.

Whether we get too much or too little, she mused, the consequences seem to be similar: imbalance. She was as wary of commitment as Dulce was, but for different reasons. She was as distrustful as Carrie of being blamed, but for different reasons. She was as tuned to possible exits as Abby was, but for different reasons. She was as ambivalent about group identity as Beth was, but for different reasons.

No wonder we consider ourselves "cutting edge," she thought later: we play the edges constantly--particularly the threshold between *in* and *out*. We don't have to *"come* to the edge," as it says in the Apollinaire poem--that's where we live, I guess.

The next day she ran into Gail who became tearful again as they discussed the clearing of their site, confiding that she and Dulce had almost broken up over the extent of destruction. Even though Ev suspected there was more to this almost breaking up than just trees, she sympathized with Gail's being caught up in Dulce's need to clear enough space for herself so she could feel like she belonged. She herself sometimes felt overwhelmed by Carrie's processes, particularly those which included her frayed dynamics with these old friends.

Gail told Ev that Dulce claimed the group was attributing all their Shiva (Destroyer) energy to Dulce instead of claiming it for themselves. Ev thought that might be true. The projection trap. We like to be creators, like Brahma; we don't mind being sustainers, like Vishnu, but we're afraid to be Shivas. Ev rolled the word "She Va" around in her imagination, savoring its various connotations, like "Go Girl!" Was this archetype the source of the "power" she both sought and avoided? The Shiva energy? Would her being a "destroyer" cause others the same kind of pain she herself had suffered? She could certainly identify with Kali energy, which seemed every bit as destructive. She tucked these questions in the back of her mind, saving them for the next conversation with Dulce.

"You need to watch out she doesn't assign all the creative energy to you since you have the plans, skills and information." Ev warned Gail.

"Oh no, she's had a lot of input into the design."

They talked about the design until Gail cheered up and headed off with new enthusiasm for implementing it. Ev mused over how her wigwam site was now being intruded upon by the location of the proposed octagon. She regretted the distraction of all this building, everyone busy pounding settlement into form instead of camping out lightly on the land as they had in past summers. Not only did it create endless noise and conflict, it diverted group energy away from the processing, exploration, and shared creativity which so engaged and grounded her there.

Ev went off to weed the garden and think about the Alice Miller books she'd been reading. The more she read, the more depressed she got. The subtle kinds of abuse which Miller described had been thoroughly woven into her later childhood through her parents' efforts to socialize her. But her grandmother's early love for her had fortunately been unconditional. For that devotion Ev would always be grateful. It had given her a core of sanity and possibility which helped her weather the emotional storms of hot wind and sharp ice which assaulted her family life. Her siblings regarded her as the one they came to in times of confusion, although at other times they weren't adverse to siding against her in support of parental dictums or competing with her for scarce moments of affection and appreciation.

Jerking out the entangled roots of weeds helped ease Ev's sadness about her past. Carrie found her in the garden and suggested they dig up the last garden plot and plant some tomatoes she'd bought. As they dug, Ev talked about her sadness and wondered if she'd inherited it from her mother, who'd never quite pulled out of the post-partum depression which afflicted her when Ev was born. Ev suspected a more severe diagnosis, but her father had protected his wife from further intrusions of the mental health establishment after they'd administered electric shock treatments to pull her into a semblance of sanity, with limited success.

Carrie assured her that sadness could be quite normal. "I got depressed when I read Miller too. It's a natural reaction to having your illusions about family shattered."

"But I didn't have any illusions. I knew it was awful from day one."

"Yeah, but you also downplay how bad that was for you personally."

Making something new, a mound of fresh earth, cheered Ev up. A garden is a commitment to hope, she thought as they planted the delicate young tomatoes.

That night the whole group discussed Alice Miller's *The Drama of a Gifted Child*, focusing on parental narcissism but ending up, somehow, comparing Jewish matriarchy with Irish. Ev found the talk too abstract, distant from her own hollow feelings. Matriarchy, however narcissistic, was not an issue for her. Then Ev realized Carrie 's feelings had just been hurt by Dulce's claim that the book applied to people like Beth but not to people like Carrie, implying, Carrie apparently thought, that Carrie had been neither good nor gifted—when Dulce probably just meant that Beth had been a "good girl" while Carrie had not.

Sometimes Ev felt fatigue in the presence of so many conflicting emotions. The next morning when Carrie started muttering about Dulce's judgmentalness, Ev got frustrated and told Carrie straight out that she had trouble responding to Carrie's blaming tone because she couldn't feel any love behind it. Surprisingly Carrie didn't get defensive, but agreed. "Yes, it feels awful to me too." They tried, without much success, to figure out what lay behind the blame.

"How can we affirm authentic experiences without re-enforcing false selves like the Victim?" Carrie asked, returning to the Alice Miller discussion.

"Maybe when the whole self feels safe and affirmed, she can let go of the false self."

"Yeah--whenever I go after someone's false self as if it were a shell that could just be removed at will, the person gets even more attached to it," Carrie said.

"Like the crab." Ev's moon and Carrie's saturn were in Cancer, so they both understood about the crab archetype. They exchanged a glance of recognition, then a smile.

"Because the so-called false self (persona, mask) is composed of the same elements--personality, talent, feelings--as the true self."

"Maybe the true/false distinction isn't quite accurate," Ev said. "Maybe 'shallow' and 'deep' describe it better. When you try to pull out what seems shallow, you discover its attachment to what is much deeper." She thought of the weeds she'd just been pulling out of the garden, their tendrils stretching down and out, clinging to rocks and even more subterranean other roots. They weren't just individual stems, they all networked as part of a much larger, more tenacious system. Life was, underground, deeply entangled.

Having said all this, Ev, a short time later, still snagged by her own melancholy, found herself exhibiting the same kind of scorn she'd just criticized in Carrie. Suddenly she found everything Carrie said annoying. When Carrie said it felt like lunch time, Ev accused her of living by a routine which prevented her from being fully present. She could feel herself being taken over by that haughty, scornful voice which often tormented her, and there was no way she could protect Carrie from its lash. It's like she'd gotten caught in her own mirroring of Carrie's recent mood. Fortunately Carrie did not run away, get her feelings hurt, or start apologizing as she sometimes did. She just kept Ev talking until suddenly that layer of defense cracked open and Ev dropped from anger to hurt. Her voice grew younger as she expressed to Carrie, one of the few people with whom she would share her "private" self, some of the punishment and isolation she'd experienced as a child.

"You're afraid it's going to happen again here, with us?"

"It *is* happening!"

Carrie's eyes filled with empathetic tears and Ev, who could empathize with everyone but herself, just stared back, blank. She couldn't feel anything. She certainly couldn't feel sorry for herself. Instead she just felt morose—stuck.

Carrie just waited. Finally Ev put her head on Carrie's shoulder and sobbed. When Carrie held her, stroking her hair, Ev felt soothed on some deep level she often forgot even existed. Ida, her grandmother, had been soft like this. She was touched when Carrie said how comfortable it felt to have her head resting on her shoulder. She wasn't a burden? That's not why Ida had to let her go?

Finally comforted, she told Carrie another installment of her ongoing story about the alien babies, how they'd ventured out from some other galaxy, somehow got lost and landed up on earth. You could tell someone was an alien baby by a trancelike open-eyed stare (something apparent in Carrie's baby pictures) and by the fact that they spoke in tongues (something Ev could still do). Carrie offered the opinion that her animals might also be alien babies, but somehow Ev didn't think so, despite lore about past life transmutations, Buddha as a bunny and all.

"Do you think you and I are from the same planet?" Carrie asked.

Ev pondered. "That's a question."

"How will we ever get home?"

"That's a question." Actually, home was not an archetype Ev embraced quite as whole-heartedly as Carrie did. Clearly she wasn't driven as the others were to make a home for themselves here in the woods.

Later they joined Abby and Beth for meditation. Sitting around the Grandmother Tree they chanted, meditated for an hour, then shared dreams. Ev told her dream about the land group being like petals in the garden and her distress that they'd forgotten to name the little cabattos, a hybrid of the kohl family that had aboveground a flowering cabbage and underground, potatoes--with a digression about Luther Burbank and his ability to make thornless roses and apricots whose seeds were almonds. And how when she woke up and told Carrie the dream, Carrie told her to go back to dreaming so she could name the cabattos.

But when Ev went back to sleep, she dreamt about being kissed by an older teacher who'd taught her Japanese literature. Then, later, the woman flew into a rage and accused her of leading the other students astray. But later still the teacher asked her home for Thanksgiving and chatted with her about black mica and citrine.

Then Carrie shared a dream about Beth and Dulce climbing something high and complicated. Beth, as usual, was sure-footed, but Dulce was scared and stuck half-way up. So Carrie reached up and lifted her down (as if she were much smaller and younger), saying affectionately, "We have to be careful--we tend to leap before we look."

Ev reminded Carrie of a story she'd heard from a friend in the city about the baseball fan who grabbed for a fly ball and almost fell out of the stands. He was saved by four men next to him, who held onto him and pulled together as hard as they could. Ev appreciated how everybody held this story in their heads for a moment of silence, imagined being the guy falling, imagined being the guys holding onto him.

After discussing everybody's dreams, they each drew a tarot card. Ev's card was Strength, a woman with a lion. She was surprised. Although she admired Carrie's ability to relate to animals, she'd never felt much connection with them. She'd even found herself feeling cross with Carrie's dog when she felt irritated with Carrie. She just couldn't stand how dogs followed people around with those soft, trusting eyes. It annoyed her as much as when people described her own large brown eyes as "puppy dog." It was all too mushy.

Finally they named issues they wanted to work on that summer. Carrie said disappointment, Abby said anxiety around responsibility, Beth said anger and Ev said power and powerlessness. They discussed each in turn, asking questions, making suggestions, offering tentative analyses. For Ev the issue of power was related to authenticity, being able to share her relational abilities, artistic talents, and intelligence without encountering envy or negative projections. Her mother had both denigrated and tried to exploit her gifts. Her sister had envied her. Her father projected his own failures upon his children. The issue of powerlessness was just as profound for Ev, that sense of being trapped and helpless which had plagued her childhood. As a bright, gifted and sensitive youngster, she was damned if she did well and damned if she didn't.

Beth proposed that instead of defending themselves against unpleasant feelings (anxiety, disappointment, anger, hurt and humiliation), they should just let themselves experience these feelings and get help from the group in dealing with them. Ev noticed that Beth had left fear out of her list of difficult feelings. Having established this permission, Beth expressed some hurt at Ev's mode of "cooling out," of distancing herself, as if out of sight meant out of mind. Rather than feeling defensive, Ev was touched that Beth had noticed her withdrawals.

This little tension resolved, Beth brought out a huge bubble wand Helene had given her. She and Ev blew enormous bubbles while Carrie and Abby went about their businesses. Mesmerized by the rainbows in the bubbles, they starting spinning them. Ev loved how playful she could be with Beth. It was another language, free from worry or caretaking. They chased bubbles, blended them, watched them disappear into the sky.

That night they planned a campfire. A couple of Abby's friends were coming to camp on the land overnight. Around dusk a car stopped near the shack so its inhabitants could look at the beaver pond. Since Ev was sitting by the pond playing her flute, she went to greet the two women in the car who looked like kindred spirits. Even though they said they were going on to the lake, she invited them for a tour of the land before giving them directions to the lake. Despite the fact that it was growing dark, she was able to show them the stream, the garden and one of the shelters. Only when they ran into Abby, who obviously didn't know them, did she realize that she'd just invited two strangers to stay with them. After they thanked her for the "open house" and continued on their way, she chuckled. Having benefited from an open door policy, she was apparently curious to try the practice.

And frankly, she was ready for some new faces, someone she could play more with--among the land people, the relationships felt too constrained, everyone too much like sisters or in-laws, somehow off limits or taboo. Sometimes she longed for the good old days, the large loose women's community of the women's movement when one could play with all sorts of folks without instigating rivalry or jealousy or hurt feelings. She wasn't ready to confine herself to just one experience. She needed a wider roof over her head than the "family" container could provide. She still needed to explore a larger world.

The campfire that night was fun. One of Abby's friends, who arrived later, played the guitar and sang a song she'd written called "City Woman, Country Child," which captured two of the dimensions currently playing through Ev's consciousness. As the full moon rose, they sang feminist songs, land originals, old favorites. They stood, they chanted, they omed, they danced around the fire, improvising and harmonizing. Ev cringed to imagine how corny some of her more cynical city friends would find this. How girl scout campy. But secretly she loved it.

Connecting through music began the first summer Ev spent on the land. For an experiment Carrie had filled some coke bottles with different levels of water, then roped them in a line between two trees and played them as chimes with a well-chewed beaver stick Hearing her from across the stream where she'd pitched a tent, Ev joined in with her flute. Tuning into this duet, Beth started playing a drum. Through the woods, at quite a distance from each other, they played together. Later Abby joined in with her recorder.

This experience reminded Ev of one of the best summers of her life, the time she was fourteen and was chosen to attend an arts camp for six weeks. Not only did it allow her to escape from the hot city and crazy family, Camp Wiawaka was in itself heaven, a place where creativity was honored and practiced in the context of beautiful natural surroundings. Everyone was talented, everyone was appreciated, everyone could play.

Whenever Ev was most happy, often when she was alone and being creative, she could feel music pulsing in her throat. Sometimes she chanted to herself, sometimes songs played through her head, sometimes she recalled melodies her grandmother, maybe even her mother who'd taught her the blessings, had sung to her in other languages. Sometimes she woke from a dream with the songs still sounding. But usually as soon as anybody else entered the scene with a few discordant emotions, the music disappeared.

At some point while they were still singing around the fire, suddenly out from the woods danced a tree--with bark, branches, roots and all. Tapping each of them on the head with soft pine branches, she danced around their circle. Ev was enchanted.

She knew, of course, the tree was Beth, wrapped in the bark she'd peeled from one of the dead pines Abby had felled for her. A revival of the tree spirit, a healing, Ev hoped for, after all this cutting down and clearing out.

At first light of morning, after singing all night, Ev and Carrie walked over to the beaver pond to look at the full moon. It was misted by clouds, like a huge round gem in the sky, a baroque pearl when reflected in the water. When a beaver slapped its tail at them, they felt blessed. Ev held her breath, afraid to care too much about this beauty lest it be taken away from her. One way she'd been punished as a child was having whatever she loved most removed from her: her paints, a favorite stuffed animal, a book of fairy tales.

Later that week, for a dose of reality, Ev visited her sister. Much as she cared for her, family was always a complicated experience. Driving back, she comforted herself by discovering along the route back a tourmaline mine, pulling off for a satisfying detour, rooting around for some lovely rocks. Either because a teacher once called her "a diamond in the rough" or because some gems glowed with the magical blue light she'd seen as a child outside in the grass when she sat by the window at night, Ev was a rock hound. She whose own identity sometimes seemed so fluid loved the solidity of minerals, the clarity of their shapes and colors.

A few weeks later a friend of Abby's, Ceci, showed up with veggies from her garden, plus some psychedelic mushrooms she'd been given by a shaman in New Mexico. Since Ceci was in fervent recovery from alcohol abuse, they were surprised at this gift, but she treated the mushrooms as sacred, which seemed to make the difference for the group. Reverently they decided to share them with her that very day.

Ev was hesitant--she was not fond of drugs; their effects reminded her of the unpredictable swings of her mother's illness. But the *I Ching* gave her "Deliverance," so she decided to partake with the others, not without a great deal of trepidation and earnest reassurances from Carrie and Beth. She evoked her spirit guides for protection.

They gathered around the Grandmother Tree, a huge, many-armed cabbage pine, and solemnly ingested the mushrooms through a nervous ritual of sharing. Then they meditated until the mushrooms began to take effect. As they did, Ev felt herself folding down toward the earth, leaning her ear into the ground in order to listen to its pulse. After a time she answered that pulse by putting her lips to the earth and sounding a long, deep, resonant tone.

Except for Gail who went off by herself, everyone then wandered into the meadow. There at the site of the big house they were still building, each of them leapt into one of the eight post holes and gazed up at the huge clouds drifting across the sky. Then Beth crawled out and wandered off, followed by the dog who returned a short time later with a huge sunflower leaf pinned to her collar. Beth called them to join her in the garden.

When Ev couldn't climb out of her particularly narrow hole, the others lifted her out. At first she seemed as heavy as one of the rocks they'd dug out the day before, but as they lifted her up, she felt light, a puffball which could keep on going, floating higher and higher.

In the garden they lay down in the furrows between the mounds and looked up at the sky. Abby cried out that two bees were mating on a sunflower, but it turned out to be just one bee, fat and lazy, who'd fallen asleep from too much nectar--or so, heavy themselves with ambrosia, they conjectured. Ev merged into the sounds for awhile, listening to the soothing murmur of friendly voices. Then the people turned into vegetables, their sounds simply vibrations.

Dulce came over from the pond, where she'd wandered to see how Gail was doing, to say there was a beautiful sunset. She tip-toed around the circle of vegetable people as if deciding which one to pick and eat. She identified Ev as a luscious tomato and Carrie as spinach. Sensing Carrie's vulnerability, Ev explained, "No, she's the earth."

When they reached the pond, Beth tossed in pebbles while they watched circles ripple through the reflected sunset. Ev found herself mesmerized by the circles, as if she were as permeable as water, entranced as they expanded toward the reflected horizon line of the mountains. Is this immersion what it's like to die? she wondered. Her grandmother had died in a nursing home, alone. Had she known how much Ev loved her? Had Ev ever told her?

Beth took out a sparkler she'd been saving and lit it, holding it up so it matched the intensity of the crescent moon which had just risen over the pond. Then while it was still glittering, she tossed it into the pond. Quickly it was extinguished. A lesson about the relation between fire and water, Ev realized.

Carrie, then others, started throwing pebbles in to create patterns of expanding and connecting circles. Ev noticed Abby sitting quietly on a rock to the side, as if listening to inner voices. Surprised to see her so still, she recalled Abby telling of a mystical experience near the ocean where she'd heard speakers from ancient cultures sharing their lost wisdom. They didn't speak through her but to her, for which she had to go into a much greater stillness than she ordinarily allowed herself. That must be where she was now.

Going back to the shack for more sparklers, Ev found Gail, weeping. Without asking what was wrong or trying to analyze her pain, Ev wept with her. Gail's sobs waned and she looked up surprised, saying, "You've taken my hurt away." Ev smiled, then led Gail out with her to the pond. First she lit two sparklers at the same time and gave one to Carrie. Then she handed a sparkler to each person there and they lit them all together. One light, many branches, each with its own pattern of light--at one point they merged into one design and at other points each had its own dynamic, while beyond them the sun slowly set and the moon quickly rose.

When it grew darker, they gathered around the campfire. Beth played the drum with a strong rhythm while Ev marched, Egyptian fashion, around the fire. Then, Ev sat down and gazed into Abby's eyes. "Wow," she said, putting her hand on her heart, as Abby mirrored her gesture. She felt she was peering into the eyes of an ancient sage with a wise, kind, steady heart, a deep part of Abby usually hidden. "Wow." As Ev described Abby's heart to the others, Beth, tearful at this recognition of one she loved, affirmed Ev's insight. But what Ev didn't describe was how remote, cool, detached this heart was. She felt it couldn't be touched personally, not by her anyway.

When Carrie spoke of auras of light she could see around each person, Ev felt confused.

It was as if at this point she was not quite present but was hovering in some nearby space, not connected to her physical self or the group in a way she could recognize. She had a different sense of dimensions.

Suddenly terror coursed through her. She didn't know where she was, who she was, or how she was. She heard a scream. She didn't know if it was hers or someone else's or if it had actually occurred.

Responding to Ev's fear, Carrie gently stroked her back, intuitively touching the heart space while Ceci handed her a rock and a stick "for grounding," then started to tell her jokes. From a distance Ev understood with appreciation how humor and natural things could ground her. Intrigued she let it work.

Though still in some altered state, Ev felt she was reconnecting with her body as a container, a vehicle for insight. Fear passed as people began to chant. Suddenly as the chanting sounds rose with the smoke from the fire, Ev sensed geometric patterns forming. And with each pattern came to her its own color and movement. Ev felt both curiously separate and fully present, with no concerns about losing her mind as she'd had earlier with the terror of disintegrating. The sense of ego had dissolved. She began to look at each person. As she did so, slowly focusing on an individual entity, she could receive information about this person, sense a sound or pattern or color that was needed. She knew she could send pattern or color through a sound that could convey the necessary missing quality.

Focusing first on Gail, she told her, in a voice that was slower and stranger than her own, different in timbre and cadence, not to be afraid to feel, that she wouldn't be abandoned, that they *could* feel with her. Then she gave Gail a sound of grief with a scream buried in it and everyone else (except Dulce who was muttering in the background about "a rat in the woodpile") murmured comfort. Then she gave Gail a sound which the others could join. She told Gail that her colors were blue and gold.

Since the scream was still unexpressed, Ev suggested that Gail push the golden air up from her solar plexus into the blue of her throat chakra. Gail gasped that her throat was locked. Ev described an image of a tight screw rusted shut.

Ev sent Gail a sound, while Beth amplified it, both conducting it through a precise channel of focused energy. It felt to Ev as if together they were melding their voices to construct a conduit that was specific in direction and vibration, bringing it into alignment with the previous vibration until Gail released a ragged scream, then sobbed with relief.

"Could you help with my gas," teased Ceci and everyone laughed.

Despite the laughter, though, the others were sensing and supporting Ev's perception and practice, allowing it to express itself. Throughout the process, Ev could feel the steady assistance of Abby's heart, the generating energy of Carrie's spirit and Ceci's skillful grounding as Evi continued to explore feelings wanting expression, drawing them out through sound and color. Beth assisted Ev by listening, fine tuning with voice and touch what was present so that it could aid in what wanted expression. Ev and Beth continued to blend sounds together until the tones came together into one sound, sometimes harmonious, sometimes discordant, until it seemed complete and then ready to subside. This was a new form of teamwork for them. With Carrie's hand on her back, Abby's silent focus, Ev's voice and Beth's voice joining, it felt to Ev as if they had become one molecule of healing energy.

Gail's voice, when it joined in the healing for Ceci, was powerful. Ev asked Ceci to spit out what was blocking her and when Ceci coughed into the fire, the flames flared up as if being fed by something substantial.

For Dulce Ev gave a growl and the color green. She could see that the passage from Dulce's solar plexus to her heart was blocked. Dulce needed to let her anger burn like fire up into her heart and clear out the stagnant energy. That was the space Dulce needed to claim. But she could palpably feel Dulce's resistance.

Suddenly sobbing, Ev realized that what Dulce needed first was a kiss, something she herself could not provide in this particular state. When she urged someone to give it to her, Beth went over to Dulce and kissed her.

But Dulce was upset by Ev's intensity, the mask of grief Ev's face mirrored. "Evie," she said honestly, "it upsets me when you look at me like that."

Ev looked away, unable to change her expression as long as she was "reading" Dulce. She shifted her focus and told Dulce that she saw above her head a dove with a cross and a light. Dulce looked startled, then shared that her father had called her "Little Dove" in Spanish when she was small.

Ev turned back to the group, only to notice Carrie sitting there with her hands clasped toward her neck, her shoulders hunched in self-protection. "I have trouble opening my throat too," Carrie whispered. With a deep, sonorous voice which sounded from afar, Ev asked, "Do you want to?" As if she were responding directly to a teaching spirit, Carrie replied, "Yes."

So Ev gave Carrie an intense blue color and high sound which started in her throat and went down into her chest. While Ev and Beth accompanied her, Carrie closed her eyes to see an image of her aunt just after she'd died, her mouth open to release her spirit. As Carrie described the scene, Ev wondered if Carrie had taken on her aunt's death, after many months of caretaking for her. Was that residue of grief or fear blocking her throat? Ev sighed deeply, counting on Carrie to do the same in response. As oxygen rushed into what had been clamped shut, Beth pushed Carrie's shoulders down so she could let the weight drop away and breathe freely again.

Then Ev found a white light at Beth's third eye and focused on Beth's fear and on her resistance to fear, but without Beth's own assistance, Ev could only note the pattern. She couldn't sound it out.

Suddenly Ev experienced physical fatigue. She told them she couldn't go on. She pulled back her energy and withdrew into some internal place. She put her head on Carrie's shoulder and fell asleep. Soon they all quietly left the circle, wandering toward their individual shelters, and Carrie led Ev off to bed.

The next morning Ev and Carrie woke early and walked down to the waterfall. As they watched the water pour over the rocks, they rehashed the night's events. Ev felt uneasy, needing assurance that she hadn't been crazy or possessed or taken up too much time. Carrie pointed out the power of Ev's authority. "You said you wanted to deal with power and powerlessness this summer. Well, last night you were some powerful." Ev dismissed this idea. Something else was bothering her as well, but she couldn't quite identify it. After her mushrooming clarity, she was now in a complete fog. All she knew now was that she was feeling very "mere."

They both recognized that a crash after such intensity was inevitable, that Ev especially should take it easy after her evening's exertions. Carrie assured her over and over that her insights had not caused resentment or envy, that her actions did not in any way diminish another's. And they both acknowledged that inevitably in an experience like last night's, the theme of power was bound to flip over to the issue of powerlessness, which was what Ev seemed to be feeling at the moment.

It wasn't until later, when Carrie started to go into town, that Ev realized what was happening. She didn't want to go with Carrrie, but she couldn't bear to let her out of sight. Like a toddler, she wanted to cling to her. So she asked Carrie to curl up with her for little while. Safe in bed with the covers over her eyes, Ev plunged to her own tender spot.

Clutching Carrie, she was rocked with the grief and despair of a three-year-old, which had almost crippled her at the time she'd been wrenched away from her grandmother and deposited with her cool relatives. As Carrie held her, she sobbed and sobbed. She must've cried like this as a child--at first anyway, before she realized it was hopeless, that she couldn't go back to her grandmother and her grandmother wasn't going to come back for her. This time she felt comforted for her loss, not resented. This time there was compassion, not punishment, for her grief.

Later, reunited with the group at the shack when they gathered for supper, Ev felt intense embarrassment when they spoke of her as a healing medium. Picking up her anxiety they tried to find out what was frightening her, but since this revelation suddenly felt "public" to Ev, discussing her fear felt dangerous, too much exposure. She was particularly wary of receiving any projections from them, even or especially if they were couched as flattery.

"Power, I guess," she finally admitted as a fearful subject, "—and maybe going crazy." Almost anything she had done, successful or not, had been threatening to her nervous family. How did she know whether this land family wasn't also threatened? Would they punish her, or, worse, hobble her, or never let her return, if her abilities frightened them?

"Can't you just say no if you don't feel like performing?" asked a softer, deeper Gail. Ev winced at the word "performing." Had they seen what she'd done as a "performance"? Or did Gail mean something else?

"Yeah," said Carrie, "We'll understand if you don't feel like going that deep or being that intense." Was "intense" a way of saying she'd been too extreme?

"But what was happening? It seemed I was *receiving* information." Ev asked, side-stepping the issue of threat.

"From Martha, Frank, Jack and Joan," everyone chorused, evoking the names of spirit guides given Ev by their dowser psychic friend. The mundane names of Ev's spirit guides, compared to more exotic Tibetan and Indian names others received had been a running joke. Ev laughed.

In order to ease Ev's discomfort at being caught in the spotlight, the group shifted the focus away from her and began to discuss how their various talents worked together: Abby's clarity and articulateness, Beth's mediation of energy through movement, action and physical sensation, Gail's rebalancing of physical energies through sculpture and body work—all contributed to the whole.

Just as Ev picked up Dulce's fear that no one had noticed her contributing talent, Beth turned to Dulce and teased, "What about you? What are you good for?"

Carrie described how Dulce connected feelings with images and put them into words and Dulce described how both Ev and Carrie could perceive the unconscious in situations, sense what was going on between the lines, and pull it out, Ev emotionally and Carrie, intuitively.

Later, going outside for a breath of air, Ev reflected on the possibility that people weren't threatened by anything she did as long as they recognized their own particular powers. Looking up she saw a rainbow around the moon. The colors were so intense, so unusual she called the others out to see. As they stood on the road looking up at the stars, they saw rays of pulsating gold, rose and green lights behind the mountains.

"The northern lights!" said Abby.

"Aurora borealis," explained Dulce.

Shimmering vertically, the light was like sunlight across water, dancing snakes, undulating ribbons of color. The intensity of its hues matched the colors of geometric shapes Ev had seen for her friends the night before. Not a bad sign, she thought. Her experience with the mushrooms had pushed her notions of what empathy and art might be while linking her to elements of both of them.   Taking a deep breath she gave her full voice to the blessing she sang: "*Baruch atah adonigh elohanu melehch ha olum ashare kidashanu b'mitsvoh tuv vitsevanu l'hadlik nair shel yom tov.*" As she made this connection to her roots, she realized that the grief she felt about losing touch with her grandmother might have matched the anguish her grandmother must have felt about losing her. And having grieved that loss, Ev could recall the great joy she and Ida had shared through their bond.

Later, Ev wrote a poem about that experience:

I twice viewed the Night World
with Night Eyes – canny and cunning
attentive and disinterested.

I could see the patterns
of Sound, the questions
Shape asks, the way Color
needs sleep.

The Night World is big

in the way a tiny sigh is big.
Cleaving the known, the certain
so drusy trust can sparkle.

What might be feet, find a path.
What might be ears, find coils of invention.
What might be heart, drums on
what might be the shoulders of…
　　　Wait! Don't say it! Don't say it!
　　　Its severity shuts Night Eyes in the cupboard.
　　　Stay.　　Stay in the Night World.　Stay.

Where we are the girl whose birth was marked by miraculous light, who was snatched from her mother by her father the warrior and raised as a servant. She escaped from this drudgery into the forest where she discovered her magical powers: controlling fire to make art, healing by touching, making things happen just by describing them. Living in the forest with her circle of companions, she was finally reunited with her mother and sisters, who joined her there.

10

FAITH

Faith arrived at 2 a.m.. No one had expected her. She and the boys slept in the car because the foster dog kept barking at them. At the first hint of dawn she was awake and out of the car. The boys with their big feet hung over the front seats looked like two slumbering lumps.

After fixing a pot of coffee big enough for everyone, she left a note on the kitchen table saying she had dinner for that night. Then, walking down to the stream to get more water, she ran into Dulce who was off to the lumber yard to buy wood. Faith rode along to help and to catch up with Dulce's news. During the drive she heard all about the house Dulce was building and she told Dulce about the loss of her job, and what was happening with her kids, who were awake and hungry when they got back.

The boys were still grumpy. Allen, 15, had wanted to stay home with his friends and Jake, 13, didn't much like the idea of hanging out with a bunch of women. But the job insecurity had formed a bond between the three of them, so Faith was able to persuade them to come. Fortunately, Abby's nephew, Barry, was also visiting, so the teenage boy pack could remain intact. After Faith fixed them breakfast, the boys went off to find wood to make slingshots.

This left Faith, currently a math teacher, to help Abby with calculations for the house measurements. If only she'd brought her trig book and her slide rule, she moaned. She also consulted with Abby, Ev and Carrie on where to build her own tent platform on the new land.

Now that they'd bought the land next door, she was officially an owner, not just an honored guest. She'd been part of this "extended family" for at least twenty years now; it was only right that she own the connection, even if she had to borrow money from friends to do so. Buying those extra acres made it possible for the rest of the gang—including Ev and Gail—to become owners.

Carrie was one of Faith's oldest friends. They'd gone to school together eons ago and their lives had criss-crossed ever since. While Carrie helped Faith dig holes for her tent platform, they talked about what was going on for her--the loss of her job, her extended family news.

They worked well together, quickly, without much concern about accuracy. While Faith was quite handy, she was more than willing to improvise and make do, as she'd learned to do from her brothers. She was ever resourceful. Neither she nor Carrie were perfectionists, as her most recent boss had been, so it was a relief to cobble together this tent platform without either of them worrying excessively about its durability or beauty. Whatever they produced would be better support than the bare, rocky, often chilly ground.

Carrie was a good listener when she wasn't trying to problem-solve everything away. She'd been with Faith through some of her biggest, and some of her roughest, moments: when she was first engaged, newly married, pregnant, breaking up with Hank, struggling to make it as a single mother. Carrie understood to some extent how this job disconnection fit into the pattern of her life. For the first time in her life, it hadn't been Faith's decision to leave a job; she'd actually been laid off, not out of any problem with her performance but because the private, experimental school had fallen on hard times, with shrinking enrollments and depleted endowments during an economic downturn. Still it had been disconcerting.

Faith remembered the time her dad almost lost his job at Sparrow's Point. He who had been so steady suddenly became moody and erratic. Once management realized this, they wanted him out of the production cycle where split second decisions could mean the difference between life and death, not to mention profits and losses. She wondered now if his disorientation was the result of some kind of industrial pollution, from whatever alloys or chemicals they added to the mixture to make steel. He'd loved that job, the risk, the dramatic molten pours, the importance of the product for national security. Fortunately, the union was able to save employment for him, but they moved him off the floor, into a desk job and he plunged into a depression which lasted far too long.

"Math was never your thing, Faith," Carrie observed. They had been English majors together. "You took that job because Allen was having trouble with math in school. You wanted to be able to help him. But it's ok that Allen doesn't like math--he has lots of other talents. So do you."

Faith kept digging, but she listened. Carrie had known her long enough to help put things into perspective. "Being a mother has always been your vocation--everything followed from that, including most of your jobs:

waitressing, teaching kindergarten, then grade school, now this. You've been keeping pace with the kids. But you're only slightly more of a mathematician than Allen is. You can't expect to turn that around in just one year."

"I'm not sure I like teaching that much anymore."

"That's part of it, too. Maybe what you need to do for them now is model the next stage, autonomy, by figuring out what you really love to do and figuring out how to get paid for it."

What Faith really loved to do was gardening, swimming, boating, puttering around her house and hanging out with friends and family. Except for the gardening, nothing to live on but plenty to survive on. And did she really want to model independence for the boys? If mothering had been her guiding light, what would she do when they left? Where does the mother bird go when the fledglings fly from the nest? Flight seemed the only option.

"What about houses? You love old houses."

Yes, she did. The old brick rowhouse she'd grown up in Baltimore, the old country houses where her aunts lived, the old house she and Hank lived in when they first married, the wood frame house she lived in now. "But I'm tired of fixing them up. And not trained for it."

"I wasn't thinking of fixing, I was thinking of selling."

Ahhh, interesting idea. Faith mulled it over. Real estate, she knew, was a risky business, especially these days. But she'd be good at it, she knew. She imagined herself showing houses to a young couple.

"You know enough about fixing to be able to tell what a house needs. You can diagnose, then get somebody else to fix it."

"Actually, I've been thinking about going back to school to become a social worker."

Carrie looked surprised, then said vigorously, "You'd be great at that too! But it's a lot of work going back to school."

"I'm not afraid of that. I like working hard."

"Yeah, me too. It's jobs I can't stand." They laughed.

It started raining, but they worked on, getting muddy as they finished digging the holes and leveling the posts Abby had cut with the chain saw. When the sprinkles turned into a downpour, they ran into town, to three different hardware stores, to find galvanized nails, a miter box, and a replacement circle saw blade. When they got back to the site, the rain had stopped, and they were pleased with how the water had run off the platform, between the boards and off the slight slant. As soon as they finished the damp platform, Faith put up her family-sized tent and the sun came out again.

Throughout these activities, Faith gave a running report to Carrie on everyone in her family, each one of whom Carrie had known vicariously for the past three decades. Faith was especially pleased to tell Carrie the latest about her adventurous younger sister and her growing family. She also described to Carrie, with great enthusiasm, the recent Statue of Liberty celebration and the tall ships, as well about friends she visited in New York City. In addition to her own family, Faith was connected to a varied network of friends, including this land group. Carrie listened carefully to extract feelings hidden in the reporting of events. Faith, who tended to breeze past her deepest feelings, sometimes depended on others to echo them back to her for recognition.

Faith was pleased because her platform overlooked the steam where two natural springs arose, guaranteeing pure fresh water all the time. Secretly she felt it was a kind of holy site, like Brigid's sacred wells. She was, one might say, the keeper of the blessed water. That part of her which was Irish relished the stories of the independent Brigid who'd been born with a mysterious light over her cradle.

So Faith was horrified when she walked down into the stream bed to discover a scum of oil on the water in some of the resting pools. She picked up a leaf covered with grease. When she and Carrie explored upstream, they found soap in the water, plus two fried eggs, hot dogs and what looked like charcoal briquettes.

"They're using the stream as a garbage dump," she protested. "It must be city folk: the drain is where dirty water goes, along with garbage and shit and everything else we don't want. They must think the stream will just wash everything away like the sink does."

They continued upstream onto the neighbor's land until they found a young man trying to chop wood. He looked like he wasn't sure which side of the axe to strike against the wood and as if he were afraid the axe would bite him.

Faith greeted him with a friendly smile and some chat about the weather. It turned out he was from the City, by which they all meant New York City, and, implying she was also, she bonded with him as an outsider. Finally she asked, "Know anything about the garbage in the stream?"

He looked surprised, then guilty. "What garbage?"

"Oh, just your usual bacon and eggs, hot dogs and buns."

He tried to look innocent.

"Trouble is, it goes into our drinking water. Makes everything all greasy. Think you could ask the people you're with to toss their garbage somewhere else? Maybe even bury it so wild animals don't drag it into the woods?" She figured the reference to wild animals might get his city boy's attention. It did.

Although there was no sign of any other people he was with, he nodded, obviously glad to save face.

Then, like a native, she gave him directions to the nearest swimming beach and, like a mother, told him to enjoy himself.

Later Carrie and Ev helped Faith carry the three chickens she had baked at home down to the campfire and Faith took charge getting the rest of the dinner--potatoes, corn, bread--cooked and served. Despite the nurturing nature of her activity, she acted more like one of the boys than the earth mother she could have been, more, as Ev described it, like "the biggest brother." Efficient as she was, there was nothing martyrish about her activity. She always took time to admire an ear of corn she'd just shucked or to smell the aroma of a fresh loaf of bread she'd just sliced.

After dinner, Faith did calculations to solve the measuring problem with the house while Abby asked for suggestions for a course on Outsiders she was teaching at the prison. This led to a discussion about why the guy in the local mom-and-pop had been, according to Gail, rude to Dulce. Everyone wondered if it had anything to do with the local's perception of them as "druids and queers," as one of Abby's local forester friends had put it. Or some prejudice against Hispanics. Since Dulce was almost always friendly herself, they finally put his attitude down to "a bad day."

Although Faith had plenty of reason to feel like a classic outsider, being a single mother fond of women, she didn't particularly feel all that different from everybody else. She had at least one foot firmly planted in the regular world. Being a single mother in itself wasn't that odd these days--and with Hank right down the road from her home, ready to do his bit as a father, she didn't feel that different from her other divorced friends. Divorce had been a greater stigma in her Catholic youth than the never to be spoken of closet, but now that both her parents were dead, she rarely thought of herself even as "divorced."

As for being fond of women, the eastern shore resort where she lived was inundated by gay people in the summer. The locals might be homophobic, but they weren't about to knock their main means of support. And many of the locals, artists and writers, were also of the persuasion. So in the summer, she fit right in with the lesbian crowd; in the winter she fit right in with the struggling to survive single mothers and other economic adventurers. With undaunted optimism and remarkable fluidity, she was able to negotiate these worlds as well as anyone. Being regular was at the base of her own sanity and the foundation she intended to provide for her children. They might be quirky but they'd never be snobs. And they'd never have to apologize for who they were.

Faith's family of birth extended way beyond its center, which had collapsed with the premature death of her mother, especially now that her father had also died. Even before her parents died, her sister and brothers, aunts, uncles, and cousins had formed a network of support into which they could bail out whenever tensions grew too tight at home. Now, as the oldest daughter, she was at the heart of this network which continued to expand with the arrival of her own children and her nieces and nephews.

With her winning manner, attractive face, and up beat personality, Faith charmed her way into multiple hearts. And once welcomed, she knew how to make herself useful, how to make herself at home, how to be a homemaker in every sense of the word. She supplied in good cheer and generosity what few of her elders had been able to offer fully, being worn down to the threads with family obligations and financial pressures.

After they built up the campfire, Jake, her youngest, told a long story, The Wanderer, which he'd learned from his camp counselor. His storytelling ability, with intricate details and suspense, was impressive. Everybody badgered him with questions and comments, but he handled the attention with humor and poise. She was proud of him. While Allen, who looked so much like his father, was the child she'd shared joyfully with Hank, Jake was still in her womb when Hank left her. When he was born, she felt ecstatic: a good omen that all would be well, despite the threats of poverty and loneliness. And even with some struggles, it had been.

The next day Faith supervised the remeasurement of the post holes for the big house and then she and Carrie worked out a system by which she lay down and scooped dirt into a bucket which Carrie pulled out on a rope and dumped. Faith didn't mind getting dirty, when the dirt was soil. It made her feel like one of her prize vegetables. This way they finished the last of the inner holes. For lunch they had leftover chicken sandwiches, the fixing of which Faith took charge of. Then Faith figured out how many cubic feet of concrete they'd need for the pour they'd scheduled for the following day, while everyone listed tasks and divided them up, amid a flutter of discussion about pumping water from the stream, their only source, and shifting sand from the post holes to use in the mixer. Faith admired their frugality and was pleased to add her suggestions to their many possible ingenious solutions, impractical as some of them turned out to be.

Faith was out near the house site rechecking her calculations when a neighbor drove up in his pickup. He reminded her of her most dilapidated uncle, chronically jobless, running out of gas as he staggered from crisis to crisis. She both felt sorry for him and tried to avoid him.

Resisting that impulse now, she strode over to the truck with a warm greeting. He gestured toward a brown bag sitting next to him in the truck. When she looked puzzled, he opened the bag and she peered in. Inside were two tiny kittens, one a beautiful calico and the other, your basic grey.

"I'm wondering if you all have a lactating cat," he said. "Their mother got killed and they won't survive without some mother's milk. They're the only ones what survived."

She shook her head. All the cats on the land had been fixed. A funny word "fixed": set like cameos in a moment of time. The women on the land, everyone but her, were also fixed in a way—all of them at this point, including her, past child-bearing. She suspected he already knew that none of their cats had milk, and was indirectly asking them to take on these orphan kittens. Her heart went out to them. But at the same time she knew what it would take to keep them alive: a special formula, feedings every few hours with a medicine dropper, constant care for weeks. She herself was in no position to give such attention. All her energy had to go into finding a new job so she could keep food on the table for the boys. Nor would her old cat, Maggie, be pleased with such intruders. She was afraid Maggie would drive them away, as she'd lost Filo when Maggie arrived. Unlike people, cats did not seem to be all that communal, at least not her cats.

"I'm not much of a cat person," he said as they looked down at the tiny kittens in his hand, their eyes still closed. Their mews clawed at her heart. She knew how attached we get to the helpless ones we nourish.

No, she said to his unspoken request, I cannot, will not guarantee the growth of these kittens whose mother was killed, who have survived their siblings, though I am touched by their will to live.

"You can do it," she said, reminding him of the litter of puppies he'd nursed through the winter, the injured raccoon he'd sheltered under his house. She told him the formula, petted the kittens and wished him well. As he drove off, she sighed.

Later everybody on the land went to the lake. Getting them to go anywhere together at the same time was quite an operation, but Faith was good at shepherding. Used to an almost daily swim, she pulled them all to water whenever she came to visit. Despite a haze over its far shore, the lake was lovely, the blue green water patterned with reflections of birch and pine.

Diving in immediately, Faith gasped at the chill of the water, much colder than her more southern ocean, then luxuriated in the invigorating tingle as her body rushed to adjust to the temperature. There was nothing she loved more than moving gracefully and swiftly through the fluidity of water. It was definitely her element. Sometimes it seemed the water flowed through her as it swirled around her. It cooled the hot, dry memories of lava bursts of anger when times were hard or the desert dullness of inner landscapes when her mother's health took a turn for the worse.

She raced the younger boys to the nearest island, while Allen sat on a rock and stared soulfully off toward the horizon. What was it like to be a teenage boy? She could almost remember, even though of course she'd never been one. Growing up with her two older brothers, she'd followed their footsteps as surely as her younger sister had followed hers, in those days anyway. At the same time, being the oldest daughter, she also had to play the part of little mother. It had been quite a juggling act. But being female had spared her the worst of what the boys had known: fierce competition in sports, the fear of being drafted if you didn't do well in school, the likelihood of being sent to Vietnam, the vexed issue of success in the face of your father's frustrations. She was proud of how her brothers went off to college, one to become a doctor and the other, an engineer. She was glad they'd shown her the route out.

All those issues were softened now, for Allen and Jake, but she knew there would be a time when she wouldn't be able to go along with them and smooth the road. She prayed that she wouldn't just dry up and blow away then. Not likely. She might be single, but she was also freer than her mother had been, thanks to her own generation of feisty women and thanks to her own choices.

As she swam back behind the boys, she saw the others, her women friends, being so characteristically themselves: Abby swimming out as far as she could go; Dulce dipping in the water to bathe, then floating in a life jacket; Beth playing with a ball in the water, trying to lure the dog in to swim; Ev floating in an inner tube gazing across the sky at the curve between earth and water; Carrie sitting in the shade, reading, her camera ready to record the day; Gail peeking into the picnic fixings to see what she could nibble.

When she pulled herself out of the water, Faith lay upside down on the large, flat rock to give the vertebrae in her back a rest. Intrigued, Beth and Gail imitated her. On another rock, the three boys played cards while the three women lay, heads dangling toward the water, in the sun.

When they got back to the shack, everybody wandered off in different directions. Faith headed for the garden to do some weeding. For some reason, her mother's funeral came back to her briefly. "May their souls and the souls of the faithful departed through the mercy of God rest in peace." But that's not where Faith's memory rested. It rested on the day before the night she died. How she'd brushed her mother's hair, the first and only time she'd done anything so personal for her mother, whose touch had usually been one-way. Lost in her coma, her mother couldn't thank her, or object, but she felt somehow that her mother appreciated the gesture, perhaps even enjoyed the sensation. Faith herself loved having her hair brushed, ever since her mother brushed it when it was so fresh and fine. She loved the brushing but hated the washing, soap slipping down into her clenched eyes. She couldn't wait until she could do it for herself. Regrets, regrets, what a waste of time were regrets.

Had being a traditional wife and mother in her family been dangerous?

she wondered. It seemed that her maiden or widowed aunts were the ones who really thrived. Thank God for her Aunt Mary, whose gumption and love of life had been a model for Faith. Like the women here on the land--tough, independent, self-reliant. These were the people Faith followed when her marriage broke up, when she couldn't follow the boys anymore. Hadn't she been the tough, independent one in that relationship, anyway, despite how hard she tried to act like a dutiful wife? Wasn't it easier, less painful, to be your own self on your own? Relationships with men or with women were tricky. What endured was her family. Her aunts, her brothers and sister, her own children, her nieces and nephews. These were the people she could count on for the steady anchor of her life, the ones who guided the daily movements of her existence.

But when she was really down, it was women like these, longtime friends, she sought out. They comforted her and sent her on her way again. Like her aunts had done when she was little and had to get away from the house, had to shut the door behind her for awhile.

The boys were playing cards on the porch. She could tell, with relief, that they were having a good time, not just making the best of a bad situation.

So Faith went off to her tent to read a book she'd found in the shack about the Findhorn community, and maybe even take an uncharacteristic nap. Not only was she moved to read how this Scottish community worked, she was fascinated with how they grew enormous vegetables in such poor soil.

As soon as she crawled inside the tan canvas, she could hear thunder. The sound rushed closer and closer. Behind the tent cloth she could see great flashes of lightning. Rain poured through the windows before she could zip them shut. Then the wind roared up, ripping through the awning like a tornado. It was exciting and scary both.

Suddenly under the weight of the water, the back of the tent collapsed. The wet cloth stuck to her face for a second so she couldn't breathe. She opened her mouth to scream but no sound came out. She imagined a shovelful of dirt crushing her, burying her. She anticipated a huge rock coming down on her head.

Zipping open the door of the tent, she leapt out and ran for the shack, despite the flashes of lightning surrounding her. As she ran down the path through a hemlock grove, she saw a bolt split a tree above her and a glare burst around her, becoming a globe of deafening sound. This boom was followed by what seemed like a vacuum in which she found herself surrounded by total silence, utter stillness.

At that moment what felt like two hands reached up out of the earth and grabbed her around the ankles. She felt bolted to the ground, unable to lift her feet, unable to move, unable to run away. Then as the lightening continued to pulsate behind her, the hands just as quickly released her feet and she was tossed sideways as if slammed to the ground by a giant fist. She fell into soft earth, padded by leaves and pine needles.

Two steps in front of her a huge tree limb fell. Had she still been running forward, it could have crushed her. A tingling convulsed through her entire body. Stunned, she pulled herself up, found no gaping holes or searing wounds on her body, and ran on, determined to find shelter in the shack.

When she arrived at the shack, soaking wet and trembling, she announced she'd been struck by lightening. At first no one could believe it, but, awed at seeing her so shaken, they listened carefully to her story, even the boys, while providing towels, blankets, and hot tea. She described the hands which anchored her to the earth, saving her from the falling limb. They looked at each other amazed.

Later when the rain stopped, they all tromped out to look at the tree limb. Sure enough, the trunk of the huge hemlock was freshly charred from the inside. They were amazed it hadn't burned down. Fortunately the rain had put out any potential forest fire.

Although Faith said she felt fine, even exhilarated by this adventure, Dulce, who'd read about possible sources of injury from lightning, insisted on taking her to the emergency room to check for interior damage. The possibility which scared Faith the most was burned out lungs. She did have an ache in her womb, but nothing worse than what she felt with menstrual cramps. No injuries were found. The ache, they told her, would go away with some rest.

Apparently because the lightening hit the hemlock first and discharged into the ground, she'd served as a conductor of electricity without any blockage. Ev, who'd come along to the emergency room for support, told her that must mean all her chakras were clear. "If not before it struck, then afterwards," she added.

Faith was amused by this restructuring of potential disaster into a cleansing, maybe even a rebirthing into the rest of her nine lives. "That's comforting," she replied, feeling blessed to have been saved. As if somebody was watching out for her. She wondered who it might be, somebody who'd crossed over already perhaps, her mother or her father? Or maybe somebody like St. Brigid.

The others teased her about being a lightening rod.

"That's how Faith avoids being a victim, no matter what happens to her," said Dulce with respect. "It goes right through her."

But the ache in her womb continued for several days, and she hoped, briefly, it wasn't symptomatic of something worse, like the cancer which had killed her mother.

The next day, after the storm, was so beautiful, crystal clear and luminous that all her worries disappeared. In the morning Faith went with the boys to the dump and then to the thrift shop where Allen bought a shirt he liked and both boys vetoed a shirt she liked. Too loud, they said.

That afternoon Carrie took Faith and the boys up to see the caves. As they hiked up the path after the boys, Faith told Carrie about the camp she'd gone to as a girl. This path through birch and beech reminded her of that place in Pennsylvania.

"You know, Faith, it's such a joy for me to have you here. It completes the circle for me," Carrie said with her shy intensity.

Faith gave her a big hug. Such explicit regard both pleased her and made her nervous. She rested her head on Carrie's shoulder for a moment and gave a positive murmur. But with her next breath she started complaining about the bug bites and worrying about where the boys had gone to. They scurried on to see the boys waving to them from the mouth of the first cave.

They got there too late to see the magic rays of sun reach into the caves, but the boys' enthusiasm was undaunted. They climbed back through the largest cave with flashlights. Tagging behind, Faith loved hearing their voices floating back over the water as they discovered peek holes and various other landmarks.

She wondered what had been mined here. Carrie, who wasn't very tuned to such details, thought, maybe, iron, but Faith imagined graphite or maybe even coal. Carrie told her the story of Iron Annie, a legend in those parts, the only person who could drive the trucks up the steep, winding road to the mines. Now she lived down the road and raised rabbits.

Bunnies, thought Faith, softness and light after mining that hard, dark stuff.

When they reached the end of the cave, they climbed back out and sat in the fading light while the boys explored even more caves. At a certain point she realized that the boys had disappeared and she figured they had gone back into the big cave. Although Carrie wanted to go look for them on the outside, since she knew the way, Faith insisted they go back inside too.

So hunched over, they descended into the rapidly cooling cave and rushed along like moles or miners in search of the boys. At one point Faith put her foot down in the shadows between two rocks and wrenched her ankle, but she didn't stop until she could hear Allen calling back to them from the mouth of the cave.

Of course, the boys were ok; they were quite frisky in fact. Now that they were moving into the cool inhibitions of adolescence, she was glad to see them unreservedly delight in this adventure.

That night at the campfire Faith joined in when Ev and Abby started a duet on their flutes. With her recorder she gradually but easily adopted their method of improvisation. Suddenly their music dropped into the background and her own melody took the lead. Surprisingly it was slow and sad, almost melancholic, such a counterpoint to her cheerful, chipper persona. But she cut it off when the boys started getting restless, talking about returning to the shack to play cards, their idea of a real vacation.

Beth suggested they all make sounds imitating nature. Jake started off with a splendid rendition of whispering wind, followed by Ev hooting like an owl, Dulce bubbling like a brook, Abby howling like a wolf, Carrie pattering like rain, Gail roaring like fire, Beth rustling like leaves, Allen mewing like a cat, which made everybody giggle. Then followed sounds of laughing, shouting, crying, *ah, oh, e,* and *i* sounds.

They sang old songs until the boys got restless again, so Faith, realizing those songs were too old fashioned, suggested that they take turns: the three boys could sing a song from their generation and the "girls" would sing a song from theirs. The women listened with delight as the boys sang, Faith tapping out the tune, Ev silently mouthing the words. But when they tried to join in on the choruses of "We don't need no education," "Born in the U.S.A.," and "Tyrannus Rex," the boys objected that they were interrupting. While the women sang their old songs, the boys rehearsed their next one, only half-listening to songs they'd heard already a million times.

Finally the grown-ups pooped out and the boys headed off for their card game. As their flashlights bobbed up and down through the woods, the women sang one of Faith's favorites:

"I've got a river of light flowing out of me,
makes the lame to walk and the blind to see,
opens prison gates, lets the captives free,
I've got a river of light flowing out of me.
Spring forth the well inside my soul,
Spring forth the well to make me whole.
Spring forth the well that I might see
the light that shines in me."

The next day Carrie and Ev arrived back from town with the news that it would be cheaper to have a truck come pour cement than to mix it themselves. After pricing the rental of pump and small mixer, and considering the cost of buying sand and cement, they consulted with a guy at the hardware store who had a crush on Gail and he suggested ready-mix. So Ev called two ready-mix companies and got information and prices. But it would mean postponing the pour for another day, and Faith was worried she couldn't stay. She'd promised Allen she'd get him home in time for a job.

But when it seemed clear that Abby and Beth opposed the ready-mix, Abby because she wanted to postpone the whole foundation until the following summer and Beth because it was too expensive, and that Dulce and Gail were gloomy because the insulation they'd just put into their floor had gotten wet, Faith felt she had to help. Carrie and Ev had already put so much energy into getting this project off the ground, or into the ground. They needed her.

So she talked Allen into staying to help, told Ev to go ahead and call the cement company and tell them to come the next day, then drove Allen into town so he could call about the job, since there was no phone on the land. It buoyed her up to be able to help like this. It made her feel confident and competent, which at this particular juncture in her life was therapeutic.

Then they went into a flurry of activity. Ev dashed off to call the cement company, who said they'd be there at 8 a.m., Faith built forms with Carrie, Abby and Jake dug to the bottom of each post hole, and Beth cleared a path for the cement truck.

Faith was in her element, giving orders, working quickly, taking charge, clashing with resistant ones like Beth, then backing off gracefully. She grabbed old pieces of wood and whacked nails into them with abandon, creating forms where before had only been scraps, like one of her aunt's quilts.

At one point Faith tripped and almost fell headlong into an empty post hole. Fortunately Carrie grabbed her and pulled her out by the pants pockets. It frightened her to lose her footing. To be on the brink of plunging into a hole in the ground was like facing her own possible premature death. Funny, how being struck by lightning was an adventure while the thought of being buried alive was terrifying. But it was all over in a second. Even though she laughed and joked about her whole life passing before her, she was sure she didn't want to die like that. She'd rather be swimming into the sunset than burrowing out from some narrow cavity--or, for that matter, getting shocked to death.

Then Allen, who'd been reading all night, woke up and helped them lift huge logs up out of the path for the truck. They had been rolling and cajoling them under Beth's supervision without much success. They were all, even Faith, amazed and impressed with Allen's strength. What took four of them to lift, he could raise by himself. But to complete the job, it took all of them—the women and the boys-- working together. They gave a cheer when the logs were finally out of the way.

Faith could feel the tension and anxiety as they waited in the meadow for the truck early the next morning, seven women and two boys. Ev met the truck at the shack and rode on the running board to escort the driver down to the building site. They felt collective relief when the truck finally squeezed through the rock wall and onto the field. Faith saw tears in Carrie's eyes.

The driver, Joe, was very nice. He seemed to appreciate what they were trying to do. He told Ev to "go for it" and later told Faith he wished he could build a house for himself. He helped them scoop the last dregs of cement into the wheelbarrows and on into the holes. And he didn't charge them for overtime. He was the kind of working man Faith trusted implicitly.

The first big pour went into the ditch which would make the footing for the fireplace. Their forms held up well and everyone, including Dulce who had limped down to help, pitched in to shovel and tamp and hold the plastic in place. Then, under Faith's supervision, they divided into teams to take each of the two wheelbarrows and fill the twelve post holes. Faith was afraid they wouldn't have enough cement for the four inner holes--she should have allowed for more than enough in her calculations. But, as it turned out, they had just enough. She was pleased. Her math skills were good enough for real life.

She felt the excitement her father must have felt at his big pours. True, cement wasn't as exciting, dangerous or powerful as molten steel, but working with it demanded some of the same teamwork and urgency. No wonder he felt demoted when they put him behind a desk.

After they'd tamped down the holes and said goodbye to Joe, Faith took her tent down and packed the car, with Carrie's help, while Abby, Beth, and Ev worked on leveling the cement, Dulce and Gail went back to their building, and the boys collapsed. Then as a whole group they went down to the local diner for breakfast where they celebrated, rehashed the pour and planned future projects.

When they came out of the diner, Faith's old car wouldn't start; the battery was dead. But after a charge from Abby's car, she and the boys set off on their long drive home. Next to her was a book she'd borrowed from Beth, *The Miracle of Love,* about a Hindu guru. And in her head were all the questions her friends had asked, some of which she hadn't really answered. Lots to mull over until she arrived again, unannounced, at the crack of dawn.

Branches

11

THE MOLECULE

We called ourselves "the molecule." This metaphor was coined by one of us more scientifically adept than I am, but I understand that molecules are bonds of atoms. As elemental units, atoms are like individuals, whereas the molecule is a shared identity. As a bond, the molecule is larger than a single atom, more expansive, its character more than its diverse parts.

Thousands of specific kinds of molecules have been identified, so what was so special about ours? Perhaps nothing more than the fact that we, as individuals, chose this bond. Although we likened this association, in larger contexts, to "sisterhood," it felt looser than familiar bonds within which sisters are linked. Like "mother*hood*," it contains an element of mystery. Unlike the powerful hood of femaleness, genes and fate which sisters share, our molecule could, and sometimes did, combine with other such molecules to form one large wave. But like the primal sister bond, when we went our separate ways, we could sense between us echoes, phantom magnetic pulls which allowed us, still, to feel over distances the sorrows and joys of the others. Like the Corsican Brother twins, from the classic comics of our childhood, we felt when the other was injured or deeply moved.

Who knows where we came from originally? Stardust, they say, and bacteria, and maybe both. Then life evolved until we were part of family configurations. But gradually, whether by collision, dissolution or electricity, we were pulled into other orbits, combined with other atoms, transformed into different molecular identities. Just as we began to settle into these separate identities, some major modification in the earth's alignment occurred. Perhaps it was a readjustment, a return to ancient rhythms; perhaps it was something very new in the lives of women. I say *modification* because it didn't just happen; I believe we made it happen. But perhaps that is an illusion. Perhaps it was simply change, not choice. I'll leave that up to our historians to decide.

Whatever it was, a weak force became a strong force. What held us rooted to established ways, the gravity of tradition, suddenly shifted, allowing a different kind of energy and chemistry to split atoms apart to form new molecules. We atoms joined a united surf of solidarity and movement we called "sisterhood," a massive wave rising over the dam of patriarchy. Many, many atoms so joined made fluidity potent, formed a liquid scarf around the earth as she shook herself awake and, in the parlance of those times, gave birth to herself.

But birth, although a miracle, is only a moment, and eventually that powerful wave disappeared, falling back into the customary flux and flow of tides. Subsequent surges were not as compelling. We atoms washed ashore, some still joined, some separate, all somehow still connected, but not together. We were thrown back into an indifferent society, back against the sharp, heavy forms of hierarchy and privilege, as remnants-- poor, unmarried mavericks and deviants—bonafide wretches!

That's when a few of us, caught in a fertile estuary, consciously became our own molecule, a group of atoms bonded by promise, place, love, not just one to one but one to all. This bond was not as fluid as movement, nor as solid as family. It allowed some to stay close to home while others whizzed around in wider orbits. It allowed each of us to be part of other configurations, so that as a group we were connected to other atoms, other molecules, other systems. This expansion was possible because, although our molecule was special, it was not unique.

We all know this. But what I'd like to posit here, my friends, in case it's not already obvious, is that we were not just any molecule, we were a *water* molecule.

Think about it. Friendship between women is analogous to water molecules. Like water, we women are everywhere. Life begins in us. We contain, carry and dissolve other molecules. We participate in the chemistry of life, shaping and converting nutrition into energy. We expand when we freeze, blustering out in defense against cold. When the heat is on, we disappear into vapor or mist, fog or obscurity. We are ubiquitous, invisible, essential.

Water molecules are composed of one oxygen atom and two hydrogen atoms, like one head with two ears. "An ear of one water molecule will form weak bonds with the head of another and vice versa so that water molecules continuously stick and unstick to each other, thus forming dynamic, evanescent lattices." (*The Way Life Works*, p. 16)

As friends we're ultimately connected, in other words, by our ears. And since we can hear with both ears, each molecule can connect with, or disconnect from, more than one other molecule at the same time. This image feels more like civil community than nuclear fusion. These moist molecular shapes cover much of the earth's surface, no matter how humble, imperceptible, and amorphous they might seem. They adapt to different cultures, different geographies, different climates. They quench a variety of thirsts, clean a variety of bodies, assume a variety of shapes from raindrops to waterfalls.

Water molecules, moreover, share their own special vibes. Energy skips quickly from one molecule to another, very quickly. Because of this swiftness, a vibration can pass through many water molecules before it dissipates. Bonds can be both instantaneous and far-reaching. They can form puddles or oceans.

We used to take our water for granted. We drank from our streams and trusted our wells. Now that streams are being polluted and wells are drying up, we finally realize how precious water can be.

Where we are the daughter of the sun goddess. One day our mother felt a shadow cross her radiance and when she returned home, after working from dawn to dusk, her beloved and devoted daughter was missing. When she finally found her, the Queen knew something was terribly wrong, but her daughter couldn't tell her. When she finally realized what had happened, she chased the Moon and sliced him into lunar pieces, then transformed her daughter into a star so she could watch over her, day and night.

12

HELENE

Helene sat in a comfortable folding chair in front of her new fire pit, pleased at how the flames rose up, illuminating the river stones she'd hauled up from the brook to line the pit. Even though her back ached from that effort, it was worth it. The way the stones reflected the firelight reminded her of the cobblestones of old Quebec in the land of her maternal ancestors.

Hers was the only campsite this remote, across the stream and deep into the woods.

And, even better, it was on her own land, the neighboring parcel she'd recently purchased. Not only did it restore the last fragment of the original homestead, it was hers to control. She was proud of the bridges she'd built over the stream and its tributary to complete the loop of trails around and through the land. With her vision and hard labor she'd earned a place for herself among this odd group of women.

She was startled by the hooting of an owl almost directly above her in one of the many limbs of the ancient cabbage pines which circled her campsite. These trees reminded her of Hindu goddesses with their multiple arms. These matriarchs kept her company now as she waited for Beth to return from her trip to town with Abby to attend a peace vigil. Helene glanced into the porch of her tent to make sure the treats she'd bought for this campfire were still ok, not being nibbled upon by mice or raccoons. She hoped that Beth would still come that night, even if it was late. Beth, who promised little, said she would try. Helene was on the land so rarely these days, she felt she deserved Beth's undivided attention. But it was hard to compete with something so momentous as war and peace. She shivered and pulled her colorful Indian blanket around her. Wonderful that she owned this land and that her campsite was so wild, but sometimes it felt a little lonesome. She wondered if she should have pitched her tent closer to the road, on the ridge where she planned to build her log cabin.

Unbidden, scenes of her life at home rushed through her head, particularly of her beloved mother, now blind because of the slip of a doctor's knife, more dependent than ever on her only daughter. Thank the lord her younger brother, having dropped out of seminary, was at home to fill in for Helene so she could escape occasionally to the land. But soon he'd be going back to school, getting a job, maybe even finding a relationship, and she, once again, would be the sole caretaker.

The Buddha was so right, all of life *is* suffering: *Dukka, dukka, dukka* No matter how much pleasure she took in life's treats, dukka always raised its ugly head. She could bear her own suffering, her back going out, the pains, the recurring nightmares, but she hated to see her mother so vulnerable, no longer able to do the cooking and needlework which kept her life busy and meaningful in the chosen confinement of their home above the family business, now managed by her elder brother since their father's death. When her aging mother first grew ill, she'd clearly wanted Helene to stay with her and take care of her. Helene vowed she wouldn't send her mother away to a nursing home as her mother had allowed her father to send her away to boarding school when she was only five. So she gladly gave up her secretarial job and moved in with her mother in the hometown of Manfred Springs where she'd grown up.

Helene took out her special ceremonial pipe and her smooth leather pouch, filled the pipe with a pinch of what she called her "medicine" As she inhaled, she felt the medicine ease the tension in her chest, and release its energy through her legs; she stretched back and looked up through the interweaving branches of the circle of cabbage pines. A flow of dark hills ringed the eastern edge of her land, and over the nearest one, a sliver of moon was rising. She wasn't sure if it was waxing or waning. Beth would know.

Helene looked up at the trees surrounding her. They were so huge that each branch itself looked like a smaller tree. One of these trees, then, was a whole village of trees, all connected to one main source, each taking off in a different direction, yet bound to the same allotment of earth, to the same portion of sky. She felt small and protected in their collective embrace. These particular trees reminded her of her French Canadian aunts, tall, strong, and powerful. Those sisters were devotees of Saint Anne, grandmother of Jesus, mother of the Virgin Mary. Helene was convinced that she, Anne, was also an ancient Goddess, a remnant of the matriarchy which preceded the patriarchy of French Catholicism. Her aunts' support had sustained her and her mother throughout the challenges and conflicts of their family life.

"Duukaa, duukaa, duukaa," Helene started singing, turning that familiar evocation of suffering into a chant. The trees seemed to be listening, responding with brief nods of their towering tops. Whether their roots were Hindu, Christian or pagan, they felt like sacred presences which protected and blessed her. She started talking to the one in whose lap she'd planted her campsite. *I never thought I'd ever camp out, much less enjoy it, but I'm proud of the fact that my camp is farther "out" than any of the others. It's fun to find an environment tuned to my expanding consciousness.*

Much as she enjoyed life's luxuries, Helene also credited herself with being adventurous. Trying to keep up with Beth and her "counter-phobia" helped hold most of Helene's many fears at bay. But living out here, alone in the woods, offered other challenges. As it turned out, Helene's well-furnished tent was pitched along an animal path, so she was visited at night by all kinds of scurrying creatures from deer to raccoons. Some nights she'd been awakened by the huffing of rutting buck. Not a comfortable feeling being caught in between all that testosterone, but not unfamiliar either.

One night something so huge bellowed through the canvas that she sat up the rest of the night trembling. Turned out, according to the newspaper, there was a moose on the loose in those parts, and Helene convinced all the land folk that her midnight visitor was that same moose.

Remembering that sleepless night, she decided tonight to discourage such visitors by bringing out her portable tape player. She turned on a tape of Native American flute music. Then she marveled over the fact that she who couldn't imagine life without cream sauces had slowly, but dramatically, become a nature lover. Responding to Beth's challenge to face her fears rather than flee them, she was surprised to discover not only that excitement is the flip side of fear but that such a simple activity as camping in the woods could be such a high.

And amazed it could be so healing. For once in her life, she was able to live simply, free from the world which had treated her at times harshly. Out here, she felt like a refugee from patriarchy.

As soon as she'd quit her office job to take care of her mother, Helene had decided to become a healer. She'd studied therapeutic massage and practiced on her land friends, delighted to have something to give them which they so obviously appreciated.

But, tonight, as she mulled all this history over with no one to bounce things off of, she felt impatient waiting for Beth, unsure if she were coming or not. She'd been drawn to Beth during a three-month meditation retreat. Nobody else except the teachers seemed so disciplined, so able to withstand the rigors of sitting still day after day. Beth had the ability to stay in a trance for hours on end. Then when she moved, it was with grace and liveliness. Like most good Catholic girls Helene knew, Beth also understood how to bend the rules and avoid the strictures of the spiritual life. Which made her, Helene had decided, a worthy companion on the spiritual path,

Helene knew this crush was just another "Vipassana romance," not to be trusted, the predictable result of allowing your imagination to have full play in a setting where no one spoke and even eye contact was discouraged. But then later, when that effect had worn off, they were both on staff together and she grew fond of this lithe, lovely woman, full of humor and understanding, such a balm to Helene's many dukkas. So, with a determination made iron will by boarding school repressions, she set out to win over this elusive person. Like the elephant man-god Ganesh, she was adept at removing obstacles, having had so many in her life. One obstacle, in this case, was the fact that Helene wasn't really into women. Dealing with men, having grown up with three brothers, was her forte. But with the clarity of mindfulness she knew she was supposed to connect with this woman. With characteristic drive, she set about capturing her attention.

First she had to make peace with Beth's absent partner, especially after they'd left the meditation center when Beth returned to the land and Helene returned to her mother. But, as it turned out, the process of re-connecting also included dealing with the whole land group. At first Helene could care less about belonging to a group of women. The whole scene reminded her of the boarding school where she felt "incarcerated" at such a young age. Nonetheless, Beth pressured Helene to join everybody on the land whenever she visited. During her first visits, the tension was palpable. She didn't feel like eating just vegetables, even the ones they'd harvested that day from their garden. Everyone tried, in vain, to guess Helene's sun sign, while they devoured the two dozen blueberry muffins and box of Godiva chocolates she'd brought them. They assumed from her generous treats that she was an earth sign, but they were wrong--she was a fire sign. At the time they were all crowded in the shack which was hot, stuffy and buggy. She was appalled by the squalor and lack of basic comforts, like a flush toilet and running hot water. Sometimes everyone would go off to their separate shelters leaving Helene on the porch of the shack with the bugs. Sometimes she retreated to her car for sleepless nights.

One time after taking Beth to visit the family shrine to Saint Anne in French Canada, Helene spoke with fervor about the Sacred Heart. They were all fascinated with Helene's story of how her French immigrant grandfather healed a woman in the name of Saint Anne, then received a vision that his farm, where the miracle took place, would become a great healing center. He built a small chapel there which still stands on the grounds of one of Canada's most powerful shrines.

Fresh from that trip, Helene described the high energy of the healing service she and Beth had attended. They all discussed the possible goddess roots of the worship. Helene told them about the statue of the Sacred Heart which, when you stared at it, changed features to become more feminine. She and Ev spoke French together, and even though their accents were quite different, one from France and one from Quebec, each was delighted with this opportunity to connect with those roots.

Another time when Helene and Beth returned from Helene's first women's music festival, Helene was so enthusiastic about the "total freedom" of the event, Ev and Abby felt obliged to fill her in on the scandals and fracases at previous festivals until Helene felt a bit deflated. Then while she withdrew, the others got into a frenzy of playing music, as if to show off that they could be just as exciting as any music festival. They weren't. Finally Beth claimed her dulcimer was "out of tune with itself and with the other instruments." Abby accompanied her on the drums but her pace was so much faster than Beth's that Beth at first tried to keep up with her, then abruptly stopped. Harmony could not be forced, Helene realized. But that wasn't her fault.

The next day Abby was nauseous, for some mysterious reason that may or may not have been a result of the food Helene'd cooked over the campfire the night before. After some feeble jokes about Abby having been poisoned, Beth and Helene offered to give Abby a Reiki treatment. This offer she couldn't refuse actually lifted Abby's spirits quite a bit. After Abby scurried off to visit some friends, of which it seemed to Helene she had no end, then Helene and Beth also did a treatment for Ev, who entertained them afterward with a routine from "Sister Evie," her invented smart-mouthed Jewish lesbian southern preacher, who told a story about a "Buddha Baby," named Helene, who was the youngest in her family and her mother's darling. Ev described how this Buddha Baby had set out on her spiritual path to find someone who was the soul of asceticism and then lavish her with attention, pampering with all sorts of forbidden luxuries. It was the Buddha story in reverse. Helene and Beth laughed, cheered by this light-hearted acknowledgment of one aspect of their connection. Helene felt recognized and accepted for the first time.

Then Carrie popped in and the Reiki team gave her a treatment. Through her sensitive fingers Helene tuned into a weakness in Carrie's second chakra, and "saw" there an ancient red goddess whose many arms formed a wheel. She recognized the image but wasn't sure if it was Kali or Tara. She knew that Carrie's anger needed to move out, be expressed, or she would become very sick. She didn't know her well enough to say that, so she did what she could with her own energy to release the negativity. But when she finally described the red goddess, Carrie smiled, apparently recognizing this symbol of her own anger.

Giving these healings to Abby and Carrie felt like a breakthrough for

Helene. She enjoyed hanging out with Carrie and Evonne, the easy flow of humor and honesty, and she could tell they empathized with her. They didn't say anything but she could tell from the way they shook their heads that they sympathized with her outsider position. Apparently each of them knew what it was like not to be the chosen one.

Things got worse before they got better. Abby told Helene she really didn't have to bring treats every time she visited, that she would be welcome without having to bring gifts. It was a nice message but the tone suggested that Helene should take the risk of finding out whether people liked her without the "bribes." So Helene, against her better judgment, arrived the next time empty- handed, and of course there was nothing waiting, no food, no treats, no nothing to welcome her. She should have known better than to count on others, especially these others, for her basic necessities. Finally Ev suggested they go out for pizza. Pizza was not on Helene' list of desirables, but she went along to entertain the others with lively tales of her flirtations at the meditation center. Later Carrie pointed out to Helene that while Beth was pressuring Helene to come to the land, what she really seemed to get from Helene was an escape route from the group. Caught in Beth's own contradiction, Ev speculated, Helene might be in a no-win situation: if she fit in with the group, she wouldn't be useful as an exit; if she served only as a bridge, she would never really belong to the group.

Armed with this insight, Helene began to invest in the more comfortable option, treating Beth to the most lavish vacations she could afford, resisting all Beth's attempts to economize. Huge chunks of her salary went into renting condos with jacuzzis, fireplaces and views of oceans or mountains. After frigid winters and no plumbing, even the frugal Beth couldn't resist taking pleasure in these luxuries.

Everything shifted when the land next door went up for sale. Helene jumped at the chance to buy her own land, make her own place, establish her right to be there, no longer dependent on the group's generosity. Carrie was pleased at the prospect of the land fragments becoming whole again. Ev was glad for more company, while secretly wishing she could afford to buy her own separate piece of land too.

Despite this progress Helene remained still wary of group pressure, sometimes resented Beth's insistence that they were all, or should be, one big family. Her own family had hardly been a model of harmony and her experiences in boarding schools with the harshness and rigidity of some of the nuns made it difficult for her to trust any group of women, despite her devotion to particular women. It took quite a few breakthroughs with various land individuals before she stopped thinking of them as meddlesome strangers. But gradually her irritation gave way to admiration, even friendship.

Despite the fact this progress had been made, the longer Helene sat there in the dark, tending the fire, the more morose she became. The longer she mulled over the history of these land connections, the more her back started hurting. Why bother to keep the fire burning? Why not just eat the treats herself and go to sleep? Beth wasn't coming. She probably wouldn't even remember she'd promised to come, no matter how late it was. There was no way a peace rally would have gone on this long.

A light through the trees caught her attention. Had the moon crossed over the sky already? No, the light was moving too fast, bobbing up and down, disappearing and appearing behind dark tree trunks. The glow followed the path Helene had built, over the bridge and down into the grove of gigantic pines. Just one light.

"I'm glad you're still up," said a smiling Beth as she stepped into the light from the fire and turned off her flashlight. No apology for her lateness, but still Helene was delighted to see her.

Later as they talked over the fire and shared the treats, Helene recalled more pleasant memories of her time with the group. One wintery Friday afternoon, she'd arrived laden with packages. Greeting Carrie with a big hug, she cried out, "Ready to party?"

And party they did. Friday she cooked chicken in pastry shells, Saturday she cooked fish, and for the combination Hanuka/ Solstice/ Christmas celebration on Sunday she cooked turkey with fabulous gravy and stuffing. She also brought decorations for Hanukah and Christmas--fountains of Jewish stars and Ho's Ho's which looked on their sides like double women symbols; strings of tube lights; a red table cloth and Hanukah plates and napkins. Beth had just arrived home from a three month meditation retreat (another cause for celebration) with a string of lights which blinked on and off to the multiple Christmas carols they played.

On Saturday evening Helene and Beth decorated. They strung lights around the spruce in front of the house, strung lights around the bay window, the door and the octagon window, strung lights along the wall near the arched windows and put the singing lights along the birch balcony in the back. With reflections in the double windows and angles in all directions, the whole octagon lit up like a giant spaceship.

On Sunday night Helene gave everybody presents--lovely little pouches from Thailand and beautiful shirts with nature scenes or animals on them. They teased Helene about her generosity, such a contrast to frugal Beth. Helene loved to shop for the unique and exotic item which was just right for someone. Receiving was more difficult for her. But nonetheless she was pleased that each of them had found something special to give her—a book, a tape, a shirt, a painting.

What she appreciated most was the opportunity to get away for a few days from the burnout and burden of caretaking her aging mother. Recently her mother had fallen and broken her hip, which required total and constant attention from Helene and her younger brother.

During this trying time, Helene kept dreaming of wrestling with a black panther, usually one of her allies, which kept sinking its claws into her arm. Ev interpreted the panther as Helene's own strength turning against her when she insisted on doing too much for others. In many ways Helene was heroic in her endurance of circumstances which would drive weaker people batty. Yet she was a champion worrier. For all her bouts with therapy, she'd never been able to get to the root of her anxieties.

Helene was grateful to the group for their support during this difficult time with her mother. They'd taken turns comforting her, encouraging her, supporting her. Beth bore the brunt of this process but she, busy with her counseling job, with family, with Abby, wasn't always available. So Helene got to know Carrie, Ev, Gail and Dulce better. And gradually, bit by bit, almost accidentally, she recognized herself as part of the group.

The next morning, after a hearty breakfast cooked on her propane camp stove, Helene wandered back to the stream to check on her new bridges. As she walked through the ordinarily quiet woods, listening for the occasional bird song, Helene heard instead the whine of a chainsaw from the parcel next to hers. She figured her neighbor Karl was doing some logging. Nothing unusual this time of year. A few dead trees for firewood. But when she kept hearing thump after horrible thump, loud enough to make the ground shake, several times in less than an hour, she began to worry.

Karl was a hunter. He did not live on the land, he camped there, up on the hill next to the road, in the fall, with his gun, his beer, and his red plaid friends. Occasionally in the summer he hung out with his family in a trailer. Helene had met him and found him friendly enough. He seemed to love the woods, seemed loath to shoot the deer, seemed interested in the beaver colony which momentarily had settled into his part of the stream. All points of connection, it seemed.

She discovered only later, after she'd accidentally wandered onto his land, that he lured the deer with tubs of food because he was either too lazy or too drunk to chase them. One day shots rang out as Carrie walked the dogs on the loop path, so close that she said she could see the smoke rising from the barrel of the gun. Helene had to ask him not to shoot toward her land. But except for weekends during hunting season, Karl was rarely there--which seemed better than having a live-in neighbor.

Apparently Karl's wife was not so enamored of the woods or they were in need of money because several times since he bought that parcel, there had been a "For Sale" sign up. The realtor was a local businessman who also doubled as a forest ranger for the National Park within which this property lay.

Several weeks ago, when it was clear Karl's property was not going to sell before the winter, Helene had heard some clearing going on, but it sounded nothing like this. By the time she got over to investigate, the damage was wide-spread and persisting. Not only had they cleared the top of the hill near the road of every tree except the fragile birches, they'd stripped all the land down from the hill of every tree, leaving a mangle of branches and trunks sunk in mud--a slash of devastation. One could easily imagine a potential house sliding down through the mud and erosion into the stream.

But worst of all, they had cut a wound of road across one of the most beautiful spots along the stream, a place where there were wide rocks and wonderful sun. With their bulldozer they had pushed aside the massive rocks, dirtying the stream and gashing up into the circle of huge pines which was half on Helene's land and half on Karl's. From her campsite the destruction made a slice of emptiness where before there had been only forest.

Helene was horrified. She ran to the octagon to call the Environmental Protection Officer. He said he'd come by that day to investigate. Later he stopped in at the octagon to tell her he'd checked but there wasn't much he could do, even though it was a protected stream, because the men had a permit. He added that they must know they were being watched because the forest ranger was also there. Helene muttered something about *conflict of interest.* The forest ranger, of course, was also the realtor, who'd probably been the one to suggest this clearing to enhance the value of the land for building, and to assure its sale.

In Manfred Springs recently she'd watched all day as a team of men gracefully and respectfully put to rest an enormous dead tree. One man climbed up with incredible courage and agility to the very tips of its wide branches and, after tying a rope around the middle of the part he was going to cut, pulled up the chainsaw which was hanging from another rope around his waist and delicately cut. Piece by piece, he methodically and steadily whittled away at the huge tree until by the end of the day it was completely gone. He was assisted by many other men, some holding the rope by which each piece was lowered after it was cut, some slicing up the fallen pieces and hauling them away, others raking the stray branches and leaves, and another using a machine to grind up the branches and then the remains of the trunk until all that was left was a pile of sawdust.

She thought the men were speaking another language, and in some ways they were, but then she realized it was English with a Caribbean accent. They worked together with such trust, efficiency, and cooperation that Helene was impressed. But it wasn't until she came upon this destruction in her woods that she realized how much their treatment of the giant tree was also loving--a funeral rather than a massacre. As she watched the Caribbean men cut the elderly tree down, she could appreciate the spirit of every out-flung limb, every curve and notch of its towering presence. Because their lives were at risk if they didn't observe each of its features with respectful attention, these men treated the tree as the ancient matriarch she was. In doing so they not only honored the tree but themselves, and each other as well.

On the land the trees were as venerable--towering cabbage pines almost two hundred years old. Each was a unique and beautiful presence. Even after parts of them died, or fell, they continued to be key inhabitants. The sacred circle they made curved across the artificial boundaries which divided the land into real estate parcels. This circle seemed almost mystical, perhaps because it was hidden away from the road and human habitation and because the light filtering down through its pine needles and nearby maple leaves on misty days was particularly magical. Now half of that circle had been cut down.

Helene was horrified when she realized how totally these loggers were destroying the huge pines. She'd been reassured by another forester that the cabbage pines were safe from loggers because they were no good for lumber. They were too curved and gnarled. Loggers preferred tall straight trees.

Not these loggers. They seemed hell bent on knocking down any tree in their path. There were only two of them, but they had a backhoe and a bulldozer so they didn't need any delicate operation, or respect either. How dangerous is it to push a tree over with a bulldozer? What difference does it make whether the trees are dead or alive?

It was ominous how these weren't just strangers who were killing their friends, the cabbage pines; these men seemed like enemies. They were killing particular tree presences who had been more than friends, who had also been, for Helene, guides and gurus, giving her peace, teaching her how to live naturally.

The pines are so much bigger than we are, Helene thought, *so much older, so much more rooted. I have, in a way, worshipped them. They've taught me so much about living on this land. In their own shapes they've shown me beauty and they've held up for me, in spider webs and birds' nests, the beauty of others. We've climbed them, meditated upon them, leaned against them. I sought their company when I was lonely and they comforted me.*

Seeing their fresh bodies massive against the earth, she was reminded of the slaughter of elephants. For the same purposes of greed: kill a sacred animal for its tusks, kill an ancient tree for 30 pieces of firewood. Some of the trunks were so large the loggers couldn't even haul them out. The scarred remains were wide enough across to make a banquet table.

Finally, she decided to go over in the midst of their interminable carnage to protest. Melodramatically, she was going to drop to her knees and make the sign of the cross in front of the bulldozer--almost as if she were dealing with foreigners who might understand this traditional body language. She was too angry to pay much attention to the possible risk of encountering the enemy, herself unarmed in the middle of the woods. If they slaughtered trees with such impunity, they might also regard women with similar bloodlust.

To her surprise, one of the men walked toward her waving. He wanted to talk. He didn't expect to meet such an angry woman. When she shouted, "Why are you doing this?" he seemed taken aback. He mentioned Karl's name. She continued, loudly over the whine of the other man's chainsaw, to complain. The first man, whose face seemed ravaged by tobacco, alcohol or poverty, protested that these trees were good for lumber. People could build houses with it.

Startled, she, who was already planning the log cabin she wanted to live in, stepped back. He saw what he was doing as a public service? But his ravaged face reminded her of something else, something she couldn't quite name but which disturbed her. Something familiar.

Although he was quick to defend himself, the logger was more curious about her, where she lived, who she was, who lived in the trailer, where the boundaries were. He wanted to know if she was Annie Greene, an older woman up the road who had a reputation in those parts for being the only person who could drive trucks up the twisting road to the iron mines and for knocking a man across the dance floor of the local tavern after he made a pass at her daughter. Although Helene wouldn't mind the shield of Annie Greene's toughness, she declined the identification.

The second man came up as she was complaining about how the circle of trees had been broken. They both followed her gestures and nodded. They'd been in those woods long enough to know what she was saying was true. But what was one more circle of trees? They protested that Karl specifically requested they take down the big pines. She muttered something about how he must be desperate for money. They replied that he planned to build a house back up on the hill.

"And is he going to use these trees?"

This question seemed absurd to them. But the other one, taller and younger, pointed with some pride at the clearing they'd made on the hill. "It's a beautiful view now," he said, "with all the birch left." She saw the artist in him and again felt a pang. This man was not really the enemy, although the gap between them left no possibility he would ever be a friend.

"We have to do our job," said the first man, "we have to make a living."

"I'm not blaming you," she almost apologized. "It's just your job. But I sure am mad at Karl."

"He said he'd clean up this mess," the other one said feebly.

"I doubt that," she said and they nodded, as if agreeing.

They pointed out the scrawny trees they'd left standing. But she was not to be reconciled to the loss. She left them, strangers in the woods-- but no longer, cut and dried, enemies.

Finally the loggers finished their job. Those horrible thuds of falling trees were over at last. But of course no one cleaned up the mess. The woods remained a tangle of branches and stumps. A muddy scar of road still cut down across the stream and into the broken circle. What would happen to the birds and chipmunks and squirrels and myriad insects who'd made their homes in those trees? What about the deer and raccoon and fox who found protection and shelter in their presence? She remembered the chipmunk at the meditation center who would eat out of her hand and even ride on her foot, her special friend.

Eventually the snow would come to cover the corpses. She was reminded of images of the dead at Wounded Knee. What would be left was not the silence of winter, wind through the branches of ancient trees, but the silence of barrenness. Not the reverent hush after a funeral but the mute desolation after a massacre.

And yet, even with its bed destroyed and muddy, the stream found its way again and continued to flow, refusing the damming. Without banks or rocks or restoration, the energy created its own path. Perhaps, Helene told herself, inspired by that vitality, the open space will bring with it new light to help the young trees grow. But that might take forever. Whatever happened, she realized that never again when she walked in that place would she feel she was in the middle of the woods. Suddenly she stood at its edge, vulnerable again.

At first Helene was so upset, she retreated to her tent to cry. When upset, she could speak only French, the language of her childhood, the language of her emotions. At first she didn't want to talk to the others about the rape of the land. It was her own private grief. When she finally spoke about it with them, she could tell the others were also devastated. Yet somehow for her the desecration struck closer to home.

A few nights later she began to have her memory dreams: stories of abuse she thought belonged to other women. After all those years of silence and loss of memory, she felt some relief at finally discovering the root of her anxiety, the cause of so much of her dukka, The suffering in her body was not malingering, not imagination, not punishment--it was real. The more she remembered, the more her back gave out. Finally she could no longer do the massage work which had given her such satisfaction. She couldn't now earn her own meager living.

No longer able to heal others, Helene turned to her own healing. Beth heard from Abby about a Vietnamese doctor who practiced Chinese medicine and acupuncture after years of being a Buddhist monk. When Helene went to him, she felt the same peace come over her as when she first met one of her Buddhist teachers. He told her that because her womb had been blocked in childhood, the vital energy, or chi, could not fully reach her heart. As a result her heart was overtaxed and in danger. That was why she had trouble sometimes breathing and why she was beginning to feel palpitations.

Grateful that his diagnosis of blockage confirmed what she suspected about the abuse, she was religious about taking her daily dose of the bitter herbs he gave her. The hopelessness of her condition, so many years of energy trapped in her body, began to ease. She was delighted when he told her that the herbs came from the barks of trees. *Tree medicine.* She herself had been cut down before she'd even had time to grow tall like the venerable cabbage pines. But like the Chinese herbs which healed her, she could herself become like medicine. Even bitterness can provide a cure.

The burden she felt about caring for her mother, that trapped feeling, lifted as she discovered, once she got up the nerve to tell her mother about the abuse, her shock, horror, and grief over what had been done to her beloved daughter. Her mother believed her. Her mother's response expelled the anger Helene felt at her for having been unprotected, then sent away. This revelation deepened the love between them.

When it eventually became clear, under these conditions, that Helene couldn't afford to build a log cabin on her property, she borrowed money from her Canadian aunt and bought a trailer, complete with hot running water and a flush toilet, plus many more amenities, so she could visit the land when it was too cold to camp,. She felt at last that she'd established roots in this new world.

That's when she recognized the tensions that were splitting the group apart, issues that had little to do with her but which concerned her. After all those years of hanging off the edge of the group, she'd finally gained entrance--and now the group seemed to be disintegrating. *Just her luck.*

At first Helene thought this splitting apart was simply symptomatic of the normal tensions of group living. People get on each others' nerves when they live so close together. That's why she'd gotten her trailer, so she wouldn't have to live with anybody. She had enough of that closeness at home with her family. It's especially tough to live with grown siblings, like Beth and Carrie were trying to do. All the old hurts and rejections get triggered so easily. Even the best of friends are rarely compatible when it comes to issues like order, cleanliness, sound levels and timing. Little things like crumbs on the counter or stinky kitty litter mean a lot. To have something in common does not always make a bond. She wasn't sure exactly what the particular issues were in this case, but she could imagine.

The original foursome, the core of the land group, which had been exclusive in some ways, began to crack. The more Beth and Carrie tried to reinforce a family unity modeled by their own compulsively close family unit, the more Ev and Abby, whose experience of family had been somewhat oppressive, rebelled. Abby took long exotic trips whenever she could get time off from work, and spent most of her free time with outside friends when she couldn't. Ev withdrew to the shack to deal with her own issues of welcome and rejection. Beth went off on long retreats and Carrie, tied down by the animals, was left to keep the home fires burning. Two long hard winters, with endless snow and ice which had to be shoveled and chipped away and a rapidly diminishing wood pile which had to be carried in to the stove, piece by piece, snapped the final threads which bound the four of them together.

Once Helene realized how bad things were, she decided to try to bring everybody together again. She resolved not to take sides, not to neglect any of the disconnected strands, until she could find some way to mend the situation. Back on the land in the summer, despite the many times she sat through one of their discussions in silent resistance to the pressure on her to participate, she missed their gatherings, the heady talk, sympathetic mirroring and silly play. So she invited them all to dinner at her trailer, neutral ground. She cooked one of her lavish feasts, praying that no one would back out at the last minute. No one did. Grateful, perhaps, for a way out of the morass, they showed up on time and were polite, even friendly, with each other.

While the evening didn't ring with the warmth of yesteryear, it was a beginning of reconciliation. Helene was obviously pleased to show off her trailer and to serve such a delicious meal. Abby, whose mother had recently died, was grateful for a home cooked meal and some basic nurturing. Dulce, up for the summer and equally perplexed and distressed about the rupture, used her social charm and intellectual acuity to keep the conversation lively. Carrie, noticeably relieved, was busy balancing emotional tensions. Between Ev and Beth there was, at least, respect and an occasional spark of the teasing which had been one of their major modes of connection.

Then, because it was the first night of the Persiad meteor showers, they walked down to the meadow to look up at the stars. There in the dark, complaining about the strain on their necks and vying to see who saw the most flares, they could feel the old pull toward unity. Even when one felt disappointment that she hadn't seen a flash another had seen, there was comfort in that shared familiarity.

"What is a shooting star anyway?" Helene asked, suddenly unafraid to reveal her ignorance. Sometimes with this group of bright educated women, she felt a little stupid. Unlike the others she hadn't gone to college. She hated school. She hadn't done well in boarding school at first because she didn't speak English. Then when she saw how her father pressured her brothers to get good grades, but never complemented them when they did, she decided that studying hard was a no-win situation, so she never cracked a book and felt a secret satisfaction that her grades were so bad. When, to the surprise of the nuns, it was revealed that she had the highest IQ in her class, she felt exposed, but never exactly intelligent. Just smart enough.

"A shooting star," replied Dulce, "is a meteor breaking up as it enters the earth's atmosphere."

"So what we're seeing are just fragments?" mused Carrie.

"I guess that's how we came to be made of star dust," said Ev.

Helene recognized how this group was like one shattered star. Each fragment had its own particular flash and dash as well as density and doom. Shining together, they were absolutely radiant, a full spectrum. But these days that unity was a rare event.

Had she by her healing action tonight pulled this rainbow back together again? Like Humpty Dumpty, they'd had a great fall. "All the kings' horses and all the kings' men couldn't put Humpty together again." But perhaps some healing was possible. Humpty Dumpty was an egg, after all, and even though one couldn't repair a broken egg, one could cook a great omelet. After all, from the splintered tree, tree medicine.

Suddenly one huge star arced across the sky with its fiery plumage and finally everyone saw it at the same time. They breathed a collective sigh of wonder. A star falling out of the sky is like a child being born from her mother's womb, Helene thought. A healer is like a midwife assisting the baby into life, allowing wholeness to emerge from apparent emptiness, a black hole. Now that Helene was beginning to heal from her own wounds, she wanted again to help others heal too.

"Well, then, what is a comet?" Ev asked.

Although everyone was willing to hazard a guess, no one seemed to really know.

A comet, thought Helene, is more than the sum of our parts.

Where we are, in the same moment, the girl, pawn for the warriors, who escaped her captivity and lived with the snake people. But she disobeyed their orders not to mess in the pond and was almost struck dead by the toad magician. After the snakes begged for her life, she then killed herself by trying to imitate the birds. The snakes by their singing this time restored her to life. Recognizing their beauty, she became a healer.

13

G A I L

Gail was not happy. The porcupine was on her porch and on the table waddling across her mushroom samples, spore prints, and cotton sculptures. Then, having thoroughly investigated the table, it eyed the post holding up the roof.

To prevent the animal from climbing up the post and heading for the rafters, to chew on them as it had done a couple of night earlier, Gail tried poking at it with a long stick. It turned its back to her and raised its quills: The ultimate insult, the ultimate weapon. It was too slow, fat and lumbering to be much of a threat otherwise, but she kept her distance. How to get rid of it? She retreated into the house to check her book on wild animals. Yes, porcupines like to eat wood. They seemed particularly fond of plywood, Gail had observed. But there were no suggestions in this book for discouraging such behavior.

It was getting dark and she was alone. Dulce, of course, wasn't there. How ironic that they'd broken up the summer they built the house. That was how many years ago? Now it was rare when they were in this house together.

She turned on all the lights and shone a huge flashlight beam into the porcupine's eyes, tiny black beads hidden within its blustery hair. It rotated and climbed the post, as she watched, partially horrified and partially fascinated with its huge black claws.

She tried to remember the endless discussions on the land about keeping out unwanted wild guests without poisoning them: soap, red pepper, garlic spray. She checked the cabinet for cayenne. If Dulce were here, there would be plenty, but now there was none. Tomorrow she'd go to the vet and rent a have-a-heart trap. But what about tonight? Would the roof still be standing in the morning?

She went back out on the porch and watched the porcupine sniff its way to the beams, then gasped as it started to chew on the plywood with a sickening crunch, crunch, crunch. *Oh no.* If only it knew how much work putting that plywood up there had been. Why couldn't it find some old rotting tree to munch? It wasn't like there was any scarcity of food. They were surrounded by trees. Why did her roof have to be the one piece of wood it couldn't do without?

She felt like screaming. This impulse, which she didn't indulge, brought to mind one more strategy: *sound.* She didn't have one of those high-pitched devices designed to scare away animals, but she did have a drum.

She pulled out the big drum, scarcely used since the days when she and Dulce took African drumming together. After a few flubs, the old rhythms came back to her with the steadiness of her own heart beat. She fell into them with her characteristic concentration. She almost forgot about the porcupine as the drum beat blurred the noise of its teeth gnawing at the plywood.

Once she had been so involved in her artwork that five firetrucks had blocked the street below her window in the city before she even noticed that the building next door was on fire. Only the red light pulsing onto her wall finally alerted her to the danger. Fortunately, they'd put the fire out by then.

The sounds of antelope hooves galloping across the plains of the Masai Mora, the elephant trumpeting before it threw back its ears and charged toward them, the lions lounging in the branches of exotic trees, the giraffes striding in their fluid fashion: yes, these were the sounds of animals on the move. If anything were to inspire that porcupine, these rhythms would. As she played, Gail remembered the adventures she and Dulce shared the summer they traveled through Africa together. The rhythm of her drum retraced the trail of their explorations.

Sure enough, the porcupine began to move. Slowly, carefully, it climbed backwards down the pole, its dangerous tush tucked under it like a koala bear. Under different circumstances Gail might even have called it "cute." Either it didn't care for her drumming or it had eaten enough plywood for one meal. It eased itself onto the table, pushed past the mess it'd made earlier and lowered itself, tail first, off the table. After glancing rather arrogantly at her and her bothersome drum, it descended from the porch and waddled slowly into the woods.

Gail continued to play the drum in the dark, caught up in and soothed by its rhythms.

Looking back to when she first came to the land with Dulce, she realized how untamed she'd been, almost clueless when it came to getting along with groups of people. An only child, she'd never really had much experience in groups. She'd always been pretty much of a loner, or at least pretty independent. She'd had friends in high school and college, but she related to them more one to one than all together.

When she first came to the land, what she loved most was the land itself. Her work, huge bronze sculptures, was full of nostalgia for nature: hollow shapes, thin arms reaching toward a larger world, now lost. After one summer on the land, her own hunger started to ease. What she'd been longing for was here in this place, in the woods. It wasn't something she'd ever really known, having grown up in a Chicago suburb, but it was something she'd been missing all her life. A place where she could really sink her roots into the earth, without having to dig through asphalt or concrete or brick.

But she didn't know how to relate easily to people in groups; she'd resisted collectivity so effectively that simple, open exchange seemed impossible at first. It had taken all her energy to ward off her mother's attempts to make her into a bourgeois housewife like herself, to wrap her in the shields of propriety and property which characterized suburban living. She knew those shields couldn't muffle completely her grandmother's fear of "the poor house." And while Gail did not, like many in her generation, embrace squalor, downward mobility or a classless society, she channeled her ambitions elsewhere, into her art. Rather than decorating a home, she concentrated on shaping her sculpture; rather than becoming a clothes horse, she focused on bodywork. And when her marriage failed, all her considerable determination and energy went into what she called "catching up" with her art.

That same determination and energy had gone into building the house with Dulce, or for Dulce. She recognized in Dulce, and shared with her, the need to create and control her own space, a place of safety and protection from outside influence, from the group as well as from potential invaders. Although Gail had grown up in relative security and safety, without the angst and disruption Dulce had endured, she had suffered her own invasions, like the casual first date which became a rape. And all her life she had tried to create her own environment to ward off the manicured milieu her mother kept trying to force her into. So even though her intent was to help Dulce build a house she never could have built by herself, Gail knew that the house building also extended the trail which her art had helped blaze: toward a way out.

She knew how to construct huge, intricate sculptures, but the real building of a real house which real people could live in was, everyone assumed, a male domain. Only men, she thought, knew the secrets of such practical structures. What she discovered by working with lumbered wood and measured forms was that she could trust her own intuitive sense about such matters, and through this construction she became empowered in a way she hadn't quite been before.

She still argued with Dulce about the necessity for women's liberation, honing her as yet not fully developed argumentative and rational abilities against Dulce's "masculine" logic, hurling her considerable stubborn will against Dulce's skill at debate. Then she read Adrienne Rich's *Of Woman Born,* and her resistance collapsed as their building rose. Though she was still not a raving feminist, she had undergone what one of her Catholic friends would call "metanoia."

But that conversion didn't make it any easier for her to relate to the group. She never realized before how much of an introvert she was. It amazed her how much time they all spent together and how much "processing" they did. While they analyzed whether or not the group was working, she reflected on how much time she'd lived alone. From this vantage point she could also see some of their contradictions. When Beth insisted that the group wouldn't work unless they got together more often and worked at more depthful relations, Gail pointed out how much Beth herself seemed to be fleeing the group and avoiding people.

She hoped it wasn't her they were avoiding. Though they welcomed her as a relative, a kind of in-law, she had trouble feeling comfortable with them. In all sort of subtle ways, she knew she was still not trusted, that she was being held at a distance, that she was not fully accepted. The evenings singing around the campfire were the easiest, but even when she could tell they appreciated her flute playing, she felt like she was on probation. And truthfully, they weren't the center of her attention either. Perhaps they continued to exclude her because for her *they* continued to be peripheral.

Underneath the frenzy of housebuilding was her fear that Dulce was going to leave her. It started the previous fall when Dulce spoke to her about getting involved with someone in her therapy group. Although they had agreed to have an open relationship, Gail went into a tailspin. As it turned out, Dulce's amorous inclinations at this point never got past the fantasy stage, but Gail's defensiveness stirred up a hornet's nest of feelings within and between them. The next thing Gail knew, Dulce was being hotly pursued by a woman at her school, and Dulce was not particularly resisting. Almost daily, letters were arriving on the land for Dulce, letters the others didn't seem to notice or chose to ignore. Whenever the subject of "paramours" came up, it was treated lightly. Dulce, it turned out, wasn't the only one with such predilections. Feeling old fashioned, Gail kept her fears to herself.

For Gail, this threat pulled at the fabric of her ego. It had been years since she'd trusted herself to be as close to anyone as she'd been to Dulce. The only other time had been with her husband--and he too had left her for another woman. That time she'd been secretly relieved; his departure, although humiliating, had been liberating: it had freed her from her mother's script for her life, and it had freed her for her art. But this time, she could see no such payback and she had every intention of holding on. She didn't see how anyone could compete with what she had to offer Dulce.

But the strain of this new person intruding on their relationship and the strain of their trying to build a complete house in just three months, and the strain of the fact that it rained almost every night, turning their tent into a sponge, manifested in their interactions. Sometimes Gail couldn't contain the impatience she felt for Dulce's ineptness with construction, or the way her accident-prone proclivities kept tripping up the process. Sometimes it felt like she was supposed to build the whole thing herself, then carry Dulce in across the threshold, like some primitive macho pioneer.

Two events that first summer helped put things in a different perspective. One was a visit from the douser, Sam, who was also a psychic healer. Even though Gail regarded him with detached amusement, something stirred in her blood at his revelations. She dreamt about her grandfather who was, according to top secret family stories, born a gypsy. Although she'd never really known him, he served as an archetype of freedom and exploration, a guide who led her away from the surburban prison. Sam, who looked and acted like a local farmer, had none of the color and flair of Granpa Jack, but the stories he told were nonetheless intriguing in the way they spoke of other worlds, other times, other zones.

He led the group to a "power spot" overlooking their site, a ledge beneath which, he said, eight streams converged. They stood there together to feel the energy. Whether it was his presence or the land's energy, the headache she'd been putting up with disappeared, and her attitude toward the group shifted. As they held hands and raised their arms into a circle, she felt herself part of a huge cup open to the sky, holding a world full of energy. It was as if their feet were so rooted in the earth that they could draw upon the hidden streams for the flow which filled this bowl constructed by their bodies.

Then they sat around while he told them about "the pole shift," a disaster of global proportions which had been postponed so more people could be saved. He assured them they would all survive although he seemed less certain about the land itself--which made Gail realize with a pang how attached she was, not just to any plot of woods and stream but to this particular place.

He told them what their lifestones were: hers was sapphire. These stones had been given to them when they underwent their "spirit change" to indicate where each of them was supposed to work when the "transition" came. Surprised, Gail realized she was disappointed when he said they wouldn't all be together. But she was pleased that Dulce's stone was also a sapphire, which meant *they* would still be together.

Even though some part of her believed all this was a lot of nonsense, maybe even shadow projection on his part, she was intrigued when he told Evi about what happened to her when she took the magic mushrooms: "mediumship," he called it. He said the rush Ev felt in her heart was probably her spirit reentering her body through the heart chakra. Her feeling of abruptness was probably a jolt of fear over what she'd experienced while "out of body." He identified the spirit which spoke through her as "God." Then he explained that Jesus was in charge of earth, God in charge of the galaxy, and the Creator in charge of the whole universe.

Later, discussing this ultimate neatness of patriarchal hierarchy, they chuckled at how "God" had been demoted and decided the Creator had to be female, the Procreator.

Gail's experience of Evi as a medium had been different. Before they'd gathered around the fire, before the voices seemed to speak through Ev, Ev had come to Gail in her grief and pulled her out of her despair in the most human way. Perhaps it was divine guidance which enabled her to tune in so deeply to the sadness Gail had dropped into and couldn't climb out of, but it was warmth and a remarkably refined empathy which enabled her to reach in, touch the wound, and send a resonating balm to heal it. By crying with Gail, Ev seemed to be drawing out the grief, as a surgeon lances a boil or a shaman sucks out the poison.

When Sam told them about their past lives together, Gail was amused at how entangled the group was, whether it "worked" or not: Ev and Abby had known each other 34 times: 11 times Ev had been Abby's mother and 13 times Abby had been Ev's. Ev had been mother to all of them; Beth and Carrie had been everybody's sister. Gail had been mother and daughter to Carrie, but Carrie and Dulce had never been relatives. Gail had been sister to Beth, mother to Dulce, and daughter of Abby. Oddly enough, according to him, all of their past lives had been female ones.

Later they also corrected this information, by imagining in what combinations they had been son, brother, father, lover and husband to each other in their many past lives. They skirted issues of enmity, murder, incest and betrayal, however, wondering in only the mildest of ways whether any of them "owed" another something because of what had happened in a past life. They figured by this point all debts that were going to be repaid had been repaid. They preferred to face the future together with a clean slate.

While this event placed her impending separation from Dulce into a cosmic context, another incident brought home to Gail the raw reality of change. At one of their last campfires that summer Carrie brought out a suit which she'd been holding onto for several months. It was a work outfit which had belonged to a friend of hers in the city, the clothes Dora wore the day she died suddenly of heart failure. Carrie had promised the friend's lover, the person in the couple with whom she'd been close, that she would "dispose" of the clothes on the land, but she hadn't been sure how until that moment. Somehow burying them didn't seem appropriate, given the shock of Dora's sudden departure, so Carrie'd postponed doing anything.

But the night before she'd had a dream about Dora's death and about a mutual friend who was still mourning, unable to disengage from her attachment to Dora. So Carrie asked the group to help with a ritual of letting go. After she and Ev told them various stories about Dora and about her grieving friends, Carrie prayed that with this symbolic gesture, Dora's spirit would be released from the karma of a weak heart and that her friends could release any blocked grief. Then out of a brown bag, she pulled a skirt, a jacket and panty hose: Dora's professional uniform, which felt to Gail like being "in drag." When Carrie finally dropped the skirt into the fire, it smothered the flames. Beth lifted it on a stick and held it over the fire while it melted.

Gail was awed. The transience of form, of shape, of structure was never more apparent. Although this ritual was a grim reminder of the fragility of material existence, it also offered relief as the shell disappeared and whatever lingered of Dora's spirit rose like smoke to join her Creator. As the jacket burned, Dulce played the drum, Abby sang through her recorder, and Ev breathed music into her androgynous clay pipe figure from Mexico.

Gail felt tears well up into her silence, overwhelmed by the power of the experience but unable at that point to name its full significance. She was impressed with how quickly one could destroy what took so much care to create: a jacket, a work of art, a house, a relationship, a person.

It wasn't until the following summer that Gail allowed the group into the empty space created by her separation from Dulce. That fall Dulce did leave her for someone else, someone so different from her that it was difficult, even in her most generous moments, to understand what the pull was. At first it seemed that Dulce could achieve the perfect balance by relating to both of them, but finally she told Gail that she was drained by the effort of giving them equal time so she was choosing the other woman over Gail. When Roger left her, Gail vowed she'd never allow herself to be that vulnerable again. But here was Dulce letting her go, rejecting her, and this time she wasn't sure she'd ever hit bottom.

But eventually she found her way out and when she did, she discovered she was, like Alice on the other side of the looking glass, somewhere else. Some kind of wonderland where things were not what they seemed and everything kept turning into something else. A land of fairies and little green people. Her heart was empty but wide open.

On the land that summer, she discovered that while it was still a site for building and struggle, it also served as ground for much deeper realities than those surface dramas. One Saturday, out of gratitude for their help on her house and suddenly appreciative of their company, she helped the others with the big house, digging the drainage trench and raising the posts.

When the neighbor who was going to operate the backhoe expressed skepticism over the project, muttering that it was the weirdest thing he'd seen in thirty years, she shared their amusement. She joined in their admiration of the graceful, almost delicate, way he dug the trench for the pipes. After one particularly skillful maneuver, they cheered and he chuckled, "Aren't I good?"

Then she crawled into the ditch with the other "girls" to fill it with stones for better drainage. She and Carrie worked together to load the wheelbarrow with stones and hand them down to Ev, Abby and Beth. The men, impressed with their teamwork, helped too. Then while the men took a lunch break, the women finished lining the leach field cavity with rocks. It began to look like a huge bowl, firmly set in the earth. For lunch Gail, who up to that point had more fame as a consumer (some even dubbed her"The Cookie Monster") than as a cook, fixed sandwiches for everybody.

After lunch it was time to raise the posts. The men called them "trees," which indeed they were--having been hauled, stripped and measured from the trees which Dulce and Gail had cut down on their site. Gail's heart filled with joy that they were being transformed this way. That kind of metamorphosis, after all, is what art is all about. When she saw the four trees standing tall again, she knew they had forgiven her for cutting them down in their prime. Once the trees were in place and secured with ropes and braces, it looked like an ancient sacred site or a children's playground.

The backhoe man made out the bill to the "Five Ladies Contractors." Finally Gail felt included; she was the fifth person. He added how glad he and his family were to have them as neighbors. After the jokes about "druids and queers," hearing this was a relief. They discussed their mutual devotion to saving the beavers and warding off the forest ranger/real estate agent who was buying up all the available land and chopping it up into small parcels to sell.

After the job was done, the five ladies went down to the diner to celebrate. In the course of their discussion Carrie mentioned plans she and Ev had made for building a winterized cabin on the hill overlooking the beaver pond. Gail responded that she'd hoped to build a studio for herself on that particular spot. This seemed to put a pall on the conversation. Carrie and Ev just glanced at each other and changed the subject.

The next morning Gail joined the group at the giant cabbage pine they called the Grandmother Tree for meditation and dream sharing. Carrie described a dream of floating in space with whole worlds floating toward her.

Rather than being terrified by this, she had felt exultant. Abby had a message dream about how greed never satisfies. Ev dreamt about a crippled child with half his face missing, who then turned into a person in his thirties, someone with a goatee. Gail wondered if this person was her--since artists are often pictured with goatees, and she in fact had shared with them her fascination with goats. But instead of asking about that, she shared her dream of grinding up stones for a sculpture, then flying away with an eagle's eye vision over a snowy field. They shared her delight in the flight and interpreted it as a new kind of vision.

As the group broke up, Gail asked Carrie if she could see the site she and Ev had chosen for their cabin, so they could negotiate sharing it in some way. Everyone looked stricken and Carrie went catatonic. Finally she muttered that she'd have to think about it, and scurried off to her shelter.

Only a few minutes later the rest of them heard Carrie screaming, "No, no, no!"

This piercing rejection from someone with whom Gail had felt warmth was like a bolt of lightening. Confused and puzzled, Gail turned to the others with moist eyes. They sat down with her in the middle of the woods. Ev explained how, since she and Gail weren't really owners of the land as a whole, they shared a part-timer status. Both Abby and Beth claimed that Carrie was entitled to first choice of a site, even though she already had another site for her shelter, but the basis of that claim wasn't clear to Gail.

"Besides," Abby added reluctantly, "that's not land you own."

Gail was shocked. Having bought into the new land, she'd assumed shared ownership of the land as a whole.

Gail didn't discover until later, when she and Carrie realized a deeper bond through sharing the experience of being abandoned by their lovers, that Carrie was caught between two conflicting impulses: one was holding onto Ev by building a house for just the two of them, a place where the foster child in Ev could truly feel at home; the other was to hold onto her role as big sister, the one who is supposed to sacrifice for the others, to share, to hold back until everyone else is served, to put all her energy into the communal house.

At the time it just felt to Gail like they were ganging up on her. But instead of marching away as she might have done in the past, she held her ground and dropped into the empty bowl of her rejection. Through her tears she described how tight the four of them were and how left out she sometimes felt. Suddenly there were eight arms around her (Carrie had rejoined them, looking sheepish), holding her, comforting her.

For over an hour they listened to her describe how hard being left by Dulce had been, an experience Beth, her predecessor, who'd also been dumped in much the same way, could empathize with. She was intrigued with their insights into her relationship with Dulce and heartened by their encouragement to become closer to them, now that Dulce wasn't there as a buffer/guard. Opening up to them, she could show the vulnerability and sweetness, sensitivity and depth she usually kept hidden. They fed her breakfast and sent her off, happy now, to work on her board and batten, her project for the summer.

A few nights later the group met at the building site for a full moon celebration. Like Picasso's Three Musicians, Gail, Abby and Ev played while the moon rose over the trees. Then Beth climbed up on the structure while Gail and Ev jumped into what Carrie called "the kiva hole," dug into the earth at the center of what would eventually be the ground beneath the floor of the octagon. Carrie'd insisted they dig a hole there for various reasons: symbolic, as a place for roots; pragmatic, as a root cellar; paranoid, as a hiding place or shelter in case of disaster.

Beth dangled from the scaffolding a rope with a twisted rebar for hook, as if Gail and Ev were fish she was trying to catch. Ev, in turn, teased Beth about being a bird, quoting the Appolinaire poem, "Come to the edge."

Although being with the group did not have the kind of depthful intimacy she shared with Dulce, it did provide two things she didn't have with Dulce: a kind of easy nurturing and a playfulness. Gail was so used to playing by herself, playing with her art, playing in her head, she didn't realize that dimension could be shared so fully.

She'd had a hint of this potential the first summer she met them when Dulce invited the whole group to the pouring of one of Gail's bronze sculptures. While they sat around in the foundry waiting for the bronze to melt, Beth started playing one of the metal barrels as if it were a drum and the others joined in with improvised instruments and vocal sounds which rose to a crescendo as Gail supervised the pouring of the golden broth, the nectar of sculptors, into the waiting forms. Once the forms hardened, she would piece them together to make the head of a small goat opening its mouth to a full udder.

Remembering this, Gail realized that these were not just friends but playmates. She liked how Dulce became playful with the group, but she herself usually felt too inhibited. Sometimes she couldn't tell if people were laughing at her or with her, and she wasn't sure she wanted to risk that discomfort.

While Carrie described the yet to be built floor as a stage upon which they could enact a musical based on Noah's Ark--only Noah would be a woman and the animal couples, gay as well as straight--and Abby showed off a t-shirt from the women's music festival of women dancing in a circle, Gail pulled a blanket over her head and started dancing, flying like the eagle in her dream.

Through the dark cloth she could hear murmurs of admiration as she soared and glided.

Suddenly she stopped, lifted her arms in a half-circle, like an bowl, with her hands out. Slowly the blanket slid off her head and she could see the others. Solemnly, innocently, they joined her, lifting their arms, holding out their hands too. Together, as one, they embodied the Receptive.

The next moment, like a miracle none of them could have predicted, a huge shooting star, a meteor or perhaps even a comet arced slowly across the sky. Even with a full moon, it was totally visible. Its tail was yellow, orange, red. Ev said later she also saw purple. Gail was awestruck. They were amazed. It was like no other shooting star they'd ever seen. They were convinced it was a sign--but of what?

Later Beth pointed out in the night sky the Pleides, the Seven Sisters. Ev quoted one of her new age friends as saying that the Pleides was the source of signals from outer space, a potential home of communicative aliens. They stared at the circle of stars, but received no message. Carrie wondered whether it was their home star, where some of their ancestors might have arrived from, then realized that original star was supposed to be Sirius, the Dog Star. Abby wondered who the Seven Sisters were, mythologically speaking. And Gail, counting the members of the group, realized that she was the seventh of them, she was the Seventh Sister. At last she, who was sisterless, had a wealth of sisters.

That night she dreamt she had a female twin who had supposedly been born dead. But perhaps she was still alive, sent off to exile or an orphanage. When she told the others the next day, everyone was intrigued. They wondered whether she was Gail's opposite self or shadow self or soulmate. They held forth on theories about the doppelganger and told stories about twins separated at birth who ended up marrying men with the same name and smoking the same brand of cigarettes and suffering from the same kind of accident at the very same time. Beth and Carrie described the Corsican Brothers, siamese twins separated at birth who had such a psychic connection that when one got run through with a sword, the other, an ocean away, doubled over in pain.

The rest of them all had sisters, she realized. The dead twin tended to take on the countenances of their sisters. She had no sister. But the twin, resurrected, became more and more real to her as she moved in and out of her dreams and fantasies.

This twin, having suffered much, was compassionate and generous. She was a writer, with extraordinary psychic abilities. She was silly and playful and liked all kinds of people. She was very tuned to the circumstances of ordinary people and very concerned about protecting the environment. She spoke to trees and cared for stray animals. She moved slowly and was not particularly concerned about getting things done.

In her company Gail herself began to slow down. Her peripheral vision improved and she wandered purposelessly around the land, up to the ledge or down along the stream. She discovered patterns in cobwebs and decaying wood, she stared at the shifting shapes in the stream, she gazed at clouds mutating across the sky.

Looking back at that summer, she realized that's when the magnetic resonance began between herself and the land, a resonance which seemed to involve an exchange of molecules. Her hunger finally felt satisfied. She wasn't longing for something she didn't have, she had no more nostalgia for a place she didn't belong, and she could feel her roots sinking deep into the earth. From that point on, her art began to change. The polarity between city and country blurred, as she began to see organic form in manufactured objects, like tires and machine parts, she forsook the expensive legitimacy of bronze and moved to softer, less elite forms like cloth and mud. And in the face of natural beauty, her supreme self-confidence, which had been dazzling in its simplicity, became more humble; she knew she couldn't compete with nature, she could only honor the earth. When her discussion group in the city kept insisting that "nature" is a construct, she knew, despite all her postmodern sophistication, that, if so, nature constructs herself in an infinite variety of ways, many quite unpredictable.

And with the earth curving softly beneath her and the sky arcing above her, she also realized that she was an essential part of the group. On the last weekend of that summer Carrie talked everyone into going to the lake to see the full moon on the water. People were tired and reluctant to go, but once they were settled on the big rock which stuck out like a boat into the water, they felt soothed by the lapping of waves against the rock.

Realizing her own melancholy about having to return to the city, Gail felt the same sadness in the others. It was manifesting in various complaints: headaches, bad backs, twisted shoulders. Going from one to the other, Gail listened through her hands for the blocked energy, massaged until the body began to trust her touch. Then her twin started whispering in her ear instructions about how to fix the particular ailment.

Her artistic skill guided her hands as she adjusted misplaced vertebrae, straightened out twisted muscles, realigned hip bones. Either they were too tired to resist or they actually trusted her as necks cracked and shoulders dropped and legs grew longer.

When the moon rose, so did they, standing together to greet the white light. As moonlight struck the mountain behind them, they could hear the howling of wolves or coydogs. From across the valley on another ledge a single responding howl echoed. It sounded like the ram's horn Abby's sister had given the group, the shofar which calls people to high holy days of the new year. But they knew it was not a human sound. Was it a lost wolf calling to its pack?

Each one of them thanked her on the way home for the healing she'd given. From that point on, the issue was not one of belonging or not, but of identity. Yes, they were like an extended family, but as she told her therapist in amazement when she got back to the city, she'd never realized before that one's Self could be collective as well as individuated, and that the two were not in opposition but connected, as the fruit to the tree, the tree to the land, the land to the cosmos.

Now, five years later, she felt at home on the land and comfortable with the group. She and Dulce still shared the house and each was involved with someone else. She had expected that her next lover would be a man, but it turned out not to be so. Tess was compassionate and silly, generous and psychic. She spoke to trees and adopted strays. She shared Gail's concern for the environment but challenged her to become just as concerned about suffering people as about endangered trees.

Thinking about Tess at her work in the city, missing her, Gail decided to wander the trail to the waterfall, which Carrie had told her was full of mushrooms. True to her Russian roots, Gail had become an avid mushroom hunter. With her eye for detail and taste for adventure, she loved the challenge of distinguishing one from the other, the poisonous from the delicious, the mundane from the mystic--deciphering gills, parasols, stains. Sautéing a delicate chanterelle or a hearty bolete was the garnish on her new freedom from hunger.

She bent to investigate the spongy bottom of a bolete, took out her pocketknife and cut it at the stem, sliced it on its tan surface to make sure it didn't stain red, and finally tasted a bit of it and spit it out. If you spit it out, even if it were poisonous, it wouldn't kill you. This one stained blue and its taste was delicious. She put it in a small bag attached to a loop at her waist.

As she ambled along, Gail thought about the significance of mushrooms, their extensive underground root system which connected and reproduced the individuals which sprung up from it. What she found most meaningful about mushrooms was how their relation to various hosts was symbiotic, not parasitic, how in processing the waste of a decaying tree, they were transforming matter, not destroying it. That process was the essence of art.

She also thought about the connection between the words "matter" and "mother" and "matrix," grateful that finally her mother was resigned to the fact that her daughter was a creator, not a carbon copy of herself.

Along the trail was a row of Caesar's Amanitas. Gail paused to admire their shape, like an extended egg, with the cup at the bottom and the dome at the top. Their reputation was so potent she hesitated to touch them. Remembering the psilocybin mushrooms the group had imbibed so many summers ago, she wondered what it would be like to take a hallucinogen now that she herself was so changed. What had been cathartic then had no appeal now.

Beyond the path she could hear the roar of the waterfall. Abby had told her that if she took the bridge across the old beaver dam, she could come from the other side of the waterfall into a cave. So after musing about chaos theory as she watched the water hurl over the rocks and plunge in an array of patterns, she took the trail which led down into the cave.

Once inside the deep red rock, engulfed by the sound of rushing water as it burst its way through the passage, she felt a gush of intense emotion, emotion she couldn't quite name. Tears rose in her; they weren't tears of sadness but of joy. This must be, she thought, what Dulce calls a numinous experience.

Then she had a vision of a sculpture she wanted to make: an earth bowl with a fountain springing out of it: the receptive and the creative as one, the group and the individual united, body and spirit together. She felt the energy inside her merge with the flow of water and realized the balance of her body was as sturdy as the rock.

She'd discovered a secret they all needed to know, how to grow out of the earth womb which had sheltered them, how to emerge from the birth canal without becoming alienated from the mother, how to let go of what you produce without experiencing loss. This was a secret known only to mothers and artists.

As she climbed out of the cave, she was lost in thought--as she planned how to ask the group where on the land she could build the bowl, imagined its shape and texture, figured how to construct it and what materials she'd need to build the fountain. Shaped out of rock and water, it would be something that neither fire nor porcupine could devour. She wondered about attaching it to her house, as a model of environmental art, useful for recycling water, filtering toxins, drawing warmth.

How beautiful her vision; what fun its actualization would be.

14

THE OCTAGON

At my center stand four whole maples who once lived at the foot of our mountain. Stripped of bark and limbs they rise above my main roof line to provide views in the four directions while supporting a higher roof--which looks like one hat shared by four beings. These four guardians allow light to pour into my deep heart's core. These trees were a gift from Dulce and Gail. My second roof was designed by Abby and Carrie. Faith and her young boys helped haul and anchor the trees.

At my root is a hollowed out kiva, dug deep in the meadow from which I sprung, once a source of chanting and visions, now silent as a waiting drum listening to the life above. This kiva was dug by Beth and Ev, scooped out of the earth by cupped hands making together a large bowl.

Built first as a concession to the many frogs and snakes whose habitats had been disturbed by the violent actualization of my incarnation, this space was initiated by a ritual of birth which included the planting of a crystal while meteors streaked across the sky above. Although first envisioned as a root cellar, this cavity is now covered by mesh and plywood, not to be revealed, perhaps, until I myself dissolve back into earth.

On seven of my eight sides are windows of varying shapes and sizes-- round, diamond, octagonal, oval, arched, bayed, rayed--letting in light from all angles. On the eighth side, vertical logs, in ascending steps, frame my massive stone fireplace and chimney, made of multi-shaped, many sized, different colored river stones. This curve of fireplace, following the course of the sun, brings light and warmth to the northern edge of my structure. At its center an egg shaped stone face gazes out from above the flames with the dark eyes of a goddess.

Opposite this northern border is my southern wall of windows, its arch bowing to welcome the sun all hours of the day, with a glass barrier only between the people and plants within and the birds, squirrels, chipmunks, raccoons and deer living on the other side, their shadows vibrant in the cold, their shapes often moving. At night moonlight and starlight pour in. Before the panes were put into the window frames a curious bird flew through one opening and out another without fluttering a wing. Beyond these windows the weather passes, snow falling into the light from the house, golden leaves blowing sideways, hummingbirds hovering over blossoms on the deck, new green sprouting on bushes around the yard.

I am a square on its way to becoming a circle. As a square I provide stability, security, predictability, centeredness. As an octagonal mandala I represent transformation in my reaching out toward the ultimate circle, the round which is totally inclusive and expansive. My curves mirror the natural environment which surrounds me with its spirals and cycles, the globe of earth which is our shared home. But I myself am not a sphere.

Unlike a true sphere, I have level floors, straight walls, and angled roofs, many corners, sharp edges, hidden lofts, abundant holes, and dark recesses. I was built by humans for humans--plus a few other animals, mostly small cats. Despite my often open door, I am not all inclusive, only half way there, but still able, a lot better than a box, to imagine how wholeness might feel complete.

It took many hands to bring me to fruition, skilled craftspersons' hands—the backhoe operator, the mason, the electrician, the plumber, the well digger, the carpenter--as well as the unskilled laboring hands of those who designed me and have lived within me, the hands of strangers and the hands of friends, the hands of those who now live within my walls and those who live elsewhere.

I am the synthesis of many visions, many designs, desires and needs. Each element—my roundness, my levels, my encircling porch, the capacity for my inhabitants to see the night sky, the larger contexts of the seasons and the weather—had to be integrated into my overall design. Each person involved had a say about my integrity. Nature outside—the nearby trees, stream, road, mountain view-- also assimilated themselves into my overall design. The old orchard was cleared to allow our apple trees to grow more fully, a large, circular, eight-petal garden was planted behind me, various evergreens and flowering trees now cluster around me.

I have more entrances and exits, including a cat door, than I have inhabitants. I have private spaces, lofts and wedges as well as public spaces, open for communal meals, meditations, and conversations. Within me is a natural flow through shared space from front to back, with private spaces on my sides like wings.

I am, as a whole place, like a whole person, multifaceted and multileveled--from kiva cup to ground floor to lofts to catwalk, ascending like a spiral, like chakras. I am a vessel in both senses of that word, containing life while sailing forward. Within my structure I protect, shelter, offer hospitality. Over the years I've become fuller and fuller.

Because of my shape I blend into my natural surroundings. In summer I look like a mushroom. In winter, like an igloo. Lit from within, I glow. Lit from without, I blossom.

15

US NOW

"Rainbow Person, Rainbow Person,
Go where you have to go,
Be where you have to be,
And love will follow you."

Two of us live in the big city, two in small towns, two in the country, two in the woods. Three live where they lived before we bought the land, one after a long period of living in her partner's home. Two still live on the land. Three live in new homes in new places. We live in a Brooklyn brownstone, a Vermont farmhouse, a Soho loft, a cottage by the sea, a homemade octagon, a small town duplex. We've each made our own nest, found a context which works for us. Vicariously we enjoy the homes the others inhabit.

All but two of us live with partners or ex's. The partner of one of those two lives around the corner. All of us are involved with other people, other than land folks. One lives with a partner's growing child. One is a grandmother of two. Half of us still consider ourselves bisexual, but have stuck with women. Some of our new lovers love the land; some have never seen it.

Three-fours of us are teachers, five college teachers, one Professor Emerita. Three of us are parents, one a grandparent. Three of us are counselors, one a meditation teacher. One is an unemployed healer busy with her own healing and her partner's. Four are artists, four are writers, eight of us are gardeners. We paint pictures, take pictures, make sculptures, write poems, books, novels, cook meals, nurture plants, write letters, and care for others. One of us, the one who worked while others played, worked hard and at the same job for many years, is considering retirement. She has earned this privilege but it scares her. A few of us are poor, all are comfortable, some can afford to be expansive, none of us are rich. Some of us are spendthrifts, some of us are tightwads.

Four of us are orphans. Four watch out for aging parents. One's life changed dramatically after the death of her mother, for whom she'd cared for years. Only two of us have both parents still alive. Two have lost sisters. Deaths in families have been sobering, inspiring, devastating. So have deaths of friends.

Some of us are healthy, some are not. We suffer from arthritic hands, damaged feet, crippled backs, sensitive stomachs, allergies, impaired hearing and creaky joints. Despite scares, none of us has had cancer. Our hearts are strong. Some of us rely heavily on western medicine; some of us haven't seen a doctor in years. We all use alternative treatments, from acupuncture and body work to Chinese herbs and homeopathy, and each swears by a different one.

Some travel to foreign countries to see grand vistas, to wander the streets and visit museums, or to work; only a few prefer to stay home; some travel to visit relatives, some to visit friends, some to hike and camp, see wild animals, have adventures or stir the imagination. Despite problems with mobility, most of us love to explore new places or rediscover old favorites, one of which for some is the land.

We are, not surprisingly, aging. Four of us have turned 60. We celebrated this event together on the land, but some of us were missing. Only one is not yet, but almost, fifty, and she has always been an "old soul." Only one of us contemplates moving to a warmer clime, and for her that would mean going home. Those who live in the city long for the country. Those who live in the country long for easier winters.

When we get together, infrequently these days, we celebrate our friendships, bemoan our aging bodies, share our ideas, talk about politics, the environment, our work and families. We've known each other for twenty, thirty, forty, fifty, even sixty years. Friendship is one of our most valuable shared accomplishments. We know that what counts most for us is not what we do for a living, or who we live with, our past mistakes or artistic success. We recognize in all of us a shared fountain of energy as well as its unique expression in each of us. Whether near or far, plus or minus, our psyches are full of each other's energies.

Placed in the context of the natural energies described in the Chinese book of wisdom, the *I Ching* or *Book of Changes*, we embody a variety of movements: For some it's Ch'ien, a rush of creativity; for others, Kun, a quiet listening; for all, it's Lu, the excitement of exploration; for most, it's Kan, the risk of going into darkness; for many, it's Ken, meditative awareness; for most, it's Sun, a gentle questioning; for some, it's Li, a soothing hand; for everybody it's Tui, a joyful shout.

For all of us, each of us is a totem for a certain kind of energy which we share. We have discovered, through the others, its source in us, yet we still need each other to experience the whole.

For this we are grateful.

Blossoms

16

A PLACE FOR US

"When you clearly penetrate the 10 directions, there is no inside or outside."
--Ying-An, Chinese philosopher

Years ago a band of us young, alienated, marginal, mobile Americans used to sing, "Somewhere there's a place for us," as we drove together to some antiwar or civil rights demonstration. One of the more earnest, yet ironic singers was our friend Harry who died a decade later of AIDS. As he was dying he called his suburban familial dwelling to see if he could come for a visit. His parents' response was "How could you do this to us?" He never returned home.

One of the great loves of his short life was *The Wizard of Oz*. Like Dorothy he was whirled away from home, not by a tornado but by the movements of the 60's. Unlike Dorothy he never knew what it was like to go home, to appreciate the view from his own backyard. His home, if he had one at all, was in a different sphere, the hidden space occupied by those who shared his lifestyle, his values, his brief path, his habitat.

Perhaps there is a place for everybody, but not everybody gets to live in his or her own place. Place is where people, animals, birds return year after year, where we choose to be with everyone else in that place, strangers or friends, animals or trees, flowers or insects. It's simple, it's basic, it's at the root of all our psyches and over the roof of most of our heads, but only those who've lived in the same place from season to season, year after year, know what it really means. Locomotion has displaced location in our souls. But any place, even if we stay there our entire lives, is temporary. Mobility is practice for mortality. Perhaps because we are a nation of immigrants, stability feels like death; mobility, like freedom. Fight or flight, we've chosen to flee. But one can dissolve in motion just as fully as one can freeze in place.

What if everyone had a place to claim and a home to live in? Is there enough room? Were there ever as many migrants, exiles, displaced people, crowded cities and starving children as we have today? For everyone with 50 acres and a mule, there are many single acres with 50 to 100 people living on them. Why are there so many references these days to cannibalism? Perhaps a sign of our no-taboo culture, it may also be a signal from our psyche that we're running out of room on this earth. How much easier it becomes then to push those who do not fit in over the edges. Or eat them up. Or let them starve. Or kill them. What a depressing vision of the future of our earth!

These issues are one reason why place matters. Without place we are dots before the hungry zero. With place we are vibrating loops of vibrant energy, some of which shrinks when others approach, some of which expands. Place is what gives us a chance to be where we are. Home is where we are attached to the earth--where our quantum singularity connects with cosmic complexity. Even though our feet were made for walking, transparent threads, like tenuous roots, tie them to the earth. Weak though gravitational fields may be, they force us to lift our feet if we expect to flow along. For reasons we rarely understand gravity pulls us into a particular pattern, texture, time, community.

Scientists talk of ten dimensions, most of which are curled up into little knots of microscopic space. They've mapped the up/down dimensions, the left/right dimensions, and back/forth dimensions, all of which we encounter every day in our psyches and in our politics. There's always someone above us, always someone or something below us. We move to the left on some issues, to the right on others, consider "on the one hand, on the other hand," dialogue between the left and right hemispheres of our brain. Back and forth, we deal continually with the approach/avoidance dilemmas and dramas of our lives. And despite what people of wisdom tell us about the presence of time, we shift habitually between past and future, between memory and planning, swing back and forth through the fourth dimension of future/past.

What scientists don't talk much about, except in regard to the hidden knot of the other six dimensions, is the inside/outside dimension. Despite the discovery that the earth is not flat, our contemporary lives tend to appear, although do not feel, as flat as lives on tv screens or computer monitors. We forget about the caves deep inside our round earth where bones are preserved for centuries, where shit survives, full of information about what our ancestors ate and suffered, where art and magic interact in images which still speak to us.

Home is the inside dimension of place, whether it has a particular location or not. It's deeper than territory, which is mostly, I think, about ego. It cannot be plumbed, squared, or leveled, yet others can be invited in through a process as simple as hospitality.

Travelers as many of us are, we return to different places at different times, like migrating birds but not always with their predictable rhythms. Even the poorest of us can occupy different zones simultaneously. Unlike trees, most of us these days are not rooted, nor can we grow as tall as trees do, in their mediation between earth and sky. We animals move from place to place, from job site to home, from city to forest, from shore to shore with as multiple a sense of place as we have of personality and culture. We chart our progress from different points, locating ourselves by measuring distances, angles, and degrees. So where do we *belong*?

Belonging in the contemporary context seems to emerge not out of a sense of place, but from a sense of identity. Of all the mysteries of life which intrigue us—death, synchronicity, evil, divinity, psychic phenomena—none is more compelling when we are young than the mystery of identity. *Who am I?* is a question which, while not always overtly expressed by youth, is constantly pondered by us as we come into our own.

Tied up as it is with puzzles of profession, mission, purpose; tangled up as it is with riddles of inherited identities of family, race, culture, and nationality; invisibly bound with enigmas of whether we originate from snails or apes, are lost sparks of a divine being, seeds from an alien visitation, part of a progeny fallen from grace seeking redemption, a lost remnant searching for the rest of the whole, or an evolving species; and fettered by contemporary perspectives regarding id, ego, superego, animus/anima, shadow and persona, the conundrum of personal identity is fraught with individual choices, each of which has collective reverberations. It takes a great deal of courage, we discover, to wrestle one's way through all the expectations, obligations and principles to an authentic and compassionate acceptance of one's own limited but promising individual identity, promising in relation to potential growth. It takes a lifetime to fully comprehend who we are in relation to the persons with whom we come in contact and choose to connect with.

Looking back on our community now, I realize that while I miss that rare and simple sense of belonging we briefly shared, I can no longer imagine belonging to any one circle. Our greatest illusion when we were young was that our identity could be shared by a group, that individual identities could dissolve into a collective identity. Many of us, already outsiders for a variety of reasons, longed to belong, to find "a place for us." Maybe that pure primary sense of native unity is still true for some people, maybe it used to be true for many, but in our multifaceted culture, identity is prismatic, not indigenous, even for original peoples. I belong to many groups, each of which reflects an aspect of who I am, but my identity is my own complex layering and faceting of self responding to the complex layering and faceting of my worlds. No one can own that diamond self but me, even though we are never as individuated as we think—we are shaped by many collective contexts, all shared with others. But how we connect with others is unique to each of us, and ultimately understood only by ourselves. In that sense we can never wholly belong to any one context, but we also cannot exist without those connections. Who I am is unique to me, but who we were together is essential to my own identity, now still as much as before.

Places within the place where I live now speak to me of movement and stillness, the poles of survival. In front of our house are two gigantic maple trees inhabited by a plethora of creatures—chipmunks, chickadees, grosbeaks, thrush and finch, some residing in their holes, some just passing through. Squirrels dash, blue jays swoop from tree to tree. In back, I sit in the swing to watch our fountain flow out of the pond we built, surrounded by the distinct personalities of two apple trees, one crabapple, one tall conifer, one weeping birch, one smoke bush, one young blue spruce, overlooking the garden we planted in a yard full of wildflowers visited by deer and moose. This, for the moment, is home for all of us here. My role in this is different from the chipmunk, jay or deer. I walk on two legs between sky and earth, a mediator between above and below as the animals mediate between regions of wild and tame.

I have finally found a place where I can live, I who have always been a stranger, a newcomer, outside the common rhythm. Here I am at home, literally and figuratively, even though I do not always feel at home here. I'm here for survival's sake, because I landed here, because here is where I could afford. I've settled down temporarily like my wandering ancestors. But this place for me is blessed. Here, finally, is a place where I can rest, if not root. Maybe it's not my role in life to be a steward of space or a keeper of time; maybe I am here to remind us of the hidden dimensions, to be a caretaker of stories, an archivist of dreams.

I like to believe that one reason our place here is blessed is not just because we've blessed it by paying close and affectionate attention to it but also because it's on the edge, on the verge of a hill overlooking both a rim of road and a boundary of river. It's one well designed juncture on a margin of sacred space, this particular speck on the periphery of a metaphoric Third Eye. A friend discovered on the internet our tiny, tiny town identified on a line of geomantic points within a New England configuration of electromagnetic fields. These points, according to the website, correspond to the Hindu system of chakras, the spine of mountains paralleling the human spine, the energy centers in the earth similar to energy centers in the body, like collective chakra points. One mountain top next to our town, up the road from our house, was identified by the internet site as the Third Eye. Fantasy or not, this symbolism makes sense to me. I feel at home in the Third Eye region.

But my *home* is not only here. Inside more hidden dimensions home is also with people I love, some who share identity by blood, some by lifestyle, some by values, some by history, by our caring for the same people and things. The place we share is not just one or the other but all our places together. Shared space.

In the bigger picture, we all live in the same space. Natural territories are not marked by fences which shut others out, but by interacting zones which exclude others of the same kind. Ironically, swallows tolerate bluebirds in their nesting zone but not other swallows. Ironically, too much of the same type in the same place is not enough. Diversity is essential to survival. Isolation, ghettoization, gated communities, iron curtains not only make those behind them vulnerable to attack; the lack of diversity also weakens the whole. It's healthier in the long run to soften the fences, leave the gates open.

Like people places can change. They too can be eaten up, pushed aside or left to starve. Our American pattern of hunger, migration, and greed has led us to devour the native wilderness, exploit the earth's riches, plunder the ground upon which we stand and into which we once longed to root ourselves. Trauma—of exile, immigration, discrimination, slavery-- has blunted our sensitivity to place. Sometimes it seems we've been content to crawl into shallow holes and watch the world around us wither. Having left our ancestral homes, we cannot trust the one we've discovered. Better to cement over the ground than let it fail us with blighted potatoes or burned crops. Have we forgotten what it's like to have a place to come home to, over and over again and again? It seems we're content to eat up places like they were fast food.

What makes a place distinctive is not the locations of nests, which often shift each year from branch to branch, adjusting to changes in trees and bushes. Even the most stable of families or clans change from year to year, finding their own way through the seasons, while around them abides the larger context which doesn't seem to change at all except by tiny permutations or violent disruptions. What makes a place special is the pattern woven from the moving strands of those who share the space, each distinctive, each unique, each intent on its own purpose and expression, all interacting together to make a harmonious whole. While the swallow brings joy with its silver blue flash, the red breasted robin delights with its inquisitive hop and glide.

Whether I move through this landscape or not, these birds, I pray will continue to soar and glide in and around each other, sharing this space with chipmunks and deer—even other humans and, of course, the resident ghosts. If we cut down all the trees in a place or endanger all the animals, we deface that place.

Now that a certain plot of land is no longer what binds our particular band of friends together, I'm searching for another metaphor to describe how we still belong in the same place. In some ways we are a flock, nesting at different points, flying free at the same and different points, coming together to share a meal, a moment, flying through other worlds separately yet simultaneously.

This image works only if we remember that each specific place is contained within an environment inside a state of mind, inside a region of space, inside a country of origin or choice, like nested bubbles, one as tiny as the first microorganism, one as large as a galaxy, and at the heart of each is home. Within such a perspective, the distances between us shrink. We inhabit the same place at the same time with our diverse identities, sharing it by describing to each other how we've moved from zone to zone within it.

Those hidden dimensions the scientists search for are nested inside us, within our skin, within our organs, within our cells, within our molecules, within our atoms, within our particle/strings, each its own place within a larger place, as we ourselves are places within the expanding dimensions of space, our home, our neighborhood, the landscape, the planet, the cosmos. It's not stability that kills us, it's our clinging to one single tight sphere, our failure to go outdoors to find out how expansive even our most rooted lives can be if only we witness the reach of trees, the luminosity of clouds, the messages of stars.

Within this sequence of nested bubbles, these ever expanding spheres of growth, exist our small miracles—the fact that we can plant trees, plan gardens, grow vegetables--and our small secrets--how we resonate together even when apart, as a piano key sounded in one place can cause a guitar string to vibrate in another because they are tuned to the same frequency. Our music does not reside in the specific location of key or string but in our shared vibrations.

This now is a place for us.

Who knows about tomorrow?

17
BEGINNINGS REVISITED

We are she who floated in the swing, her hands clutching the ropes while other hands, firm, strong on her back, pushed, pushed until she swung free of the hands, soared into the hot blue sky under the cottonwood tree, swayed with the wind through her hair, rocked to the rhythms of leaves, fell into a trance as the heat rising from the horizon blended into the hills and gave her visions of what her life would be, out there, over there, rising and falling, coming and going.

We are she who'd been an unplanned child, a surprise to a weary womb, a challenge to a mother sick with this unexpected pregnancy so soon after the birth of her last child. The womb felt cramped but she clung to life in there, emerged reluctantly, hesitant perhaps about her reception. When finally she did come out, she was held so warmly, so tightly by her confused but honorable mother, she longed to burst free. But she also loved that embrace and what it taught her of home.

We are she who watched the stars from the bedroom window, who saw them descend as fairies, twinkling outside the panes, calling her out into the night where she was forbidden to go. Their tiny gossamer wings beat a tune for her, their luminous blue bodies gestured to her, their tiny, tiny gold heads aglow with an inner light. She quietly raised the window and tossed out to them her tiny jewels of light, rhinestones from the dime store, gifts of kind.

We are they who, as if by signal, both leapt out of the bathtub and ran giggling in opposite directions, their aunt's hands not quick enough to snatch them up, no diapers to catch hold of. Hand in hand they helped each other stand and walk. Whisper to whisper they found the hidden cookies and shared them. Eager beavers they filled up the gas tank with sand while their parents innocently played tennis.

We are she who shared a room with her older sister, so tiny that only on their separate beds could they avoid bumping into each other. Being in each other's face, each other's business, was a given. Outside, in the park across the street from their apartment building, she felt free to move at her own pace, to stretch herself to her fullest. She biked across New York, hiked across Europe, joined movements for equity and justice from Boulder to Birmingham.

We are she who, when the girl pushed her from behind, turned around and pushed back. The girl pulled her long hair and when she struggled to free herself, they fell into the dust and rolled around trying to bite each other. They stopped just as the bell rang, just before a teacher could catch them and sit them in opposite corners of the classroom. It was a draw. They became the best of friends.

We are she who sometimes dropped into the bowl her caretaker'd pushed her face into when she was little, after she'd asked for more. In its center was a hole, like the drain in a sink, through which she fell, deeper and deeper into emptiness she tried to ward off by keeping to herself. Given clay in an art class, she found she could shape it into a bowl. The lump could form both an inside and an outside. She could make it wide and shallow or deep and full. She could let it get hard. She could paint it different colors. She could use it. She didn't have to shrink and disappear inside it.

We are she who was amazed when her friend dropped out of the May Day procession, out of the line of uniformed girls singing, "Mary, we crown thee with blossoms today," to watch an ant carry another ant along a winding trail. Tentatively she joined her to help cheer what they decided was one ant friend helping a wounded ant friend get back to their nest. They followed the pair all the way back to the hole, even though it meant that Sister Immaculata put her on probation and called her friend's mother to warn her about their special friendship. When Sister made her apologize to the whole class for spoiling this sacred moment, she stood before them and said, "I'm sorry if I did anything wrong."

We are they who built a "fort" in the vacant lot next door, using old packing crates. It had two stories, an entrance you crawled into, and several windows on the top layer. They hammered and nailed. They covered the top with canvas. They fixed up the top room with blankets and pillows so they could sleep overnight in it. But a storm came, full of lightening and thunder. The roof filled with rain, then began to leak. Finally they chickened out. They ran back home, drenched and disappointed. Next time, they vowed, they'd do a better job.

We are she who, as she grew older, followed her brothers out. She tagged along behind them, going fishing, playing baseball, smoking cigarettes in the alley. When they won scholarships to college, she worked hard in school so she could go to college too. That was the way out. That was the way she went, the way of the boys. Her family was not a safe place for women who didn't follow the boys. Her mother died young, only in her forties. Her sister-in-law died young, only in her forties. Her youngest sister had breast cancer at the age of thirty-five.

We are she who was allowed to run free only at the place of the sacred springs, her dog as companion. She'd visit the holy waters with deep reverence for the healing they'd inspired. There she'd pray for her saintly mother while her dog, her best friend, sat beside her, the warmth of her body a comfort in the chilled early morning air. Then she'd wander through the woods where she felt safer than she did in her own home. She talked to the trees and flew with the birds. She felt the sacredness of the outside world, despite her mother's fear of it.

We are she who, when she was lucky enough to get the window seat, edged as far away from her siblings as the cramped space would allow, tolerated the dog crawling across the seat of laps among the piles of comic books, and gazed out at the many houses they passed, farm houses, shanties, mansions, suburban boxes, to wonder about the people who lived in them. As they crisscrossed the country, she dreaded the cheap motels, wished she could be inside one of those homes where the lights were now on and people probably gathered around the dinner table instead of being stuffed inside a car. She imagined what their lives were like. She was tired of being outside looking in.

We were better off than most other females, this we discovered. We hadn't been tossed out on a winter hillside to die because we were girls, our feet had not been bound, we'd not been sold as children into slavery, we hadn't been gang banged, we hadn't been orphaned by a military junta, we didn't have to work in a sweat shop to support our families, we hadn't been driven with our families into exile, we hadn't been given in marriage at the age of ten to men old enough to be our grandfathers, we weren't, exactly, homeless runaways, we hadn't been marched with our mother and sister into a concentration camp, we hadn't been beaten to a pulp, we hadn't been pulled out of school to work in the fields, we hadn't become pregnant at thirteen. We were, we discovered as we became women, for the most part, lucky girls.

We are she who realized that school was her oasis. There her talents were not a source of sorrow for others, a threat to their sense of self; there her intelligence was applauded, her talents were celebrated. And there she could be of assistance to others, students who weren't as quick or as cagey as she was. Her teachers became her parents in absentia and she was as devoted to them as she longed to be with the awkward adults who parented her.

We are she who was a tumbleweed, not by choice. She longed to sink her roots somewhere, anywhere, even in the desert. But she kept moving, afraid that if she didn't keep her family in sight at all times, they would disappear, drive off without her. Or, if she complained too much, they might stop the car and dump her out. Even after she'd left them behind, she kept on moving, automatically, afraid to get attached to any place or any person.

We are she who was ignorant of politics but impassioned about justice, who found herself at the first national civil rights march on Washington. Never before had she seen so many black people together, smiling, talking, singing and cheering. Not sullen or wary or silent masks of servitude in a white world as many had seemed--those, at least she'd observed from a distance, not the few individuals she knew in school. Now herself the minority she eventually suspended her chalkiness as the thrilling words of Dr. Martin Luther King set the course for liberation, not just, although mostly, for the black folks there but for all of them. "I have a dream." This was the first step of her long march toward liberation.

We are she who listened as her friends told tales of their anti-war activity, blocking traffic in D.C., marching down Wall Street, sitting in at the Justice Department, and boasted of their arrests, being dragged into paddy wagons, locked into stadiums, tossed into jail to spend the night with prostitutes and drunken disorderlies, while she was tied down out of choice, one child in a stroller, another inside her. She hated the war worse than any of them, missing her brother, afraid already of losing her toddler son, but she'd passed the point of youthful recklessness. She had a family to care for. All such adventures would have to come later.

We are she who'd been wary of entering the Christian Church where the Girl Scouts met, a star at Hebrew School who could not believe her good fortune when the women's movement started. Consciousness raising groups with women from every kind of background, supper groups, ecumenical New Years, feminist Passovers, writing groups, political action groups, a show for women artists, play writing groups—it was, on earth, a world beyond the world she'd known. A heaven of expansion after a hell of confinement.

We are she who'd taken the only route of escape available to her. She couldn't afford to go to college, although she was smart enough. She was tired of dead end jobs. She was sick of living at home. She was in love, not for the first or the last time. The lure of marriage wasn't how lovely she looked in the wedding gown or the thrill of a honeymoon or the piles of presents, no. She knew for someone like her, that walk down the aisle toward the long trek of matrimony provided the only gauntlet that could lead eventually to independence.

We are she who challenged boundaries ever since she was little. Warned against climbing trees, she'd head for the highest branch with the agility of a tight ropewalker. Frightened by the steep cliff of a mountain, she'd plunge over the edge. Restricted by her religious upbringing from the simplest pleasures, from excesses of any kind, she'd dance with abandon, drink till she dropped, kiss another woman, push all limits at least once. Forbidden to enter, she'd find a way in. But just by the fact that as a woman she pushed the limits, she found herself outside the pale. Only the need to make a living and the strictures of her many jobs eventually penned her in. Then one day, locked in after hours because she had so much paperwork to catch up with, she faced a choice: spend the night on a hard desk, or raise the window and jump out. She chose the latter, even though the only exit was through a second story window and the ground below was cement.

18

THE LETTERS, FRONT TO BACK

If **A** is where we begin, legs planted, head up, **Z** is where we end, like the snake who knows the end is the beginning is the end.

If **B** is our first lesson, the message of the double helix, **Y** is our last hurrah, the "Yes" to our life.

If **C** is how we first greet the world, with open arms, **X** is what we find, the mystery within the world.

If **D** is how we defend ourselves, softly closed, **W** is how we store our life's treasures, in two open chambers.

If **E** is how we engage the world, with both hands and head, **V** is how exuberant we feel when we are successful.

If **F** is how we converse with others, open faced, hand extended, **U** is how the world holds us, nested.

If **G** is how we offer hospitality, table prepared, **T** is how we walk the tightrope of closed borders, arms extended.

If **H** is how we hold our ground, balanced and secured, **S** is how we flow through life, avoiding obstacles.

If **I** is how we assert ourselves, **R** is how we rest, curled but ready to move again. If **J** is how we step back from danger, **Q** is where our questions lead us, to the next sprout.

If **K** is how we step boldly forward, **P** is how we pause to reflect.

If **L** is how we turn a corner, **O** is where we are born again, where all is one around the zero.

Which leads us to the middle ground, where we live in this moment, the tension between **M**, both round and edgy, steady and responsible, and **N**, which announces with a flourish that it is ready for action, however risky.

This, the alphabet of Europe and the Americas, traces the stages of our lives, developmentally, linearly, matter of factly. If we place this line of letters in a circle, as I've done here, it delineates but does not fully describe the mysteries of our lives. For other dimensions we must turn to other letters, other alphabets, other languages.

First there are the vowels, fundamental tones of our bodies which sound the energies of our chakras, from **U** at our bottom, **O** at our solar plexis, **A** at our heart, **E** at our third eye, **I** at our crown. Variations of these sounds express the range of our emotions. They do not come and go in orderly sequence; they rise and fall like colors through the fabrics of our lives. Like the Northern Lights.

For deeper mysteries and meanings, we turn to the runes, Greek letters, Hebrew letters, Chinese hexagrams, ancient pictographs.

In the runes, **X** is not negation, it's a gift. This gift comes from a world where the only difference between a man and a horse are the extended lines of the man's legs around the horse's belly, like another X. A world where "ear" is a letter which also means earth and where the letter for "sound" means wisdom.

The Hebrew letters serve as husks for seeds of mysticism buried within, seeds which, understood, give rise to the Tree of Life, at whose crown is not worldly attainment but pure being. When the mystic goes through the letter Daleth, she enters the door to enlightenment. When she understands the letter Yod, she sees the hand of G-d. When she opens the letter, 'Ayin, she finds ecstasy.

The Greeks gave us Alpha and Omega, the beginning of our beginning, the end of our end, and the wisdom that Alpha and Omega are linked, not just front to back but also back to front. It's no wonder we use these letters to describe the rhythms of our brains, the fast Beta, the relaxed Alpha, the blissful Theta. These letters are like piano keys to our internal pulses.

The Chinese hexagrams are the elements of our world: sky, earth, thunder, water, mountain, wind, wood, fire, and lake. Each letter gives us one fundamental impulse out of which our world and our lives alike are formed: the creative, the receptive, the arousing, the abysmal, keeping still, the gentle, the clinging, the joyous. The earth and we are one.

To understand our lives we must be multilingual. To express our love, we have to settle for the letters we know. Such as these letters, seen, sent or received:

"Seems kind of amazing how the years add up. So many, many memories. The first picture that comes to mind is you sitting so cute with your lively face and ringlets. 'Such an imaginative child,' as Mother would say. And you always were!

You had so many good ideas for our play—and plays you wrote for us three to perform. Things to do! Places to go! I was lucky to have such a fun and innovative sister. A helpful guide into the world. I treasure that picture of us in our snowsuits and you helping me to walk. You were dear. You were a big help to me. As I look back, there were many times you were a protective buffer for me 'in the world.' I'm grateful for that. All those times we had to move, leave friends and enter a new environment, you were always there. It sure helped to be able to go through it together, to have your companionship.

"Oh, so many memories flood in! How can I do this for 59 years worth? But it makes me realize what a lot of fun we had together, what an adventurous life.

"Everywhere you went you made a contribution—of yourself. You made a difference. You were out there with your multifaceted gifts. You also gave your emotional richness. You felt strongly, reacted strongly, stirred things up, sparked people's growth—a catalyst—helped them move (sometimes even before they were aware of that need—which was hard on you—and them too, but beneficial.) I know I myself have realized things later: 'Oh yeah, I see what she meant.'

"I don't think you've gotten enough recognition for how much you've given. You think of others so much, encouraging them to reach their potential, creating vehicles for them to manifest their own talents. Speaking up for the unrecognized, rarely promoting your self. Attempting to break down unwarranted hierarchical boundaries and include everyone. So many people have been touched and uplifted by you. That's a wonderful legacy."

*　　　　*　　　　*　　　　*

"You are one of my oldest friends. The first kindness you did me that I remember occurred after I had just narrowly escaped being expelled by Sister Therese…

"I've serious regrets about some of what I have and haven't done in our friendship. I remember once sitting around a campfire on the land. We were all talking and singing. Suddenly you got up and began running in place, facing the fire, sharing with us your fantasy of being a bear. You wanted someone to join you in this spontaneous imaginative exploration, and I was too inhibited to do it. But I admired your courage and self-manifestation—and regretted that I was not able to meet you. I hope someday we have another chance like that together.

"One of my goals in life is so to live that I don't, as Thoreau warned, die knowing I haven't lived out what I could. You are a friend who has lived your life, written, painted, taken photographs, built houses, tried primary relationships with a man as well as with women, nurtured gardens and animals, and taught. You've taught me a lot. I love you."

*　　　　*　　　　*　　　　*

"I thank you for the friendship, the moving on and through. The friends, the houses with varieties of wallpaper, the farm, the friends, the trip to see you the day after Kennedy was shot, the trip with the roosters in the car, the friends, the years that followed and were connected by many celebrations and projects to join in and bring to fruition and live in and enjoy. I'm thankful for the ways your awareness and love of beauty is shared and deepens my own."

*   *   *   *

"This card—"the constantly changing colors from near black to deep purple to shades of orange and gold to the brightest yellow"—captures something about your wonderful colors and depth and intricacy and beauty and something about the complexity, depth and intricacy of our connection during all these years. So many years, pictures (in my mind's eye as well as in my stacks of photographs), stories, and experiences from the 30 years I've known you, first in Wisconsin, then in Baltimore, then on the land, and now in Vermont.

"I can see us all climbing Buck Mountain, all swimming and floating around in Lake George and in the rubber boat, can hear you singing your land song and all of us sitting around singing. I picture you playing your autoharp. I remember the very cold time in January when you visited us in the shack and we all slept on the second floor as the snow piled high and soft and beautiful and cold.

"And there were hard times there, too. A lot of coming together and moving apart. A bit like that deep and textured photo on the card. Complex.

"And now, I think how much respect I have for your good work, of your generosity, wanting everyone to get a higher salary, wanting to give recognition for everybody's good work. Your sense of fairness, justice, and compassion. (And did I ever tell you about one of your acts of great compassion that I remember vividly, the giving me the lit candle that day in church so that I would not feel alone and in the dark?) I think too how kind you were when my mother died. Thank you."

*   *   *   *

"On first impression you were a little scary. You seemed dour and to be totally uninterested in patching it over with superficial politeness or pleasantries, unwilling to make a concession to those sorts of conventions. It's part of what I've come to value most about you—a kind of extremeness of authenticity—willing to go (and to show the going) wherever you are feeling—and a great range in where that takes you.

"Two moments come to mind:

"The first is a dramatic one. We had one of those group meetings under the grandmother tree, about the land, what, when, where sorts of things, and I was actually finally feeling comfortable enough and brave enough to say I was thinking of building a studio on a site near the beaver pond. The meeting broke up. Five

minutes later a blood-curdling scream issued from deep in the woods. (I gathered you weren't too happy about my idea.)

"And the second and equally vivid memory is of you cuddling a little sandy apricot furry thing in a towel, patiently opening its mouth and gently squeezing pipettes of nourishment into the little shaking body—and doing this again, and again, and again—tendering this sweet creature into life.

"I've come to love this person of these extremes, and of what's in between."

*   *   *   *

"Once upon a time there lived a woman in a small hut in the forest. Whenever she went, dogs and cats accompanied her. She would stop to smell the flowers, hear the birds and the sounds of trees sighing in the wind, touch all that there was simply to feel the texture of nature. But seeing was her favorite. Her 'magic eye' would capture Mother Nature's elusive side! And, oh, what an eye! She captured the spirits of many beings, great and small, in her camera—a joy for others to behold!

"She could be seen rambling along going nowhere and everywhere. Sometimes she looked like an old bear blending into the forest scene. She always brought a smile to my being. She is a gentle and compassionate creature. She was always there to lend an ear when I needed someone to listen to me. I always felt better when leaving her.

"Then one day the old bear and all her animal friends just up and moved on to a new forest. But she never forgot her old friends. I'm proud to be counted as one of them."

*   *   *   *

"DEAR COMRADE,
> *I've known you since*
> *your hair was coppered*
> *and your form lithe*
> *with confusion*
>> *and now when I run*
>> *my fingers through*
>> *the silver milkweed silk*
>> *of your head and hug*
>> *the thicker frame*
>> *of your body of knowledge*

> *I remember*
> *when we were pebbles*
> *nestling in the aggregate*

of some tall wall of stone

left by receding waters
and movement
to bake and splinter
till separate
tumbles of navigation
required our attentions

    and yet by dint
    of some gothic
    unforgetting

    and its long long
    shadow cast over
    those lithic days

I can sigh relieved
that sour lessons
of perspective's
path of parallels

end down the distance
where all vanishes
to a shared point.

        *   *   *   *

"It is an honor and a joy to have you as my long time 'search and settle' sangha soul-friend—for the search—you've served as the best compass, pointing towards all things crucial; for the settle—you've provided the best of nests, offering a safety few are lucky enough to find. Together, the search and settle elements look much like the proverbial magic carpet in mythic days."

        *   *   *   *

"I can't remember life without you. I think we cut our teeth on 'otherness' by observing how you were not me and I was not you, in subtle ways. Mom always thought we were so different and that is apparent now, but it wasn't then. Yes, there's that photo of me holding your hand while you first walked, but from then on, it was you leading me up into the trees, up over the wall, down into some arroyo. I'm pretty sure I wasn't the leader when it came to physical daring do, and I know I wasn't the mastermind when it came to stealing cookies or exploring some

forbidden realm. That became quite evident when we left home as young adults! You trod down every exotic path before I even knew where they were!

"*But I'm jumping ahead. What do I remember from when we were children? I remember you stirring the chocolate pudding so carefully. I remember your quietness, your big eyes which took everything in, your squirming off adult laps to run off and play, our joyous laughter, your puzzlement over Granpa's joking, our wonderment at seeing the stars from the roof in Tucson, our amazement at the dressed fleas at Mrs. Beards, your affection for animals, your sense of adventure but reluctance to leave. Many of these are Mom's stories too, but it makes sense that you were the one who asked "Can we go home now?" after one more unwelcome move. I remember our going with Mom and Grandmother to Perpetual Adoration, your prayerfulness, that deep sharing of silence among the four of us, the foundation, I believe, of our spiritual life (more than Mass or Catholic school).*

"*One of my fondest memories is of lying in bed on a Saturday morning listening to you play the piano. You played so gently, it was very soothing. And I recall how very proud I was watching you play baseball or basketball: thinking "That's my sister!" when you'd scoop up a line drive as shortstop or drive deftly through the crowd to make a basket. Oh my! I felt the same exhilarated pride when later you climbed to the top of the Grandmother Tree. I remember my delight after Mom discovered your impishness, when you were teasing Sally once, and how you disguised it under that aura of innocence. I remember us almost drowning from giggling when we had to 'rescue' each other in Red Cross water safety class. You had a gift for flowing quietly to wherever you wanted to be.*

"*I think despite your and Mom's devotion to each other, you were often hidden within the family complexity, the chaos and conformity of so many moves. But secrecy was also a cloak which allowed you to become more of who you are. I recall how startled I was to see photos of you as a teenager hamming it up at some party with your friends (in those days where there was a strict dividing line between my friends and your friends). I hadn't seen you free like that, with that dramatic flair, since childhood. I've been happy to see it again on the land.*

"*But before the land reunion there was a longer period of separation and secrecy, while I went my way and you went yours, all the way around the world in fact…when you came to St. Louis as I was leaving, then up until you and Dulce settled into Sea Gate. I only had glimpses into your life as it was then. I recall your flirtation with the Peace Corps and my worry about you going off like that, your time at the Pride of Judea, your studies at Naropa, but it felt like we didn't really reconnect deeply (although in some way we also never really were that far from each other in terms of geography and also visiting each other) until the anti-war movement erupted in D.C.. I remember so well standing outside that huge fence (the D.C. coliseum?) tossing food over to you, Abby, and Bill. There I was terrified of being arrested (having squirmed away from it a couple of time) and there you were, delighted at the adventure of it. I used to think you were fearless; now I think you are brave (not just counter-phobic)*

"*Around that time, as I recall, you embarked on your many spiritual explorations. This was a realm I probably would not have explored on my own and I am so grateful for the insights and richness of perspective which I gained from following you, more like a tourist than the navigator you were--to Naropa, to Kashi Ranch, and to IMS, where you introduced us to the practice of Vipassana which has changed our lives. You have been, and continue to be, a wonderful guide and teacher in the ways of the spirit. Nothing was off limits, no culture too strange or without value. You carried our heritage of many cultures into the spiritual world in ways that have been quite healing and transformative. But this was not just curiosity; you have deepened these insights with commitment and practice that is inspiring. I'm grateful for that.*

"*I am also grateful for your gift of listening, your capacity for hearing our stories and responding lovingly. This capacity for paying attention to others, whether human, vegetable, or animal, is very nurturing, very loving, perhaps at the heart of why we are on this earth. I have been sustained by your receptiveness throughout my adult life, but especially after my separation from Ev when I was so devastated. Not only did you listen patiently to all my moaning and groaning, blaming and self-doubt, you encouraged me to keep the connection with her alive, and you reminded me that relationships can be 'dormant,' can still survive. I can't tell you how valuable that support and advice was.*

"*It was particularly delightful when we were able to share as a group on the land, so that you were as much listened to, supported, and challenged as you listened, provided support and challenge. Those exchanges were among the deepest human dialogues I've ever had. Not to have them has been a great loss for all of us. And of course there was all the play, work, music, psychological processing and analysis which created the soil for that deep sharing: singing and playing around the campfire, our trips of the psyche, concerts through the woods, the building of our shelters and discoveries up the mountain, at the pond, in the woods, all so much fun, so life-changing, so empowering.*

"*I learned particularly from you how to see more closely, how to observe not just the big picture but also the detail, the unique individuality of each plant, rock, flow of water, rush of wind, each moment of change from season to season. My winter trips to visit you and Abby at the shack are particularly vibrant in my memory because I'd never experienced winter out of doors like that. I remember you leading me across the frozen pond, our snow-shoeing up the frozen caves, watching the water under the ice in the stream--how beautifully you recently captured that experience. You have the gift of seeing as well as hearing, and it is evident in your video shots, in your natural sculptures and in the wonderful way you have created gardens and outdoor places of beauty on the land.*

"This sight emerges out of another thing I've learned from you, how to slow down, how to experience each moment more fully, more deeply. This is not easy for me, but I've valued your pace enough to emulate it when I can, whether meditating, puttering, or just moving slowly across the land. Slowing down to enter an experience more deeply.

"Your ability to maintain your own pace in the face of increasingly frenetic social busyness is particularly admirable. It emerges partially out of your stubbornness--which manifested itself in the building process, where you showed such incredible patience, hope and perseverance in the face of what seemed to me insurmountable physical frustrations and obstacles: "We can do it!" you'd say and most of the times we could. But mostly it comes from your integrity, your commitment to being yourself no matter what the consequences, no matter what anybody might say.

"Our sisterhood had indeed been powerful, and our friendship even more so. I can't imagine life without you."

Whether writing to or written about, each one's signature is as vivid as the distinctive flight of a bird: swallow, dove, robin, chickadee, hummingbird, heron, woodpecker, bluebird. Each body, seed, self, soul is unique--with her own colors, her own song, her own flight pattern, her own territory, her own zone of connection--and each a part of the whole. In their own languages, birds sing in cadences tuned to the tones of the spheres out of which they emerge, through which they fly.

These are the letters that matter. The lines that count are the ones that connect. These letters are ours. These lines we claim. This is our language.

19
C L O S U R E

"Will you go, will you go along with me?
To the land that we will discover,
To the country where we will be free."

I am the friend with city blood, country dreams, who visits every year. I love to fill my lungs with clean air, my eyes with beauty everywhere, my ears with songs of birds and rustle of leaves, my nose with fresh smells, my mind with new ideas, my heart with the exchange of gifts. I've come for solace when grieving, for inspiration when depressed, for companionship when lonely, for adventure when bored. I've buried my pets beneath the Grandmother Tree, taken pictures of autumn leaves, helped dig and helped build. I'm the guest who never stays. I'm always welcome.

"Where the inaudible note of the ninth planet
completes the perfect tune, breaks and
remakes the octave." Sara Maitland, *Three Times Table.*

I am the lover who experiences the land as a rival. I am the place which competes with the land. I live in the city where everything happens. I am the city where all things converge. But no matter how much security, comfort, stimulation, entertainment I provide, I cannot win the whole heart, I cannot keep her from leaving, I cannot have her all to myself. Can't she see that I am her home, I am her family? I'm sick of singing the Stay-sis Blues. What do the land and the group provide that I don't? On some level I don't understand, I can't compete. So I hang at the threshold, waiting for her to return. They invite me in but I won't stay for long. I don't like being a guest and I refuse to belong. But don't for a moment believe that you are whole without me, that the land is all that matters.

> **"The earth is our mother.**
> **We must take care of her."**

We are the children you sometimes forget, the ones who've grown up and gone away, the ones who've played in your springs and hidden in your trees, helped you build sheds. The ones who were never born, whom you feared and longed for, dodged or carried briefly, who were born to friends and relatives. Or the ones you knew and cared for somewhere else, played games with, told stories to, scolded, comforted and taught, who've never walked on the land, never climbed the mountain, never camped near the steam. You often forget us between our birthdays, when sometimes you send cards and gifts, as we forget you, but you miss us nonetheless. Some day you will remember. Who will you leave the land to, if not us? You are not the end.

> **"Rocka my soul in the bosom of Abraham,**
> **Rocka my soul in the bosom of Abraham,**
> **So high you can't get over her,**
> **So low you can't get under her,**
> **So wide you can't get around her,**
> **Oh, rocka my soul."**

I am the grandmother you loved so deeply. I'm honored by your Grandmother Tree who is just about as old as me. I am the Bubbie, I am the Nana who spoke the wordless language to you when you were too little to talk. I watch over you now, though you can't see me, I guide and comfort you still. My spirit hovers in the wind, speaks through the stream, calls with the birds. Yes, it's the ancestors' voices that you hear in the water, it's the grandmothers' voices that you release when you sing. You are the women we wanted to be, you are the future that we have become. You have broken the cycle of our oppression and for this we thank you. In the strength of our silence, the creativity of our endurance, we planted the seed that you are now harvesting. Women before us prepared the soil. Neither you nor we were the beginning.

> **"All I want is a room somewhere,**
> **Far away from the cold night air,**
> **Lots of coal making lots of heat,**
> **Lots of chocolates for me to eat,**

**Warm hands, warm face, warm feet,
Wouldn't it be loverly?"**

We are the animals who share the land. The first of your dogs to climb the mountain, to bark at the beavers and howl at the moon, who died licking your hand, whose spirit wags at your knees. The second dog, whom you found crumpled in the city street, given up for dead, the little lame prince called Midnight who recovered from his shattered hip to sit on many laps and run down many trails. The neighbor dog who made this her second, then first home, a natural in the woods and ponds but a klutz in the house, the one who rescued other animals and guided them to freedom and safety, the savior of motherless kittens, yet eternally jealous. The abandoned dog, wary of confinement, probably abused, who begged to be able to stay, refused restraint but voluntarily became a couch potato. The three old cats, the matriarch and her two companions, yin and yang curled up together, imported from the city, now buried beneath the Grandmother Tree. The city kitten, his mother wild and wary, snatched up in a storm from under the front steps, wet and scrawny, and carried to the land. The country kittens, one borne in the mouth of the dog, the only one of her litter to survive, the other two, from different litters, one coon, one calico, following their friend, the dog to a better land, they knew. A chorus of canines, a phalanx of felines, we are the voices which haven't been heard. Ours are the tales which continue to wave.

**"Hey ho, nobody home,
no eat, no drink, no money have I none.
But still I will be merry."**

Oh yeah, well, what about us? We're animals too. Only we were here on the land before the rest of you came and we'll be here, hopefully, after you're gone. If it weren't for the domesticated barks and meows, you'd hear lots more from us. Remember our singing inside our lodge, below the surface of the pond, our chomping at night, and the slaps of our tails? Remember our soft brown eyes and twitching ears as we stared at you from across the stream, pawed at the brush and flagged our white tails? Remember our masked eyes and busy fingers as we sampled cat food and peered at you from the porch of the shack? Remember our pretty quills which we left as mementos for you after you chased us away with your prickly broom? Remember our little turds by which we marked every bite we took from your latched cupboards as we carried our wide-eared mouselings from nest to insulated nest? Remember our paw prints as we ran over your cloth ceiling in search of more feed?

Speaking of others, let's not forget us birds. The heron am I, majestic and awkward, as I rise from my fishing and sail over the pond. The kingfisher, I, raucous and dashing. Owl am I, elusive but hooting. Hummingbirds darting from flower to flower, swallows soaring down to the nest, woodpeckers tap, tap, tapping, and grosbeaks congregating. Birds of every shape, color and personality, orioles, jays, tanagers, finches and robins, we are. And I, companion in both winter and summer, a small package of courage, the chickadee who comes again and again to the window each day to thank you for your gifts. Don't forget us. We live here too.

"Somewhere over the rainbow... somewhere there's a place for us."

And so do I live here too. I am the one who is telling this story. I'm in and I'm out, belong and beyond. I'm of this circle and of other circles too, the hub of my own pinwheel. From the circle of story-tellers I know how each of us exists in other dimensions, how each of us lives simultaneous lives as different characters. And in those other dimensions, we are both the same as and other than who we are in this dimension, on the land. We are the animals in Noah's Ark, surviving disasters, the neighbors in Winnie the Pooh, being our greedy, gloomy, playful selves in our various, fitting shelters, the friends of S'ster Rabbit escaping our myriad troubles.

We were the children of the blue ray, the daughters of the dog star, Sirius, the alien babies, sent here to heal the planet, sisters in a circle like the Pliedes, like the Irish circle of stones, strangers in a strange land, lost and afraid in a world we never made, stardust. We were the immigrant menaces with our foreign germs and mutant genes. Such were our dreams.

Old souls in new bodies, higher selves in lower incarnations, we faced earth changes, pole shifts, tribulations, walk-ins and ascensions. Between the abuses and the disasters, thanks to our spirit guides, our guardian angels, our dream mentors, we fulfilled the prophesies; the future became us. Soul mates, soul family, we rediscovered each other. Fractals in a hologram, we are reunited, separate pieces become one. Adopted by earth, we know we are not alone in the universe. Such are the messages.

There is Malka, the exiled princess, who kissed a frog which stayed a frog and did not turn into another princess. She was banished by her father because she would not acknowledge that all power flowed through him. She was sent into the wilderness with other outcasts and eccentrics. And there she made a world of her own, a world of harmony and equality, a realm which came eventually to rival her father's kingdom. Such was our vision.

There is the Pied Piper, Elijah without a place at the table, the lavender messenger, the radical teacher, the feminist outlaw. She played the flute which led the animals, the children, the other women into a new land. She is the genie in the closet who disappears as soon as she is recognized. She is the travel agent who sings the lullaby and chants the dirge which mark the borders between here and there. She guards the zones between life and death, she witnesses the comings and goings of our lives. She is the sentinel on the edge of life, the place where people disappear and emerge. She is not wife or mistress, but midwife. Such is our mission.

We fairies are like water molecules in the air, like dew evaporating or drizzle from clouds. We whirr through air like tiny motorcycles. We hold our shapes briefly by hovering over green grass, our wings sparkling in the light of a brilliant spring sun. Movement keeps us alive. This rhythm's not just a sign of life. It is life.

There are the natives of the land, the ones born in burrow or lodge, hollow or cave, nest or hive. We are the beaver's extended family. We are the mating dragonflies, head to foot, head to foot like floating, synchronized swimmers. We are the eagles who thought we were ducks, the ducks who knew we were swans, the snakes who knew we were healers, the spiders who knew where to build, the bats who knew where to hide and the wild iris, day lily and black-eyed susans who knew when to bloom. Such is our reality.

"This land is your land, this land is my land,
from the gulf stream waters to the redwood forests...
This land was made for you and me."

I am this land.

I know you tend to take me for granted, but I feel, since I was the first word, I'm entitled to have the last word. I'm this land you claim as your own and I am land you have not known. Beyond familiar curves of my thighs and breasts are dimensions uncharted. Deeper than womb-caves are unmapped sources. Beneath my surface are levels of ocean never to be explored and layers of depth never to be plumbed. Beyond my contours is energy untapped, unrecognized, my breath, tears, emotions, aura felt through wind, rain, comets, light and movement. In my veins, gems abound, rivers originate. Within my bones crystals mark change. At my core, fire creates daily miracles. What is molten shifts shapes. What is formed makes new worlds.

These lateral slices you make across my skin to mark property boundaries may scar me, but they cannot divide me. You think because you walk all over me that you can own me. You think that because your spirits soar toward the sky, that I am beneath you. Little do you know that most of the time, your heads hang down into the blue like babies just born; all that holds you to life is the gravity at my core, my invisible hands around your tiny ankles.

You feel you are aliens, sent from other stars to save me, but alienation is a state of your own minds, divided from themselves, from each other and from me. If only you could sink your hands into your own soil, plant the only seed you were given and nurture its unique shoot, the breath within you, then you would know all I have to teach you about comings and goings, stability and change, growth and transformation, timing and light, feeling and form, death and loss, fertility and resilience.

Your myths tell you that you've been banished from the garden of eden, the divine orchard, the perfect place. How can I convince you that those of you most marginal have been cast *into* the garden, invited *to* the wilderness, sent *into* the forest which is your real home? You're the chosen ones simply because of the choices you've made.

In truth you were not banished. In many ways you never left me. Whenever you bring spirit to this body and ground your spirit here, you recognize me as your home. I am not hell to a heaven someplace else. I myself--earthy, not filthy--am sacred. What sustains you grows out of me, what you suffer can be buried in me. I am the She who is the ground of We.

I know we're not alone in this universe. I know the complete spectrum beams many more than our seven colors and the whole hum sounds more than just eight notes. But before you abandon this luminous globe, remember our history, and listen to promises which wait within me to be born.

If you do, my cluster of friends, you'll know that what you're experiencing now is not just death pangs but also growth pains. Not just fire, flood, earthquake or drought, but also sprouting, rooting, budding. When you nestled in the seed pod together, you felt as one--warm, cozy and safe. But scattered out, busy sinking into the rich dark for nurture, reaching up for light, you bumped into each other, wrestled for space, groped for direction and, branching out, collided. All this common ground was forgotten as you discovered your own particular form, as you must to survive.

Don't worry. With ripeness comes the sweetest time, the deepest unity. Allowed to season fully, no one feels excluded. Allowed to grow, each finds her place here on this land, this earth. This much I hope. This dream I know.

20
FINALE

Slow, graceful, all parts ascending in one full gesture of departure, everything shifted at once.

I find it heartening that some of those lost people are just ahead, around the next bend. If there is any greater joy than the discovery of friendship, it is the rediscovery of friends.

For Carrie it's Ch'ien, a rush of creativity; for Beth, Kun, a quiet listening; for Abby, Lu, the excitement of exploration; for Ev, Kan, the risk of going into darkness; for Helene, Ken, meditative awareness; for Dulce, Sun, a gentle questioning; for Gail, Li, a soothing hand; for Faith, Tui, a joyful shout.

She was a love dog. Love was the food of her soul. She'd go through any hardship to give and receive it.

We fairies are like water molecules in the air. We hold our shapes briefly by hovering over green grass, our wings sparkling in the light of a brilliant spring sun.

In their own languages birds sing in cadences tuned to the tones of the spheres out of which they emerge, through which they fly. These are the letters that matter. The lines that count are the ones that connect.

When we came together, we had wonderful times, around the fire, on the shore of the lake, climbing the mountain, listening to the stream.

We resonate together even when apart, as a piano key sounded in one place causes a guitar string to vibrate in another.

Fruit

21

THE KEYS, FIRST AND LAST

The First Keys

The Dreamer Poems: PIVOT

I go to bed, my back out,
sore, cramped, twitching,
stiff as I toss fitfully.

In a strange city
on a cramped porch
we meet a crippled man
whose bed, a board,
is his back.

He croaks like static
words we can't grasp,
but in tones we can hear.
Is this an impediment
or does he speak from a distant star?

An ancient witch doctor,
instead of curing him,

cries out, "I must bury my own body,"
then starts to dig a grave.
The dreamer sees through earth
which already holds
the body of a young person
fetally curled
between death and life.

The first man, now walks
easy, blithe,
plays with a rope, shows the dreamer
how to find the pivot point,
how to swing free.

We ride a tram
high above ground,
each in a separate car
when he calls out,
"Now swing free!"

and we sail a great arc
above the whole earth,
as if leaping out
on a giant's rope,
up the South American coast,
across an ocean dotted with islands,
up our east coast,
awestruck by shining shores,
blue and white rolling
into brown and green.

Landing in a big city,
the dreamer shrinks at the toes of skyscrapers,
sad to be so small
and powerless again.

In her circle of people
she cries, "We all must've
landed together--
in New York City,"
and someone replies,

"We landed together,
but not all in New York,"
and she figures some landed
in Boston, Baltimore or Philly instead.

Each must have followed her own
momentum, found her own
pivot of balance,
though somehow we all
swung free together.

When I wake,
my back no longer hurts.

The Dreamer Poems: CROSSING BORDERS

Lost in a foreign city,
the dreamer sees her sister
blended into a rock wall.
Once so light, so agile,
now a butterfly mired in mortar.

She asks some youngsters
directions to the airport.
They point to a nursery
full of children
who seem pleased
to have her join them.
A plump, quiet caretaker
sits there, sewing.

Feeling constraint
in how the children move--
babies wiggling some
but older ones tied
into their bodies,
she offers to teach them how to fly
and, almost imperceptibly, they stir ,
but a woman in charge,
stiff gray suit, stern face
stuffy tone, says "No."

Caught imitating the dreamer's flight
the children turn it into a line
dance, showing her,
as the matron watches,
acceptable steps--
not too much bounce or lift--
twisting ankles
while the dreamer imitates them.

Suddenly "the American girl"
stuck there by accident
rushes out of the room and down

to the beach, exciting the children,
alarming the adults.
The dreamer is allowed to run after this girl.
A little boy with wild hair
and funny face tags along
down the steep steps to the beach,
even though the grown ups yell
at him to come back.

An official from the school
with a stricken face
trudges up the steps toward them.
Assuming the trapped girl
has drowned herself,
the dreamer sends the little boy back
to protect him from the horror.

Down at the beach, people
encircle the drowned girl,
now entwined with another girl,
both naked.
Did one try to rescue the other
from drowning
or did they both wash up together?

Suddenly the dreamer sees
one is her sister
and the other, her friend.
Growing out of their
apparently dead arms and legs
are roots, in long, messy tangles.
Shocked and grieved
the dreamer glances away.

The crowd gasps.
The dreamer looks back to see her sister
and friend standing up,
their arms covered with down.
As the dreamer stares,
their arms grow wisps
which stretch into fluffy brown sails.

Astonished she realizes
they're demonstrating
with gestures only
how roots turn to feathers
as they grow into wings.

The dreamer rushes back to the nursery,
knowing it's not too late
to teach the children how to fly.

The Dreamer Poems: DIMENSIONS

Hummingbird's caught inside.
Such amazing
shades of green blue.
Suddenly, without help,
she's free...
a hole in our screen.

"None of us speak the same
language," cries a friend.
"We'll never, ever
communicate."
Caught in her worry,
the dreamer senses how unique each
one's word is,
how resistant everyone is
to discussing
this problem unnerving her friend.

Suddenly herself flying
she notes how each sweep, turn
dive, glide, soar,
and somersault says
how she feels,
what she believes.
but when she tries to show others,
no one bothers--
everyone's too busy.

Riding by on a bike a young girl
says "hi." When the dreamer asks her
to give so-and-so a message,
she says "No,
I want to be innocent,"
and the dreamer laughs, hugs her,
says, "You're right
to say no."

An older boy asks her to read
a paper he's written
and after she says she likes it,
he disappears,
as if sucked down a drain,
into a hole in the ground.
Distressed, she stands firm,
waiting for him to emerge
and explain himself
until she realizes
this burrow
is **his** dimension,
his home.

Delighted with this insight
she rushes to reassure her friend,
"It's all right--
we're all in different
dimensions, simultaneously--
each one special."

"But we must be
with Christ,"
the friend replies tightly.

The dreamer blurts out,
"Jesus is just a screen.
He protects us
when we're scared,"
Caught by her friend's anxious face,
she quickly adds,
"Christ is everywhere--"
not just one dimension."

Suddenly she flies away,
free of worry,
a hole in the screen.

The Dreamer Poems: LETTING GO

"Denying my distress
over your disappearances,
you don't understand when I say
it feels you've fallen
off the face of the earth.
But when we come to a street
which drops off abruptly
like a cliff,
you step back in alarm.

"Next to us a woman speaks
about letting go
and suddenly starts sliding
down the grassy part of a hill
not as steep as the cliff,
gone with a swoosh and a giggle.
She glides over
the lawn into the street
under a truck's huge wheels
and together we see
how to fall
as we stand there in shock
until the truck stops
and she slides through unhurt."

But tough men
on the other side
mean the other woman harm,
so the dreamer and her friend
run down the hill
to save the one who fell.
But before they get there,
the men grab her
and one, still standing,
rapes her,
forcing himself into her.

Seizing a knife

the dreamer reaches him first
and stabs him in the back,
right behind the heart.
He staggers but doesn't fall
and sensing the danger she's in,
she pauses long enough to make sure
the woman and her friend escape--
then flees before
she can be arrested.

"No time to say goodbye
before I disappear.
I know now how it must
have been for you."

Back up the hill
she flies over a fence,
waves to a woman in the yard
amused by her flight.
Beyond the yard police
are after her.

Suddenly a door opens,
a woman pulls her inside.
A prison matron, she knows
prison's a good place to hide
where they'll never think
to look. Sympathetic
with the dreamer's plight,
the matron helps with her disguise--
heavy makeup, sexy hair
clothes of a streetwalker--
and the face
of the dreamer's earth drops off.

The prison's a train.
Riding with the dreamer
are two children,
one about ten, friendly, sweet,
the other much younger
who calls her "Mommy"

and slides down her knees
with a joke
about just coming out.
Hugging the young one, she sees how jealous
the older one is and she smiles at her
as the baby settles into her lap.

Outside they pass through slums
where a woman sleeps
in a crate with three men--
and our prison train feels safer.
We drift into a port city
past many huge ships--
southern California already?--
the dreamer glances in a mirror
and sees she's now Asian.
Will she start a new life
or live forever in disguise?
Will she reconnect
with her friends?
She's dropped off
the face of her life.

Still protective,
the prison matron
cleverly hides the dreamer,
sticks her head under blankets,
whenever officials come through.
But a big inspector
finally zeros in on her.

Now she feels like a man
disguised as a woman,
so to fool him
she cuts off a piece of her hair
holds it above and below her mouth
in precise imitation
of the inspector's own
mustache and beard
which he just admired
in the mirror--

and she talks exactly
as the inspector does,
like Chaplin mocking Hitler,
embarrassing him
so he hurries away.

Suddenly a little card
appears in her hand
saying, "And then a ripple
of laughter passed through the room,"
and she stops to see how much
other prisoners
enjoyed this action.

She knows now this story is over,
she must go out into the world
as herself, without disguise
or protection.
As she gazes out the window,
the matron whispers, "The private goodbye
was the hard one for me,
but I prefer the non-dead to the dead."

"Now," says the dreamer,
        "I understand why you
too had to leave."

The Dreamer Poems: MAGIC

When I sprinkle water,
a fairy appears
with a tiny butterfly
both of them fragile
and luminous--
but they shrivel up
when I stop sprinkling.

Running down a hill
the dreamer hears a voice saying
"And we never grew up--
we turned ourselves into fairies,"
while she turns a full flip,
hoping to land on her feet.
And she does.

We're parading
down the road
while she describes a musical
we'll all create--
After a first
enthusiastic flush
I hear a doubting
silence full of questions.

Then a gigantic woman
on my left picks me up
and holds me in the air,
declaring with a challenge,
"Who do you think you are?"

Calmly I respond,
"How long do you think
you can hold me up
like this?" Everyone laughs
and she laughs too. I shake
her hand and say, "Thanks."
But when she puts me down

my dream begins to shrivel.

The dreamer, her dipper high,
sprinkles us and we all rise.

The Last Keys: Land Poems

In the Woods

I meet a holy rock
set in a hollow
padded by ferns
under a large curving pine
in a circle of trees rainblack
waiting for winter's mourning,
transformation's freeze,

am startled by my impulse
to step on her,
sit on her.
Instead I speak with her,
noticing her grey textures,
brown stains, aqua lichen,
tuft of green-glow moss,
fur of pine needles,
wonderful wavy water lines,
earth creases and wind smooth
features above
a wry smile
between several distinctive
well-populated cracks,

place my hands
over her blind eyes
and ask for insight,
touch her silent mouth
and ask for wisdom,
cover her tired ears
and ask for solace.

Then I bow to her,
lean my face upon hers,
hoping for her solidity,
her endurance,
her view of the sky.

The View from the Top of the Mountain

is not what I expected:
gorgeous canyon vistas,
alpine panoramas,
all sides visible
from one fixed point,
the sharp edge.

No--this summit's round
like a head overgrown
with brush, but balding,
spotted with modest
clearings: a clump of rocks
where no trees grow,
a garnet ledge, the
bare space circling
a tall pine.

When I close my eyes,
light tilts into my dark space
like sun bowing into a cave
or the pulse of a finger.
Sitting here against the pine,
inhaling scents of needles
and sap, I receive warmth
and see nothing
but a bright slant of blue sky.

I am so full of peace
a dragonfly settles
on my knee.

The view from the summit
is not what I expected
but the view of the summit
is much more
as I rise with the dragonfly,
our wings of light
double above the mountain.

Nothing Doing

Out in a boat I row to the lake's center,
crawl into the bow, lean back to rest,
shoulders soft against the metal,
sun on my face, breeze through my hair,
while the boat drifts.

Across water on shore I hear hammering.
Beyond beaver dam, ducks cluck, paddle,
nibble at buoyant tidbits.
men tease each other,
voices vigorous with pride of action

while I do nothing, float, limp,
fluid, open, musing about other zones,
planes, dimensions, circles,
simultaneous spheres, past and future
intersecting each other at the same time,
imagining someone upside down from me
the other side of earth wandering down a river
or staring into an empty rice bowl
this same moment.

As water moves deliberately over the dam
and wind's will makes itself felt by leaves,
I flow beyond human drive, animal instinct, natural forces.

The sun dwindles, water chills,
I notice how far I've drifted,
consolidate my multiple zones,
compress my body toward rapid resolve,
hoping for shore before dark.

Light Knows

When they dip and glide
through setting sunlight,
the swallows seem to know
how luminous their wings become.

Butterflies dangling from the comfrey bush
as sun begins to rise
harvest radiance
like blossoms in their sails.

The firefly
flirting in the dark
understands his flickering light
beneath the falling stars.

The spider
weaving her web after a rain
recognizes the flash of prisms
from each bright strand.

I have no wings which catch the light,
no body which glows at night,
no shining silk I weave out of myself.

Only through witnessing
spider, firefly, butterfly, swallow
can I spy my own translucence.

Leaving the Land

Settled today in the current,
my chair at the point
where both streams meet,
beaver and trout,
muddy and clear,
still and rushing--
up the flowing curve beyond the merge
flew the heron
no more than ten feet over my head,
following the twist of the stream,
to cast her shadow across me,
landing on the crown of a dead beech
I called my enlightenment tree
to name a time the reality/ illusion
of stability/change
first struck me.

As she poised at the peak of the tree
(what's left of it now wind, bugs
and rot have collected their tariffs),
gazed into the distance,
her grey neck extended
with only a stationary stretch,
I saw her so clear --
tall as my heart, straight as my back, grey as my hair,
but her neck fluid as she lowered it down
into its nesting Z,
the rest of her still as a monk
as she mused at the top of the tree, mindful.
She stirred slightly at the splash
of dogs in water,
edged gently when I stood to watch her
didn't move until I turned to emulate her,
flexing my neck, tilting my elbows,
curling my feet in place.

Then, as if to mentor me,
she gathered her many awkward parts,

rose above the range of leaves,
slow, graceful, all parts ascending
in one full gesture of departure
everything shifting at once,
a bold unifying whoosh of flight,
arcing like the seasons over my head,
her grey body soft against the sky,
wings flaming
as she charted a future
I'd yet to imagine.

22
REFLECTIONS AND COMPLAINTS

Differences

Differences make friendships interesting. Even if we choose friends who are almost carbon copies of ourselves, which we may do if we're feeling particularly insecure, eventually the mirror image will cease to imitate our movements, will strike out on its own, lighting a cigarette to our horror, or maybe even sticking out its tongue. Variety, as they say, is the spice of life. Not just spice, actually, more like the substance.

Differences can be viewed both telescopically and microscopically. At a distance, differences can blur into categories we either identify with or judge, respect or reject. These categories become a kind of check-list by which we welcome the stranger or cast her out. Many such categories can be verified by eyesight (ethnicity, gender, clothes) or confirmed by a simple inquisition, the filling out of some bureaucratic form (age, income). Some of these can be fairly superficial, having little to do with friendship, while negotiating some other categories has a lot to do with friendship. They are hurdles we must face in order to meet on a deeper level.

Imagine watching a friend advancing toward us as if viewed through a long telescope. At each crease in the extended telescope, we see this person more clearly, more individually until finally she is face to face with us. The closer she gets, the less we're able to label, categorize, or sum her up. We know, as she steps through each of the rings which contribute to who she is, that they have helped make the difference between us, but they can't fully tell us who she is.

Viewed under a microscope, the mystery remains. Looking inside we can see all the facets, contradictions, complexities of this person; we can even examine in detail the changes she has undergone, is going through this very minute. But we can't begin to unravel the mystery of who she is. And despite understanding all this, we may have just as much trouble negotiating our differences with her in the real world as we ever did. Understanding someone does not seem to help that much when it comes to actually dealing with those differences. Isn't that the challenge?

Yet there is rarely a complete difference between two beings. If one perseveres, eventually there is always some common ground to share. Even when we are attracted primarily to the difference, which happens often when we're too young to know that what draws us can be a projection of our own unacknowledged selves--or, perhaps, when we're old enough to know ourselves so well that we welcome a change of scene--we will discover, at some point, if only temporarily, that we are in some respect similar. That, in fact, can be a turning point. We might realize that what we thought was only in the other is actually part of who we are, and our need for that person in our life suddenly drops away and we go on alone. Or we recognize that this particular person is much more than a screen for our hidden selves and we decide we still want to be friends with her.

What I wonder about in friendship or potential friendship, is what happens to make differences non-negotiable? Any difference, it seems, could be enriching in itself but not necessarily a basis for friendship. Unless of course we are completely narcissistic (and even then, from what I've observed, differences can be challenging: *how can I get this rather odd person to reflect me to me?*). If we knew the answer to this question, of course, we could maybe cure most of the world's ills. But only if we could negotiate all the differences based on money, status and power--a daunting task, given social, political and economic structures, and, some would claim, human nature.

But just on the level of friendship, such differences are instructive. As long as they are unrecognized, unspoken, they seem to be non-negotiable. It's not that someone has more money, power or status than I do which blocks our friendship: it's when he or she either fails to see how this makes a difference between us or when I fail to admit that it makes me jealous or angry or resentful. Usually the person in the privileged position has no reason, no experience of deprivation, to know what it might feel like not to be so privileged. Although some rich people have once been poor, guilt often prevents them from remembering what it felt like. Straight people who've been gay can be especially paranoid about closet doors creaking open. But very few men have ever been women or white folks have ever been black. And unless they can tap empathetically into some other experience of discrimination or oppression or exclusion, it's seems highly unlikely we can ever be deep friends with someone who is—except, perhaps, when we are very young or very old, cut off in a leveling way from the centers of power and privilege.

The middle years seem, in fact, the time when difference is most challenging. Looking back at friendships which have lasted many years, I suspect that in our younger days, we are so busy differentiating ourselves from the matrices we grew up in, the institutions we grew out of, that we welcome kindred spirits without much awareness of how varied we are. Especially in our youth when barriers between us were momentarily lowered, we embraced an amorphous diversity without fully realizing how rigid some of those boundaries had been and could be again.

Entering middle age, particularly in more conservative times, we realized the difficulties of diversity and tended to fall back into the familiar. Religious identities reemerged, class assumptions asserted themselves, racial bonding increased. Only in certain disadvantaged communities, like gay and lesbian enclaves, where everyone was still an outlaw, did diversity continue to be intimate. In the rest of the world, even in progressive communities, bonds across class, race, and gender lines, even in the deepest friendships, were strained.

I've worked hard to be aware of whatever in my identity is a structural barrier to friendship with others, first of all privileges which militate against equality, the necessary foundation for friendship. In some cases, when possible, I have even given up those privileges, sometimes finding myself on the other side, feeling the inhibitions of the deprived. In other cases I have fought to obtain the privileges, to free myself of the envy and resentment that blocked friendship. In other instances, of course, I had no choice: I am still white, I am still female. I am still hidden. But I haven't found these to be the major barriers in specific friendships. As our lives change, these walls shift, sometimes even shatter. Equality seems more like a see-saw than a fixed balance. The funniest things can shift the balance: one's health, one's luck, one's size, one's employment status.

The barriers which used to seem insurmountable to me are the ones rooted in personality, things like extroversion and introversion. While I enjoy the energy of my most extroverted friends, I can't help finding them shallow at times. While they appreciate my reflectiveness at times, I'm sure they find me too much of a loner, too secretive. Introverts, I hear, tend to regard extroverts as too self-centered whereas extroverts regard introverts as too self-absorbed.

But these things shift too. I have become more extroverted in my life; my outgoing friends have been forced by experience into more introversion. It's a matter of balance, for continued survival. As Jung observes, some men become more nurturing at midlife while some women become more active in the public realm; thinkers have to integrate their feelings, and intuitive types develop more sensory awareness. I like these changes; I like watching my friends finally incorporate their shadows--actually, it's a great relief, though tough going in the process. I like seeing them expand their repertoires, polish up their facets, grow to fullness (with or without gaining weight *or maybe both*).

The differences which are not negotiable are ones which don't allow for such changes. I don't mean that change should involve the elimination of differences. Quite the contrary. As we all age, we seem to become even more peculiar, idiosyncratic, unique. The differences gain shape, color, texture, solidity. This I love, even when I don't love some of the peculiarities. I love them because they are owned, acknowledged, sometimes even loved.

The lack of change which does not seem negotiable is the failure to acknowledge the differences, the refusal to look at them or to view them from other angles. I guess narcissism is the extreme example of this: an inability to view another as other, a determination to force them to deal within one's own frame, to play a part in one's fixed script. What this comes down to is an inability to recognize the difference in the other. Along with the tragic inability to appreciate that difference, and thus to celebrate difference itself.

This seems like a cliché. But that's really what I find non-negotiable about differences: my or another's refusal to recognize them. Whenever I make a judgment against another, I'm refusing to recognize our difference as a given, acceptable whether or not I like it. Whenever I feel caught up in another person's script, I feel invisible; I feel unrecognized for who I am, different and unique in my own terms.

Recognition doesn't mean I or you have to like those differences. Some differences in some of my closest friends still drive me nuts. But they're negotiable, and that has made, still makes, all the difference.

Caught in Between

Even worse than the situation where two friends become so enamored of each other that you feel left out is when two friends stop talking to each other. It's not that everyone you like has to like everyone else you like--we can't expect friends always to like friends. While negative connections within our intimate sphere can be irritating, they can also be instructive, sometimes even amusing. But when two of your friends have been close and then stop being close, it can be torture.

First you have to listen to their complaints about each other. Then, if you decide to put a stop to that, you can still hear the unspoken objections every time you say something complimentary, or even just descriptive, about the other, the low growls, the hurrumphs. You have to tip toe through the shattered trust which lies on the floor like fragments of glass. Even when you repeat something nice about the other which one said before the estrangement, you can be greeted with a sneer or a dismissive wave, which says, "That was before I found out what a --- she is."

You feel like a bird caught in a box, beating your wings against the walls. The trick is to keep your balance, not to favor one side against the other, to hold your loyalty to both. There is a constant temptation to set upon this conflict your own unresolved complaints against one or the other or both and let them ride along. But to do this is to risk perpetuating the conflict, even fixing it in cement, with no hope for resolution. It is also to risk being blamed for the whole mess once they work out their differences privately.

The greatest temptation, however, is to try to fix the situation, get them to resolve their differences before they are ready. While many fights do benefit from having a referee and many stalemates require a negotiator, be careful. Unless you're very skilled at these translations and not particularly invested in the outcome, you can make matters worse. If either one is going along with a settlement just to oblige you or to take care of your discomfort, the other will smell the insincerity and either hypocrisy will set the tone, or the whole thing will blow up again.

What I've discovered is that sometimes people just need more time to get over their anger, or to root around for deeper causes of distress, some of which may only be triggered by this conflict but need to be resolved within the person at a deeper level. To force immediate resolution may not allow for this process, may guarantee that it will erupt again, perhaps around the same issue with the same other person or perhaps around another issue with someone else, like you. Sitting with the ambivalence takes a lot of discipline and patience.

Recently, I've been experiencing a conflict between two friends which has dragged on so long that all my buttons have been pushed. First I empathized with the hurt of one who felt rejected by the other. Then I empathized with how the other felt rejected in turn. But then I got hooked into the parental indignation that the one was being so unreasonable. Then I flipped over into feeling how the other was scapegoating the first one. Each position was excruciating for me and the whole situation was agony.

I could see, however, that the others were not suffering as much as I was, who was listening to all sides. They were going about their business--with closed hearts, true, but nonetheless otherwise rather determined and peaceful about the inevitability of it all. I was the one who turned into a seething mess of disappointment, frustration and rage. I finally had to get out of there, bide my time.

It is, however, worth it to endure such times, which, however prolonged they seem, are only moments in the whole lifetime of these mutual connections. Because friendship is rarely simply one to one. It is part of a whole network of links which give us community, which sustain us multidimensionally. The layering of surprises and discoveries as well as securities and consolations which sustain us through the decades are possible only because some of our friends also care for other of our friends. And where there is caring, there is inevitably conflict. And where there is conflict, there is also the potential for growth.

And plenty of opportunity for worry.

Betrayal

The hardest thing about friendship is how much power friends have to hurt you. No matter how many times such a violation happens, often with the same people in the same ways, it hurts. In order to love, the heart has to be open. An open heart is vulnerable. Openness requires a kind of tenderness which is not necessary or useful in ordinary commerce. Given the callousness, competitiveness, scarcity dynamics, and self-aggrandizement which characterize our ordinary commerce, it's no wonder people get hurt.

What has hurt me the most have been two things: being left out and unfair judgment.

Being left out is probably the more understandable of these betrayals. After all, everyone can't be invited to everything all of the time. But I'm not sure that's why exclusion hurts. It's not even that I want to be everywhere or anywhere I am not wanted. The issue, it seems, is power. To exclude can feel very powerful, especially if one has suffered from the powerlessness of having been excluded. To invite one and exclude the other lets one assert her taste, that most powerful of faculties in a bourgeois society. But sometimes what is really motivating the exclusion is an avoidance of conflict. If two friends are not compatible, the easiest way to resolve one's tension (since often each represents some pole of inner tension) is to choose one over the other. Better to be the chooser than the chosen, because being the unchosen can be very painful. We've all had to make these hard decisions. To protect a certain group dynamic we leave out Uncle Bill who, we know from experience, will dominate the discussion, or our neighbor whose recent bitter divorce will skew the conversational balance.

Sometimes one is left out because for some unacknowledged reason she threatens the person leaving her out. She's too loud or too emotional or too popular or too pretty or too smart. To the person doing the leaving out the particular trait matters greatly but to the person left out it may not be apparent and whether it is a vice or a virtue is irrelevant. I have even been left out because I was too important to the person giving the party, so important that my presence might threaten some of the other less important, less secure guests. But this is either flattery or a setup, certainly not friendship--because it ignores the part of me which doesn't feel all that important.

I have some friends who specialize in exclusive relationships. They are constantly murmuring privately in front of others. They trade in secrets. They condescend to include you in their twosomes and threesomes. What I have discovered about them is that they are terrified of being left out, so scared that they have to block out what it might feel like to be on the outside looking in. And while they have their generous moments of opening the door and inviting you in, they are just as capable of turning you out again if you're not sufficiently grateful.

Often, I've discovered, to be left out is a blessing in disguise. To be an outsider is untold freedom. Sartre was right, hell sometimes is other people; compulsive relationship is the worst kind of prison. But no matter how much I enjoy being alone, I must say I'm still subject to a pang when I'm deliberately excluded. Or not so deliberately forgotten by someone who supposedly loves me. And no matter how much I love someone, it takes a real act of generosity--prying open my heart with a crowbar--to feel sympathetic joy for an event from which I have been excluded.

But as I said this pain feels less a betrayal than unfair judgment does. Whatever causes such exclusion is usually not malicious; it's weakness of some sort, or expediency, or simply insensitivity. And while it certainly can trigger self-judgment, feelings that I am unworthy or odious or not well-liked (no matter how realistic I am about the fact that who I am is not the issue at all), it does not set off the potential self-loathing and despair which unfair judgment can unleash.

Unfair judgment is a real trap, one usually set with a great deal of disguised anger or malice. Often it is a naked lie dressed up as straightforwardness. And while I understand that it can be projection, some despised aspect of self put onto another, I still find it hard to accept. One hopes that one's friends will put the best spin possible on their characterizations of us. We certainly don't expect them to throw mud on us, much less assassinate our character.

And since unfair judgment leaves one feeling so vulnerable it's difficult to confront. We all indulge in gossip, usually not malicious or deceitful, but sometimes callous or misinformed. And never in front of the person talked about. Slander by a stranger can be taken to court, but there is no court for the back-stabbing that can occur in friendships. It shouldn't come as surprise that even our best friends can be mean-spirited, but it does. Never mind that we ourselves are, far too often, mean-spirited, even deceitful. It just isn't fair when the knife comes from a trusted hand. It feels more like a direct blow to the heart. Especially when in the past we have been both just and generous with that person (although, obviously, not entirely or always, since the judgment usually has some shard of truth.)

It doesn't matter that what was said might be so far from the truth that other friends who hear it are not likely to believe it. It's not a question of paranoia really, though it certainly does set that off. It's not a question of exposure either. We know we're capable of being regretfully mean and petty.

But what if the slander describes something you couldn't in a million years imagine doing? What if you realize that all these years this so-called friend was secretly viewing you as so much worse than you are, obviously not seeing you in all your complexity? You might understand it if your weaker traits were viewed with some understanding or, perish the thought, compassion, but unfair judgment is like being pinned under a microscope and then labeled falsely. And while you know it reveals much more about the viewer than about the subject, it still hurts to be seen as something you are not.

This pain, however, can be a source of compassion and action. Having suffered the bites of exclusion and unfair judgment, one can refuse to perpetuate systems of racism, classism, sexism, homophobia, which cut people out and pin them into negative categories, all to the benefit of the people making those choices and judgments, never with a fair judgment of the individual thus pinned.

It's inevitable in friendship that we recognize each other's weaknesses and failings; it's quite another thing to bear false witness against one's neighbor. Maybe it's too much to ask that we love the stranger, that we open our doors to the homeless, that we forgive those who have hurt us, but the bottom line for any kind of human kindness is that we give each other the benefit of the doubt--even, I guess, when that other has falsely judged us.

Estrangement

One of the most disconcerting things about friendship is when friends turn into strangers. I've never known a friendship in which this hasn't happened, at least temporarily. And I've known many which haven't survived the transformation.

This is not to say that all my friends past are now strangers. At least I hope not. Sure, there are people I'd just as soon never encounter again, some I've forgotten, some who weren't really friends, some who never were friends and some who began and ended as strangers.

Friends who turn into strangers but never make the perilous journey back to friendship have fallen into a neutral zone, a kind of no one's land which is neither the heaven of friendship nor the hell of enmity--a limbo of stuckness, I guess. Past a certain point of negotiation these situations seem hopelessly irretrievable. Waiting for another life for redemption, perhaps. But you never know. Under different conditions (like a natural disaster, perhaps) or in another context (a shipwreck) they might become allies once more. One can only hope.

But in a more flexible pattern friends who remain friends are always slipping and sliding in and out of that category, the stranger. Sometimes several times a year, or a month, or in the case of new intimates, perhaps even several times a day. Estrangement, rather than hate, is probably the other side of love. While I'm not sure what this says about love (one reason I'm writing this tome might be to describe what I have experienced as love), alienation is definitely integral to every relationship, rearing its ugly head at every opportunity of frustration, conflict, betrayal and ego-challenge.

We are all disabled by our egos, or, as they say, "ego-challenged." That's the first reason friends turn into strangers. They simply aren't meeting our needs. We're disappointed in them. They're not the perfect mommies or daddies or siblings we never had. Their plans and processes do not meet our expectations. We construct them as dreamboats and then feel betrayed when they run aground or sail off in another direction, sometimes without us even on board, sometimes with someone else on board. Fearing our anger will destroy the friendship, we neatly and unconsciously project our anger upon them and then distance ourselves, thereby undermining the friendship, at least temporarily. This kind of experience is usually the first line of defense a friendship must survive. If one cannot or will not express disappointment or anger without blame or guilt, then chances are that's the end of that connection. One can spend many sad years performing such disconnections until she or he (or I) runs out of any friends at all or loses the energy to connect in the first place.

If this estrangement is chronic, it probably, as therapists will tell you, repeats a childhood pattern, the loop de loop of rejection or disappointment by which we ultimately hang ourselves if we don't stop to untie the knots. But hopefully at some point along the line we meet a worthy opponent, someone who won't let go until you fight it out, or will hang in there when you try to fight it out--and you break through to another dimension, one in which someone can hurt or offend or drive you bonkers and still be your friend. This is a place of grace in friendship and the beginning, I believe, of love. It doesn't always feel so good; in fact, until you establish rules of engagement, it can really can feel like torture.

Having experienced this, I expect nothing less from new friendships.

Which may be another reason those friendships can flounder. But I'm not sure I'd trust the relationship until I'd crossed over that line. I've watched with some curiosity relationships where that kind of opposition was not part of the connection, wondering how long they could last, like explorers traversing some very thin arctic ice. Some seem to go on for lifetimes, like in arranged marriages held together by the glue of routine and physical safety and a veneer of propriety. Since there is little or no communication between them, one never needs face the fact that the other doesn't have the slightest idea what one needs or wants or really feels. This may work for marriage but it rarely works for friendship.

The other reason friends turn into strangers usually occurs further into the relationship and is not so easily negotiated by a loosening of the ego. This is when we run into the shadow selves of our friends. Again, I've never known a real friendship where this hasn't happened. If we're lucky we can remember enough of our friend's story to look the stranger in the eye and recognize her or him: *Oh, this is the nun who locked her in the room in the third grade; oh, this is the jeering older brother, the abusive father, the crazy mother.* That's easier when we're all younger and still peeling away those family layers. In honest relationships, we can reply: "I'm not your mother..., father, sister, brother, son, daughter," etc." since what we're encountering in the friend is often the mirror image of their projections, if you know what I mean. Or if driven to the wall, we can shout, "You're not my mother!" and then in a moment of calmer reflection, point out to them, in a compassionate way how they may have introjected some negative figure from their past, and, having so recently suffered from it ourselves, we may be able to sympathize with how they must have suffered: "Wow, now I realize how you must have felt as a child!"

But this kind of consciousness-raising gets a lot trickier when we age and begin to discover that our shadow selves are in fact deeply integrated into the very fabric of who we are. A friend's mockery might not be just a distant echo of past hurts, it might be part of her perfectionistic, exacting nature, some of which has proven to be very useful for her, and, perhaps, for us. Another friend's procrastination might follows, as the night the day, from her loving, relational value system by which stopping to chat is more important than getting a job done. One friend's pattern of promises, promises, promises is part of her need to be liked and respected and cannot be separated from the fact that she is indeed a helpful, kind person. Another's irritating abstraction comes from the same core of insight which makes her brilliant.

Not that these recognitions are sources of estrangement, of course, but they can be, especially when they are not fully recognized by the friend herself. And they are not easy to point out in the course of a regular friendship, whose smooth flow often depends on a certain mutual tolerance. One can put up with a friend's habitual lateness until it comes down to missing your plane to Greece. *Oh, sure, she's greedy, it's because...blah, blah, blah,* until she decides she wants *your* lover. Yeah, she is kind of competitive--but not *with me?* Surely her frugality is a virtue until she's stingy with, or even cheats, *us.*

That's the problem. These negative sides are usually so ingrained they are habitual, more often than not unconscious, and they make no exceptions for us, no matter how deep the friendship. We, on the other hand, feel disappointed if someone runs roughshod over us, even though we've seen them do the same to others. These flaws seem petty enough or forgivable enough until they play themselves out on us.

Unlike old family specters, these traits are not so easily sympathized with. For one thing, they are often not self-destructive; they are serving our friends very well. Some of these traits protect the softer, more vulnerable sides of the person, the aspects we particularly love. If we're honest about it, we know the qualities which can drive us crazy are inseparable from those qualities which delight us. One friend is so spacey that her life is a constant dizzying route of distraction from distraction. It's hard to keep up with where she's been or why. But, on the other hand, she can be the most fun, the most spontaneous, the most here in the moment of any of my friends.

Again, these traits, even the negative ones, can be loveable, special facets of that unique person, until we run afoul of them and then it seems unbelievable that this person just cannot control herself or wrench herself into consciousness for our sake. "How could she...*at a time like this?* You'd think, *given how I'm feeling,* she could *for once in her life* stop this behavior." But of course she can't, it takes a major life shift, a cataclysm, for people to be aware of their behavior, much less change it, and sometimes I wonder if people ever do change or if we just adjust our consciousness to greater and greater degrees of acceptance, from zero tolerance to, at least, 180 degree tolerance. Some people soften more than change, perhaps, but often not soon enough for us to avoid their hard edges.

The hardest thing for me is to become myself a stranger to a friend. It's easier for me to work around my own anger and hurt than someone else's. Sometimes this happens because I have been obnoxious and I know it. That's the easiest to deal with. We can apologize, explain, promise never again and perhaps they will forgive us. Sometimes this happens because they've run afoul of one of our unconscious negative selves. We, of course, remain innocent. "I didn't do anything; what's with her?" But ultimately we have a choice either to opt for righteous indignation or go with empathy.

Sometimes when I'm stuck in this dilemma, I have one of my empathy dreams, find myself without conscious permission in the other person's position and then I can feel what they felt, aside from issues of blame or guilt.

This is almost always a point of personal growth as well as a leap forward in a relationship if I can express that empathy and the other can hear it. It leads indirectly, among other things, to some owning of one's own shadow and some necessary self-forgiveness.

The hardest kind of negotiation occurs around someone making you into an enemy for no good reason at all. For reasons of self-rejection or projection, I guess. Projections are just as likely to happen with strangers as with friends, via stereotyping or bleed-throughs, various overlays or deja vu's, but it's a danger with friends too. Suddenly with a friend, usually with little or no warning, you're not just a stranger but an enemy as well. When this happens, I find it doesn't help to try to deal directly, at least not right away. I prefer to walk away from behind the screen of that projection and let the person shadow-box for awhile. It's the kindest way not to make a fool of them in the process. And it's the safest way to keep yourself unscarred. Then you hope and pray they keep on going past the mirage or come to forgive you for whatever you haven't done or love you in spite of it all. And sometimes with the very best of friends, you can even point out later that who you are is not who they hated at all.

But don't count on them understanding that, and don't make or break a lasting friendship on just that recognition. Maybe what they're forgiving in you is not something you actually did, but chances are you have done other things just as bad they never even noticed. So it balances out.

To the Limits

One difference between friendship and romance is that in friendship one does not push another's limits, at least not intentionally. In romance higher expectations, demands, hopes for compatibility and generosity are inherent. Whereas they often lead to illusion and disillusion, disappointment and sometimes ever bitterness, they also push us into a deeper intimacy which, in turn, can transform us as well as the other into a fuller, more genuine, more honest or at least more humble person. Friendship, by its nature, is looser and less earth-shaking. One of the tests of friendship is one's ability to look the other way, to tolerate quirks, to forgive transgressions. And if we find ourselves unable to do this, we don't break up dramatically, we just fade away.

But over the long haul, even friendships push our limits and shove us to the margins of acceptance and endurance. The first wall we encounter in a friendship is usually the one of difference. We discover that because of her background or her experience (or lack of) or her mode of perception, she is simply incapable of understanding us or empathizing with us--and you can be sure she is, at the same time, realizing a comparable insight about us.

226

I've found that the best way to deal with these differences is to acknowledge them, analyze them together (unless, of course, one or both of us is allergic to analysis), point them out in practice, laugh about them and live with them. You're a neat freak, I'm a slob. You're outgoing, I'm a hermit. You're easy going, I've got a temper. The assumption, despite the teasing, jockeying for recognition, loaded language, is that differences are equal. Being an introvert is not objectively or inherently better or worse than being an extrovert; it just feels different.

This kind of difference, when negotiated well, can be an endless source of discussion and delightful sharing across the fence. It allows that looseness of connection which friendship thrives upon. Even when the labels shift (from astrological signs to learning styles), the conversation flourishes because it gives equal time to exploring who you are and who I am and who we are, face to face.

The harder kinds of limitation we have to deal with in friendship are the walls we run into when we're side to side or back to back. Side to side, we begin to spot parts of each other which are unknown to the person herself: the hidden parts, the false selves, the phony smiles. These are not so easily named and pulled out of the closets for closer scrutiny. I know my teeth get set on edge when I hear that syrupy tone in your voice or see you try to cover up your hurt or anger with that chuckle, and if I thought about it, which I try not to, I realize I have mannerisms you find just as counterfeit or camouflaged. It's hard to resist the impulse to grimace or groan or laugh when we know our friend's not being genuine. But experience has taught me that if I speak directly to what I perceive as real, you could deny it or withdraw from me.

Often it takes a greater intimacy and years and years of patience to dig around to the sources of our false selves, the subtle or not so subtle forms of abuse or neglect or control which produced these automatic defenses and pretenses. Unmasking them, I've discovered ruefully, doesn't get rid of them; it gets rid of the friend. The only hope of dismantling the false self is to affirm whatever glimpses we get of the authentic self beneath the mask, along with relating joyfully and appreciatively to the genuine aspects of the other which are revealed in our daily interactions.

And yet, even with the oldest of friends, false selves can persist. Sometimes it seems, although this may be grandiose, some false selves are even exacerbated by our presence, either because our friend has known us so long, she reverts to that mask when we appear because of our familiarity (just as we often revert to our childlike selves when we reenter our childhood homes or reconnect with our families). Or perhaps something in us is so threatening that the false self is essential to our interaction. Ironically, what might be most threatening is the fact that we know the self is false. Sometimes we just have to go along, albeit not cheerfully, with the pretense until it just drops away like old dead skin.

But the highest wall to climb, the most difficult limitation in a friendship, is not when the other person cannot see a false aspect of self, but when she is actively invested in denying her whole self. Usually this means she is refusing to integrate her shadow self or is identified only with her ideal self. The false self might be irritating and disappointing and never to be counted upon, but the ideal self, I've discovered, is really dangerous. Woe unto anyone who points out, like the child who observed that the emperor was naked, that this person is not 100% the loving, nurturing, sensitive, generous person she thinks she is, that in fact she can be mean, spiteful, grudging, and nasty at times, that she hurts others by her active hostility or by her passive withholding.

Often this ideal self never has a feeling which can't be rationalized, often by blaming or scapegoating somebody else (watch out). She's never unduly angry (only righteous), never envious or jealous (except when she's been victimized), never hates anybody, only pities them.

But those who are most successful at acting out of the ideal self--those good girls and boys whose very value originated at a very young age from their usefulness or their docility or their sensitivity--can hide their investment with humor, with humility, with playfulness and innocence which totally disguise the rigidity and judgmentalness behind their behavior. One must observe not how they talk but what they do.

And, in fact, it's usually as a result of something they've done which hurt or angered us, not once or twice but over and over, that we realize this limitation. When we try to express the hurt, they sympathize but never apologize; they console but never validate our anger. We often end up feeling, if we're prone to self-blame, that somehow what went wrong was our fault, even when the offense is objectively quite blatant. I used to resort to rage when treated like this, but then the blame was more easily laid on me. Now I pull back and guard my clarity with silence.

But that does not make anything better. It doesn't bring the other closer to wholeness and it certainly doesn't bring us closer together. This is the wall I find insurmountable. I can't climb it because it runs right through my friend. I can't kick it because that will hurt me.

This kind of wall is a wailing wall. All one can do is insert in one of its chinks a prayer and hope for a larger blessing that will show this friend that even though she can be a jerk, we all love her anyway. Show her the kindness she tries, not always successfully, to show others.

Time

Friendship, more than any other reality, convinces me that time is not linear. In our friends we see ourselves not only reflected in time, we see ourselves both coming and going, as we were when we were young and as we are now.

Once, many years ago, when I first ventured into a foreign country without parental protection or guidance, I was obsessed with time passing. I'd just graduated from college, moved permanently away from my family who were overseas. My grandmother had died the Christmas before, one person who'd held a stable home base for us and one source of unconditional love in my life. I was full of sadness. For a vacation I drove down to Mexico with two of my friends. From the back seat I could see the landscape receding in the rear view mirror, the Mexican desert stretching all the way back to the Rio Grande, as I watched my childhood disappear. In Arizona where my grandmother lived we'd played in desert much like this, the same desert, actually, despite the prickly border which cuts it into two countries.

Then at a certain point on our way down toward Mexico City and the pyramids (hurtling forward into our futures while sliding back to an ancient past), we were parallel with a train going the other way and could see our little yellow Chevy reflected in the windows of the train, leaping from window to window until our image was swallowed up by the solidity of the caboose, before we were liberated into thin air again.

Since that point I began to understand the view proposed by Stephen Hawking, that time is going forward and backward simultaneously. Like a flower, the seeds of time's beginnings are in its ending. They meet each other somewhere in the middle. While our lives move forward in their inexorable way toward whatever destiny our seeds and our luck have mapped for us, our minds are stretching back to bring everything with them, to remember, to connect, to include all we've ever known and loved. Much as we would like to drop the extra baggage of trauma, grief, disappointment or failure, that detritus too seems to stick to us like burrs. These sacks of sorrow we carry with us into our futures.

This makes me wonder about past lives, how much of them still adhere to who we are and who we choose as friends. The odd thing about past lives is that we don't actually remember having known these friends before, unless we're psychic or have particularly revealing dreams. I suppose if we did remember, we might drop right back into the same old self, and embrace the same old connection we had with them, which could really hobble the new self. But who's to say we don't do that anyway, perhaps even more compellingly because we don't remember? Still it's comforting to think that death might not be as decisive a dividing line as we think it is.

With some of my dearest and deepest friendships, it feels like we have known each other for many past lives, with many variations of role and relationship. Once four of us visited a woman psychic who "read" your past lives by describing what appeared on a kind of screen behind your head (or aura). She said they appeared as different films. I've forgotten most of mine now (how reliable memory is, even within one lifetime) but I could see how as a composite they added up to who I am in this life, personality wise. She talked about how I was abandoned by my family during the destruction of Atlantis (the same family I have now--a shocking revelation), I was ill-treated in a harem (fuel for my feminism), I was a barbarian (given to rape and plunder and carnage, apparently) and I was a saint (a female St. Francis type), I was an artist, and I was an Indian.

Of course aside from our own individual scripts, what fascinated us as a group was where our scripts overlapped, not necessarily in the same time frames: we had all either died or survived one of the many disasters in Atlantis, for instance; we'd all suffered the proverbial triangle, the unfaithful wife or boyish lover killed by the jealous husband, or the jealous husband killed by the illicit lovers. We weren't sure if this revealed the limits of the psychic's imagination or the limits of the human story. Wisely perhaps, this psychic did not identify us as other players in each person's script. So we weren't able to analyze whether we had been comrades in battle, enemies or allies, victims or violators, we could only speculate whether our roles in this life vis a vis each other were reversals or repeats. But clearly, even before these revelations, we all felt we had known each other before. Knowledge of detail, while available like water in a well, did not need to be raised to consciousness for us to recognize that.

This kind of recognition is true of most of the people described in this narrative. And yet, paradoxically, at the core of these friendships is a commitment to letting each other change. This permission, in fact, is at the heart of friendship. When a connection is driven by need for nurture, for sex, for love, for protection, then any change the other makes can be threatening. She or he will no longer be available to feed us, make love to us, speak for us, take care of us, for us to take care of, for us to feel sorry for, or whatever.

Some of my very best friends are former lovers. We have passed the test of true friendship by allowing each other to move away from that kind of tight intimacy into a looser and freer connection. Sex, I've heard and often felt, can be, among other things, the glue of a relationship. But if it holds, it must do so lightly, not like superglue but rubber cement, so the relationship can grow beyond that attachment without shattering. It's not hard to imagine this potential for detachment could have taken lifetimes of being in relation to each other as parents and children, husband and wives, murderers and victims, owners and slaves, bosses and workers.

What can be useful about past life symbology (aside from generating healing narratives) is the unraveling of compulsive connections which do not feel like genuine friendships. We've all had some bond with someone with whom we have nothing much in common. Sometimes this can make for fruitful exchange, but sometimes it can feel like an albatross around the neck. The blessing that can drop that load could be a past life memory: *Oh yes, this person nursed me during the Crimean War when I was dying of my wounds; she fell in love with me and I was so grateful for her tenderness that I am now ready to devote my life to her even though I'm already married with children and a career in jeopardy.* Such an enlightenment, rare though it may be, could perhaps free us from disaster by offering another method of showing one's gratitude, one which might be all the more welcome to her, who is also married with children and a career as a doctor on the line.

Sometimes the reappearance of old friends, even in this life, can be more disconcerting or boring than exciting. Have you ever gone to a reunion and discovered you have more in common with the person who was known then as the class nerd or clown or someone you hardly paid any attention to than with your 'best friend'.

Of course, not all friendship depends on having a lot in common. Sometimes the differences themselves make the exchange worthwhile. We may share much in perspective and values with such friends despite obvious differences in lifestyle, background, even culture. Are such attractions because we were friends in a past life? Or simply the lure of variety in this life?

What really puzzles me about time passing, however, is not whether we lived before but whether, and how, we survive death. Is there no memory because the self, or this self, is no longer viable? When we die do we merge completely back into the all-in-all or is it more like taking off one body of apparel and, eventually, putting on another?

Is this life the fullness of who we are? Aren't our friends precious because we'll probably never know them, as they are now, ever again? I am captivated by this mystery of past lives because our individual life spans seem so limited given the vast history and prehistory of our cosmos. I am enthralled even more by the preciousness of life. It is so fragile, so tenuous, so quickly gone. Yet the existence of each unique person, whether this means personality, little self or big Self, ego or soul, is such a miracle, such a blessing.

It does seem true, though, that the ego is probably the least unique of all these individual manifestations. All ego seems to be made out of much the same mold: rigid, self-centered, quick to envy, competition, and power-mongering. Some part of everyone I know is enveloped in this little nutcase.

It's great for survival, but not so great for relationships or for growth. It's not hard to imagine that this element is the hard core of matter which drops with the bones and sinks back into the embrace and teaching of mother earth while the spirit, the soul, that person of us, passes on into whatever is to come.

When I asked my friends what their perspective is about past lives, one said she wonders if they are simultaneous, layered not linear, like time itself might be. That makes sense to me. Just as we have reptilian brains, and carry in our bodies the whole history of evolution, so we are layers of lives upon lives, each level an adaptation to the context and time in which it takes shape and grows. The place of growth is the present moment, the critical place where we are right now.

But there are bleed-throughs. Seen with the laser eye of the spirit, we are multiple exposures, one variation superimposed upon another, synchronized layers reflected in the manifold facets of our friends. Sometimes, perhaps, more than one layer is tapped into and a new synthesis or a new conflict emerges. No wonder our present lives are so complex. No wonder friendships are so challenging.

Some friends just fade away, without the cutting line of death. They've moved on, we still remember them, but we are no longer actively connecting. We've lost touch, the last address is a dead end for mail, the phone number is answered by a stranger. Or they've stayed put and we've moved on, into realms no longer communicable to someone whose life has seemed so stable, so seemingly ordinary. Or, since no one's life is really ordinary, the shell of convention around them is so secured that there's no way we, caught in our own orbits, can crack it. Or maybe we just don't have the energy to try. Or we simply drift apart and get caught up in something so extraordinary that the most we can do is immerse ourselves in it, never mind write a letter. As a result that old friend disappears with the passage of time as we swing out in diverging orbits.

But lately life has been tossing me some surprises. Old friends have been turning up, as if, in fact, they'd been there all along, in some other dimension, just waiting to pop out and start chatting again. A name tag at a party on a familiar but much older face prompted one such reunion. A name on an envelope at work, addressed to a co-worker, inspired me to write and reconnect to a dear friend who'd moved away south, entered a new life, and seemed lost forever. A chance encounter at a conference between two old friends provided my phone number and led to another meeting with one I hadn't seen for at least a decade.

Sometimes these loops of time are just crossings of paths, never (*never say never*) it would seem to cross again, but sometimes they make a whole, a remembrance, a meeting of the minds which makes me realize this is a friend for life, not was a friend once. The name tag led only to a sharing of old photos, memories of a time together not to be recaptured. But the envelope led to a deeper encounter, a visit, a sharing as lively and looser than any that had gone before. And the conference convergence yielded a conversation that seemed like a time lapse it was so natural, easy and trusting.

My life has been so mobile, has crossed so many borders, never to return, that I have been under the illusion that nothing is ever the same, and in most ways, it's not. It's true that "you can't go home again." Home itself changes. And so do friends. So much so that the postmodern or Buddhist objection to the "self" seems to be true: peeled away like the layers of an onion, there is no self, only personas, personalities, clusters of socialized attitudes or networks of neurons. And when we die we'll probably discover that what we called our unique selves were simply containers for a larger energy or spirit, vessels shaped by the conditions of body and society and environment into which we were born. Chances are more than likely that we are each different containers for the same spirit.

But in the meantime, living in this world of constant change, I take delight in the fact that despite all the differences and all their changes, I can recognize a friend when time loops back and allows us to commune once more. I know this person, and this person is unique-- I have never met anyone quite like her or him since --and since I too am I unique, so is our connection. We are each in some way as irreplaceable as precious gems and as solid, despite the evanescence of our lives. Something recognizable abides at the core, even, perhaps, across death, into other lives. We can know each other that way even when we don't know how we know.

Hawking's view of time as simultaneously moving forward and backward has been criticized, I understand, for the implication that, in fact, time is standing still. I don't know enough about physics or metaphysics to debate the issue, but I can imagine in a curved universe, time could go both ways and meet in the middle.

What if all this were true? On one level aren't we moving forward, playing out our plots in linear time, caught on a certain historical trail, victims of progress we can't control? On another level we are flowing backward, remembering, reconnecting, reconstructing our lives as we go. And at some deep fluid core of unique identity (let's not call it "self") we are standing still and letting it all happen around us like swirling ethers.

But all this speculation leaves me feeling like a spectator at a tennis match, when in fact what time's changes feel like from the inside is how my life is like a sphere, both growing and curling back into itself at the same time.

When mine was a baby sphere, my growth seemed so phenomenal, so rapid, I could hardly keep up with it. My life filled up, a seed blessed by sunlight and raindrops. The fuller I grew, the more time seemed to slow down, the more fixed my identity became in design, function, destiny. Like a sunflower, at my peak it seemed as if I would stay full forever. Now I'm beginning to droop a bit, losing only seeds which birds have taken from me. Eventually, I assume, my decline will feel as rapid and as inevitable as my rising and flowering did. Perhaps. I wish I could remember where both ends met in the middle. For such remembering, I need my friends. And a place where together we can receive whatever comes to us from the outsides of our shared context, all we all are gifted with daily in this beautiful world of ours.

However we emerge and dissolve, we live on the edges of a revolving globe of earth inside an expanding universe within a network of tenuous lines which connect us, friend and foe alike, with every other being, self or other, human or animal, whether we like it or not. Given that each one's experience of this network is unique to some extent, and given how we're each subject to a complexity of competing forces, it seems a miracle that friendship endures at all. We never know, despite heroic efforts, when someone will disappear. We just know that inevitably they will. And so will we.

But in this slightly deflated, rounding the midlife pinnacle, over the hill, perhaps, time of my life, I find it heartening that some of these lost people are just ahead, around the next bend. Because if there is any greater joy than the discovery of friendship, it is the recovery of friendship.

In this experience alone time herself can be fulfilled.

23

OTHERS OF US

Before venturing any further in recounting the past, let us pause a moment to reflect upon one of the central patterns within the fabric of friendship-- judgment. Lovers we dare not judge. Friends are another matter altogether. We are always judging our friends, maybe not with the same degrees of sympathy and loathing with which we judge ourselves, but certainly with the same range of feelings: admiration, scorn, justifying, condemning, excusing, accusing, forgiving, congratulating, reviling, defending, and so on. And when we're not judging in terms of value, we're comparing: *she's more outgoing than I am, he's more selfish than she is,* and so on and on and on. Sometimes I wonder if you took judgment and comparison away whether there would be anything left to talk about between two people.

What's interesting is what happens to judgment and comparison when, in fact, it is within an *I and You* situation rather than as *She/He/They.* Have you noticed how your judgments soften face to face with the person you're judging, how suddenly, unless you're very angry, what you felt as a judgment becomes merely an observation, couched in flattery, pillowed with affection. Everything changes: tone, words, even intent.

I know of a holy man who decided never to talk *about* people, only to them. I wonder how it worked out. He must have been silent much of the time. I, for one, think gossip is invaluable. It can lead to compassion as well as to judgment, it can provide that crucial piece of information which can turn a negative judgment into understanding: *"The reason she's acting weird is because her lover just left her for someone else."* I can't imagine never talking about people, but his decision really raised my consciousness about *how* I talk about people. I try at least to understand now, to give them the benefit of the doubt.

What strikes me as funny is how we revere judgment. Teachers who are judgmental are often the most respected. Their judgments, however damaging to individual students, are considered to have the authority of "truth." Yet, in truth, there is rarely anything more subjective than people's judgments. Invariably, the harshest of judgments reveal one's hidden deprivations, deepest wounds, greatest lacks. Yet no matter how much we know about projection and dismissal, we still regard judgment itself as the sharp edge of truth. Perhaps our regard for it is born of fear. Judgment in our society is what creates the hierarchies we live in; a judgment when believed, especially if supported by a prejudice, can knock us off one precarious rung onto a lower one, can keep us down no matter how hard we try to stand up.

What gives judgment the sound of authority, even though it actually undermines its reliability, is the fact that judgment stands apart, separate from, apparently detached. "Oh would the power the gift he gi' us, to see ourselves as others see us," as Robbie Burns puts it.

Of course, as I stand apart here, pontificating about Judgment, I am uncomfortably aware of the fact that all I am doing so far is talking ABOUT other people. Am I, in fact, just indirectly talking about myself?

I'd like to explore that issue right now by describing a group of other land friends I've lived with. I'd like to check out my hypothesis that our harshest judgments often flow from unresolved issues, particularly hurt and anger. I've noticed over and over how quickly our judgments about others just melt away once we have cleared up some difficulty between us, once we have found some expression for our grievances. Blame is often the cutting edge of judgment and when the reasons for blame can be understood and resolved, the judgment itself often becomes irrelevant.

So I'd like to talk about these eleven persons I've actually lived with, just to see whether, in fact, there are hidden resentments on my part, or subtle projections, or unresolved issues I still need to deal with. Consciously I am not aware of any such subjective distortions. You be the judge.

(While I haven't asked their permission to tell you about their lives, I'm sure they won't mind. They're admirably detached from all those issues of privacy and shame most of us worry about. I will, however, protect their identities by using only their pet names.) What I plan to do here is just give you a series of quick portraits. Don't worry about remembering who is who. If that information is important, I'll give you a fuller picture later in this story.

In the order in which I have known them:

Radhi: She is beautiful, smart, courageous, quick and lively. She's a good mother and a good provider. At least she was smart until she had a bad accident which left her with a broken jaw and a huge lump on her head. She has fully recovered, but some of her friends whisper that she seems a bit addled now. True, the accident did nothing to relieve her major neurosis, an eating disorder. Even though she has always been slender, she goes nuts for any kind of protein or dairy. When you live with her, you find her in your face whenever you open the refrigerator door. Now that she's older, she's almost gaunt in appearance, but her hunger is palpable. And she's still quite clever in her ability to get what she needs. She's also a bit hyperactive. (Here I'm afraid my judgment is clouded by the judgment of others.) When I first met her, I found her energy attractive. But her nervousness is not soothing. She's affectionate, but rarely can sit still long enough to be cuddly. I think her desperation stems from her traumatic separation from her mother and siblings at a too-young age. She was passed around a bit before she found a home. I love Radhi; she carries some of my most precious projections, but just as I know I can be hard to live with, I knew she can be too. It's sad now because she's been such a joy to me, and I want to give her respect as she ages.

Chi: Where Radhi is hyper, Chi is phlegmatic (*Note*: comparing). He's remarkably affectionate, but some people regard him as a bit of a wimp because he lacks ambition and is such a homebody. He may go out for a walk sometimes, but he's certainly not a hiker or even an outdoors kind of person. He's more like Ferdinand who preferred to smell the flowers to being a big, bad bull. Although I know nothing about his early life--he's quite a talker, but has revealed little about his past--I do know that he may have reason for not venturing out that much. When I first met him, he had a gash in his leg which took some time to heal, and I'm pretty sure from what I observed that it had been inflicted upon him by a hostile presence. In any case, it has not made him into a fighter himself; he'll go out of his way to avoid conflict. But he genuinely likes all kinds of people, and gets along with just about everyone.

Flame: Flame, on the other hand, has only one real love in her life--Chi. While she ignores just about everyone else, except her mother, Radhi, whom she treats with respect, she dotes on Chi. Flame in her day has been compared to Elizabeth Taylor: dainty and pretty as a young one, she ballooned to humongous proportions as she grew up. Even though she has slimmed down in middle age, she is still quite hefty, a far cry from the white socked pre-teen with her high, sweet voice. For all her ponderous heaviness, Flame has an adventurous streak and likes to explore, on her own, new territory, when she's not busy lying around in the sun.

Obsi: In his younger days, Obsi was a bit of a rogue, apparently. Although he was raised in a loving family, his single mother worked nights in a hospital and Obsi was left to the whims of the older teenagers in the family, and often left alone. He was known to escape the confines of home and yard, parading his freedom to the consternation of his peers who remained "under protection." But his loose and wandering ways eventually got him into trouble, and when I first met him, he was suffering multiple injuries from a car accident. The doctor wasn't sure he'd be able to walk again. I called him my "lame prince" because he so rarely complained about his pain, and he was so gallant in his efforts to become mobile again. Now you'd never know he had been so crippled; only a slight bounce to his walk signals the compensations he made to walk again. I'm not sure if Obsi was as affectionate and trusting before his accident as he is now, but unless you interfere with his eating habits (while he doesn't seem to have an eating disorder, he is neurotic about food, perhaps as a result of having been the baby of the family, teased too much around mealtimes), you couldn't have a more loyal and devoted friend.

Mukti: Another freedom lover, Mukti has a reputation for squirming out of any circumstance not to her liking and for choosing conditions which suit her better. She is remarkably intelligent and can size up a situation almost before you know what's happening. She's quite courageous and will risk any amount of discomfort to get what she feels she needs. She is also quite affectionate, but in a detached sort of way, as if she learned early that excessive devotion could be painful. When she likes someone, she can be demonstrative, and when she doesn't like someone, she may express some irritation, but usually she just disappears. She is fond of Obsi and they have been companions for some time now. But while she has enjoyed sex in her day, marriage is not to her liking, and she seems as content with female company as with male. With more schooling, she might have been quite accomplished, but she has seemed content enough with her own talents for exploration.

Guppie: One of Mukti's dearest friends is her step-sister, Guppie, who is quite a character in her own right. Large, boisterous and awkward in company, Guppie longs to be small and cute. She'd climb right into anybody's lap who would let her. She's strikingly handsome and a terrific athlete. She is as at home in nature as anyone could hope to be, jogging down the road, climbing mountains, plunging into cold mountain streams. She's devoted to a fault, falling in love with the most unlikely candidates and persevering in her affections despite the obstacles. Some of us have concluded that Guppie's problems can all be attributed to the fact that she's an ACOA (Adult Child of an Alcoholic). Instead of looking with you at the rest of the world, she tends to keep looking at you for reassurance. She can never get enough. Mukti, of course, suffered from the same condition, but she was adopted when she was more mature, and she had enough sense to get out earlier, to make a life for herself with Obsi. Guppie, instead, remained pulled between the old and the new, running back and forth between family members, trying to make everybody happy so she can be happy. She's actually very nurturing and is always taking care of some new waif, some of whom have actually followed her into our community.

Riddle: One such waif, but not one brought by Guppie, is Riddle, who showed up on our front porch in the middle of a thunder storm. He had been living on the city streets with his mother who could no longer care for him, so she apparently urged him to find shelter with us. Later I heard that he was completely wild and unapproachable, but that night when I saw him, drenched and bedraggled on my doorstep, I invited him in, and he came quite willingly. Despite his obvious need, he has never been overly dependent. He has always been the polite guest, resourceful and independent, well-trained by his mother in survival skills, and suspicious of but not hostile toward strangers. He can be affectionate but he is not overly demonstrative. The only other person besides his mother to ignite his passion has been Peche, who I found out later bore some resemblance to his twin sisters who wound up on another doorstep.

Peche: Peche was another waif delivered to us in a storm, by Guppie, an infant whom we weren't sure would survive. We fed her baby formula from a tiny bottle and carried her in pouches next to our hearts until she grew big enough to crawl around on her own. Three of us took turns nursing and holding her, watching her every move. As a result she is very trusting, very affectionate, and very spoiled. Oddly enough the only other person her age whom she trusts is Riddle, who batted her around terribly when she was a baby. Since she was the one who came after him, he was jealous of her, just as she was jealous of Thai, the next one after her. But as often happens with siblings, abuse turns to admiration and fascination, and Riddle soon became quite fond of Peche. They had great fun playing together, and although they have outgrown that stage, they still hang out together sometimes. Riddle is the only other young one Peche will tolerate. A teenager now, Peche is fluctuating between home and the outside world. For days at a time she will be completely absent, and then suddenly she'll be lying around home as if she'd never been gone.

Vincent: The real loner in this bunch is Vincent, who is both shy and independent. Caught between two generations, he is wary of the older ones and awkward with the younger ones. While he would like to play with the children, he seems hesitant to relinquish his hermit status for any length of time, which results in everyone treating him as kind of a stranger. He is quite resourceful at taking care of himself and only drops by for a meal now and then. He can actually be quite playful and affectionate, but tends to be somewhat disdainful of commitment or engagement. I know nothing of his early history, only that he was abandoned at a certain point in his young life.

Thai: Another relative stranger was Thai who showed up almost full-grown, decided he liked what he saw and stayed. He was another friend of Guppie's. Unlike Vincent, who flees from the resentment of others, Thai seems supremely self-confident, plopping down in the middle of our lives without a doubt that we would enjoy his handsome and easy-going presence. Like Obsi, he has a bit of a limp, from some previous accident, yet does not seem to be hampered by it; it gives a sprightly jaunt to his walk. Although we saw him as quite peaceful--unflappable--at first, we came to see that he has a combative side. We called him "Thai" which means peace, but found out later his original name was Tiger. As the newcomer, he tends to pick on Vincent whom he saw as an intruder (even though in fact, Vincent was a longtime resident and Thai himself was the intruder); and as Peche's "replacement" he has had to defend himself from her frequent complaints. But on the other hand, he has protected and befriended the very newest of the gang, Cassie, another of Guppie's waif friends.

Cassie: Cassie was young, thin and pitiful when she arrived, but so pretty and good-natured, it was hard to turn her away, even though everyone else tended to resent another mouth to feed. It wasn't long before we all fell in love with her, to the total disgust of Peche, so recently the recipient of the same nurturing energy. But where Peche grew up with an abundance of caring, Cassie survived with less admiration, and is content with less. While she knows how to take care of herself in the food department, she is smart enough to take a backseat to the demands of others, to wait for her turn, and to shy away from everyone else's favorite chairs. And she keeps us all entertained by her games; everything is a plaything; everyone, a potential playmate.

As you may have guessed by now, these eleven persons I have just described are not only friends. They are animal friends. And while it may seem respectful at first to refer to them as if they were human, what I realize in the process of doing this is how these descriptions make them vulnerable to the barrage of judgments we subject our human friends to, most of which are self-referential: the degrees of affection we feel for them and how difficult it is to train them to do what we want them to do.

And these descriptions also block out what makes these particular friends special as cats and dogs. Boxed into the strictly human realm, I couldn't tell you about Obsi's airplane ears or Cassie's motorboat purr, I couldn't share with you some distinctions which they might consider important (other than gender) such as which are dogs and which are cats, nor could I share some other distinctions which they could probably care less about, such as color and pattern, important as those are. And being human I can't communicate in their language other distinctions which must be crucial, like texture and smell (other than the "doggy" odor some folks find odious). Some of the most impressive detail about species and individuals gets eliminated by this comparison with humans.

Radhi, for instance, is a renowned hunter whose range has been reduced by her advancing age to the kitchen and dining areas. Her wildness is deemed unacceptable behavior only because it is played out in this domestic context. Much as I dislike her flying after a bird in the woods, I am even less enamored of her hurtling across the counter to grab a chicken wing out of my grasp. And Flame, the Elizabeth Taylor of the cat world, is only a year younger than her mother (Imagine getting pregnant at the age of five).

Obsi and Mukti are both dogs, as is Guppie, of course. Obsi is seven years older than Mukti, so she has kept him younger, while he has provided some much needed stability in her life. Although many people think they look like siblings, his tail is like a fountain while hers is a plume, his ears are fox-like, while hers are spaniel. Both are of uncertain age and parentage; both are mutts; both are strays; both are black. Obsi used to jump over the back fence in his city home and roam the back alleys until he was struck by a car and almost sent off to be put to sleep before I came along to rescue him. Mukti was tied to the back of a pickup truck at a country diner before she escaped and wandered down the road until she found us. All we knew about her past was that she had a passion for girls and chocolate, and distrusted men, which suggested to me that her first love was a little girl who fed her chocolate and whose father, for whatever reasons and by whatever methods, got rid of Mukti against her will.

It's their stories that make them special. How Guppie, the rescuer, brought Peche in her mouth to us, a little ball of wet fur we couldn't quite identify since her ears were down toward her mouth and her eyes were so big; only her purr revealed she might be a kitten. . As it turned out, Peche was the only one in her litter who survived. The other kittens starved to death after the mother was hit and killed by a car. How Mukti was attacked by pit bulls, how Flame got lost on Long Island for three days (after jumping out of the hot car at a rest stop, before we began to believe in cat carriers), how Guppie hung around outside the shack all year, even through the cold of winter, without being fed, just to be with her true love, Abby, how Thai and Cassie both followed Guppie a mile down the road to discover our kitty haven.

But I won't go on. These friends are probably too many for you to keep straight. Even if you are an animal lover, you don't necessarily love *these* animals. You might instead be ready to tell us about your animal friends.

Instead, let's turn back to the issue of judgment. Clearly my brief descriptions were loaded with judgments, and many of those judgments were self-centered. So how much of what I said about these friends was purely subjective, simply projection? Since there's no way you can answer that, and no way I will, without a whole lot of prompting and soul-searching, let's flip the question and ask the animals themselves.

How do you imagine they would describe each other? What do they really think of each of us? No doubt their individual descriptions would be just as subjective as mine are, but nonetheless potentially insightful. As for judgment, well, if one more waif wanders down our dirt road, we'll have a full dozen, enough for a jury. On the issue of human nature, what would their verdict be? Possibly kinder than ours is.

24

THE STORYTELLER

Well, I guess it's been up to me to get this story going. *Why?* Am I the only one who remembers, who cares, who wants to tell, who chooses what to tell? Or am I just trying to evoke that law of synergy which arises when the "I" asserts herself? Must the "We" then respond?

Surely I'm not the only ego in this collection of egos who needs to speak out. The only pearl who wants this oyster to open, who's willing to risk being cast before…if not swine, then certainly an indifferent, saturated audience.

No one else, so far anyway, has spoken up. So I'll go first, but hopefully not last. I don't want to be the only one keeping the lamp lights burning.

So, who am I that I should be the first one to speak?

I 'd like to be able to announce that I was appointed Storyteller by the "tribe" on the basis of my commitment, objectivity, and eloquence, but such a sinecure I can claim only in my imagination. Indeed, my previous attempt to tell our story elicited a few squeaks, then silence. Besides, we're not a tribe, not even a clan, just a small pool of friends. So, let me make it clear, right away, that although my memories are limited and my selections suspect, I'm not just a blabbermouth My spirit guide, my muse, my astrologer all assure me I'm meant to start telling this story and let it grow from here. *So here goes.*

As for me, personally, I've wanted to tell you about Dulce perched high on a mesa overlooking mountain and desert, planning how she'd travel further than the farthest horizon, around the world itself. About Beth climbing mountains like a goat and jumping out of windows to freedom. About Carrie meandering through the messes and meanings of it all, in and around trees, animals and people. About Faith in the gardens of her life, planting, weeding, harvesting. About Gail shaping sand, clay and metal while researching mushrooms. About Abby exploring the wilderness, escaping from prison. About Helene at the springs, lost and found, losing and finding. About Evonne on many shores dreaming of golden eggs nesting in favorite places on the land. About our friends, the trees, from whom we learned about roots and flexibility, and our cousins, the animals whose four toned paths we followed as they flowed through the woods.

I also wonder. With all our processing and consciousness-raising, have we, between us, achieved our ideal of love? Did we share fairly enough, with liberty and justice for all? How did living on the land change us? Could this remembrance serve to reconnect us?

So, how can a storyteller tell our story without revealing our secrets? Must I speak in code? For me to tell who we are, I'd probably have to reveal who I am. I'd rather remain anonymous. For self protection, of course, from the us, as well as the you, *dear reader.*

In telling the story of our lives, it is difficult to avoid what one writer friend of mine described as "exposing and exploiting" one's family and friends. I've often wondered how writers manage to keep their friends after they've described them in fiction or with a "bold honesty" in memoirs. I imagine writers must be a lonely lot, not just because they have to be alone to write. Sometimes after reading contemporary novels I cringe at what the author's friends must feel when they read them. Is our need for recognition so starved that we accept shame as fame? Is there some relief when secrets are told? *Now they know...* How does the writer, then, manage to keep her own nose clean?

One's own life is never a clear and separate strand; it is intrinsically tangled up with the lives of others. No one is an island, entire of herself, and so on. It is, in fact, how much we are a part of each other that fascinates me. Much of who I am now is a result of who I have chosen as my friends, and if some psychics are right, who I chose to be my family (or *whom*, as my mother might remind me). *The who, who, who of owls in moonlight.*

None the less, when it comes to exposure and exploitation, it is of course easier to focus on the others than on oneself. The view in a mirror is almost always one-sided while our angles on our friends are multiple. Odd isn't it? We feel ourselves in multiple ways but see ourselves in fixed ways; we see others in multiple ways but feel them in fixed ways. We can see others from the back, from both sides, from above or below, when they are sleeping or drunk or otherwise unable to see themselves; we can even see through them, or so we think. The judging mind, the comparing mind assesses a variety of friends as we carve out our own self-identities. The compassionate, empathetic heart chooses a few to love, though solitude and company, thick and thin.

Sure, we can avoid our constant dialogue between the self-flattering ego and the self-deflating critic by focusing on the talents and foibles of others. But what happens when we describe ourselves in fixed ways? How does this make us feel? Do we still feel a need to defend or explain ourselves even as we are loosening our attachments to these particular, limited personalities we've lent life to?

So what's the fair and honest thing to do if we wish to tell an authentic story? One can, of course, lie. Biographies are full of them; as our lives are full of self-deception. But if one is telling one's story as a way of getting at the truth of it, then lying is, at the very least, somewhat self-defeating.

That's where fiction comes in. Invention can be a duck blind behind which we can take as many potshots as we wish. On the other hand imagining stories may be the only means we have for discovering, revealing, and shaping truths.

Many years ago a friend of mine wrote a fascinating novel, quite inventive, with a mythic connection to "reality" as we know it. Years after it was finished the book turned out to be a map to memories of a childhood abuse which had been totally buried. It routed the psychic territory she then had to travel by more painful means to bring it all to consciousness and to healing.

What about fiction not individually referential? How about using imagined stories to protect our friends? Can we play with story itself to explore deeper truths than surface facts? Is that my hope in spinning these tales?

Once I start telling you about my friends, I realize I'm speaking with you as if you are, in fact, friends. Then I notice that some of you are, indeed, already my friends--and some of you are the very friends I am talking about as well as to. That's where this fictive narrative gets tricky. That's when this storyteller must become very careful.

*   *   *   *

This story is my feeble defense against loss. It takes only one death for us to know too many people have died. We are both many and one. Feeling our unity and our separateness at the same time can be revitalizing

I know that time is running out on us, even as we run from it. As we review and renew our lives, death keeps calling. Close, far, horizon and heart, here now, gone tomorrow are constantly shifting. One moment we're wondering where we're going, the next day we discover we're heading the other way. Is this what Stephen Hawking means when he says time goes both ways at once? Does the Phoenix speak the truth backwards?

So, as we grow older, let's also grow younger. As masters of going both ways at once, of following divergent streams while keeping up with the tides, let's try now to map our whole terrain, and beyond. This land and its distant shores.

One reason I'm telling this story is to help keep my friends alive. This flow of mutuality is essential to my well being. Who my friends are says a lot about who I am-- especially at those rare harmonious peaks when our different strings and keys sound varied notes to create a shared melody.

At this point, I believe, it's time for us, as we go over the crest of the hill, to recall our scattered pieces and pull ourselves together again. This story is more about remembering than about what each of us can now recall or has forgotten.

So, as we bend down again toward our toes, let us gather our fullness within our roundness and fall not like tear drops into that vast ocean. Instead let us flow together like steams joining one of those leisurely Chinese waterfalls, majestic in the deep of rugged mountains.

*   *   *   *

When I first stepped into this storyteller role, I imagined by the end that I would step out from behind the curtain of omniscient narrator and reveal myself. I would unveil the mask and announce: I am so and so from such and such a place, with such and such a history, and this kind of personality. *Ta Ta! Here's who I am. Here's where **I** fit into this story.*

But suddenly I realize when this story is over, so will I be as the narrator. As an oyster sinks to the bottom of an ocean, I will dissolve back into the silence. This pearl may go on to become one of many in a necklace or set in a ring, but I, the storyteller, will disappear as this story winds down. Story and storyteller, of course, are integrally related, like hydrogen and oxygen when they become water. But this story is, as it turns out, bigger than the actual storyteller, as a lake is bigger than the stream which feeds it. So this story may go on, but without me as the story-teller. I am not, as it turns out, the pearl I first imagined myself to be. I am the oyster. Maybe someday I'll produce another pearl. But until then it's time for me, if you'll excuse the metaphoric side- step, to clam up.

I hope that I have been able to give you our stories without telling you our deepest, most treasured secrets. Those of you who can read between the lines, like those who can read people's minds or faces or codes, may guess some of our secrets, maybe because your secrets are like ours, but nobody can't know our hidden sides, no matter how clever they are. And that is as it should be. We don't know their secrets either.

I believe it's not just me who has been or will be changed by and since these events, and the telling of this story; we all will have been. After all, we are already not the same people we were then. As I have changed just in the

246

telling of this, we all have changed with these changing events of our lives, these self-revelations, self-discoveries, self-transformations.

Who we were at the time of these events was only the raw material for who we are now. We cannot be fixed, even by our own partial, and certainly distorted stories—distorted, I confess, by me, the storyteller, who is after all, only one limited point of view. Fortunately it is in the nature of who we are to welcome change, seek self-knowledge, embrace transformation. Mine is only one slant of light on our collective story, and hopefully not the last one.

But before I go, let me enter into the core of this telling and distill the story for our great grandchildren, grand nieces and nephews, students and young friends: As a story ours is very simple: When we land folks came together, we had some wonderful times, around the fire, on the shore of the lake, climbing the mountain, or listening to the stream. Our lives together weren't happily ever after, we each had too many different other things we had to do. But because we knew each other, we did live fully, and for the most part happily.

We sometimes thought of ourselves as our animal allies—tiger, wolf, horse, elephant, mole, squirrel. We sometimes imagined we'd fled destruction, discrimination, disaster, development—and we were experimenting on how to survive with much, much less (our Noah's Ark fantasy). Later we took on the positive characteristics of our animal neighbors—beaver, raccoon, deer, heron, bear, moose. We had to be careful not to stereotype them, or ourselves, projecting single characteristics upon each other as if we were only furtive, anxious, busy, growly, bossy. We learned to soar, root, gnaw, burrow, nest as if we were them. We rooted ourselves in nature.

Despite occasional set-tos, we had fun together. We sat around the campfire at night and sang. We explored the forest, climbed the mountains, wandered through the stream, and swam in the lake. Other creatures like owls, horses, even an occasional dolphin flew, galloped, or sailed in. They joined the busy beavers building and hauling, the kingfishers flashing and fishing, the coydogs howling and hunting.

That's the narrative. Here's another, more practical, more current reason for writing this: I'm wondering whether we can or should, or should not, sell this land—now that we're getting older and in need of money for retirement. What about a Land Trust? What are our obligations to this land? What do we owe to what we own? Can we secure this home well enough to guarantee the safety of those who share it with us, those who have no property rights, like the deer and the fox? How can we share this ground's blessing of belonging? With whom? What of this land is our legacy to the future?

Who's to decide? Me, here at my desk, away from the land, and its flow of streams, chorus of wind, hush of trees, songs of animals, chatter of birds, paths in the forest. You, still rooted on the land. You, off on another mission. Or you, waiting for someone to call you back?

"*I wonder if the ground has anything to say about this? I wonder if the ground is listening to what is said. . . .I hear what the ground says. The ground says, 'It is the Great Spirit that placed me here.*"

This was spoken by Young Chief of the Cayuses while refusing to sign away tribal lands because the people had no right to sell the ground which the Great Spirit had given them for their support. *(Touch the Earth)*

"*The earth moves under our feet.*"

Can we feel her now again, listen in concert as we used to do? The earth speaks into our feet. Can we hear what she has to say?

Let's all turn now as we did when we moved through the woods, hand in hand in the dark without flashlights or maps, following the soles of our feet as they felt for the path beneath twigs and rocks, leaving our footprints embedded in the soft ground, our scents on the wind. Let's move, again, as one. As we feel the earth under our feet, let's go with her, not against her or away from each other. Neither too rigid nor too fluid let's go. Slowly, meditatively, carefully, hopefully, let's move together now.

25

THE NUMBERS

Zero

Zero is the point of pointlessness. The time when the end is the beginning; the beginning, the end. The place where both ends meet and become a circle. The hole of the whole. Out of whom the numbers rise and into which they fall. The ocean of annihilation and bliss. The voice between "Oh!" and absolute nothing.

Zero is when death dances with birth. The great primordial soup where A shakes hands with Z and 1,2,3 multiply into hundreds and thousands and millions of nothing but nothing is everything. The frightful melting pot where oppressors slide beneath oppressed, colors blend, everyone turns inside out.

Zero is when the I's turn to We, when the We's dissolve and reform to generate more I's. Zero is where we are both one and many. Zero is how parallel universes converge. Zero is where our synchronous stories are simultaneously told by the storytellers. Where, listening, we feel how fully they describe our life as one.

One, Two

First, last and always there is one. The one which is We--earth, mother, world, family--out of which Me emerges. Who gradually turns into other but still stays mine.

The one which is me contains two: two eyes, two ears, two thumbs to suck, two nostrils to stick two fingers into, two arms to wave, two knees to crawl.

One times one is also fun: the shadow in the glass, the shape in the tub, the one who stares through the sunlit window. And the one who giggles when I giggles, who peeks back when I peek back and hides her face when I hide my face. The one whose song echoes across the pond. So shocking yet so predictable.

But two is most intriguing: the one who giggles when I cry, the one who runs when I peek, the one whose silence meets my "Hi." The other who is not mine. So terrifying yet so alluring.

With two one has eyes in the back of her head, four legs for getting places two legs would not have dared to explore, four arms for lifting burdens far too heavy for two. How exhilarating.

With two one hears thoughts felt too deep for words, feels feelings too naughty to tell, dances to music one never heard before. How mysterious.

With two one fights over things one simply took for granted before. With two one is envious of qualities one never even knew existed. With two one feels despair that isn't even one's own. How exhausting.

No wonder. We live in a binary universe. One is never enough but two is more than one can handle.

What possible need could there be for three?

Three is two plus one. The extra one pulls us out of the lock step compromise, the march of one, two, one, two, one, two, one, two and moves us forward. One, two, three--weeeeee!

Three, Four, Five

Three's the oddest balance, that extra leg to trip over, use as a crutch or tilt us into new worlds like the head of an arrow. Such a small number, the first odd beyond one, it allows room for someone to enter or to feel left out, someone else, the other than the pair, the challenge to the couple, the catalyst for triangulation. Yet three is also one among others who is free to come and go, to discover on her own, to lead the way or follow. When no one is the excluded middle, triangles combine to form domes. To become water molecules. The Triad, the Holy Trinity.

Odds and evens. Evens like symmetry, balance, fairness. Odds like that extra edge, the solitary point, surprises. As alternating rhythms, they make a wholeness, complete the range of possibilities, the scale of measurable experiences, the ambling path of numbers. Rescued from the lockstep of linear progression, they make music, they dance.

One and two together are two legs walking. One and two alone become a march. When three, four, and five enter in, the march turns into a dance. A dance with variable rhythms.

Four is steady, sturdy, the earth, the foundation, the four-footed life of the world. Four is two plus two. Four is a horse trotting over the horizon, four is a dance between two people. Four, like the legs of a table, we can depend on. Four, like the sides of most houses, gives us shelter. Four, like grandparents on both sides, is rootedness. *"The symbol of heaven is the circle and that of earth is the square. All square things have their origin in a straight line and in turn form solid bodies... " (I Ching, 14)*

Five asserts the odds once more. Five is two plus three, one plus four. Five is the five pointed star, the human body with its points of feet, hands and head. Five is cartwheels and sparklers and vital movement. Five is the unexpected leap, the spark which emerges from nothing to make its own point. Five is the absolute fullness of oneself as human when no one else is around to expand the self beyond the boundaries of skin, bone and brain. Five is the foxtrot, the jitterbug, the samba.

Three and five break the ties that bind us to one or two, while four makes sure we have ground to stand on while we grow.

Six, Seven, Eight

With six, seven, eight, we discover expansion and completion. The growing globe moves out from zone to zone. The square becomes a circle, the circle becomes a spiral leading from and to other realms, the circle stretches into an oval, the egg which is our beginnning and its own ending.

Six is the hexagon, the shape of each cell in a bee's hive, the first stage of community. It makes the square three- dimensional, it extends the cube toward points on the horizon, east and west. It synthesizes two triangles, balancing those tensions to make a six pointed star, which integrates what is below with what is above, earth and sky, spirit and matter.

Seven is a lucky number. The seven chakras, points of energy within the whole person, the nerve center for the egg aura which envelopes each one of us. Seven grounds us while connecting us to all that is. Seven are the colors in a spectrum, the rainbow. Seven stars in a circle are the seven sisters in the sky.

Eight are the notes in an octave. Eight are the sides of an octagon, symbol of transformation, of the middle ground in the transition of square to circle, of cube to globe. Eight completes the round, connecting the loop which marks it whole. Eight is the eight-petaled flower and the eight bedded garden in which it grows. Explorer, Priest, Magician, Shaman, Philosopher, Mother, Artist, and Healer. Eight is the final note, the completion of the group, its boundary and its end.

"Wait a minute. Where do I fit in? This can't be the end. What about me?"

"And me?"

"And me?"
"And me?"
"And me?"
"And me?"
"And me?"
"And me?"
"And me?"

"Who are you?"

We are the daughters of our starving villages which have stopped practicing the old ways of adoring the goddess, honoring the earth and all living creatures, respecting women. Not afraid to speak with ghosts, we went to the ancestral groves and sang lullabies to the old people. In return they reminded us of the rules of our mother, the earth. With these guides we saved our dying villages and became leaders of our peoples.

We are, simultaneously, the girls who chose to be hermits, who decided to meditate, not marry. When our angry fathers ordered us killed, we were saved by tigers and transported to other realms, where we rescued captured spirits, met the Buddha, became enlightened, and went into seclusion. Out of our solitude we rescued people in distress, even saved our fathers' frightened souls, and decided to stay on earth until every holy living thing knows that it is holy.

Nine, Ten

Nine is the feminine cycle, the coming to terms of our human identity, the pregnant pause before each birth, the gestation of hope, months of blood and tissue forming new persons.

Nine is the American team, spaced out, mobile components of baseball's unit of play, individual players with separate roles whose coordination cuts that thin line between win and lose, success and failure.

Nine are the planets in our solar system whose slow cosmic revolutions around the sun, abiding yet precarious, dance on the edge of an immense universe, dots of light in a vast sky.

Ten is one plus zero. The one who knows that zero is where we return and out of which we came, who in that knowing is no longer merely nothing. The zero which shadows the one, reminding it that unity must inevitably dissolve, that what we experience of oneness with each other spins on those single, solitary units which are each of us alone.

Ten is as far as we can count, the final digit beyond which the mind does its tricks of adding and subtracting oughts and naughts. Ten completes any cycle designed by humans and turns us back upon ourselves.

Ten is one human, one world, a single line, a whole circle, the completion of our lives, both empty and full.

Ten is our radiant earth and one person who cares.

Eleven, Twelve, Thirteen

But ten, as we know, is not the end. It's as far as one human can count on her fingers but not as far as humans together can go. With eleven, east meets west. In the eastern *I Ching* eleven is peace, three broken lines above, three straight lines below, the receptive supported by the creative in perfect harmony. In the western numerical system, eleven is two ones side by side, balanced like the scales of justice, equal in size and shape, in perfect harmony. From the east the balance of top and bottom meets the balance of side to side from the west.

Eleven is about relationship, about fairness and equity, what can happen when both ones work together in a synthesis of equals. It's relationship in a stiff sort of way. What's fair is fair, what's yours is not mine. It recognizes the space between the ones. It honors boundaries. It provides a balance beyond the entitlement of ten, reminds us that fullness of digits, both hands forward, is not all there is, introduces the other one whose territory is not ours, whose hands, perhaps, reach elsewhere.

Twelve is about relationship of a different order. It's where microhuman meets macroworld, where our two hands stretch out to the wholeness of twelve moons circling the wholeness of seasons. It pulls us out of the human circle into the larger world of nature. It pulls us also into a flexible in-between of hospitality, rapprochement, tolerance, compromise.

Twelve introduces the bending of knees, the swaying of options, the bowing to otherness which the 2 suggests in form and in meaning. Twelve is truly one plus two, not the one plus which merges into three but the dozen of abundance. As in the miracle of the loaves and fishes, twelve can be multiplied in every direction: three fours, four threes, two sixes, six twos. If one expands in every direction with no subtraction, one draws a mandala which includes everything: the directions of the earth, the changes in the sky, and the configurations of our minds.

Thirteen is a magic number, how we go from inclusion to love, how the mandala opens up to welcome what's new. Whether through the mysterious chemistry of a coven or the alchemy of the last supper, Christ plus his twelve apostles, thirteen is the baker's dozen where that which cannot be measured enters in and blesses what counts. The one of each of us is sanctified by the double curve of the double helix, the sacred lemniscule, the breasts of mother earth. 13 is where the numbers meet the letters to form the holy mandate: B.

And so we be, thirteen of us, times thirteen times more and more and more of us.

ACKNOWLEDGEMENTS

Jackie Brookner, *Urban Rain, Stormwater as Resource* (City of San Jose, 2009).

Inez Martinez, *To Know the Moon* (Brooklyn, N.Y.: Sandia Press, 1993)

Bernice Mennis, *Breaking Out of Prison: A Guide to Consciousness, Compassion, and Freedom* (iUniverse, 2008).

Patricia Monaghan, *Wild Girls* (St. Paul, MN: Llewellyn, 2001)

S.B. Sowbel, *Wooing the Muse; The Mole; Curious Georgic; A Looser Place to Shelter; Of the Persuasion* (D'esperanto Publications from Tiny-Tiny-Topsham Press, 2000).

Special thanks to Kathleen A. Herrington and Evelyn Torton Beck for manuscript review and illuminating suggestions.

OTHER BOOKS BY MARGARET MOORE BLANCHARD

The Rest of the Deer: An Intuitive Study of Intuition
From the Listening Place: Languages of Intuition
Restoring the Orchard (with S.B. Sowbel): A Guide to Learning Intuition

Hatching (fiction)
Wandering Potatoes (fiction)
Who? (fiction)
Queen Bea (fiction)
Change of Course (fiction)

Duet (poetry, with paintings by S.B. Sowbel)
Beyond the Keys (poetry)